Breaking EVEN

E.A. Schreiber

BELLA
BOOKS
2018

Bella Books, Inc.
P.O. Box 10543
Tallahassee, FL 32302

First Bella Books Edition 2018

Editor: Medora MacDougall
Cover Designer: Judith Fellows

ISBN: 978-1-59493-576-3

About the Author

E.A. Schreiber currently lives in upstate New York. While not entertaining new ideas for stories, she enjoys challenging herself to try new sports now that she is retired from collegiate athletics. Outside of training for some new event with Katie where one of them is inevitably injured, she can be found hiking, golfing, playing games with her family or relaxing with a new book. While her career path is still winding, she is passionate about the influence of culture on policy and pursues projects in the non-profit field.

Acknowledgments

First of all, thank you to Bella Books! I've loved reading the incredible stories you bring to the world, and now you've given me the chance to share mine. Thank you, thank you, thank you!

Mom and Dad, thank you for raising me to be confident in who I am without condition. Your love and support surrounded me to the point that I never had to question myself or who I loved; I always knew you would love me. That gift is something that inspires me every day. You are the best people I know and have modeled for me what it means to be caring, honest, and open every day of your lives. Thank you for sharing your love with the world.

To my sisters, Ashley and Chelsea, thank you for encouraging me through all of my insecurities and doubts, painstakingly reading through multiple versions with me, often at the most inconvenient times. Knowing I have both of your unwavering support and brutal honesty gave me the confidence to forge ahead despite myself. You two make me laugh, drive me crazy, and keep things interesting. Ash, thanks for all the long-distance chats, what the hell, it's Christmas! Chelsea, I know I forced you to abandon your homework and spend hours picking through sections piece by piece, but look, you got your own section out of the deal! (How about that second chapter?) Greg, don't think you didn't make the cut! Thanks for being the best addition to our insane family, accepting me and my antics, and giving me all the life/academic/tech guidance I need!

I have to thank Katie, Lindsey, and Maria. You deserve more credit than I can give for supporting me as I continuously change my mind in life and in writing and for always listening to me vent. Katie, thank you for, well everything. You're the best, that's all there is to it. Lindz, thanks for listening to my readings. Maybe the next book will be filled with magical powers. Maria, I don't have the words, but I suppose I never have. I'm so lucky, and so grateful, that seven years later you're still here and still helping me navigate the chaos. I love you. Thank you all for being patient, critical and supportive, as well as for providing much needed distractions throughout this entire process. I love you all and would not have been able to finish this without each of you!

Finally, to my editor, Medora. I will forever be grateful for all that you did in helping me shape this work into what it is today. You put up with all of my annoying writing habits and rookie mistakes to guarantee we arrived at the best possible version of the story. Thank you so much for making me a better writer!

Dedication

This book is dedicated to all those who have summoned the courage to ask what they want out of life.

CHAPTER ONE

May

As evening settled in around her, she gave in to fatigue. Collapsing on the reading chair they'd just packed in the back of the moving truck, Chloe took some time to regroup. Hannah was in the apartment, probably feigning exhaustion, a heap on the floor.

It had been a long day. Moving out of a third-floor apartment didn't make for a relaxing weekend. All things considered, it could have been much worse—like last year when they moved Hannah and her seemingly endless supply of belongings from a second-floor walk-up to the industrial loft she currently occupied. Talk about a gauntlet of scraped forearms, tight corners, and endless stairways.

That's what you get for having a lawyer for a best friend—a pantsuit collection to rival HRC's and enough law textbooks to fill six bookshelves top to bottom. They had to have weighed a ton or more. She shuddered at the memory of the aches and pains they'd caused.

Hannah had no room to complain about the quantity of things she'd helped Chloe move today. Hannah's things had not only filled the largest rental truck, they also flowed over into Chloe's Jeep for the trip across Baltimore. In contrast, Chloe's belongings hadn't even filled the smallest U-Haul.

No, the most draining aspect of this move was not the physicality of it; it was the emotional toll it was taking on both of them. Together they had navigated their fair share of challenges since undergrad, but Chloe had assumed they'd moved past that stage in their lives, that maybe things would settle down as they each transitioned into their chosen fields. That hope had evaporated rapidly. Chloe could see in Hannah's face every time she didn't bring it up that she knew Chloe was truly struggling.

A slight breeze rattled her neighbor's chain-link fence, reminding her that kicking back in a full moving truck in downtown Amherst might not be the most prudent thing to do. Then again, she had proven this year that prudence was not her forte. After three years here, she was escaping under the cover of darkness, departing for a leave of absence, thanks in part to the efforts of a faculty member she had once idolized.

Time and space, that's what she needed. There was plenty of both in Maine.

CHAPTER TWO

September

Wednesday

The sound of an old-fashioned car horn blared its way into Chloe's consciousness. The warmth of the covers tempted her to remain motionless, but the alarm on her phone would not be ignored. Grudgingly reaching out from under the blankets, she silenced it. Seven thirty felt incredibly early from the vantage point of a cozy bed. Realistically she didn't have to wake up this early; the shop didn't open until nine. But ever since college, when she'd discovered her potential for productivity in the morning, she developed the annoying habit of setting ridiculously early alarms. While it helped her finish papers and get readings done on time, she had much less to prep for when heading to a retail job. As she set the device back on her nightstand, it vibrated. Curious, she reached out from her cocoon one more time and checked to see what had come in.

A text from Nora. Chloe stared at the notification on her lock screen, blinking twice to make sure it was really there. She felt the familiar tug of guilt. She couldn't bring herself to deal with it, not this early in the morning. Really, though, responding later would be fine. That's what she would do.

She rolled over and pulled the covers closer still. Staying in bed meant sleeping, which meant not thinking. With her eyes resolutely shut, she told herself in two minutes she would get up.

Another blaring car horn roused her from sleep and she groaned loudly. This time when she checked the clock, she knew she couldn't possibly allow herself to drift off again. In her head she calculated the amount of time she needed to shower, make breakfast, change, and be out the door in time for work… She had at most a half hour.

Ten minutes later, toweling dry, Chloe began searching for chinos and a T-shirt. Finally finding some wrinkle-free pants, she dressed, made a bowl of instant oatmeal to eat on the way, grabbed her keys, and headed out the door.

The roads were still wet from rains that had fallen sometime last night. It must have been quite the storm; the ditches were nearly overflowing. The sky held promise now, though—no signs of any more storm clouds. There was virtually no traffic, which was helpful, considering she was cutting it rather close. Having a ten-minute commute was great but leaving twelve minutes before she needed to be at work was less than ideal. Driving a little too fast, she made it to the harbor on time, barely. Jacob wouldn't be upset or surprised about that.

Before meeting Jacob, she had imagined all lawyers as stern, unfeeling, corporate types. Not Hannah, of course, but retired ones like him she always envisioned the same way, out of laziness and maybe a touch of social conditioning. Jacob had blasted away any and all stereotypes she harbored. Finding him entirely approachable and generally wonderful, Chloe easily fell into friendship with the older man, appreciating his mellow demeanor and quirky humor. She was grateful not only that she found a job in his store when she desperately needed one, but that she also somehow managed to find a good friend in the process.

Pulling into the parking lot, she wolfed down the last few bites of her breakfast and dropped the dish unceremoniously on the passenger's seat. The street was quiet as she stepped out of her Jeep and headed toward the back door. The sun, cresting the tops of the nearby buildings, had lost its biting heat from earlier in the summer. The stillness that had gripped the town through much of August, when it was too hot to move or breathe, had loosened its grasp. She could almost feel change moving in; the weather was finally beginning to reveal traces of the onset of fall. She loved to watch the mellowing of summer as it gave way to the cooler dawning of autumn.

Chloe's focus shifted to the Boatery, situated between the town hardware store and the Moosehead Café on the corner of one of the older streets in town. Boothbay was a tourist town. The streets bore the unmistakable signs of tourism, but the town retained its character and charm thanks to the variety of historic buildings dotting the streets. Ever-faithful year-round residents kept the town alive during the harsh winters when the flocks of tourists returned home.

Chloe returned her attention to the Boatery and headed to the back door. A gust of wind ushered her in, rustling her honey-colored hair. Catching a glimpse of her reflection on the door, she realized that the short cut she had been sporting in May now resembled a shaggy mane, long enough for strands from the front to fall into her eyes. Capturing the rogue hairs between her fingers, she brushed them back into place.

Hanging her coat on the wall-mounted hooks, Chloe stepped in front of the small mirror Jacob had hung nearby. Though her face was still framed by the remnants of a tapered fade, the longer hair on the top which she liked to style was now nearly too long to control. While her mom was always shocked that someone with Chloe's feminine face might be misgendered, Chloe knew her athletic, six-foot frame and close-cropped hairstyle did not register immediately as feminine and wasn't bothered by it. She wondered if Pink had the same problem.

Hannah had teased her that out in the country she might be able to embrace her inner woodswoman, and she realized she *was* beginning to look a bit more rugged than usual. It was always a challenge finding hair stylists who were comfortable cutting masculine styles on female customers, and she had yet to find a barber or hair salon in the area where she was confident that the stylist would cut her hair the way she liked it. She might have to dig out her clippers and trim it herself while she continued her search. She could at the very least maintain the cut until a professional could touch it up properly.

Thinking of Hannah, Chloe was pretty sure that it was this week that she was starting at the new firm. They had texted last night, but that had primarily been about the best method to cook asparagus. The discussion had begun with a picture from Hannah of her dismantled steamer captioned "help."

Chloe shook her head. Considering how incredibly intelligent the woman was, it was impressive how flummoxed Hannah could get in a kitchen. And how resistant she was to admitting it. That was certainly one thing that hadn't changed since their time rooming together as undergrads. Chloe had let her continue to delude herself last night while she coached her through the subtle art of steaming vegetables. She smiled. Though they were currently separated by more than five hundred miles, they still relied on one another for the most basic of tasks. Yes, she was definitely overdue for an actual call.

Noting her arrival, Jacob, who was reading from *Anna Karenina*, greeted her with a flourish, bowing his head. He nodded toward an ominous stack of boxes in the back corner, then returned to his reading.

"Jacob, how'd you know I'd rather unpack deliveries all morning than read even a chapter of Tolstoy?" Chloe called out.

"It's a gift, *dorogaya*. Thank me later."

"Seriously? Russian?" she called back to her boss. She could hear the chuckle emanating from somewhere deep in his chest as she made her way toward the boxes. She reminded herself to fact check Jacob's Russian, assuming "dorogaya" was a real word, to see what he had called her. While he was well read and very intelligent, he had a penchant for fabricating details to add a splash of color to his conversations.

She headed for the latest delivery, ready to ease her way into the morning. Receiving inventory was mind-numbingly boring and required little to no mental alertness. The most difficult chore of the entire operation was managing to use the box cutter without slicing the packaging that encased the products—she checked the packing list—in this case, pairs of snowshoes. That and avoiding cardboard cuts. The bastard cousin of a paper cut, these had become the bane of her sporting goods existence. She liked Jacob's choice of snowshoe. Incredibly lightweight, they were made entirely from recycled materials. The ergonomically designed packaging was environmentally conscious, too, which Chloe appreciated. The minimalist design eliminated excess packaging materials, which was great, but it was a pain in the ass to unpack.

Then again she knew to expect nothing less. After all, Jacob was a passionate hipster from way back. His enthusiasm was generally contagious, at least after eight in the morning when Chloe was fully human.

Jacob's ownership of the Boatery was about as unplanned as Chloe's employment there was. Experiencing a strong sense of wanderlust, he'd retired from practicing law and traveled the country. Finding himself in Boothbay, he'd come into the store and apparently never left. That was fifteen years ago. Jacob had fully assimilated. No customers ever guessed he was originally from Raleigh. Or what his previous profession had been, for that matter. Or that she was a physicist. Talk about some highly educated sporting good rental clerks.

Soft music began playing on the stereo system, drifting through the store. The sound instantly lifted Chloe's mood. Jacob liked music, but it was really Chloe's presence that reminded him to play the mix CDs she had brought in for him to sample. Chuckling to herself, she stretched to relieve the kink in her back and decided that a little John Legend in the morning was never a bad thing.

* * *

Around twelve thirty Jacob left his desk at the front of the store to find her.

"What sounds good for lunch today?" he asked.

"Whatever you want. I'm assuming you realized I didn't pack anything," Chloe answered, excited by the prospect of any sort of lunch.

"When you barely manage to stumble in on time, I generally assume your preparation for work is minimal. You're pretty easy to read."

Smiling sheepishly, Chloe shrugged in a what-can-I-say manner.

"I'll head out and see what tickles my fancy and bring us back something. Can you handle this baby on your own?" Jacob's question was all for show; they both knew full well they might get all of two customers while he was out.

"If you see smoke, come running. Otherwise, I think we're all set."

Jacob nodded and started out the door into the afternoon sunlight. Chloe's gaze followed him along the street toward one of the many cross streets. There sat the post office and Montino's, one of the local pizzerias and one of the town's best-kept secrets. On her first day on the job, Jacob had invited Chloe to join him for lunch. Instead of going to one of the many trendy little tourist cafés and cute shops, he had walked them to Montino's. Chloe had pegged Jacob as a thoroughly healthful eater upon meeting him. Setting the tone for their friendship, Jacob had surprised her by striding into the comfortable pizza shop and insisting she try the pizza special.

After a forty-minute absence, Jacob returned.

"Reuben or tomato mozzarella," he announced as he tossed their lunches gently on the counter.

"I'll take the tomato," said Chloe as she gathered up the food to take to the benches out front. "I hope you told Susan hello for me while you wooed her," she added, bringing the hint of a blush to his face. His flirting with the owner of the café was adorable and highly predictable.

Outside, the slight breeze brought with it whispers of the autumn that would soon descend upon the coast. An opaque smattering of clouds muted the blue of the sky, casting shadows throughout the town. Though this kind of weather was perfect for a midday jaunt along the coast or up one of the nearby creeks in a kayak, most of the college and high school students were back in school and many of the tourists had left with the close of the weekend. As they enjoyed their lunch, Jacob mentioned a climate change panel that had been on the news that morning. As usual the two of them ended up despairing about the pseudo-science that contributed to the overall scientific ineptitude of the country. As a scientist, it was maddening to Chloe to see so much ignorance.

"I wish I could sit down with some of these climate change deniers. I really want to understand what goes on in their heads."

"Darling, it comes down to ignorance and refusing to listen to reasoning. And I doubt a display of your temper would do anyone much good." Jacob tilted his head slightly, raising one eyebrow at her, waiting for the objection Chloe couldn't contain.

As Chloe began to rebuff his claim that she would lose her temper, he continued, "I vividly remember hearing your dulcet tones one day while talking with Andrew while you two were on break." Clearing his throat, he went on, "And I quote, 'As a fairly informed person who occasionally thinks thoughts about the world, I'm warning you if you don't shut up right now I will rip my own arm off and beat you with it.' End quote."

Chloe's laughter escaped against her will. "Come on, first of all, it was funny. Second, we both know he was purposely trying to get me going. It was only fair to warn him what was coming."

"Right. Well, in the interest of your remaining limbs I say we don't encourage any interventions with true deniers out there. Leave that to Neil deGrasse Tyson and Bill Nye."

"Hey, maybe I could work with them to spread some science around!"

"I suppose that is an option, but uprooting and starting over in show business is a long shot," Jacob countered. He wasn't the slightest bit worried about her actually pursuing a YouTube career, but for a minute the idea intrigued her.

Giving up hope of Internet stardom, Chloe went on, "At this point, as long as I've still got all my limbs I think I might find a carpentry apprenticeship. Tool belts, work boots, using my brain and my hands, it makes sense. If not, then I'll hope to someday become manager here and by the time I'm seventy I might have my student loans paid off."

"Oh, that's reasonable. Abandon academia entirely in favor of perpetual splinters." At this, Jacob smacked Chloe lightly on the head and returned to eating his Reuben. He thought she was kidding. And she was—for the most part. She had secretly been considering the possibility of staying on with Jacob at the Boatery indefinitely. Three months into her escape from UMass the sense of direction she longed to find was still eluding her. Her grad program would not wait forever. In fact, the university was only going to wait nine more months.

Jacob's penetrating stare broke her concentration. "Listen up. I am more than happy to keep you in my employ for now. Your work is decent and your company tolerable." Try as he might he couldn't keep the serious tone going.

Chloe nodded her head solemnly as he continued. "But you are not going to cruise this life riding the coattails of my retirement. You know you wouldn't be happy doing this; it isn't stimulating enough. You want to talk about wormholes or how fast Justin Bieber would fall if you dropped him from a building in a cat suit or something."

"I can't believe you read my master's thesis, Jacob. You really do care!" Chloe nudged his arm as another deep laugh rumbled out.

"Anyway, aside from your strange love of ridiculous physics problems and quantum particles, we both know you want something that inspires you. And even though it terrifies you, you know you want to create some change. To top it off, we both know you are capable of anything. Well, anything except diplomacy. Beating people over the head with the bluntness of your arguments isn't always the answer."

"I can be diplomatic. You never see it, though, since it's always your hard head that I'm trying to beat the truth into," Chloe countered, shaking her head in mock exasperation. They teased each other easily as if they had known each other for years, not months. Jacob was always patient with her, a gift owed partially to his temperament and partially to wisdom born of experience. He had recognized early on that she wasn't always the most forthcoming of people, especially when it came to her emotional status.

"Well, if you can get me to see the truth, you obviously have what it takes to get some high school kids to see it as well."

"Impressive how you always manage to bring it back to this. If nothing else you're," Chloe paused, exaggerating the effort involved with choosing the right word, "persistent. And that's putting a positive spin on it."

Jacob had come to the conclusion that the most logical progression for Chloe would be to try her hand teaching high school. She had gotten certified and considered teaching as a career early on in her undergraduate days, though that had been eclipsed by her immersion in experimental particle physics while in graduate school. This past year, though, had done a number on her confidence. While she had regained control of her personal life to some extent, her professional life was an entirely different story. While it was a saving grace, her leave of absence left limited time to figure it all out. She could hardly believe that it had already been three months since she left UMass.

"This job is not the least bit stimulating for you, and while your customer service skills are great, you are contributing nothing to society here."

Chloe interrupted. "Well, thanks for that. Talk about your picker-upper."

A glimpse of exasperation flitted across the older man's face, immediately replaced by a tender, almost fatherly affection.

"You are gifted, charismatic, and passionate. According to my calculations those are some of the most critical elements in teaching," he offered gently. He added, "Even if you don't pursue it long-term, while you're here why not use your brain a little? You might even impact a student or two." Chloe sat with his words for a moment, trying them on for size. Though still undecided, she was warmed by his appraisal.

"Thank you. I really do appreciate your help, you know." Chloe paused, thinking, then carried on, "Honestly, I don't know how I'll relate to high school kids. I wanted to pursue higher-level physics. I don't want to kid myself with unrealistic expectations again. That didn't exactly play out as planned."

"Nothing ever does, but alas, you landed here with a wizened sage to guide you."

"Wizened sage, withered eccentric. Potato, potahto, I guess."

"I'll take that sass as a sign that you know I'm right." Jacob bowed in a gesture of supreme smugness, a contented smile playing on his lips. "In all seriousness, I'm glad you've put your résumé out there and are going to get the chance to substitute. You have sincere motivations, ones that I think will serve to sustain you. I know you are going to surprise yourself."

Chloe let the reassurance Jacob provided sweep over her, knowing his words were genuine and hoping they were right. They lapsed into quiet thought for several moments, and then Jacob offered another bit of advice.

"If all else fails, Chloe, remember this…"

"Lay it on me."

"If life gives you lemons, throw them at people. I'll be in the back room starting inventory. You man the register." And with that, Jacob headed inside, leaving Chloe's laughter behind him.

* * *

"Your phone's ringing!" Jacob called from inside the office. It was nearly four o'clock and the sun was beginning its slow descent toward what promised to be an enjoyable summer dusk. Chloe assumed the call was from her mother and jogged in to answer. The number didn't register in her contacts.

"Hello, this is Chloe Amden."

"Hi, Ms. Amden. This is Maryanne Pruzzi from Wiscasset High School. I'm calling to see if you are available to substitute for us this Thursday—tomorrow—in the physics classroom. On your application you had indicated a high level of comfort with physics, is that correct?"

Chloe was so surprised to be receiving this call, she answered quickly, her nerves clearly showing. "Oh yes! I have my master's in physics and am certified to teach!"

"Well, that sounds wonderful, honey. Are you available tomorrow?"

"Oh yes, yes. I'm free."

"Well, then, classes start at seven forty a.m. Most substitutes come in around seven fifteen or so to get their pass and get set up in the classroom. You can park around back by the gym. Those doors will be locked that early, but you can head around to the main office. The doors there will be unlocked and I'll be here to show you to your classroom. As long as your fingerprints are on file, you should receive your check within two weeks. Our pay rate is one hundred and fifteen dollars for the day. Do you have any questions?"

"Only one. What grades will I be working with?"

"Oh yes, Mrs. Flore teaches two junior/senior combined classes. The one is an AP-level physics class, the other is Regents-level physics. Mrs. Flore also has a study hall with juniors and seniors. Anything else, Miss Amden?"

Chloe was so startled by this sudden change of events she was drawing a complete blank on the questions she should be asking.

"No, I think that's all I have."

"Lovely. I will see you tomorrow. Have a nice day."

"Thank you, you too." With that, Chloe ended the call, cocking her head to one side, losing herself in thought. As understanding began to set in, Jacob's voice entered her consciousness.

"You accepted pretty quickly for someone not wanting to teach." Despite his gentle teasing, his support was too genuine for Chloe to be annoyed. "Looks like you'll be needing Thursday off," he said cheerfully as he came out of the office.

"Apparently I will. Is that okay? I guess I should have asked before I said yes. That's what normal employees do, right?" she responded, raising her eyebrows at him with mock concern.

"I suppose so. Are you excited? I'm tickled pink. Now you can start doing something about this pipe dream so we can move on with our lives," he joked back. She knew full well he was as invested in listening to her and helping her through this transitional period as he would have been for his own child.

"Excited, nervous, anxious, terrified, completely overwhelmed…" Her voice trailed off. After a moment she continued, "I'm not processing it completely yet. I'm sure everything will hit me when I pull in the parking lot. I haven't been in a high school classroom since junior year student teaching. Thank God I don't have to plan a lesson."

"True. Don't get too worked up about the nitty-gritty. You'll most likely be watching some video from the 1960s. Best practice your stern, quiet-down face for the kiddies. Maybe they'll think you mean business—for the first five minutes, anyway."

"Hey, I'm intimidating! I can control a classroom!" Chloe balked. It may have been four years since she last did this, but she was older now. She didn't want to be thought of as a joke.

"High school kids are tough. Don't be a total pushover and you'll be fine," Jacob replied. "Assuming you can get there on time," he added. With the satisfaction she saw on his face, Chloe realized he had only said what he had to get a rise out of her. And as she usually did when her father baited her, she had given him exactly the reaction he'd wanted.

"Funny. Wait until I come back here traumatized. I blame you. It was your half-baked idea in the first place for me to get into this."

"The burdens I bear are mine and mine alone." Jacob sighed, leaning on the counter for support from his figurative troubles. His flair for the dramatic was just genuine enough to be endearing.

"The heaviest burdens go to the strongest of men," Chloe returned sarcastically, bowing with a grand sweep of her arm as she headed for the back of the store to continue unpacking the newest shipment, several cartons of beginner ski poles.

* * *

When five thirty came around, Chloe was seven poles away from completing the shipment. Jacob called out to tell her that it was time to "skedaddle," and she returned to the front of the store. After locking up, she walked out with him. Not wanting to let the beautiful day go to waste, she decided to drive over to the point at Barrett Park to take a run along the trail that ran parallel to the beach.

Rifling through the contents of her Jeep, she located her bag with a change of clothes and sneakers. She kept a spare set of shorts and T-shirt handy for days like today when she could sneak in some extra workout time.

There were only three other cars when Chloe pulled into the well-maintained parking lot near the point. Noticing one man and his dog walking down toward the beach on the east end, she wondered who else might be out today. With the breeze off the coast, the air was cooler here, tempering the brightness of the sun. There were easily three hours of good daylight left. Grabbing her water bottle and pocketknife, she went into the bathroom to change. She was glad she had packed her long-sleeved shirt. It never hurt to have clothing options in the often unpredictable weather in Maine.

* * *

Emerging from the bathroom, Chloe inhaled deeply, wanting to memorize everything about the evening. The light wind was soft, dancing on her skin. The tide was lapping calmly on the rocky shore, bringing with it the cool air from the sea. Rays of light filled the horizon with shades of gold and orange, pink and purple, mixing and swirling as if painted on the breeze.

Stepping on the grass to stretch, Chloe shook out her long legs, waking them up from the lazy day at work. If she didn't loosen up first, her knee would ache later. After tearing her cartilage in college, she couldn't do much without a warm-up. The trail she was going to take was an easy, flat one, winding between the rocky shoreline and the forest. The path, made of fine gravel, had few potholes so she needn't worry too much about her footing.

This late in the summer there wouldn't be very many tourists either. The beaches had pretty much emptied out by now. She set out, gravel crunching under her feet in time with her breathing. In the pocket of her shorts her cell phone bumped rhythmically against her leg, reminding her of the early morning text from Nora. She pushed the thought away. She was being a coward, but the situation was too complicated for her to face at the moment. She was becoming adept at avoiding dealing with it, but that wouldn't last forever. After all, Nora and Elaine were central to the entire mess and to her current lack of direction.

Chloe blocked those thoughts, deciding to add Nora to her list of burned bridges, even though, in all fairness, she had to concede that Nora had never been malicious. Merely young. All the more reason to step back and give her time to grow up and learn from Chloe's mistakes. That was the best decision. Keep running.

She shifted her focus to her physical run rather than her metaphorical one, stretching long legs in front of her with each stride. The air felt so good on her skin, cooling her as she started to sweat in earnest.

And then there was the scenery… Each time she passed one of the old wooden docks or a picturesque vintage fishing vessel she became a little bit more enamored with the area. Even when the ocean wasn't visible from the path, the sound of water lapping against the boats and the creaking docks reminded her of its magic.

The tourists came to Boothbay to enjoy the obvious beauty of the area, the lush greenery, untamed forests, and rocky beaches. But she loved the feel of the place most. It oozed history.

If only she could feel as strongly about her own direction as she did about this region.

Increasing her speed each time a disquieting idea clawed at the edges of her consciousness, Chloe managed to leave most of her negative thoughts behind. When she reached the oldest marina in Lewis Cove, she turned around. She swatted the fourth black fly of the night; her patience was wearing thin. It was definitely time to head back.

As she drove back to her apartment, the calmness that had enveloped her while running evaporated and was replaced by new thoughts. Hopping out of her Jeep and walking up the front steps to her portion of the old colonial house, Chloe shivered in the cooling evening air. She was so glad to have found the first-floor apartment. The original wood floors and abundance of natural lighting were wonderful perks, though Chloe would have signed the lease without either after meeting her landlord. Joanne, a retired state trooper, lived in the second-floor apartment and had her own separate entrance. Chloe had minimal worries about the house, its upkeep, or her own safety, though she admittedly never saw her landlord. The rent was affordable too.

The flickering light of fireflies danced on the horizon. Throughout her entire childhood fireflies had been the guardians of summer nights. The little beacons of light conjured memories of family and friends and even better weather. Thinking back to easier summers, Chloe continued inside. Walking through the door, she lobbed her backpack onto the floor, locked the door behind her, and settled in for the evening.

Once she sat on the couch, she allowed herself to start trying to process the phone call she'd gotten earlier in the day from Maryanne Pruzzi. It was simply an opportunity to substitute teach, nothing to get too thrilled over. Being a high school substitute was a far cry from a sustainable career. She didn't even know if she would like it or, God help her, be good at it. Either way, there was no going back now. The nervous excitement she was feeling was better than the hollow nothingness that had preceded it.

She went to the closet to get her guitar. She had missed jamming while in grad school and was now trying to get back to it; it had been a fixture in her college days. Her fingers became reacquainted with the feel of the smooth neck in her hands, the vibration of the strings, and soon the chords began to resonate within her. Once she had played the rust off, she moved on to an Ed Sheeran favorite of hers. Playing from memory, she started to relax again. Good music, no matter how poorly she might play it, never failed to help her mellow out.

Unaware of how much time had passed, Chloe stood finally, unfolded her body, and stretched enthusiastically. Her shoulder sometimes ached after playing. And then there was the crunching in her knee. Her meniscus wouldn't ever be the same from the damage inflicted over the course of her college career.

At six feet tall, Chloe was naturally athletic. Whereas Hannah, with her long blond hair and curves, presented as distinctly feminine, Chloe was a study in angles, lean muscle, and androgyny. Her toned arms and legs, the product of a workout routine she'd perfected in college, gave her the appearance that she had had when she was still playing, thin and muscular.

If only she were still playing. She'd never aspired to a career in basketball, but playing meant having a goal that was singular and simple—winning a game, winning a championship. Personal goals were much more difficult to discern and articulate. There wasn't a clear-cut path to long-term "be happy" goals the way there was to improving on the court.

By the same token, winning championships did little in the way of fostering a rewarding and workable life. The last time she checked student loans couldn't be paid off with layups and sweat. Her academic career had always been much more linear, undergrad, graduate school, select a lab and advisor, publish, then get a tenure-track position. Walking away from familiar, previously established protocols meant answering questions about herself that she wasn't sure she was prepared for.

Rather than continuing down that rabbit hole, Chloe directed her attention to getting ready for her first subbing job. Truthfully, all she needed to do was prepare for a simple day as a substitute without placing too much importance on succeeding at the job. The problem was it felt much more important. Despite the fact that it was a one-day gig, she still wanted it to be a positive experience—for herself and for the students. That meant she needed to take a step back from the experiments she'd been working on at the CERN Hadron collider exploring the fundamental building blocks of matter and reorient herself to the basic physics principles she was sure to find in the lesson plans waiting for her. Running away from academia didn't mean she also forgot everything from her education. Rifling through her old textbooks, she pulled out her introductory book from freshman year and her notebook from student teaching and started reviewing. Sticking with the basics was the best plan. After she felt like she could pass as a reasonably well-informed physicist again, she called it a night.

CHAPTER THREE

Thursday

For mid-September, it was a warm and peaceful Maine morning. The start held the promise of a comfortable day. Chloe drove in with the music turned up, partly to distract her and partly because she loved the Mumford and Sons in her CD player. She always got lost in the acoustic harmonies they pumped out.

Crossing the bridge over Cod Cove into Wiscasset, Chloe saw shimmering reflections on the water. *I am living in a postcard.* Living in the northern regions of the East Coast her entire life hadn't lessened her appreciation of nature's majestic design. Sure, the black flies here drove her to the brink of madness, but the beauty surrounding her far surpassed the irritation caused by the pesky insects.

It was an easy drive to the high school, only nine miles according to Google. Chloe had woken up an hour before her alarm this morning, her nerves propelling her out of bed with an abundance of time to get ready. Beset by last-minute qualms, she wondered how her androgyny would be received.

She had opted for gray chinos, a blue floral-print button-up layered under a maroon sweater, and her brown suede chukkas. She felt comfortable, but she wasn't certain she wouldn't stick out like a sore thumb. She hadn't really met any open hostility as a result of her sexuality while at Saint Michael's in Vermont nor while she was in Massachusetts. Entering a school in rural Maine, however, might be another situation entirely. She'd been asked if she was in the correct bathroom multiple times while out shopping in Boothbay. She was cautiously optimistic about Wiscasset, but only because she couldn't bring herself to consider the alternative.

The high school was nestled against a forest on the outer edge of town, and the parking lot out back that Maryanne had instructed her to park in was small. Not many of the other teachers had arrived yet, judging by the fact that there were only four cars in the lot. Chloe tried to relax, remembering her student teaching days and the kids that she had loved working with. It had been terrifying at first, but eventually the kids seemed like they could relate to her in some way. She hadn't been a pushover, and she had seen a respect in most of them that gave her hope for today. The only problem was that today she wasn't a student teacher; she was simply another sub.

* * *

Once Maryanne had given Chloe a quick tour of the school, she dropped her off in the physics room to prepare for the day. Mrs. Flore, the veteran physics teacher, had left detailed instructions for her substitute typed up neatly in a manila folder left on her desk. She included a printout of her entire schedule, which was convenient since Chloe had never been exposed to block scheduling or "A" and "B" Days.

	"A" Day	"B" Day
First Block	Regents (General) Physics	Regents (General) Physics

Second Block	Free Period	Regents (General) Physics
Lunch Break		
Third Block	Study Hall Supervision	Planning Period
Fourth Block	AP Physics	Study Hall/Senior Release

The school secretary explained the "A/B" day schedule to her, informing her that the letter days alternated throughout the week, and she would only see one set of students each day. This type of scheduling added flexibility for holidays and snow days, and students still had equal instruction time for both sets of classes. This Thursday, she learned, was an "A" Day and she'd be teaching a general physics class and an AP physics class. Next Thursday would be a "B" Day and the other two general physics classes would be meeting.

The teaching load consisted of just two classes each day, with a total of four overall. Mrs. Flore agreed to drop to a .8 position to save the school money as she neared retirement. The first period today was the general physics class. They would be going over the homework that had been assigned. The remainder of class time would be spent watching a movie and answering a set of questions from the textbook. Chloe allowed a hint of optimism to ease her nerves. First block, at least, was navigable.

The AP class would be her fourth block. She hoped that class would be uneventful too, but remembering the smart-ass high school boys she'd had to deal with in her own AP classes, she knew better than to try to predict how it might go.

The second-block time slot was a free period. While that might be a good time to bone up on what the AP students were working on, she thought she'd covered most of that in her review last night. Last-minute cramming tended to make her more, rather than less, nervous. Good thing she'd brought along a book to read.

As she contemplated the rest of her day, she found that the idea of walking into a staff lounge without knowing a soul was about as appealing to her as teaching stark naked. It was a bit antisocial, but eating the lunch she'd brought with her in her classroom sounded pretty good. She would make a decision about that during second block, she guessed. During third block she would monitor a study hall in the library with Miss Levit, one of the English teachers. At least she wouldn't be thrown to the wolves during that block. Probably. Unless Miss Levit was some kind of cream puff. She would find out soon enough.

After getting her bearings, Chloe took stock of the classroom. Typical wooden lab benches with solid black countertops lined the room, reminding her of her own physics classroom in high school. The classic momentum cars with magnets and Velcro on opposite ends, the kind she'd used then, were sitting out on student benches. Some were resting on the miniature metal tracks that accompanied them for the Newtonian mechanics lab. Piled in the back corner were various clamps, stopwatches, and motion sensors for the lab work.

The outer wall of the classroom was lined with windows, which overlooked the soccer pitch and track. To her right, Chloe found the entrance to Mrs. Flore's office. It was small but filled with books and toys for demonstrations during class. Lining the walls were hundreds of pictures from students spanning decades. It was clear that Mrs. Flore was well-respected; students didn't give every teacher signed pictures. The walls were lined with quotes from notable scientists, some relating to physics, others describing life in general. The warmth of the office was almost tangible, welcoming.

After collecting the materials Mrs. Flore had left for her, Chloe sat down at the front of the classroom to prepare. Reading through the homework questions and the accompanying answers, Chloe was confident she would be able to field any questions the kids had. It had been a while since she had been immersed in the mechanics of introductory physics, working through assigned lessons instead of doing research, but these concepts were so thoroughly a part of how she viewed and interacted in the world she was actually excited about the chance to explain the science behind a few of the problems. Poring over her notebooks last night had definitely made a difference; the physics component would be manageable at least.

Running her hand through her hair, Chloe wondered what the students would be like. Would they follow direction or take the opportunity to act out? Chloe began tapping her foot on the floor, her mind racing nearly as fast as her bouncing knee. She was really about to try her hand at teaching high school kids.

On the one hand, if she loved substituting, she faced struggling to find long-term substitute positions and waiting it out until she could nail down a long-term career. On the other hand, if she hated everything about working with the students, she would have to tick another career opportunity off her list and remain as far as ever from a clear sense of direction in her life. If she was totally ambivalent about the entire experience, she would remain in the post-grad purgatory that held her unsatisfied and underachieving.

How the hell does anyone find a job that's rewarding and fulfilling? Is it naïve of me to hold out for that?

Wiping off her sweaty palms, Chloe forcefully shook her head in an attempt to refocus and read the rest of the instructions. The video was in the VCR and ready for first period to watch. The only thing left to do was to find a textbook so she could read out the questions the kids had to answer during the movie. Where was the book? There had to be one, but aside from lab equipment, nothing else was on the benches. Pacing the room, she saw nothing. *The office!* Letting out an audible sigh, Chloe grabbed the book from the office desk and felt her heart rate return to normal. Inhaling deeply, she spread everything out on the front bench and waited for her students to head in.

* * *

When the bell rang signaling the end of first period, Chloe was amped up. Her first eighty-minute period as a substitute was over, she had managed to accomplish everything on Mrs.

Flore's list, and none of the students had been jerks. To top it off, she surpassed her own expectations leading the class. She'd managed to answer the few questions about the homework easily, even getting a few laughs out of the students.

Now that she had a free period, lunch, a study hall, and only one other class to teach fourth block, she decided a walk around the school would not only be a good use of her free time but also a way to work off some nervous energy. With the majority of students now in classes, the hallways were nearly empty as she set out. Winding her way through the corridors, Chloe found herself in a hallway lined with trophy cases. Two large sets of doors, immediately familiar to her, stood open.

The polished wooden floors, aluminum bleachers, and basketball hoops she saw inside put her at ease. Having dedicated a vast amount of her time to practices, workouts, games, and watching games over the last twenty years, that wasn't surprising. Whenever she walked into a gym, she itched to feel leather in her hands. This time was no different.

She liked this gym. It was pretty big with bleachers on all four walls and eight baskets on the perimeter along with the two main hoops. The bleachers were relatively new, but the banners of the opposing teams in the conference had to be from the seventies. Walking across the gym toward the cage of basketballs, Chloe noticed the feisty Wiscasset wolverine painted at half-court. There were worse mascots than wolverines. Judging by the banners on the walls, the Wolverines had been pretty successful for a small school.

Finding the equipment cage unlocked, Chloe plucked out a ball and turned to face the center of the gym. Absentmindedly she spun the ball in her hands, a habit deeply ingrained in her. In a seamless move, as natural to her as walking, her dribble was down, between her legs and falling into the rhythm of her body as she walked toward the basket. As she shot, she discovered that she had acquired an audience.

"Can I help you with something?" The question came from the far corner of the gym, where an office was located.

Chloe spun around. "Oh, no. I'm sorry. I'm substituting today for Mrs. Flore. This is my free period. The gym was open. I couldn't help myself."

"And your name is…"

"Chloe Amden… I have my visitor's badge. Hang on." Chloe palmed the ball in her left hand while fumbling in her back pocket to fish out her badge. She handed her pass over to a slightly shorter, muscular woman with glimmering blue eyes and was relieved when her face broke into a smile.

"I didn't mean to scare you, but for the safety of the kids, I have to be pretty vigilant. I can't allow any yahoo to walk into my gym and start playing, even if they're decent shots." The woman extended her hand for a firm, yet friendly handshake. "I'm Taylor Rafferty. I teach physical education and I coach the varsity girls' team. I haven't seen you around before." Taylor paused, pushing a long strand of brown hair out of her face. "How did you end up at Wiscasset?"

"Well, I work part-time at the Boatery in Boothbay, and I'm trying to get my foot in the door to start teaching and hopefully coach some basketball. This is my first time substituting here. Well, anywhere, actually."

"What do you want to teach? I'm always curious about people that want to join in the insanity that is high school education." Taylor laughed as she cocked her head, waiting for Chloe's reply.

Chloe had done some serious growing during her higher education, becoming more comfortable stepping outside of her bubble to get to know new people. Moving away for graduate school had demanded that of her. With a little effort she generally managed to find some commonality with the people she encountered. That did not necessarily mean she genuinely enjoyed each interaction. Taylor, the affable gym teacher, was turning out to be one of those interactions that was just easy, as if they were old friends.

"Ideally I'd like to pursue a position teaching physics. But right now I'll take anything I can get. I haven't done anything since my junior year student teaching."

"Why so rusty? Your junior year can't be that long ago. Have you even graduated yet? And you coach? Answer any of those questions you feel comfortable with and in no particular order." Holding her hands up for the pass, Taylor caught the ball and took a shot, waiting for Chloe to answer.

Chloe appreciated Taylor's approachable demeanor. She was friendly, genuine, and patient enough that her questioning didn't feel at all pushy. She looked to be somewhere in her mid-thirties. Her dark brown hair was pulled back in a ponytail, and she was wearing khakis and a Wiscasset girls' basketball T-shirt. She was shorter than Chloe by at least three inches. Clearly defined muscles peeked out from underneath her short sleeves with each shot she took. Chloe had a sneaking suspicion that Taylor was not straight.

Grateful for the warm welcome she had offered, Chloe responded easily.

"Well, I'm rusty because I graduated three years ago. Even though I apparently still pass for a student, I'm really a twenty-six-year-old bum with two expensive degrees and no direction. I coached during my summers in undergrad. We only won a couple of tournaments, but with the talent we had that was basically like winning the World Series. I loved my kids to death and they played so hard. They did everything I asked of them and grew so much in three summers."

"That's nice you got to stay with the team for that long. I'm assuming you played in college, where? Oh and don't worry about having no direction. I only have One Direction," Taylor added as an afterthought. That was until she raised her eyebrows and nodded at Chloe, waiting for the joke to sink in. Chloe took a second to process which direction Taylor was joking about, then finally it clicked. Chloe couldn't suppress the corresponding groan. That was enough acknowledgment for Taylor, who let out a loud and enthusiastic laugh.

"So, where'd you play? You aren't terrible." Taylor took another shot.

"I played at St. Michael's in Vermont."

"Division Two. I'm surprised. I pegged you as a Division One player. I'm assuming you got offers, but you chose St. Mike's for the academics?"

"Yeah, I knew I wanted a small school and I felt like I fit there. Vermont is beautiful and it worked. I'm from upstate New York so it was close enough to get home but still feel like a new place. You must have played. Where did you go?"

"Hartford Hawks, baby! But you were probably in third grade while I was playing. Pffft." Taylor gave a dismissive wave. "Here, let me quick beat you at PIG."

With that Taylor spun on the spot and hit a turn-around jumper from the wing, officially starting their game. Chloe stepped up and replicated the turnaround, the ball hanging on the rim and gently falling through. Taylor grabbed the rebound and started walking around the court, deciding which shot to take next. Settling on a three from the baseline corner, she drained her second shot. Chloe checked the time. This could take a while.

"You said you're the varsity coach here? How are you guys going to be this year?" Chloe asked as she too hit the shot from the baseline.

"We have three senior starters from last year and four juniors that are ready to contribute way more this year. The biggest thing we have to adjust to is that we lost our post last year. She graduated and went to play at St. Bonaventure."

"Do you have any other size?"

"Nope. And I don't have any young guns that I could pull up either. We're going to have to adjust to compensate, but let's be honest you have to do that every year anyway. It's the core part of my job. I'm going to have to be creative with our speed, primarily on defense, to make up for it. But that's what I love, figuring out the different strengths and utilizing them."

"How did you do last season?"

"We ended up losing in the championship game. That was a tough loss, but it's definitely motivated some of the girls this offseason. They're turning themselves into college prospects for sure."

The conversation slowly shifted to different offenses to run that would work well for a smaller team, discussing the strengths and weaknesses of each. Not only was Taylor friendly, she had a great coaching philosophy. She could learn a lot from her, Chloe decided. If nothing else, she would be going to plenty of their home games—and most likely the away games as well. It wasn't like she had other pressing plans.

Taylor took a three from the twenty-eight foot line, missing a touch long. As the ball rebounded across the gym, she turned to Chloe. "We only have five minutes until lunch! Let's rain check this game, but I want to pick your brain about the motion offense you ran at St. Mike's. I love that style of play, but my kids need more structure than that. Care to continue this in the staff lunch room?"

"Wow, yeah, that'd be great! I have to grab my food. Who knew? I thought I'd be the lame new kid eating alone in her classroom today."

"Well, you are still the lame new kid. I'm a bleeding heart."

Chloe laughed, heading to the gym door to get her lunch with the promise of meeting up with Taylor shortly.

* * *

The halls were as empty as they had been at the start of the period, but now they were filled with a palpable energy that only the impending lunch period could bring. Chloe quickened her pace to beat the mad rush to the cafeteria that was about to ensue. Sliding into the staff room the secretary had pointed out on their early morning tour, she spotted Taylor right away at a table near the windows. Waving, she headed over to join her.

"I feel like I should do something to haze you, but since you're only a sub for the day, I'll only ask you to bring me a napkin from the coffee table over yonder."

Chloe changed direction to grab Taylor's napkin, but as she walked she called out, "No problem. Every action has an equal and opposite reaction, but the laws of the universe don't apply to PIG scores. You opting not to haze me doesn't negate the fact that I'm up on you."

Laughing, Taylor responded, "Okay, hard-ass. Have a seat. This lunch period flies by."

Chloe sat down and opened her lunch. The salad she'd packed the night before was much less appetizing when compared to Taylor's homemade enchiladas.

"Those look delicious!"

"Thanks, they are. My partner Anne is an incredible cook. It's a good thing too, or I'd be eating sandwiches every day."

Resisting the urge to celebrate that always accompanied finding another lesbian, Chloe played it cool and brought their conversation back to the finer details and variations of the offensive schemes available for a smaller and faster team.

In college Chloe had been a part of a motion offense, one with a high degree of structure with ball screen and off screen reads built into it. After she described the system, which relied heavily on the guards reading situations and the point guard signaling an initial read option which would waterfall into corresponding reads, she and Taylor concluded this particular offense, while elegant and effective at the collegiate level, would be much too complex for the group of girls Taylor was expecting to come out for the team.

Two offenses stood out as the front-runners when they turned to options that the team could conceivably handle. Chloe favored a one-four high option, with lots of on-ball screens and back screens, whereas Taylor had been considering a flex option that was highly structured and offered more opportunities for mid-range jump shots.

"At least now I feel confident that I have two potential systems to implement. If I feel totally ballsy maybe I'll put both in. There's a fine line between brilliance and insanity. I passed it a long time ago, but that's a minor detail."

"That's the spirit, Coach. Motivate the troops with your supreme confidence," Chloe responded, generating a loud burst of laughter from Taylor.

The pair turned their attentions to their long-forgotten lunches with vigor, realizing that the lunch period was very nearly over.

"Oh, I almost forgot. Are you busy tonight? We play pickup about twice a week here and we're down one tonight. We usually get at least eight and manage to get a couple good four-on-four games going, but damn Levit has a game tonight so she can't make it."

"Levit? Does she teach here? I think I have study hall with her next block."

"Yeah, she's tragically boring. Poor thing was a soccer player. But we still let her come play every week. It's really because we're the closest thing she has to a social life. Like I said, I'm a bleeding heart."

"I'm not going to lie. You don't exactly have me jazzed for this study hall."

"Don't worry. For a soccer player she isn't half bad." Taylor paused, then added a grin. "Some days I even like her."

* * *

Since Chloe had no papers to grade during the study hall and prepping for class for another hour would only increase her nerves, she decided to bring her book and read something other than physics while "monitoring."

Rounding the corner that would take her to the library, she saw two teachers talking near the opposite end of the hallway. They appeared to be one of those couples that tended to pop up in high schools, a tall, black-haired man with perfectly coiffed hair and perfectly tailored clothes and a brunette wearing tortoiseshell glasses and a patterned scarf. He was obviously flirting with her. When he placed his hand on her arm, though, she tensed and pulled away. Making the decision to keep as far as possible from any lovers' spats, Chloe sped up and ducked inside the library.

In the far left corner a door stood ajar to a room labeled "Quiet Study Area." She assumed this was where study hall would be held but decided to check with the librarian to be sure. Walking up to the main desk, Chloe approached a woman with graying hair and rimless eyeglasses.

"How can I help you?" came the soft voice of the librarian.

"I'm subbing today for Mrs. Flore and I wanted to make sure the room in the back, the quiet study area, is where I'm supposed to go…"

"Oh yes, none of the students have come in. I haven't seen Madeleine yet either, so you're on your own for now. You might not have any students today. I believe the juniors are on a field trip, and I know for a fact that the two seniors on the roster have early dismissal. I'm Mrs. Ross, by the way."

"Thank you so much! I should probably head in and wait to see if I have anybody to supervise." The librarian nodded in polite acknowledgment and told Chloe to have a wonderful day before heading to the computer room to complete some other task.

Wondering where Ms. Levit might be, Chloe meandered into the study area. Inside were four large tables, each with six chairs. Another, smaller table stood at the front of the room with two more chairs. Assuming this was her table, Chloe sat in one and spun it to face the door.

Chloe was removing her bookmark, preparing to immerse herself in her book when a flurry of activity at the door grabbed her attention. The brunette she had seen outside the library minutes before hurried in the room.

Her hair hung loosely in a low braid, with auburn highlights now visible. Chloe hadn't noticed the satchel that she carried earlier. It was swinging dangerously now as she stormed into the room with more than a hint of frustration. She wore black pants that clung to her legs, knee-high brown leather riding boots, and a loose-fitting maroon blouse. She reminded Chloe of the English graduate students she'd shared many cafés with outside Boston. She was intriguing.

As she turned to the front of the room where Chloe sat, the woman jumped in surprise.

Chloe could not help but laugh, standing simultaneously to apologize. "I'm sorry to sneak up on you like this, sitting here reading in your study hall, but I come in peace." She expressed her regret with the slightest trace of enjoyment. "I'm the substitute teacher for Mrs. Flore, Chloe Amden." Chloe offered an outstretched hand to the beautiful teacher.

The earlier tension slowly drained from the frazzled woman's face as she released an audible sigh. Her features relaxed into a comfortable repose, allowing Chloe to take note of the way her hair framed her gently sloping cheekbones and full lips.

"I'm Madeleine Levit. I'm sorry for storming in here like a maniac. A stressful day is no excuse for being ready to roundhouse kick a stranger who's sitting in the quiet study area quietly studying."

Chloe shook the hand Madeleine stretched toward her, noticing as she did that she was wearing on her wrist a bright blue, knotted hair band that resembled a bracelet. Temporarily distracted, she imagined Madeleine with her hair pulled back into a ponytail. She could definitely pull off that look. Releasing the handshake, Chloe was brought back to the present as Madeleine went on.

"In my defense, you're most definitely not Mrs. Flore, so I think my surprise was warranted." The intensity in her expressive hazel eyes faded into calm composure again.

"Surprise, sure that was warranted. Jujitsu, though, maybe not absolutely necessary?" Chloe countered with a shrug. Madeleine greeted her quip with a peal of laughter, and the last of the tension etched in her face slipped away.

"I'm sorry your stress level is high enough that you're prepared to level innocent strangers. But as long as you decided not to take me out with a nasty roundhouse, I can work with that."

"You're safe for now," Madeleine answered. "But one question remains. Where are the children?" Her eyes shone as she gestured around the room. Chloe grinned.

"I haven't the foggiest idea." Both of them laughed comfortably. "Actually, according to Mrs. Ross, we get to oversee an empty study hall today. The juniors are on a field trip somewhere and the few seniors had an early dismissal."

"Well, that is fantastic news. I'll call down the attendance, and you can get back to reading without being afraid for your life."

"That sounds like a great plan to me," Chloe responded, settling in with her book for the second time. She doubted she would get much reading done. Madeleine was distracting, to say the least.

When Madeleine approached the table again, Chloe couldn't help but smile. She was sure the English teacher would have plenty to do during this study hall, but she could not ask for a better way to spend her time than with a beautiful and witty peer. Madeleine's voice broke through her thoughts.

"I'm sorry. I won't be very much fun this study hall, but I really need to take advantage of the fact that there aren't any students in today and get on top of these essays. If I don't do them now I never will." Madeleine gestured toward the manila folder stuffed full of papers that was sticking out of her bag, giving a shrug.

"No worries. Pretend I'm not here. I've got a date with *Atlas Shrugged*."

"You're reading Ayn Rand? Don't tell me you buy into her ideology," Madeleine scoffed, appraising the book Chloe held more closely now.

"Whoa!" Chloe called, tossing her hands up in the air in a mock surrender. "I read it in high school and I was intrigued by the notion of individual success. Embarrassing, I know. But now that I have a clue about how the world works and how vile Rand was, I'm revisiting it. I've got to be informed if I'm going to argue against it with my uncles."

For an impromptu defense of her perusal of a book that plenty of people thought was drivel, she thought she'd done pretty well. She was content that she didn't sound like a total moron at least.

"Okay, so you actually think about what she says as opposed to swallowing all of it. That's refreshing."

Madeleine stopped suddenly, her eyes widening in alarm, "Oh God, I'm so sorry. That was one of the most pompous things I've ever said. I get so used to forcing my kids to think about what they read I forget that many normal humans voluntarily do so. It's the English teacher in me."

She went on, her voice quiet, "You must think I'm a total ass right now."

Madeleine's outrage and then her subsequent, self-deprecating apology helped to temper Chloe's knee-jerk reaction to the roller-coaster ride this woman had taken her on in a span of about four minutes. Her eyes traveled to Madeleine's, reading genuine embarrassment there.

"What's the point of a behemoth like this one if we don't talk about it, right?" Chloe said. "But we aren't at book club, and I hear you have work to do. Don't let me keep you from it."

Madeleine nodded and set her supplies out on the table, visibly relieved at Chloe's willingness to overlook her book snob outburst. Then with the resolve of a teacher determined to be productive, she dove into grading her pile of essays.

It took Chloe a solid fifteen minutes to get through the page she had left off on. She was hardly surprised by this, as she had suddenly become very concerned about appearing scholarly while she read. This had resulted in her restarting the entire process twenty times or so.

After she had finally turned a page, she realized that for all of her efforts to impress someone that she would likely not encounter again, she had succeeded only in making it appear that she was reading at a first-grade level. Bringing herself back to reality and pretending she hadn't had spent the past quarter of an hour being stupid, she finally focused on the reading. Initially distracted when Madeleine would turn a page or scribble down marks on the papers, eventually she became desensitized to the noises and stopped noticing entirely.

About halfway through the study hall, Chloe had a feeling Madeleine was looking her way, but she resisted checking for fear of getting caught. As frazzled as she'd been when she came into the study hall, one of the last things Ms. Levit needed was unwanted interest from a substitute.

More than that, Chloe reminded herself that shifting her focus away from her future was a mistake. She could hear Hannah's voice clearly, warning her to avoid any and all "cute homos" until she could personally determine their viability. She had no doubt Hannah would tell her to be wary of any woman, let alone one who likely had a beau working at the same school. She was only now beginning to let go of some of the anger and bitterness that had filled her for the last few months. She needed to focus on moving forward. Nothing was worth jeopardizing the possibility of achieving some semblance of stability in her life, the kind of stability, as Jacob would no doubt remind her, that teaching might provide.

Chloe's thoughts drifted back to where she wanted to go with her career. She had so far genuinely enjoyed the day in Wiscasset; the kids she had worked with were receptive and she felt supported by the staff even though she was only a substitute.

Then again that's how she had initially felt at UMass.

Today isn't over yet, she cautioned herself, the realist in her rearing to life. A buzz from her pocket provided a welcome distraction—until she saw the text was from Nora.

A song by Ben Rector came on today and I smiled.

Chloe smiled too, then frowned. How was it that she was still susceptible to notes like this from Nora? Maybe because she represented something unfinished? The girl needed to realize there was no hope. She shook her head, amazed that she could be so stupid and selfish. How could she blame Nora for holding on to hope? Still, whatever Nora had represented before, now she was yet another loose end in Chloe's life. That's all she could be. She deleted the text. Perfect. Why couldn't all the other knotty issues in her life unravel and blow away in the wind?

* * *

Fourth block went by quickly. The first few weeks in any high school physics class served primarily to get the students' feet wet. This early in the year they were still in the beginning chapters of Newtonian mechanics, laying the groundwork, so to speak.

Mrs. Flore's AP kids were fun to teach, and the homework questions had been relatively simple. Chloe had successfully helped MacKenna, a junior who was very eager to learn, have a breakthrough about the interchangeability of the different equations depending on what the question was asking. She had gone out on a limb too. Deciding that the video they were scheduled to watch was old and boring, she had flipped on the projector and played a few episodes of *Cosmos* with Neil deGrasse Tyson. They were a total hit with the students, and Chloe loved watching them herself, so it was a win-win. The kids still learned about the universe so the main goal of the exercise was accomplished. She hoped Mrs. Flore wouldn't be terribly upset.

When final announcements came on the PA system and students were dismissed, Chloe was shocked that the day was already finished. Unsure about the procedure for her to lock up and whatnot, she grabbed her lunch and courier bag, turned out the lights, and headed in the direction of the main office. Most of the kids were either on the buses, heading for their cars, or in their after-school period, so the halls were nearly empty again as she passed through them. The main office was a flurry of activity, however, with teachers and students milling about finishing up various tasks. Chloe was greeted by Maryanne.

"How can I help you, Ms. Amden?" Despite the torrent of activity around her, the secretary remained unruffled.

"I wasn't sure if I needed to sign out before I leave. I turned out the lights and locked the door of the classroom."

"Typically, that would be all I would need from you, but I talked with Mrs. Flore's daughter and we're in need of a substitute tomorrow as well as the whole of next week. Mrs. Flore has been hospitalized with pneumonia." Shaking her head, whether for Mrs. Flore's health troubles or her own scheduling woes Chloe wasn't quite sure, most likely a little of both, Maryanne continued, "Are you at all interested or available for any of those days? Don't feel obligated, but I wanted to offer the time to you first as you've already helped us out today. Whatever you are not interested in I will offer to the other substitutes."

Caught off guard by the unexpected offer, Chloe gathered her thoughts.

"I would love to cover the entire time. Can I call my supervisor at my other job to double-check that he is all set without me? I can do that right now," she offered, confident that Jacob would tell her not to worry about the Boatery.

"No, no, that's all right. I'll put you down for tomorrow and you can let me know then about next week. Even if you can't take the whole week that gives me plenty of time to start calling the list." Flashing a polite smile, Maryanne nodded slightly, then returned to her computer, effectively ending the conversation. Everything the woman lacked in pleasantries, she made up for in efficiency.

Outside, the sky was clear and inviting, the rest of the afternoon teeming with possibilities. Invigorated from her first successful day as a substitute, Chloe felt tentatively optimistic. Heading to her Jeep with a lot more confidence than when she had come in this morning, she set off for the Boatery to decompress with Jacob for a while. Later she would come back to the school for a bit of pickup basketball. Finishing her evening playing with Taylor and whoever else she wrangled into participating was one of the most exciting evenings she had scheduled since arriving in Boothbay. She could hardly wait.

* * *

As she had expected, Jacob was thrilled that she was going to get a week of exposure to what he called "the unseen world of molding young minds." He told her not to worry about the schedule. Andrew was coming in every day next week, and fall was a fairly slow season until people began to rent winter gear.

They chatted about Taylor, the school, and how her classes had been manageable. Jacob smiled when Chloe spoke excitedly about her plans for the coming week. She was sure that she might get a little leeway in what to do with the classes since it wasn't likely Mrs. Flore had drawn up plans while in the hospital. If nothing else, she hoped to teach a bit of actual content, following Mrs. Flore's original lesson plan. Checking her watch finally, Chloe realized she only had a half an hour until she was supposed to be at the gym to play.

"Shit, Jacob, I have to go change and get to the gym. Taylor, the phys ed teacher, asked me to join them tonight to play some pickup games!"

"By all means, change in the back!" Jacob shooed her away. "Go forth and prosper! I'll see you for your shift Saturday!" he called after her as she raced to the changing room.

* * *

Chloe could barely believe her luck. Her first day of substitute teaching was over and now she was going to play basketball with a group of former college players. Her excitement about the prospect eclipsed any anxiety she might have had about walking into a gym full of strangers. Putting her Jeep in park, she spotted two women heading to the gym, one taller, the other resembling a springy little guard. She slid out of the car and briskly walked inside behind them.

The bleacher nearest the door had been pulled out so that the bottommost row of seats was available for the group to sit on. Strewn along its length were five women. The only one Chloe recognized was Taylor. Walking toward the group, she tapped Taylor's arm to interrupt the impassioned story she was telling the brunette next to her. Taylor jumped to her feet and hugged her, then turned to address the other players.

"Everybody, this is Chloe Amden. She subbed at Wiscasset today and lost to me at PIG."

"If you call being up P to P-I losing I guess I did then," Chloe said, shrugging. At that, the tall woman she had followed into the gym piped up.

"Don't worry. We all know better than to believe everything she says. I'm Stacey, by the way. I teach at Boothbay."

"Nice to meet you," Chloe replied, instantly liking the tall woman with soft brown eyes.

Taylor began to introduce her to the remaining players, Anna, Robin, and Jaysa. Anna was a stocky power forward who had played Division III ball in Vermont. She had a round face you couldn't help but trust. Robin had attended LeMoyne in Syracuse, a strong Division II school. Her dirty blond hair was pulled tightly back, and she gave off an aura of laser-sharp focus. Chloe had a feeling she would be very good.

Jaysa introduced herself, offering a confident hand. Her hair, haphazardly thrown up in a loose ponytail, was several shades darker than her olive skin. She was easily the shortest player, but she had that springy carriage distinctive of raw athleticism.

"Call me J, everyone does. And don't underestimate me because I'm the shortest. I can outjump all of these fools. I played in upstate New York and I'm a CPA in Wiscasset." Her bouncy energy was contagious.

Chloe found herself more excited than nervous to get out there and play. During the introductions, Taylor and Stacey had gone out to warm up and the women Chloe met had finished stretching. Chloe rushed to remove her chukkas and get her sneakers laced up. She was tempted to skip stretching, but the thought of moving tomorrow after no warm-up slowed her down enough to get a quick round of stretches in. Holding onto the bleacher, she began her routine, watching the women shoot for teams. This was going to be some pretty solid basketball. She smiled to herself, feeling utterly content. *Let's see what you've got.*

* * *

"Do you ever miss?" Taylor yelled at Chloe from the baseline.

"It has happened before…" Chloe raised her eyebrows at Taylor as she walked over to her. She'd ended the last game by draining a three. They'd traded buckets the whole way, neither team able to pull away. She, Robin, and Anna had beaten Taylor, Stacey, and J.

"I'll be guarding you next week to make *sure* it happens again." Taylor laughed and purposely bumped into Chloe as they walked toward the bench.

"Congrats on making it through the gauntlet," Stacey joked. "You can come back every week. Today was also your first day as a substitute, right? How was it?" Chloe was surprised at Stacey's genuine interest.

"Honestly, it was really great. The kids were all pretty responsive and respectful. They asked me to come back tomorrow and next week. I couldn't have gotten much luckier." Chloe couldn't possibly explain how completely that statement applied to this entire surreal experience, from subbing to meeting Taylor and joining this group to play basketball.

Jaysa called out in an impressed voice, "Jesus, I don't know how you handle kids. I couldn't do it and I love math. Maybe I love it so much because none of the numbers I crunch can roll their eyes at me."

"That or the fact that none of them are taller than you," Robin quipped. The group burst into laughter at the glare Jaysa shot Robin as she simultaneously flipped her the bird. In that moment, Chloe realized no matter what happened with her job search, she had found an incredible new outlet for alleviating her stress and she couldn't be happier.

CHAPTER FOUR

Friday

Almost before Chloe knew it, her first full week of substituting was coming to a close. She couldn't believe it. Her classes had gone almost too smoothly to be believed. That didn't mean, however, that she didn't desperately need the weekend to recover. Teaching was invigorating, but it was also challenging and flat-out exhausting. She had made it to her second block free period, with only study hall and her favorite AP class between her and the weekend. Thankfully she only had a few things she wanted to get done this block, so she allowed her thoughts to wander.

In addition to subbing, she had come to two more open gym sessions, each one more fun than the last. Taylor had turned out to be one of the funniest and most warm-hearted people Chloe had ever met. She reminded her of an older, slightly more level-headed version of Hannah. Initially they had bonded over basketball, but while they often discussed her team and sports in general, they had found so many other similarities there was never a shortage of conversational topics. As she had discovered when Taylor had invited her to join her, her girlfriend Anne, and the rest of the open gym gang for dinner after the game last night. When Taylor had asked her to join them, she had made a point of extending the invitation to "anyone special" in Chloe's life. Chloe had chuckled at the obvious attempt to fish out confirmation of her sexuality. She told Taylor that she didn't currently have a girlfriend, but she would love to find a special lady to bring to dinners eventually. Taylor was elated at the news.

Though she hadn't met Anne before, Chloe recognized her immediately when she joined the group at the restaurant. She was every bit as beautiful as Taylor had said. She had an easy way about her that Chloe instantly liked.

"Chloe?" Anne stood up and spread her arms wide for a hug. "I've been looking forward to meeting you. Taylor comes home lamenting how you beat her up at pickup, then she forgives you because you're willing to listen to her at lunch." Anne released Chloe from her hug and returned to her seat next to Taylor.

The group was small, only Taylor, Anne, Stacey, Chloe, and Madeleine. Chloe was content to relax and listen as the teachers swapped stories across school districts. Stacey's principal, it seemed, was as different as humanly possible from Mark Dorman, the well-respected principal at Wiscasset.

It was interesting seeing different facets of Madeleine's personality as well. The easy smile she was wearing tonight was the most relaxed one she had seen on her face. She had piqued Chloe's interest since they first met, and their brief conversations at lunch hadn't provided as much opportunity as she'd have liked to get to know her. The study hall they monitored together didn't offer a lot of opportunity for conversation either. She clearly had an impressive intellect. She was also clearly not only a coach but an athlete; her carriage bore the unmistakable poise and strength of athleticism. She was an enigma.

When the conversation shifted to the students and how the year was progressing, Taylor had offered an opinion that livened things up a bit.

"See, I like the standards we have for physical education. I still have the freedom to evaluate the kids individually. And the standards are pretty comprehensive. There are some that are bullshit, but I can't complain too much. It's not like what you classroom people have to deal with."

Stacey and Madeleine were nodding in agreement with Taylor, on board with her opinions on assessment for the moment. Seeing Taylor nudge Anne's arm, Chloe suspected that wasn't going to last. She winced at what she said next.

"After all—showing kids how to fill in little bubbles *has* to be stressful."

If anyone other than Taylor had delivered that line straight-faced, Chloe knew, Stacey and Madeleine might have suffered simultaneous aneurysms. As it was, their response was tempered, but it was clear from their faces that there was no way they were going to allow Taylor to poke the bear and not get *any* blowback.

Stacey inclined her head to Madeleine, ceding to her the opportunity for rebuttal.

"Taylor, I love you to death and I know that you're stirring the pot, but you do realize every time you say that a piece of my soul dies?" Madeleine tilted her head slightly, raising one eyebrow with the same intense look Chloe had seen her use to silence quite a few students in their study hall.

Taylor paused, clearly debating whether to goad Madeleine further. Madeleine spared her the decision and continued.

"You have the freedom in phys ed to build relationships and tailor your curriculum to what you imagine to be the most successful course. That's a luxury we lowly classroom teachers are not afforded. And it robs us of our ability to be as effective as we can be." Madeleine's strong hands gestured around the table to emphasize her point, and Chloe sat, her focus locked on Madeleine.

"Think about it. I guarantee each of us here tonight had at least one monumentally impactful teacher in our education, someone who irrevocably shaped who we became as people, as educators, and as thinkers. That, in essence, is what teachers do. They're charged with molding the potential of our youth. Or they should be. Instead it's like all we're doing is scrambling to get our students to pass, measured by arbitrary standards. What happened to learning, growing, thriving even? Do we really think that it is humanly possible to standardize the nuances of English literature? We expect a test to evaluate the human experience?"

Madeleine drew breath, glancing around the table quickly. Recognizing that she needn't convince this group, she turned to Taylor and added quickly, "At least they can't completely cheapen everything you love about phys ed."

It was impossible not to be moved by what she said. The cadence of her speech was eloquent even in frustration and her eyes shone brightly in the shadowy lighting of the restaurant. Chloe knew even from her limited experience that teachers like Madeleine were essential and all too rare. The system seemed designed to smother them until their fire was extinguished.

As she studied Madeleine's face, Chloe saw it suddenly shift, her features reassembling into a wry smile. "If Chloe never comes out with us again after that," she said, "I want it known that Taylor started this!"

"Are you kidding me? How could I stay away?" Chloe asked when she was finally able to speak. "It was inspiring to hear how you talk about teachers. The ego boost wasn't bad either."

Taylor's comeback was tinged with sarcasm, "Oh God, she's been won over. A little flattery and she's toast. But it's funny, I didn't hear her mention science anywhere in that rant."

"She didn't have to," Chloe said. "Our job as teachers is to cultivate the best in our students and engage them. It doesn't matter the discipline. Knowledge and understanding permeate them all. I couldn't agree with her more. Then again I did go to a liberal arts school…" As Chloe left that thought hanging, Madeleine didn't need to say a word; her expression told Chloe they were in complete agreement.

"Nope," Taylor interjected. "Definitely not. We are not waxing poetic about the liberal arts tonight. You two can find some other time to read poetry and study astrology together, some time when I'm not around." The table had dissolved into laughter at that, eventually returning to lighter subjects.

* * *

Thinking about last night's conversations brought an involuntary grin to Chloe's lips. Thanks to Taylor and Wiscasset's need for a substitute teacher, she was not only surrounded by incredible women but also actually teaching a subject she loved. Both her professional and personal life were in sync so far. It felt odd after having them clash for what felt like an eternity at UMass. Teaching high school juniors and seniors had never before been enticing, but the students were fun and she hoped she was beginning to make a difference.

On Tuesday, during her AP class, Leah, one of her most promising and quietest students, had, with a little prodding from Chloe, gone to the board to walk the rest of the class through one of the more complicated problems. A junior, she was one of only three girls in a class dominated by boys, but she and her soccer teammate Molly, the lone senior girl, appeared to be fully capable of handling the nonsense of high school boys. Emma was another story. Though she had volunteered to answer confidently at the outset, this past week she had lost her self-assurance. Chloe couldn't pinpoint what had happened, but she wanted the chance to figure it out. Emma had the makings of a solid scientist; Chloe wanted that for her. Hopefully today she could get Emma to lead the class and build that confidence back up.

She pulled her thoughts back to the present, getting excited for her fourth-block session, especially the group review activity she had planned to follow the lecture. It was a problem-solving ladder, a series of problems that required a student to use the previous student's answer to solve the next problem. She would split the students into teams and after the winning team reached a solution, they would go through the entire series as a class. The winners would get two bonus points on the quiz. It was helpful to spice up the Newtonian equation-solving they were doing so the kids wouldn't get too bored and, as a result, sloppy.

Relaxed now and a bit tired, Chloe reached into her pocket for her phone, intending to find an appropriate playlist to play in the background as she continued preparation. As she scrolled through her music library, the classroom phone began to ring. She quickly crossed the room to answer it.

"Hello. Ms. Amden speaking."

Maryanne's distinctive voice rang out. "Wonderful, you're exactly the person I need. Ms. Amden, this is your free period, correct?"

"Yes, ma'am, it is. Is there anything I can do for you?"

"Not for me *per se*, but Mr. Dorman would like you to come down to his office. He has something he would like to discuss with you and he is free at this very moment."

"I'll be right down."

"Splendid." In typical Maryanne style, her reply was followed almost immediately by the sound of the dial tone. Chloe hung up the phone and began the walk to the office. She had only seen the school's principal from a distance. He was by all accounts a fair boss, engaged with the student body, and overall quite pleasant. That did not, however, completely assuage the nervousness she felt at being summoned to his office.

At Chloe's arrival in the office, Maryanne gave no indication as to what she could expect. A curt nod from the secretary directed her to continue to an open door at the far corner of the hub of the school. The nameplate there was small and understated, unlike the ornate special order nameplates some of the faculty had chosen at UMass. She hoped that was a good omen.

Though the door was slightly ajar, Chloe announced herself with a light knock. Mr. Dorman appeared around the corner of his desk and he beckoned her inside silently. Holding his office phone up to his ear with one hand, he gestured for her to have a seat in the cushioned chair across the desk from him. He nodded his head and arched his eyebrows, signaling to her he was involved in what had to be one of the most unpleasant aspects of the job, tedious phone conversations.

Chloe took the opportunity to study both him and his office. His hair, once a deep brown, was now streaked with gray, reflecting the stress she imagined accompanied any administrative position. If she had to guess his age she would say he was somewhere in his fifties, though she wouldn't be shocked to learn he was actually much younger.

The most dominant piece of furniture in the room was the enormous wraparound desk in the corner, lined with picture frames and covered with books. A table was situated to her immediate left with three comfortable chairs scattered nearby. Chloe felt welcome in the office, something that was not always a given with administrators.

After about a minute of nearly unbroken silence, Mr. Dorman finally spoke.

"Cynthia, I really appreciate your input, but I have to apologize. I have an important meeting now and I have to go. I did write down what we discussed and I will address it as soon as…" His voice trailed off as he listened to the Cynthia character politely, if not altogether patiently.

Again he spoke, this time more firmly. "Cynthia, I appreciate the call. I've heard what you've said and I will take it from here. You get back to John and I will see you next week for the art open house."

This was followed by a much shorter pause, then he nodded and ended the call. As he turned to focus his attention on Chloe, his demeanor lightened considerably.

"I'm sorry about that. Cynthia is an engaged parent, and while we need more of them, she might benefit from a lesson in recognizing when to step back and be a parent and not an administrator."

Chuckling and shaking his head, he stood, extending his hand, and continued, "I'm sorry it's taken me this long to formally introduce myself, but I'm Mark Dorman. I've heard nothing but great things about how it's been going down that science hallway." Chloe took his hand in hers, impressed by his warm welcome and grateful for the praise.

"It's nice to finally meet you, Mark. I can't quite explain how grateful I am that I found my way here to substitute." Though she saw pride and warmth reflected in his face, Chloe knew he couldn't possibly grasp how much this school had already grown on her in such a short time. In a handful of days, Wiscasset and the people she had stumbled upon by association had helped thaw a layer of ice that she hadn't realized had crept into her life.

"You know, I'm glad you brought that up. I wanted to hear a little bit more from you regarding your experience both in the past and here at Wiscasset." He sat as he talked, gesturing that she should do the same. "I read your application to substitute. I saw your CV and I must admit I was surprised that you were branching out of academia, especially considering you were on the fast track to your doctorate."

There it was, the same confusion Chloe had seen too many times on the faces of those closest to her. The familiar line of questioning sent her emotions into free fall. Scrambling to regain control, she took a steadying breath.

"I haven't ruled out returning to my graduate studies, but I needed to take some time for myself to get some perspective. I couldn't imagine a better way to do that than to share what I had learned with current students and maybe even ignite a love of science in a few of them while I'm at it."

While this description was vague and phrased to obscure her own confusion about the direction her career had taken, it seemed to satisfy the principal, who was nodding as she spoke. She continued, "As for Wiscasset, coming here has been an absolute pleasure. Even though I am only substituting, it reminded me how much I love teaching, no matter the level."

The caution Chloe had initially been met with melted away, replaced by another emotion. Was it hope? Excitement? Now it was Chloe's curiosity that was piqued.

"Well, then, bearing that in mind, I have something that I think might appeal to you." Straightening in his chair into what Chloe assumed was the friendly principal's formal posture, he continued.

"I've been in contact with Marlene Flore's daughter and have gone to visit her since her hospitalization. Collectively we've decided the best course of action would be for her to go on leave for the remainder of the year."

Chloe's pulse began to race in wild disbelief at where she assumed this conversation was headed. Struggling to rein in her hopes, she listened intently.

"We will be holding open interviews for the long-term position that has now opened in light of Marlene's failing health, but I wanted to encourage you to apply given your qualifications and the way you have meshed with our students and staff in such a brief time. That is if you really want it—which, pardon me, I haven't even asked you. Regardless of your feelings about the long-term position, though, for the students' sakes we want you to continue subbing until the new person comes on board."

Mark finished his thought quickly and sat back waiting to hear Chloe's thoughts on the matter. Where to begin? She didn't want to appear overeager, but then again if she hesitated, what did that say? Ignoring any misgivings or doubts that were building along with her mounting hope, Chloe went for it.

"Wow, Mark. Obviously I'm concerned for Mrs. Flore. I hope that this is exactly what she needs to get well. But that being said I would absolutely love the opportunity to apply for the position. To be frank, I feel like I have found a niche here. I will gladly continue next week. Given the chance, I would be honored to work here for the year!"

Mark beamed. "I am thrilled to hear that, Chloe, I really am. I will have Maryanne send you an email with all the particulars so that we can set up your interview and get the process started."

He stood and extended his hand again, gripping hers with both of his. Wishing him a good rest of the day, Chloe left the office. For the umpteenth time since this surreal journey began, she could not believe her luck. She shivered with excitement and a bit of fear. How long would it be before this newfound luck ran out?

* * *

Returning to the classroom, Chloe looked at it with new eyes, marveling that it could become hers for the next nine months and envisioning small changes she would make, posters that might work on various stretches of exposed wall. She shook her head in disbelief. She needed to talk with someone about this stroke of good fortune. She didn't know Hannah's schedule for the day, and she didn't want to disrupt a potentially busy day for her. *Jacob*. He would be thrilled with her news. This was most likely what he had imagined when he had persuaded her to give teaching a whirl.

Chloe punched in the number for the store, though mounting doubt was dampening her excitement. Jacob wouldn't be upset, would he? Fall was a slower season for him and he wouldn't need the extra hands. It would save him money to get her out of his hair.

Jacob's expressive voice greeted her after one ring. "*Buongiorno*. What passes in the land of bountiful attitude?"

"Well, time passes. I'm sure a handful of students will too." Chloe's quip was met with a low chuckle. "How's business?"

"Not a bad day. A trickle of late season tourists came through. I'm working on one of the window displays now. It's rather uninspired, though. I'm stepping away to let something come about organically, if you will."

"I hate to interrupt a master at his craft, but maybe my news will bring some inspiration with it."

"Oh do tell!" Chloe could hear the approval in his voice.

"Well, the secretary called me down to the office to speak with the principal. Mrs. Flore is taking a medical leave for the rest of the school year and he's encouraged me to apply for the newly opened long-term substitute position!"

"Bravo! You must be doing some really solid work up there if they want you to apply so badly. I don't mind taking a moment to gloat and congratulate myself on this accomplishment, but the question is, how do *you* feel about it?"

Leave it to Jacob to pick up on her misgivings so quickly.

"I'm terrified now that I'm overthinking it, but when he first talked to me about it, I don't know—it felt right." Chloe's voice trailed off as she struggled with the tumult of emotions.

"What about the position excites you? What appeals to you about it?" Jacob asked.

His straightforward questions were difficult for Chloe to answer honestly. If she verbalized her excitement, then she risked feeling more pain when things inevitably failed to live up to her hopes and expectations.

"Well, for starters the timing is nothing short of ideal," she said, aware that she was avoiding the real reasons she was interested, the ones Jacob wanted to hear. Those were the reasons that were the scariest to articulate. "I would get some great experience to put on my résumé while working within the time constraints of my leave of absence."

Chloe hesitated. Every commitment she had made within the past few years had left her vulnerable. How could she risk that again, especially now that she was starting to feel somewhat normal? She wasn't sure she was ready to risk having something else that she allowed herself to become passionate about implode right in front of her.

"Yes, logistically it does play out quite nicely. But the same could be said for you delivering the mail, so why does this job appeal to you specifically?"

A hard edge crept into her voice despite the fact that she knew Jacob was only trying to be supportive. "You know why, Jacob. It works. I would still be able to do some physics, and it would fill my time until I make up my mind." Her response was met at first with silence. Then...

"Chloe, whatever decision you make will be your own, and that is exactly what you need right now. I know there is fear and doubt, but I believe in you. Eventually you'll find a way to do the same. But remember, there is always risk involved with reward."

He paused, almost as if he knew Chloe needed a moment to let the words swirl around her. Every hurdle would not be tackled today, but he could apply whatever emotional balm he had.

"Now, I'm entirely too old to boast about how wise I was to suggest this, so I will instead choose to return to my window display. Don't work too hard today. I'll see you for your shift tomorrow." With that he hung up, but not before Chloe heard him start humming to himself in a contented way.

CHAPTER FIVE

Monday

What a way to start the week. Maryanne had been able to squeeze the interview in during Chloe's free period so no one outside of the committee was any wiser about the whole thing. The interview itself had been straightforward and encouraging. Judging by the way that Mark and his panel of teachers had nodded at each of her answers, she felt pretty good about her chances, though her emotions regarding the prospect of teaching for the rest of the year were still prone to fluctuate wildly at any given moment.

Staring down at the stack of quizzes that needed to be graded, Chloe sat motionless, surprised at herself. She had left the interview with a clear head and was temporarily at peace. Noticeably absent was the stream of doubts and worries that had ticked on endlessly in the back of her mind when she started the day. She still wasn't sure how many applicants they were bringing in and how long it would take for them to decide. All she could do now was wait.

She had expected to spend her weekend filled with anxiety, but it actually had passed quickly, thanks in large part to Jacob and to some serious Netflix binging. Working with Jacob had been a good balance of distraction and discussion. As usual, his words had struck right at the heart of the issue.

"Chloe, what you've experienced, absolutely that's enough to dismantle anyone's confidence. But the question is, how do you respond? I know you've faced adversity in basketball. Did that keep you from playing again? You have to start somewhere."

What had she expected when she took her leave of absence—to run away indefinitely? Even if she got the job, she would still be avoiding the larger issue, the future of her academic career.

The more Chloe thought about the Wiscasset position the more she realized she was being irrational in hesitating. Nothing about taking it mandated that she remain in a high school setting. She had been strong enough to walk away from UMass. She could certainly handle a few months teaching physics to high school kids.

Talking to Hannah had also helped. They had spent a good portion of Saturday evening on the phone discussing their respective bucket lists. Hannah was hoping to visit Chloe next weekend if her workload allowed and she wanted to tick off a few things on her list in the process.

The prospect of spending a weekend goofing around with Hannah was providing Chloe with a bit of an emotional buffer as well. All she had to do before she visited was survive a period of torturous anxiety, a week of teaching, and grading the rest of the quizzes from today, which she had been staring at for the last ten minutes.

Grading was an interesting experience. Chloe actually kind of liked it. Still in the process of getting to know her students, she saw their personalities reflected in every answer, in the way they approached each problem. She enjoyed throwing bonus questions in at the end of quizzes for fun. The one on this particular quiz asked the students to calculate the mass of a group of Star Wars characters given a set of clues about their relative sizes and volumes. For an extra point, students could argue why one character was superior to the others. Chloe loved to read the arguments. Even more, she enjoyed writing responses to them.

Leah had written a particularly moving argument in favor of the newest female Jedi in training, Rey, as not only the best but the most clearly underrated and overlooked of all of the Star Wars characters, noting that she had been left out of the action figure sets in toy stores despite being the main character of *The Force Awakens*. Chloe was contemplating what feminist stick figure cartoon she would draw as a response when a knock on the doorframe disrupted her concentration.

"Please tell me one of the students superglued your ass to that chair." Taylor had sauntered into the room and now stood opposite from her, wearing an expectant expression.

Confused, Chloe stared back as Taylor waited for her response.

"Have you forgotten the outside world? Being superglued in that chair is the only reason I'll accept for you not doing whatever the hell you're doing outside. At least get some color while you geek out. Jesus, you're practically translucent."

Chloe's retort had barely formed on her lips when Taylor held up her hand and continued. "You know what, it's fine. You can make up for it by saying yes to the two things I'm going to ask you to do before I even ask them."

"Taylor, I may have only been here for a couple of weeks, but I think I know better than to agree to anything from you before I read the fine print."

"I should probably be insulted, but it really doesn't matter, you're going to say yes anyway. I'll start off with the tougher sell considering your apparent agoraphobia. Madeleine's soccer team has a home game against Stacey and her gang tonight. Six thirty. I'll pick you up. Unless you're planning on staying here the entire time…"

"Obviously I'll go," Chloe responded. "But I, unlike you who gets to have class outside every minute, have to grade these and I happen to need a desk for that, so forgive me for being inside. I won't need a ride. I'll probably stay here to finish them up since it's nearly four." She paused, steeling herself for Taylor's response to what she was about to say. "I really need to get these finished if I want to get that year-long sub position."

Chloe hadn't told anyone at school about the interview before this, not wanting to get involved in any school drama. She had contemplated not telling Taylor for fear of jinxing it, but as soon as she walked in, she decided to bounce the possibility off her. Her reaction to Chloe's statement did not disappoint.

"Wow! I had heard Marlene probably wasn't coming back this year. Did you interview? How'd you find out? Tell me everything, you fool!"

Taylor's excitement at the possibility of Chloe working at the school year-round was infectious. Chloe felt some of her nervousness melt away as she related her conversation with Mark Dorman and the interview that had taken place earlier that day. Taylor ate it up.

"This is fantastic. You're a lock for it. They're not going to find anyone on such short notice, and they've seen your potential with you being here for, what, almost two weeks straight? No question it's yours. Congratulations, kid. Either way, it's an honor Mark asked you to apply."

"Thanks, Taylor. I'm pretty nervous about it. If I get it, that means being a real teacher. If I don't, that means having to branch out and sub in who knows where."

"Don't think that way. This is a killer opportunity to work with me every single day, obviously."

"Clearly, that's the only reason I applied. I'm desperate for more time with you." Both women laughed, grateful for the other. "I'm nervous, but I've got to ask. You said you had two favors to ask me?"

"Well, I have something I would like to offer you, though technically I have to ask you if you want it first." Her tone was more serious now, no longer joking. Chloe waited for her to spit it out.

"Julie, my JV coach—you haven't met her but you would have loved her… Anyway, she was basically in a position like you, subbing and trying to find permanent phys ed jobs. She called me over the weekend—and I can't be upset about it because she deserves it—but a position opened up in Virginia. She got the job, and she's moving there this week. So obviously, I'm in a little bit of a pickle."

Chloe stared at Taylor, dumbfounded. There was no way this was happening. She opened her mouth to respond, but the words wouldn't form. Her neural network was fried; a huge surge of emotion had wiped it out, and she was no longer capable of speech. All she could do was sit there as waves of excitement crashed over her.

"Umm, I guess I can put it more plainly. Chloe, I want you to be my JV coach. The pay is lousy, but the company is fantastic. You'll still have to interview, but the job is yours unofficially." Taylor's smile dimmed momentarily as she paused, "I have to say, though, any more of this silent treatment and I might have to reconsider."

Taylor's quizzical reaction to Chloe's odd response was enough to break her silence. Giggles turned into nearly uncontrollable laughter and began pouring out of her as she jumped to her feet and engulfed Taylor in an enormous hug.

Taylor's muffled response advised Chloe that if she wanted the job she might want to stop suffocating her. Chloe stepped back, beaming. "I think I was in shock. That was so out of the blue it felt like a joke, but then it was real and…I can't wait. Can we start now?"

"That's more along the lines of what I had been expecting." Taylor laughed. "But ease it back. Technically we still have to go through Landon. He's our athletic director. And I won't sugarcoat it. He's a misogynistic asshat. But you can't have everything in life."

Chloe thought back to her lone glimpse of the AD so far, his interaction with Madeleine on her first day of subbing. He was very possessive of her. At the time Chloe hadn't known who either of them was, but the exchange she had seen outside the library that day was one she herself hoped to never have with the man. Since her future as a junior varsity basketball coach rested with him, however, she might have to endure his nonsense as well.

"I'll follow your lead. I guess I should get used to that if you're going to be my boss."

"Damn straight! I'll never steer you wrong. I've already led you to the homo sanctuary every Tuesday and Thursday, haven't I? Now I've got to go get Anne, but I'll see you at the game!"

Taylor's offhand comment about leading Chloe to a sanctuary had been closer to the truth than she could ever know. The support she had given her during their first interaction had been far from the last. Last week Chloe vented to her about her encounter going to the restroom and having an older teacher she hadn't recognized brusquely tell her she was in the women's bathroom and that the men's room was down the hall. The disgust in her voice had made it perfectly clear that she didn't think Chloe was simply lost.

When Taylor heard the story, she made some very creative suggestions about where the woman could put her bigoted head, which thoroughly entertained Chloe. She then went on to lift Chloe's spirits further by offering to explain to her colleague the nuances of gender expression. When Chloe had wondered aloud whether the administration would be open to offering an introductory level LGBTQ+ Professional Development course for staff, Taylor told her she'd need to find a way to stick around next year as a full-time teacher so she could teach it herself. The thought that that might be an actual possibility now caught Chloe's attention, but she cautioned herself not to get ahead of herself just yet.

Chloe was glad that Taylor had reminded her of the game today. Somehow she'd forgotten about it, despite the fact that both the morning and afternoon announcements had reminded the entire school about the contest with Boothbay and Molly and Leah, both starters, had worn their jerseys to class. It would be nice to show some support for the girls.

It was time for a change of scenery, she decided after an hour of steady grading. The sun was still large on the horizon, though it was slipping closer to dusk. From her seat in the classroom, she could make out the Wiscasset girls in their white home unis as they began their dynamic warm-up. She checked her watch to see how much time she had. It was 5:48. She had a little over half an hour before the game would start. She decided the quizzes could be finished in the stands while she enjoyed one of the few remaining temperate afternoons. She was excited to see Stacey and Madeleine in action. They were considered two of the best coaches in the region, and Wiscasset and Boothbay were soccer powerhouses. She hadn't really been exposed to soccer growing up. She developed an interest in the team as a freshman in high school, but that had been more about one of the captains of the team than about the game itself. She'd gotten a little bit ahead of herself as a result and lived to regret it to this day. Instead, she'd focused her energy on basketball and softball. She had watched a handful of games in college, though, and had started to pay more attention to the sport, especially the national women's teams. Now that she knew two high school coaches she had even more reason to get to some games.

She gathered up her bag and papers and grabbed her jacket and car keys. The weather was perfect for a night game, though it would be chilly. Putting on her gray, fleece-lined, vintage military jacket, she pulled out her phone and texted Hannah.

The military jacket lives on. Perfect chance to slay and stay warm.

Hannah fervently hated the jacket and had ever since Chloe had first worn it during their sophomore year. Chloe, however, loved it and refused to part with it. She was convinced Hannah hated it because her first serious crush at St. Michael's had worn a coat nearly identical to it. To her ultimate disappointment, the coat had belonged to the girl's boyfriend. Hannah had moved on to another crush, but her antipathy to the jacket remained. Now Chloe had a reason to chuckle every time she wore the coat, especially after Hannah had confessed that the jacket did suit her.

Slipping her phone back into one of the jacket's large front pockets, content that the taunt would make Hannah laugh,

Chloe stepped outside into the crisp evening air. The wind hadn't taken on the full bite of autumn yet, but the sleepy warmth of summer was decidedly absent. The sun, hanging lower in the sky, was still casting brilliant rays around the fields, and she was grateful for the sunglasses she had left in her messenger bag.

Since the science wing had a door that opened directly out to the soccer fields, her walk to the bleachers was a short one. Two large sets of metal bleachers stood on the north sideline. On the opposite sideline sat the team benches, protected from the wind by otherworldly plastic bubble huts that reminded Chloe of the public bus stops in Amherst. The field was in great shape, at least to Chloe's untutored eye. A chain-link fence with Wiscasset red plastic tubing covering its top enclosed it.

Not surprisingly, no spectators had arrived yet, though Chloe imagined eager parents might be arriving shortly. Stacey and Madeleine were busy talking to their squads at opposite ends of the field, she saw, which meant she was free to pick the perfect spot to watch the game and save seats for the rest of the group. She had been unsure whether or not she should say hi to her friends before the game. She decided she didn't want to interrupt their pre-game routines. She sat down instead and set about finishing the last of her grading.

By the time she next paused, twenty minutes had passed and students and parents had begun trickling in, filling in sections of the bleachers. The scoreboard ticked down the seconds to game time as a trail of fans made their way to the field from cars in the parking lot, and the energy surrounding the teams swelled. Excitement and anxiety hovered around the athletes, feelings Chloe was intimately familiar with and missed with her whole being. Nothing could compare to the sensation of pre-game focus.

The two teams were executing passing drills and taking shots on goal. Chloe found Madeleine on the field; she was standing just outside Wiscasset's box. Her focus was evident from seventy-five yards away. It was easy to see why she was one of the best coaches in the league. Even Wiscasset's warm-up was clean and precise.

"I hate to interrupt, but Anne and I were wondering if you saved those seats for us or if you were planning on staring into space alone all night?"

Taylor's boisterous call interrupted Chloe's observations of the coaches and players. The couple made their way up the bleachers toward her. Though Chloe hadn't spent much time with Anne yet, the easy way she carried herself made her feel as though they'd been friends for months instead of days. Taylor held her hand as the pair climbed the bleachers, and Chloe's heart melted a little. When she stood to greet them, Anne stepped forward.

"Chloe, I want you to know you have to stick around. Taylor complains about you all the time, beating up on her at open gym and whatnot."

Anne gave Chloe a warm hug. She returned the greeting happily, then stepped back.

"I'll take that as a compliment?"

"Oh yes, it is. If Taylor takes the time to rag on you, you've made it into her circle of trust."

Taylor reached out and snaked her arm around Anne's waist, "Except you, sweetheart. I never rag on you."

"Right, and I never call patients awful names in my head."

Taylor gasped, as if shocked at Anne's disclosure. Anne laughed, addressing Chloe again.

"I'm a physical therapist, it's what we do. And Taylor, she's a suck-up. She's lucky she's cute." Anne extended her cheek to Taylor for a kiss, something she was more than happy to provide. Laughing, the three of them sat down on the bleachers and got settled in for the game. The bleachers had filled in earnest with a strong showing of fans. The game clock showed ten minutes left before play would begin.

Leaning across Taylor, Anne asked how Chloe was enjoying working at Wiscasset. "Taylor told me you hadn't had a lot of experience before coming here. Now that you've got more than a week under your belt, what do you think?"

"I'm really lucky to have landed here for my first exposure to high school kids. I don't know if Taylor told you, but I interviewed for the long-term sub position today. I'm excited, but it doesn't quite seem real yet that I could be here the rest of the year."

Anne nodded in understanding. "I know what you mean. When I graduated and walked right into the job I'm still working today, signing the paperwork and going to orientation felt like a really vivid dream."

"That's exactly it!" Chloe found comfort in Anne's knowing smile.

"Even if you don't get the sub position, though Mark would be crazy not to hire you from what I hear, I can at least guarantee you that the JV job will get you unlimited meals and drinks at our house."

Taylor broke in, aghast. "Babe, am I so impossible to work with that you're sinking to bribery now?"

"We both know she'll be over anyway. Assuring her that she'll be rewarded for her perseverance is the humane thing to do, in my opinion anyway."

"I know I'll be taking you up on that offer. She called me agoraphobic today before she even offered me the job. I'm going to need sustenance this season, I think."

Taylor reached over and smacked Chloe. "Keep it up, I can always offer someone else the job. Hmm, maybe Jaysa wants it. Let me ask her." Taylor's voice trailed off as Jaysa joined them, bounding with energy and excitement for the game.

"What do you want to ask me?" she wondered out loud, glancing curiously from Taylor to Anne to Chloe.

"Yes, what was it you wanted from her?" Chloe teased, knowing full well Taylor loved Jaysa but could never coach with her. They were both too high energy to survive a practice without exhausting everyone in the gym.

"Jaysa, I was wondering if you were free this evening after the game. If so, we would be delighted if you would grace us with your presence at a postgame meal courtesy of Anne's generous PT check that came on Friday."

"That sounds incredibly formal, but I'm definitely coming. Anne, don't let Taylor throw your money around like that. I could invest it for you."

"It's okay, J. You already set us up nicely. Plus it makes Taylor feel like a high roller when she can pay for everybody." Anne silenced any retort with a quick kiss on Taylor's lips to the amusement of everyone.

With Jaysa's arrival came news that Anna, Robin, and a player named Jess that Chloe had yet to meet couldn't come for various work-related reasons, though they specifically wanted Jaysa to wish both coaches good luck in person. The group text had been going off all day long with questions about the game time and good wishes to both Madeleine and Stacey. Tonight was an important night in the season; the winner would most likely be seeded first for the conference tournament. Chloe was glad she had kept her phone in her office and on silent during the school day, since Taylor had done her fair share of blowing phones up with her group-wide trash talk about Wiscasset's superiority. It seemed safe to turn it back on vibrate now that the game was about to start.

Stacey and Madeleine were standing together talking at midfield, both looking confident and excited by the thrill of good competition. Hopping around on the sideline, staying warm, and getting focused, the players reminded Chloe of racehorses at the gate, anxiously awaiting the start. The horn sounded, signaling the end of warm-ups, and as the players ran out to the pitch the scoreboard was set.

The sound of the referee's whistle set off a cascade of activity as field players spread to their positions. Stacey's team would be taking the opening possession. Chloe spotted Leah—she was starting at right mid—and Molly, who was oozing excitement at the left forward spot. Another whistle and the game was off and running.

Chloe hadn't known what to expect out of the pace of the game, considering it was high school soccer, but this was obviously high-level play. A vibration in her pocket pulled her focus from the game. Expecting a text from Hannah, she pulled out her phone. Instantly she frowned. Another text from Nora. Opening it, she was twisted with even more guilt.

Chloe, can we talk? Things are happening here and I'm a little overwhelmed.

Chloe ran her hand through her hair, unsure how to respond or if she should respond at all. As she stared at the tiny message, her guilt grew and the option to ignore it became more alluring. The decision made, she shoved the phone back in her pocket.

As the first half raged, the action was nonstop. Chloe was both informed and entertained by Taylor's commentary, as well as Jaysa's insights into Stacey's personnel. The squads were fairly evenly matched, though Madeleine's team had an advantage in speed, particularly in their attack. Stacey's goalie was more than up to the task of containing them, however. She was being recruited by some of the top schools, Jaysa said. Apparently even UNC had sent her some letters. Wiscasset's white uniforms with red accents covered every inch of the field, but the blue uniforms of Boothbay were never far behind.

There were a string of heart-pounding moments throughout the first half, breakaways and beautiful shots on goal, but no one was able to secure the first goal. When halftime hit, Chloe, Jaysa, Anne, and Taylor began placing small wagers on the outcome of the game.

"There's no way Stacey's kids don't put the ball in the net this half," Taylor announced. "They're the highest scoring offense in the area. Hate to say it, but my money's on them. Final score two nothing. I guarantee it."

"If you're right, lunch is on me tomorrow. But when Madeleine's team pulls it out, you owe me lunch. Deal?" Chloe couldn't help herself; Taylor was too easy to mess with. She had a strong feeling that Molly was about to break out this half. She had been awfully close a couple of times so far, and there was only so much another team could do against energy and athleticism like hers.

Jaysa piped up. "I don't know, guys. This thing could end in a draw. They're as well matched as any two teams I've seen."

"Either way, both teams put up a great first half. This one is going to be a nail-biter for sure." Everyone nodded in agreement with Anne. The second half promised to be thrilling.

The rest of halftime passed quickly as they all chatted about their weekend plans. Chloe was less than fully engaged in the conversation. She couldn't stop watching Madeleine and Stacey in action. As their athletes passed back and forth on the sidelines, stretching and staying warm, both coaches moved through the ranks. Stacey, Chloe was sure, was busy reminding her team of their game plan, pumping each girl up as she walked past. She was more curious about Madeleine's coaching style. From what she had been able to see of her during the first half, she had encouraged the girls, giving them tips but otherwise relying on their preparation to get them through the game. Chloe was impressed that during the halftime huddle she had her three captains address the team. It was evident that the girls respected and valued Madeleine. It was equally clear that she loved her players.

The sound of the horn signaled that the second half was underway as Taylor returned from the concession stand to "comfort eat the stress away." She brought Twizzlers and Laffy Taffy for everyone, as well as cups of coffee to counteract the dropping temperatures. Three-quarters of the way through the snacks, Anne was sharing a story about one of her particularly stubborn patients when Wiscasset made a run. With six minutes left on the clock, Leah placed a great through ball for the streaking Molly, who chased it down, but a well-timed tackle from the defender saved the goal, giving Wiscasset the corner.

Jaysa, visibly anxious, covered her face. "I can't do corner kicks. I always feel like someone is about to get a concussion or something. I would never have survived as a soccer player. Tell me when it's over."

Sympathetic, Taylor put her arm around Jaysa and promised to keep her updated.

Chloe was excited to see that Leah was coming forward to take the corner for Wiscasset. Madeleine shouted something to her. Though Chloe couldn't hear what she said, whatever it was appeared to buoy Leah's confidence. Spinning the ball and placing it on the line, Leah stepped back, took a deep breath, and raised her arm to the official. At the top of the box, players were still jockeying for position.

Leah, dropping her hand, took her approach. As she addressed the ball, Chloe caught sight of Molly rubbing her defender off her teammate at the top of the box. The ball soared to the far side of the box, where a sprinting Molly was headed. Chloe held her breath. The players moved in slow motion. The goalie was still on her line, sliding to her left to follow the ball, but Molly, diving forward, somehow put her head on the perfect strike from Leah, sending her shot under the outstretched hand of the keeper.

It took a moment for the fans to realize what had happened. The Wiscasset players mobbed Molly and Leah, and Chloe, Taylor, Anne, and Jaysa were all on their feet, joining the rest of the hometown fans cheering for the beautiful goal. Chloe caught Madeleine turning to her bench and emphatically pumping her fist, celebrating with her bench players.

When the excitement settled and the fans returned to their seats, the urgency of the Boothbay players was ratcheted up to a new level. Wiscasset was working to maintain possession, draining the clock as much as possible. Though the Boothbay girls never gave up, with ten seconds left a desperation through ball was trapped by Leah, who cleared it to the opposite end of the field, securing the win for Wiscasset.

"Well, what would you like for lunch tomorrow?" Taylor asked, conceding defeat to Chloe.

"Let me think about it. I'll get back to you. I want to really enjoy this." Chloe chuckled, savoring her personal victory. While Anne and Jaysa gathered up the garbage from the snack fest they had participated in, Chloe and Taylor made their way down the bleachers to where Madeleine was addressing her team. Stacey and her group were getting packed up and heading for their waiting bus, undoubtedly anxious to get home. Parents with blankets wrapped around themselves were clustering near the far corner of the field waiting for their respective athletes to take their leave.

Chloe hoped that Molly and Leah hadn't left yet. Watching them play had jump-started her momma bear instincts; she was immensely proud of her kids. She had tried to tell herself that she was still detached, but after spending only two weeks with them, she was invested. Watching them play tonight had brought the fact more clearly to light; it was something Chloe could no longer ignore, for better or worse. Acknowledging her attachment to her students would make it harder to leave if she didn't get the long-term position, but at this point, there really was no going back.

Turning to Taylor, Chloe asked, "Do you see Molly or Leah? I really want to catch them tonight." Standing on her tiptoes, Taylor searched for the two girls above the flock of supporters.

"I think I see Leah. She's by the bench packing up her bag. I'm not sure about Molly. I think she might be at the center of that blob of people."

"I should have known. That girl's got one of the most magnetic personalities I've ever seen. She reminds me of someone. I can't quite place it." She ticked off a list on her fingers. "She surrounds herself with good people, talks to everyone, thinks she's the funniest person in any room. Sound like anyone we know?" Chloe asked, elbowing Taylor.

"That's the best compliment you could ever give her," replied Taylor, inclining her head regally to accept the praise. "But you're going to have to hustle over to catch Leah. I think she's leaving."

Chloe took off at a jog toward the far corner of the field. Leah was indeed packed up and heading for the back gate to the far parking lot where most of the players parked. Chloe increased her pace. When she was close enough, she called out, "Hey, Leah, hang on!"

At the sound of her name, Leah paused and turned. Chloe waved and slowed slightly. Leah's slender face lit up with recognition. When Chloe closed the gap between them, Leah spoke first.

"Miss Amden, I didn't know you were coming tonight!"

"Of course. I wouldn't have missed it!" Chloe reached out and clapped Leah affectionately on the arm. "You played amazing tonight, Leah!" Leah's shy grin was worth every bit of cold Chloe had sat through. The change in her posture and hint of color that sprang to her cheeks told Chloe how much it meant to her to have someone in the stands recognize her efforts.

"I'm glad we got the win. Boothbay's always so good." Unsurprised that Leah would move the conversation in the direction of the team, Chloe couldn't resist one more Leah-centered comment.

"They're definitely a solid team. I didn't realize what a leg you've got on you. Do you always take the corners?"

"I didn't last season. We had a senior defender who used to, but Coach had me take them in practice all the time. This was my first one in a varsity game."

"Well, an assist on your first one isn't a bad start, kid!"

At that, Leah flushed slightly but conceded. "I guess not."

"Well, it's getting cold out here and I'm sure you're sweaty and hungry after that one. You get out of here and I'll see you in class."

"Okay, thanks for coming, Miss Amden." Leah hesitated, her face reflecting the struggle of deciding whether or not to say what she was thinking. After a brief pause, she blurted out, "Now you're going to have to come to all our games. We haven't beaten Boothbay in like five years."

Laughing, Chloe replied, "I'll see what I can do, Leah. You promise to keep playing like that and I'll be there. Now go before I have to agree to paint my face for every game too!"

Her face breaking into the widest smile yet, Leah nodded and waved, turning to leave for her car. Chloe couldn't help but imagine how much more Leah was bound to grow before she headed off to college. She was clearly gaining confidence on the soccer field. A large portion of that confidence had something to do with Madeleine, of that Chloe was sure. The junior was polite, inquisitive, and a gifted athlete. Though reserved, she was a sweet kid. Chloe was proud of her, despite only having known her for a few weeks. She couldn't imagine how Madeleine felt, having worked to cultivate Leah's growth for years.

The vibration of the phone inside her pocket disrupted her train of thought. A new group message had been started in the five minutes since she had ventured over to Leah. Unsurprisingly, Taylor, Anne, and Jaysa had been too cold and hungry to wait around and had gone to get a table at Manchetti's. Chloe checked the field, curious about whether Madeleine was still around.

The final stragglers were grouped together near the entrance to the field, gradually making their way to the last cars in the parking lot. Molly wasn't in the group, nor was Madeleine. A movement in her periphery caught her attention. She spotted the soccer coach, bundled in layers of team gear, near the benches. She had made her way over to the control panel between the bubble benches, presumably to close up shop and shut down the lights. Spotting Chloe, she motioned her over.

"I'm assuming you got the fifty-seven group texts?" she asked, her cheeks tinged pink from the cold air that had settled in.

"I did. It's still September and the cold got to them. How do they survive the winter?"

"It's a little embarrassing, right?" Madeleine paused. "I can't give them too much shit. They've endured some pretty snowy games in the past couple seasons."

"I would be willing to bet there was some Irish coffee or spiked hot chocolate involved," Chloe interjected, drawing a chuckle from Madeleine.

"I'll have to ask them tonight. Now that you mention it, that one game there was a lot of giggling going on." Calling up a mental image of the group of women bundled in fuzzy hats and blankets and sipping out of thermoses was all too easy for Chloe, though she was pretty certain they wouldn't have gotten buzzed at any really important game for Madeleine.

"I have to switch these lights off. If you want to wait a minute, we can walk out together. I swear I won't ask you whether or not you've moved on from *Atlas Shrugged*…" Madeleine's tone was wry and self-effacing. Chloe nodded.

"Sounds perfect."

One by one, she shut off the giant lights, each of them going dark with a metallic clang followed by more silence. The buzzing of the electric current gradually faded until the final light fell into darkness and the world was plunged into silence.

Chloe stood still, head tilted as far back as it would go, mesmerized by the millions of stars thrown across the sky. With no lights on around them, no moon in the sky, and not a trace of cloud cover, she was surrounded by undiluted celestial brilliance. Points of light glittered across the nighttime, dancing in a chaotic order only the universe could provide. The immensity of space contained within the expanse of darkness was begging to be experienced. She turned her body slowly in a circle, savoring the moment.

"Beautiful doesn't do this justice." Madeleine's voice came drifting out of the darkness. Unable to turn away, Chloe nodded in silent agreement. She was aware of Madeleine now, standing next to her, as absorbed by the night as she was. Her voice came again, softer this time.

"I can't believe how often I forget how incredible this is."

There was a hint of something in that casual admission that resonated with Chloe. Was it regret or fear, maybe disappointment? Chloe couldn't be sure. Maybe it was the ambiguity that drew her in. For some reason, Chloe felt that Madeleine could relate to her in that moment. And it felt... Well, it felt nice.

* * *

By the time Chloe walked in the front door of Manchetti's her body was reminding her that she hadn't eaten more than a few Twizzlers since lunch. The smell of freshly baked Italian bread and pizza set her mouth watering. Taylor called out to her as she walked into the dining area. "There won't be much pizza left for you if you don't get over here!"

Chloe was at the table in three long strides. She folded her lanky frame into the booth next to Anne, who had graciously set out a plate and a slice for her.

"You know better than to believe her, Chloe, or at least you better learn that before the season starts," Anne advised Chloe.

Chloe would express her gratitude in a moment, after she got a few bites of pizza.

"Easy, sweetheart. She hasn't interviewed yet, so I've got a little more time to milk this." Taylor laughed as Chloe smothered her slice with parmesan cheese and dove enthusiastically into it. To Chloe's relief Madeleine walked in the restaurant at that point, saving her from more of Taylor's ribbing.

"Madeleine! What a game!" Jaysa shouted, her face lighting up with excitement for their friend. Madeleine smiled, then slid into the booth with Jaysa and Taylor.

"I would have liked to see them finish in the first half, but it's early in the season. They played hard tonight." Despite her reluctance to celebrate too soon, a hint of pride rang out in her voice.

"You realize that around us you can say you had a damn good night, right?" Jaysa asked, the slightest trace of frustration creeping into her response. Madeleine smiled ruefully, though before she could respond Taylor chimed in, "This is your circle of trust! I swear we won't go telling the papers you're already counting your second state title."

Chloe laughed with the others, impressed to learn that the young coach had already won a state title. Those did not come easily at the high school level, least of all from mid-sized schools like Wiscasset. The surprise must have been evident on her face. Anne leaned over to her. "They won two years ago. It was Madeleine's third year coaching. She came in and turned the entire program around. She'd never tell you that herself, of course."

Jaysa momentarily abandoned the breadstick and dipping sauce she had been making quick work of. "It's been fantastic to watch. With her and Stacey coming in at the same time, soccer around here has blown up."

"Soccer has always been big up here," Madeleine countered quickly. "When I was playing on my club teams growing up, the Northeast was constantly pumping out great talent. I think it comes in cycles. We needed to help the kids remember why soccer is exciting."

"Yeah," Taylor teased. "People do have a tendency to fall asleep when games end scoreless."

"Easy, babe. Your basketball is showing," Anne chided Taylor cheerfully. Taking the jest in stride, Taylor dropped her hand below the table, and Chloe watched as her fingers seamlessly intertwined with Anne's. A small moment all in all, but to Chloe it represented what she hoped to find someday.

Chloe considered her own string of failed relationships. If she were honest with herself the common factor in all of them had been a serious lack of equality between the partners involved. Perhaps that was why they all failed. She pulled her thoughts back to the table, where Jaysa was absorbed in talks with Anne and Taylor about Stacey and the likelihood that the championship would be a rematch of tonight's game. She turned toward Madeleine, rocking back slightly, startled, as gorgeous hazel eyes peppered with flecks of green locked onto hers.

Suddenly the table felt much too intimate. Chloe hadn't ever had a reason to sit this close to Madeleine before. Swallowing hard to keep her plummeting stomach under control, she tried to remember what she had been about to ask her. Mercifully, Madeleine, unfazed by Chloe's hesitation, spoke instead.

"Why did you go with basketball instead of soccer? With your long legs and strong hands, I imagine you would have had your choice of positions on the pitch."

Chloe managed to pull herself together enough to participate in the conversation, though imagining Madeleine appreciating her long legs was incredibly distracting.

"Honestly, I'm a little bit of a bandwagon soccer fan. Growing up I wasn't really exposed to it. It's probably better that way. I'm terrible. From the handful of times I've tried to dribble with my feet instead of my hands, I realized I should leave it to the five-year-olds."

Madeleine chuckled and thought for a moment. "You can't be that terrible. At the very least I'd wager that you'd make a great keeper."

"Absolutely not. I was made painfully aware that it is not the game for me. I'm okay with that." Chloe shook her head, trying to hide the mortification that accompanied her memory. She switched gears. "Isn't that cheating, though? I'd be in the one position where I get to use my hands."

As soon as she uttered the unintended innuendo, Chloe flushed, biting back embarrassment. The flash of emotion across Madeleine's face was so quick, she couldn't be sure if there was acknowledgment there or if she'd imagined it.

Undaunted, Madeleine went on. "It's only cheating if you have your sweeper take the goal kicks."

"We'd definitely be cheating then because I shouldn't take them." Madeleine shook her head at Chloe's insistence. "Anyway, I did start to watch my friends play in college and then I fell in love with half of the women's national team during the 2011 World Cup. I mean, come on, Megan Rapinoe, Lauri Lindsey, Abby Wambach, and Ashlyn Harris. How could I not love that team?"

"Wow, you really did fall hard." Madeleine's voice sounded different suddenly; it had lost some of the warmth it held seconds ago. Chloe was thrown by the unmistakable shift in her demeanor. She had tensed up as if thinking about that team was painful. Momentarily thrown off, Chloe continued, hoping to move past whatever just happened.

"Now I pretend to know what I'm talking about until I talk to someone who actually does know the game."

"That's refreshing. When I was playing everyone I talked to acted like they should have been coaching the national team." Apparently over whatever had passed between them, Madeleine added, "Funny, not one of those fans ever got the job."

Chloe laughed, instantly reminded of her friend Brooke's dad. "Most of the time it's the parents who are the worst, aren't they? One of my teammates, she had it rough. She was from Louisiana and her dad was a nightmare. Thankfully he couldn't make it to many games. In his mind, he could outcoach Geno Auriemma."

Madeleine nodded. "It's hard for me to watch professional games anymore, at the stadiums or in public in general. People are lunatics."

"Seriously! I always end up thinking snarky things about how they were probably awful at sports and never played at a high level. Which makes me the real asshole. Whoops." Chloe shrugged, completely unapologetic. Madeleine's subsequent laugh sent a tiny tremor through her.

Madeleine leaned forward to whisper her response. "I think the same things. Don't tell anyone that, though. It'll ruin my image." Madeleine went on, unaware, Chloe hoped, of the jolt of excitement she'd sent through her. "And, in our defense, not a lot of people have actually played high-level sports, so maybe we are a tiny bit justified in our smartass inner dialogues?"

Nodding, Chloe answered happily, inclining her water glass toward Madeleine. "I like the way you think." *Speaking of high-level sports...* "So where did you play? All I know is what Taylor told me, which was that you could have played basketball but chose soccer, the act of ultimate betrayal." Chloe was infinitely proud of her self-control; so far she had resisted the temptation to scour the Internet for details of Madeleine's athletic history. She knew her own weaknesses, and beautiful athletes topped the list. Perusing Madeleine's athletic accomplishments wouldn't help her focus on figuring out her own life.

"I love playing basketball, but soccer has always been my sport. I started playing when I was four and never wanted to stop. I ended up playing at UConn." Chloe glimpsed pain or maybe regret flash across Madeleine's face, only to be replaced immediately with composure. Unsure what to make of that and whether they were on a safe topic, Chloe faltered. Instead of continuing, she waited for an indication from Madeleine of where their conversation would go. Thankfully she didn't have to wait long.

"You downplay your skills at soccer, but I hear from Taylor that you were incredible at St. Michael's. Is there a basketball record over there without your name on it?"

"Honestly, I don't know the individual records I have." Chloe paused. She hadn't thought about those since she was playing. She had game balls somewhere from each of the scoring milestones she'd achieved, signed by her teammates. And Coach had given her some certificates and a plaque or two. "You would have to ask my parents. They have all of my stats and whatnot. Dad counts it among his personal duties to always be ready to rattle off my career stats to the extended family." Chloe remembered the embarrassment of hearing him do that during her senior season. "What I'm most proud of is that we went to the Division II Final Four three times and won the whole thing my senior year. That was one of the best experiences of my life."

"Nothing compares to winning a championship does it?"

"Not even close. So how many national titles did you guys win? I can tell you know the feeling. It's all over your face." Madeleine's cheeks went pink, a fact that pleased Chloe a bit too much.

"We won two. I was lucky."

Chloe was more than impressed. Winning a Division I championship was a big deal. If Chloe hadn't pressed her, she might never have told her that she was a two-time national champion.

"That's more than lucky, Madeleine. That's incredible. Being a part of a team that talented and disciplined." Chloe paused, processing this new information. "Yeah, you have the right to tell anyone that tries to tell you how to coach to shove it." She saw gratitude, warmth, and passion flit across Madeleine's expressive face. She leaned back in her seat. Stuffed with pizza, warmth finally back in all of her extremities, Chloe was entirely content.

CHAPTER SIX

Tuesday

It had been exactly one week and one day since she interviewed for the long-term sub position, a period of time which any rational person would understand was much too short for a school to make a decision on a candidate. That had not kept Chloe from feeling anxious and jumpy all day. The reasonable side of her personality had gone on strike. Yesterday had been her first painful Monday since coming to Wiscasset. And wow, had it been painful. At least tonight she could work out some of that frustration with the girls at open gym.

Parking her Jeep and zipping her coat up all the way, Chloe headed into the school through the biting wind. Inside she was greeted by the usual crowd. Taylor was talking to Stacey and Anna animatedly about the cruelty of Sea World. Chloe had to laugh, assuming Taylor had recently watched *Blackfish* and was feeling particularly inspired. Madeleine was sitting with Robin and another woman Chloe didn't recognize, though she assumed it might be Jess, a colleague of Anne's. Though she hadn't officially met Jess, Taylor had described her as mellow and fun.

Chloe was excited; they would have eight tonight—she had seen Jaysa pulling into the parking lot as she was walking in the door. She tossed her bag on the gym floor near where Taylor was sitting and sat down to lace up her sneakers.

"Hurry up, guys," Taylor yelled. "Let's shoot for teams. Today was a long day and I want to get playing."

Once the teams were divided, it was Stacey, Chloe, Jaysa, and Anna against Madeleine, Taylor, Jess, and Robin. Chloe shook her head. She had done a solid job of guessing who had played at which level in college, as well as picking up on people's habits and strengths. Madeleine's team was stacked. There was only so much that knowledge could do when facing a team loaded with that much talent.

Jess was the smallest person on the other team so Jaysa would guard her for the night. Both of them had played Division III ball, so it was a fair matchup. As for the rest of the pairings, not so much. Robin had played at Lemoyne in Syracuse and had been an All-American power forward. Though Anna was barely five-ten, she was pretty solid and could body up with her defensively. There was only one problem: Anna wasn't skilled enough to ever score over Robin. That meant that offensive production would fall to Chloe and Stacey. She had always made it a priority to facilitate during these games. As the new girl she didn't want to be a black hole; she'd always been afraid of being called a ball hog, even as a kid. But having lost most of her games since coming to open gym, she was sick of coming up short.

Chloe asked Stacey who she would rather guard, Taylor or Madeleine. While Taylor was the oldest of the group at thirty-four, she was also a Hartford Hall of Fame inductee who played basketball nearly every day in class and at practice. Age was nothing to Taylor. As a five-foot-ten guard, she wasn't an easy matchup for anyone.

Then again, neither was Madeleine. She had shown her Division I athleticism from the first day. She had a killer first step and was so quick it almost wasn't fair. She was a dead stick shooter too. Her only weakness was that she was only five-eight. That didn't really count as a weakness, though, since she had more than enough skill to compensate, even against much taller adversaries. Chloe couldn't imagine what kind of career Madeleine would have had if she had chosen basketball.

There was absolutely no way Stacey could guard Madeleine, but Stacey would struggle with Taylor as well, so Chloe let her pick her poison. Stacey shrugged. "I'll take Madeleine, but who knows how long that will last."

Chloe laughed and clapped her on the back in a supportive way, hoping they wouldn't get blown out.

* * *

Four minutes in, it was clear to everyone that Stacey, try as she might, was never going to be able to contain Madeleine. Madeleine was way too quick. Stacey had been scored on four possessions in a row. As Taylor went to put the ball inbounds, Chloe yelled over to her teammate. "Stace, switch with me. I'll take Madeleine." Stacey nodded gratefully.

Taylor, instigator that she was, had to add her own comment, of course. "Watch out, Madeleine. Chloe thinks she can shut you down. Take it easy on the new girl, will you?"

Chloe had played with Taylor for long enough now to recognize her playing mind games, trying to get under her skin. She chose to ignore her, pivoting mentally instead to how she'd have to play Madeleine. Chloe was at least four inches taller and had a much longer wingspan, but Madeleine was smart and quick. They hadn't been matched up before. It should be interesting.

Play continued as Taylor brought the ball up the floor, swinging the pass to Jess on the wing. Madeleine cut to the basket baseline. Seeing Robin, she changed direction up the lane, trying to shake Chloe by running her off Robin's down screen. Chloe managed to beat her to the spot, but then got nailed on a back screen by Taylor.

Fighting through the screen, Chloe trailed behind as Madeleine slipped toward the basket. On the entry pass from Jess, Madeleine went up for the layup, but Chloe had closed the distance between them. Amped up from getting hit on the screen, she extended her full length and swatted the ball out of Madeleine's hands from behind. She hadn't intended to be quite so vicious, but she couldn't contain her competitiveness any longer. She decided then and there not to hold back again.

Taylor, of course, had to let out a loud "Oooooohhhh" from the elbow as Madeleine sent Chloe some challenging side-eye.

"Our ball," she stated calmly. She tossed it to Jess at the top of the key and headed to the wing. Jess checked the ball with Jaysa and Madeleine immediately cut through the lane, popping out to get the pass on the opposite wing. Taking two dribbles left, Madeleine faked the pass inside to Robin. Chloe bit on the fake. When Madeleine pulled the ball back, Chloe scrambled to close out a half-second too late; she drained the three in her face. "Fuck," Chloe muttered under her breath. Madeleine nodded to Chloe and then jogged back to play defense. *Okay, if that's how you want it, you got it.*

Chloe brought the ball up the court and kicked it over to Anna. Cutting through the lane, Madeleine bodied her up, bumping her on her cut to the basket. Chloe stopped like she was going to post Madeleine up to take advantage of the mismatch, then popped out to the baseline for the pass. Madeleine scrambled out to Chloe. Hesitating a moment, Chloe jab-stepped left. Madeleine, off balance, took two extra steps to cut off Chloe's drive. Chloe changed directions and put down the dribble going right. As Madeleine started to recover, she brought the ball backward between her legs, stretching out completely to get separation for the step back jump shot. Damn, it felt good to be back out here. She smiled to herself as she heard the ball hit the net. Anna gave her a high five before running back on defense and Chloe knew this game was going to be a little different.

The next possession, Madeleine caught the ball on the wing and Chloe reached out to check up. Madeleine swung the ball through to break Chloe's contact, trying to get the first step, but Chloe cut her off. Keeping her dribble, Madeleine brought the ball up with her right hand, faking hard, then out of nowhere kept it and sliced left past her to take it in for the layup.

Jogging back down the court together, Chloe acknowledged Madeleine. "That's all you get tonight." Madeleine nodded at Chloe and put an arm bar on her ribs, pressing herself along the length of Chloe's side. Chloe couldn't quite focus on what was happening on the other side of the floor, the proximity to Madeleine—her hands on Chloe's side, the intensity of her golden brown eyes—currently eclipsing the game.

Wondering for a moment if Madeleine was at all affected by her, Chloe nearly missed Taylor as she picked Stacey's pocket and started the fast break. She refocused and sprinted to catch up. When Taylor tried to force the pass to Robin, Anna stepped in front of it for the steal. She quickly passed the outlet to Stacey and they ran back up the court. When Chloe caught the reverse pass, she drove right, getting the defense to collapse on her. Drawing Robin from the opposite block, she dropped a shovel pass underneath Madeleine's outstretched arms to the waiting Stacey across the lane.

After Stacey scored, Chloe offered Madeleine a high five to taunt her a little bit, but she shook her head at Chloe, playfully slapping her hand away. The two of them laughed together, the excitement of being evenly matched providing an opportunity to enjoy the challenge of one-upping each other and carrying their respective teams.

Chloe's team scored four more times, thanks to her creating most of the offense. They were only down by one, but Madeleine had the ball in the backcourt for game point. Determined not to let her score, Chloe unashamedly kept checking her, bumping her to remind her she wasn't getting through, pestering her, and keeping her from making her break to the basket. She was definitely fouling her, but it was call your own and there was no way Madeleine would call an off ball foul.

Madeleine sent a pass over to Taylor, who drove off Robin's screen. Chloe had to slide over to help the screened Stacey, so Taylor crossed it back to Madeleine on the opposite wing. Anticipating the drive, Chloe sprinted across the lane again as Madeleine lowered her head, driving baseline from the wing. Chloe stopped dead at the edge of the lane and set her feet as Madeleine left hers, hanging in the air to take the game-winning layup. Madeleine shielded the ball from Chloe, releasing the shot as the two of them crashed to the floor in a tangle of limbs.

Madeleine collapsed on top of Chloe, the full length of her body pressing them to the floor, her face within inches of Chloe's. Together they watched to see if the shot fell. As soon as it did, Chloe's focus shifted to the face inches above hers. Her jawline was set tightly in concentration, the soft features enhanced in the rush of competition, and Chloe was mesmerized. Taking in the sight of Madeleine's furrowed brows, the easy slope of her nose to her soft lips, she greedily absorbed the details before her. God, she was beautiful.

The thundering of her own heartbeat faded to the background as the sound of Taylor's celebration pierced her consciousness. Anna nodded, acknowledging that the final basket would count. Game over.

The victory announced, Chloe and Madeleine remained on the floor. Madeleine locked eyes with Chloe, grinning, sweaty, and beautiful, and Chloe's breath caught again. She didn't want Madeleine to get up. Madeleine hesitated as well, lingering briefly before breaking contact. The jolt of adrenaline Chloe felt wasn't the typical basketball-induced high, she knew. No, this had much more to do with Madeleine.

Extricating herself from the embrace, Madeleine offered her hand to Chloe. Chloe grasped the outstretched hand, feeling another surge of sensation at the contact, then pushed herself off the floor. Without breaking their grip, Madeleine pulled Chloe in for a half hug. Bringing Chloe into her personal space, she whispered in her ear. "That was definitely a charge, but I'll never admit it again."

Her low whisper and breath on Chloe's ear raised goose bumps on the back of her neck, and another surge hit Chloe, flooding her skin with energy from Madeleine's nearness. As her stomach flipped, Chloe could only manage a halfhearted nod in return, one eyebrow arching. Madeleine however appeared completely unaffected by their little exchange and walked to the sideline. She carried on, giving out high fives and hugs to all the women as they always did after the games.

"No question! That was a charge! The bruise forming on my ass is proof," Chloe called after her.

Taylor reached over and slapped Chloe's butt. "That's the bitterness talking. Nice play, Madeleine."

"I've never played better defense in my life," Chloe retorted. "Damn right, I'm bitter!" The group broke out in laughter, untying their shoes and preparing to bundle up to head out into the cold night air.

While they were getting ready, Madeleine called out to everyone.

"Guys, I have a huge favor to ask. The girls have been playing so hard and with sectionals coming up I want Saturday to be a fun practice. With that in mind, I got a bunch of my old teammates to come out this weekend for a scrimmage, old farts versus young guns, but I need some of you to play and maybe level the playing field a bit?" The look on Madeleine's face was endearing. Her desire to put together a great weekend practice was evident.

"Stacey, I'd love to have you, but I know you have practice Saturday, right?"

Stacey responded, "Actually we're having team bonding at the bowling alley, their request. But next year I'm totally stealing your idea, Coach." Everyone laughed at that, then started piping up. Jaysa, Jess, and Taylor were in, but Anna and Robin couldn't go. Madeleine turned to Chloe.

"So, are you in? You're my last hope. I don't have a keeper."

"There's no way I'm playing. I was traumatized in high school. Don't ask me to relive it. Taylor, can't Anne come?" Chloe turned desperately to Taylor.

"Sorry, sunshine. She's at a conference all weekend. Come on, Chloe, it's all for fun. How big of a wimp are you if you can't suck it up for these kids?"

"You guys don't understand." Chloe refused to relive that awful halftime experience. She had never been more embarrassed in her life. Moments like that never truly fade.

Madeleine had been quiet, a pensive expression on her face. "Chloe, I respect whatever skeleton you have in that closet of yours, but I need you, so... I have a proposition for you."

Chloe, clueless as to where this was heading, was intrigued but still disinclined to play.

"I want you to come out to the pitch with me tomorrow after school. I'll shoot five times from the top of the box. If you actually try and you can't make at least one save, then I'll figure something else out. This way you can prove to me the universe is opposed to you playing soccer."

Chloe did not want to be the asshole that messed up this great scrimmage idea for Madeleine. But she had managed to stick to her vow of never playing soccer in public for ten years and she didn't want to break it now. The high schooler in her was stubborn.

"Take the deal, Chloe. She's giving you an out. She was on the fucking women's national team. You stand no chance," blurted Jaysa, shaking her head at Chloe's hesitance.

Chloe was blindsided by this news. Madeleine had played with Abby Wambach and Carli Lloyd? The fact that Madeleine had reached the absolute pinnacle of her sport was mind-boggling to Chloe. She was fully star-struck—until she noticed Madeleine's expression. It had dimmed considerably. Though she found it odd that those memories were so painful to her, she couldn't prolong her response any longer.

"Fine, but this is going to be ugly."

The joy that replaced Madeleine's pained expression was infinitely better. Chloe couldn't help but feel herself lighten at the possibility that she had somehow caused that change. Even if it was only for agreeing to be a target in goal.

The chatter around them picked up at the prospect of the scrimmage. Chloe tried to tell herself it wouldn't be that bad. Five shots. Then she would be free.

Leave it to Madeleine, though, to pit Chloe against herself. Chloe had fancied becoming a soccer player after meeting some of the very cool, very beautiful upperclassmen on the team during her freshman year, but that dream died at the pep rally. She'd refused to embarrass herself on the soccer field since then, but now here she was, struggling with her competitiveness—as Madeleine must have known she would. Her best strategy would be to simply let the goals in, but already, unbidden, she was thinking about ways to avoid getting blown away by Madeleine.

Perfect. Another crush ruined by soccer.

Chloe froze. She had been doing so well avoiding thinking about how attracted she was to Madeleine. Well, she could continue to ignore that. Probably.

She donned her ski jacket with a renewed commitment to staying unattached. She was preparing to leave when she heard Madeleine's low voice from her left.

"And Chloe, sorry about your ass. It looks fine from where I'm sitting, though."

The floor dropped out from beneath Chloe, the sensation of free fall nearly overpowering her. *What the hell does that mean?* Chloe's mind exploded, a million thoughts buzzing around in it and impairing her ability to formulate a response. Turning, she saw Madeleine sitting, bag in hand, hair thrown into a messy bun, gorgeous face full of mischief.

Before Chloe could come up with a response or hide the flood of color warming her cheeks, Madeleine went on. "I'll meet you on the field outside your classroom after school tomorrow. Don't get lost on your way there."

Nodding, Chloe turned to leave. How in the hell had everything suddenly gotten so complicated?

CHAPTER SEVEN

Wednesday

For most of the day, Chloe almost managed to forget that she had promised to play goalie after school. Two of her classes had a test coming up at the end of the week and the kids were slightly panicked. They had kept her too busy to worry much about her appointment with Madeleine—until Taylor had dropped by before fourth block. Her observation that Chloe resembled a condemned prisoner had brought her anxiety front and center in a nanosecond.

Chloe watched her kids file out of the classroom, knowing she couldn't put off the inevitable any longer. She had agreed to undergo certain embarrassment in front of Madeleine, and if past experience was any indicator, her embarrassment would not be of the endearing sort. She stood and walked to her tiny office to change.

"Don't tell me you're running away from little old me?"

The sound of Madeleine's voice cheered her, if only momentarily.

"I'll admit the thought had crossed my mind." In truth it was still very tempting, though the prospect of Madeleine's company made the escape plan slightly less appealing, "Don't you have a practice or something? Such an accomplished coach can't really be wasting her time with the likes of me, can she?"

"Silly basketball coach. Soccer players wake up early to weight train and do conditioning. The girls got everything done this morning so they could take the afternoon off. Now, the real question is what tragedy befell you to make you so averse to a little bit of footie?" Madeleine's tone was light, but there was genuine interest on her face.

"It really is a pathetic story. Let me change and I'll consider telling you on our walk out."

Nodding, Madeleine hopped onto a lab bench to wait, agile in even the simplest movement. A flash of skin, taut over firm abs, caught Chloe's attention immediately. Pausing to take in the rest of Madeleine's appearance, she saw she was wearing a dry-fit, long-sleeved T-shirt with slim-fitting warm-up pants, tight at her ankles, that followed the contours of very muscular calves. Whereas Chloe's legs were long and sinewy, Madeleine's looked powerful, even when hidden beneath sweatpants. She looked every bit the image of the Division I soccer stud with an apparent women's national team stint under her belt as well. *Christ, what have I gotten myself into?*

As Chloe emerged from the office wearing fitted black Adidas sweatpants and a gray quarter-zip running top, Madeleine turned her attention away from the poster at the back of the room and back to Chloe. The light in her eyes remained as she took in Chloe's transformation.

"All it took was a pair of sweatpants to turn you into a confident keeper!"

"It's going to take a little more than magic pants to do that."

Laughing at the ridiculousness of their situation, the pair walked to the warm-up field. The fresh air perked Chloe up a bit. After all, this really wasn't that terrible a situation to be in. A nudge from Madeleine brought Chloe back to the present.

"Chloe, I don't want to force you to do something painful, but if you don't tell me what happened to make you swear off soccer I can't really judge if I'm being inhumane here."

"I know. I've been cryptic. It really is embarrassing that I haven't moved on from high school." She paused, thinking about how she wanted to describe what happened, then continued. "At my high school we always did these gigantic school-wide pep assembly-type things for all of the teams before they started their respective regionals." Madeleine nodded, openly curious.

"Well, my freshman year the girls soccer team was fantastic and the pre-season pick to win it all. The junior phenom was being recruited to all the top schools." Hesitating, Chloe added, "I assume you can relate." She bumped Madeleine's arm. "She was my first serious crush. I'm not ashamed to admit it."

"Chasing older women huh?" Madeleine teased. Chloe's response was a shrug and a guilty-as-charged grin.

"Well, Becca, that was her name, was in charge of this soccer shootout activity. The principal picked three students to shoot on goal. He liked to pick at least one athlete who played in a different season. Apparently, my number was up."

Madeleine's face had shifted, understanding and apprehension written on it. Chloe plowed on. "I was feeling confident. I was an athlete after all. This could be my chance to showcase my smooth moves and impress Becca. There I was walking my scrawny self down the bleachers to the box. Mr. Deloria was rambling over the loudspeaker about the talented freshman basketball player who was going to try out soccer or some nonsense. I nodded at Becca. I didn't even say hi." Scoffing at the memory, Chloe shook her head. "Then I got ready to launch the ball."

Stepping onto the grass, they walked over to the goal together. It was fitting, Chloe thought, that they would return to the scene of the crime for the retelling.

"I was ready to do the damn thing, so I started my approach. As I brought my leg back as far as I could to get the power I wanted, my gangly arms were flailing around and somehow my fingers got caught in my shoelace."

"No!" The gasp that escaped Madeleine's covered mouth was cute, though Chloe couldn't linger on that.

"Yup. I couldn't stop myself in time to recover. I went through with the kick, effectively launching myself in the air and landing in a pathetic heap of mortally embarrassed high schooler. The laughter from the stands was thunderous, but all I could hear was my own heartbeat. I remember laying there, wanting to disappear, dreading having to look at Becca."

Madeleine had been struggling mightily to contain her own laughter. Her eyes said they felt for her, but her face showed the struggle of holding back the laugh.

"You can laugh. It's ridiculous, I know." Chloe had to admit it was a bit pathetic to keep avoiding soccer over something that happened so long ago. "It's not like I didn't recover, but I won't lie: it stuck with me. I swore I'd never try soccer again in public and I've managed to avoid needing to until now."

Chloe could almost see the comment forming, then traveling to Madeleine's lips along with a mischievous grin.

"The good news is you're no longer fourteen and I'm sure you've recovered your ability to charm beautiful women. So on the whole, I'd say no harm no foul."

The corner of Madeleine's mouth twitched, then slowly turned up in enjoyment. Chloe watched as her countenance shifted, another emotion creeping in with the teasing. Sparks flared as her body reacted.

Madeleine was casually leaning her frame against the goalpost, a ball neatly at her feet, hands in her pockets. She acted as if she hadn't a care in the world, though the whole of her attention was focused on Chloe. Chills broke out along her spine.

"I don't know if I should be flattered by your belief in my charm or hurt that you implied I'm a player." Chloe felt a sudden need to defend her reputation. Even if Madeleine was straight, Chloe didn't want her operating under that delusion.

"I suppose you should only be offended if it's true." Madeleine shrugged, her demeanor casual, though her calm focus had not wavered.

"Well, my short list of past relationships and the absence of any trail of broken hearts suggest my charms could use a little work. I'll console myself with the thought that you at least thought I was smooth for a minute or two."

They laughed together, the charge that had arisen now abating. Madeleine started walking on the field, tapping the ball along. As she walked, she called back toward Chloe, "For the record, I never said you weren't smooth or that you were a player." Her voice was soft and even. "And now that I know what happened, I feel much better about guilting you into playing."

As she turned to face Chloe from the top of the box, Madeleine's posture was confident, her features clear. Chloe knew the jig was up. She wasn't going to hold out on Madeleine or the girls. Maybe she would have a little fun out there if Madeleine could train her up enough to avoid complete embarrassment. Prepared to admit defeat, she called out to Madeleine, "We can still do this whole shootout, but I'll play no matter what. I think it's a great idea for the girls." She paused for a moment.

"I do have one small request. Could you find it in your heart to give me some tips so I don't have to relive my epic embarrassment?"

Madeleine beamed, her excitement that the scrimmage was a go written all over her face. Chloe couldn't believe she had doubted that she would play. In truth she had realized she wasn't going to turn the team down as soon as she walked into school this morning and saw Molly and Leah in the halls. There was no way she was going to disappoint Madeleine either.

Committed now to the task, Chloe stretched and began her training. She was nervous at first, but very quickly found the challenge of stopping shots exciting enough to clear out the nerves. She was actually enjoying herself as she learned about keeper's lines and punching a ball out of traffic versus catching it.

She was doing a pretty bang up job picking things up, if she did say so herself. Madeleine was moving all around the box to send shots Chloe's way, giving her pointers on reading a player's body. For a minute during that explanation Chloe spent a bit too long perusing Madeleine's lithe form. When Madeleine asked her a question, she had been forced to ask her to repeat it.

When it came time to learn a little bit about striking the ball, Madeleine began sharing some of her favorite coaching stories, the stories of girls from Wiscasset and all the camps she had worked around the country filling her voice with happiness. She was a natural teacher, which of course was a large part of what made her the excellent coach she was. Under her tutelage, Chloe was becoming more confident in her striking. More often than not, she could get the ball to go at least in the vicinity of where she aimed it.

Being around Madeleine like this, getting to see more and more of who she was, was nice. The more Chloe learned, the more she wanted to learn. As they peppered the net with goals, their chatter moved toward their high school experiences, college friends, shared music tastes. The boys' team on the adjacent field was nearly done with their practice, but to Chloe it had felt like only twenty minutes had passed.

Feeling much more confident in her ability to retain her dignity during the scrimmage, Chloe stepped up for a long shot. Squaring her body, she aimed for the top right corner of the net, surprising herself when she struck it well and nailed the shot from outside the box. Pumping her fist once in celebration, she turned to see a thrilled Madeleine clapping for her.

"Holy shit, Madeleine. I never would have believed I could do that. You made that happen!"

"You did! You're a natural athlete. Your biggest issue was being inside your own head. When I was in high school that was my problem. I kept piling all this pressure on myself." Continuing, Madeleine casually, as if it required no concentration on her part, flicked the ball in a rainbow arch over her back, caught it in the crook of her foot, and went on.

"It was my travel coach who broke through to me and told me I was only as good as I was free. If I could let go of the thoughts and just play, then I could do anything. He taught me to play because I love it, not because someone else told me I had good footwork and potential."

Finishing her thought with a flourish, she flicked the ball off her foot and proceeded to drill a blazing shot into the net. The way her body moved had Chloe entranced. Raw power directed by finesse and elegance. It was a thing of beauty in every sense of the word. Watching her move freely, as if nothing could make her happier than this moment, buoyed Chloe's spirits. Madeleine was unlike anyone else she had met.

"Damn." Chloe didn't realize she had said anything out loud until Madeleine turned to her.

"What was that?" Their eyes connected, and Chloe felt fireflies dance into life in her stomach. Chloe watched as Madeleine's fingers went to the knotted hairband on her wrist and began to play with it.

"He hit the nail on the head," Chloe replied. "At the end of the day that's really why we play, passion and freedom. It's a beautiful thing we have to share, these games we love."

The moment between them stretched on for some seconds, both of them lost in their own thoughts. Chloe wanted to know more about Madeleine's experiences after college, how she had made the national team, and what had kept her from playing professionally. Now didn't seem like the right time to ask, however.

"How about we have you take a few more shots in goal now that we've overcome your fear of striking the ball? That was the deal, wasn't it?" The corners of Madeleine's lips curved upward and Chloe's heart rate picked up.

"Okay, but don't coddle me. Kick it at least as hard as Molly will. We both know she won't hold back." Chloe turned and walked back to the net. Silently she willed herself not to dwell on her body's reaction to Madeleine, to focus instead on channeling the rush of adrenaline it had caused to help her stop at least one shot. Bouncing on the line, Chloe readjusted the Velcro on the goalie gloves Madeleine had brought for her. All she wanted was one stop. She could be proud of that.

"Are you ready?"

"This is about to be a reflection of your coaching, so the real question is, are *you* ready?" Chloe teased.

"Let's do this, Amden." Her brows furrowing in concentration, Madeleine bit her lower lip. Chloe's focus wavered, torn between watching Madeleine's lips and the need to prepare as she walked to the ball. Her heart was at that familiar frenetic pace she knew so well from before games in college. She could fully appreciate now why keepers bounced on the line before penalty kicks. It was the only outlet they had for dealing with the mounting energy. Madeleine was at the top of the box, as opposed to the actual shootout distance, out of respect for their mismatched skill levels.

The wind picked up slightly, adding a slight chill to the air and carrying to her the sounds of chatter at the boys' practice and the irregular rumble of a riding lawn mower being used to groom the football field. Madeleine stopped beyond the ball, her body poised to deliver the kick. She raised her hand as if she was taking a corner to signal to Chloe she was about to shoot. Chloe nodded, gaze locking with Madeleine's until she broke the contact and began the motion of her shot.

Chloe tried to read her body, guessing that the shot was going to the upper left corner of the goal. Madeleine struck the ball, her entire body leaning into the shot, and Chloe barely had time to recover, throwing her body to the ground, desperate to block the shot as it squeaked in the lower right corner of the net. As she hit the ground, the ball grazed her outstretched fingertips. The sound of the net rustling signaled the goal.

Chloe jumped to her feet, more determined now than she ever would have imagined. Crouching in the back of the net she grabbed the ball, turned, and kicked it back out to Madeleine's waiting feet. Going back to her line, she refocused. Without saying a word, Madeleine raised her hand again, addressing the ball. In another smooth motion she connected. Even though Chloe leapt to her full extension, Madeleine had targeted a laser in the far left corner over her outstretched hands.

Landing hard, Chloe recovered quickly, not wanting to stay down long. Pushing herself up with her hands, now with another set of grass stains, she began the process again.

"You're reading me really well, Chloe. That's huge."

"Thanks, Madeleine, but I thought the whole point was to stop the ball from going in the net."

"Chloe, you've been playing soccer for about an hour. You're one of the best athletes I know, but seriously, like I said, I've been playing since I was four." Madeleine didn't act at all surprised at Chloe's frustration. In fact, her crooked smile suggested instead that she was enjoying herself.

"Yeah, I guess it's a little ridiculous to think I could shut out a national champion." Madeleine blushed. Chloe felt her face nearly split from her grin.

"The crazy thing is you're anticipating shots better than half of the keepers I played against. You're a natural at this."

"Thanks, but I haven't forgotten that I've yet to get a save. One more, for my pride. I want to say I went down fighting."

Chloe sent the ball back to her and got ready for the final shot. It was becoming more difficult to wipe the silly look off her face at the memory of Madeleine's adorable blush. The response to her compliment had awakened some of the dormant fireflies in Chloe's system. They became more and more active the longer Chloe spent around Madeleine.

One more time Madeleine raised her arm, taking aim. Chloe felt her muscles clench in anticipation as Madeleine lowered her hand and bounded forward. As she poised to strike, a loud bang drew Chloe's head sharply to the left. Her heart leapt out of her chest. Was that a gunshot? Before she could process the sound more closely, another powerful pop pulled her attention in front of her again. Back to the blistering kick that Madeleine had unleashed. And the look of horror on her face as the ball headed straight at Chloe's head.

Before she could even think to raise her arms to protect herself, the ball slammed full speed into her nose, the crunching sound reverberating in her head. Her eyes snapped closed on impact, then filled with tears. She dropped to her knees. The world was spinning. If her nose was bleeding she couldn't feel it. Her entire face stung, but it was also numb. Was that possible? She reached her left hand forward. Down? Somehow it connected with the ground and the wobbling decreased slightly.

The ground was hard beneath her hands. Kneeling forward, she took deep, steadying breaths.

"Shit! Chloe!" The gentle hands that found her shoulders were shaking. "Here, sit back. I'll help you."

Chloe let herself be pushed back slowly, her legs stretching out in front of her as she used her left hand to stabilize herself in her new seated position. The wooziness was settling down now, but pain was throbbing into being, spreading from her nose to the rest of her skull. Mercifully, though, she heard no other voices approaching. She might not have survived had any of the coaches from the boys' team come over to investigate.

"Shit, I'm so sorry. I was aiming for the lower right-hand corner and then...that damn lawn mower backfired! It startled me and I pulled it." Madeleine's voice trembled. "Let me check you out."

Soft fingers removed the hand Chloe had been using to cover her face. Placing both of her hands gingerly on either side of Chloe's face, Madeleine tipped her head back slightly tracing gently underneath her closed eyes with the soft pads of her thumbs.

"How bad is it?" Chloe managed to get out, though every syllable pounded in her teeth and cheekbones.

"I'm so sorry," Madeleine repeated. She hesitated, her hands still cradling Chloe's face. "I," there was another pause, "I think I broke your nose."

Desperate to regain even an ounce of control, Chloe opened her eyes. Control, however, was not what she saw in the face inches from her own. She found abject fear. Despite the fuzz of her addled brains, she could tell that Madeleine was seriously shaken. Her worried eyes were searching Chloe's face ceaselessly. A face which, Chloe suddenly realized, was probably streaked with tears and no small amount of snot as well as the blood she could feel dripping out of her nose.

Was that a tear on Madeleine's face too? What the hell? Her nose hurt, but she would be fine; it wasn't life threatening. Instinctively, she looked for a way to reassure her.

"The real question is, did I get the save?" She raised her eyebrows, instantly regretting it and wincing in pain. Madeleine glared at her, then turned around to locate the ball.

"If I didn't, lie to me." That got a little chuckle.

"You're in luck, keep. The ball must have ricocheted off your dome. It's a good fifteen feet from the net. Congratulations, you got the save." Madeleine smiled, some of the worry leaving her face. "For the record, though, you're supposed to use your hands, not your beautiful face."

Supporting Chloe with one hand, held warm against her cheek, Madeleine swept some of the hair off her forehead with her other hand, her touch featherlight. Her fingers combed through the rest of her hair, pulling the strands back into place, but her eyes never left the throbbing mess in the middle of Chloe's face.

"C'mon. It can't possibly be that bad. You look like someone stabbed your puppy."

At that Madeleine finally managed a short laugh. Letting go of Chloe's face, she reached for her hands, removing the gloves she'd forgotten she was wearing.

"It's already starting to bruise under your eyes and it's only going to get worse. Stay put. I'll get some stuff from the first-aid kit in the soccer teams' storage unit." Madeleine stood and walked away.

Chloe stayed put, as ordered, content to sit still for a while longer, hoping the pain would recede a bit. She pulled her knees up to her chest, wrapping her arms around them as she waited.

Returning with some gauze pads, Madeleine knelt down next to Chloe. "Stop me if this hurts, but we can't have you dripping blood all over the place." Madeleine slid her hand behind Chloe's neck, supporting her head as she tipped it back with her other hand. Chloe's skin tingled at the soft touch. She couldn't determine if it was shock, the gentle way Madeleine was stroking her face, or the rush that accompanied her proximity that was preventing her from feeling any pain. Most likely it was the intoxicating mix of all three.

Madeleine finished, leaving her fingers on Chloe's chin after gently tilting her head back down. Chloe's heart froze, then in order to make up for the lost time took off racing in her chest. She watched, mesmerized, as Madeleine dipped her face a fraction of an inch closer. No sooner had she begun to contemplate what that might mean, though, to hope it meant what she'd like it to, than Madeleine dropped her hand, a slight tremble noticeable as she brought it to her left wrist to play with the hair tie there.

Thoroughly shaken herself, Chloe leaned back on her hands, trying to get a little distance from whatever had flared between them. Madeleine stood, careful not to bump Chloe.

"We have to go to urgent care. I'm worried that you might have a concussion, and I think they're going to need to reset your nose."

That statement was enough to bring Chloe back down to earth.

"Madeleine, I'm fine. I don't need to go. I can breathe and my head doesn't hurt hardly at all." Chloe had zero intention of going to the doctor. She had been to way too many already. She was not going for a simple broken nose.

"You've got to be kidding me. I broke your damn nose. Let's go."

The retort Chloe was going to make—that she'd broken enough bones in her lifetime to know how to handle a fractured nose—died in her throat when she looked more closely at Madeleine. She was more shaken than a ball to the face should have made her.

"What is it?" Chloe stood, reaching out a hand toward her.

"Concussions scare the shit out of me and I launched a ball full speed at your head. Plus, your nose has to be broken. I feel terrible. Taking you to the doctor is all I can do about it. Please, can we go?" The impassioned plea surprised Chloe. She put her hand on Madeleine's upper arm, rubbing it softly.

"Okay, we can go. But please promise me that you'll stop feeling guilty over it. I've been hurt so many times, broken so many bones, this is honestly nothing. My family has a saying about my propensity to be injured, it happens that often. They say I always 'break even.' Every injury I've had, I've never been irreparably damaged. And something positive comes out of it. I may have broken my nose, but I got the save. It's all even in my book."

"I'll work on it. Let's go." Amusement played on her lips, though more than a shred of remorse remained on her face.

Chloe opened her mouth to respond, but shifting her facial muscles produced a jolt of pain like lightning and she couldn't bite back the wince that escaped.

"You do realize that if you keep doing that it's going to make it incredibly difficult for me to forget that I did this to you."

"You're strong. You'll pull through."

Sighing, Madeleine shook her head. Suppressing as much facial movement as possible, Chloe grabbed Madeleine's biceps with her hands and ground out in a harsh whisper, "Hurry, I haven't got much time…"

Batting Chloe's hands away, Madeleine stepped back. "You were doing so well pulling off cute and pathetic. You had to go and ruin it. Let's go, Dumbledore."

"Hey, is that a nose joke already?" Chloe called out to Madeleine's retreating back. "C'mon. It hasn't even been fifteen minutes!"

"Too soon? Weren't you the one who told me to stop feeling guilty?"

Despite the pain it caused, Chloe couldn't stop the grin that spread across her face as she followed Madeleine to the car.

* * *

The urgent care visit had been very fast. No one had been in the waiting room when they arrived and the nurse perked up, grateful for a distraction. She had ushered them to a room and within ten minutes the doctor had come in and immediately administered the concussion protocol. To Madeleine's obvious relief, she was negative for most concussion symptoms.

The broken nose was equally straightforward. He wanted to reset it, though it wasn't absolutely necessary. Chloe had resisted at first, but when she saw Madeleine's pained expression she decided to let him straighten her nose so every time Madeleine saw her she didn't have a visual reminder of the incident and feel guilty. The doctor told her it was her lucky day; she had a clean break. He could do a closed reduction then and there and she would be as good as new.

Madeleine left the room for the procedure and about twenty minutes later Chloe was doped up, splinted, and ready to go. The doctor left them with instructions to get some food in Chloe soon, as the pain pill he had given her often led to nausea when taken on an empty stomach.

As they walked to the car, Madeleine was silent. Chloe's curiosity was piqued. Why had Madeleine been so scared when she first saw Chloe on the ground tonight? She had done her best to hide her turmoil, but Chloe had seen her recurring discomfort throughout the visit to the clinic.

As Madeleine backed her car out of the parking spot, she spoke up. "What sounds good to eat?" She edged her car up to the exit of the parking lot, waiting for an indication from Chloe of which way she should go. She turned to Chloe, and Chloe's breath caught. She decided to blame the daze she was in on the Vicodin and not the way her whole body thrummed at being close to Madeleine. She watched as Madeleine's eyebrows inched upward, her face amused as she waited for an answer.

"I'm trying to be all stoic here, but you're making it difficult." Chloe balanced her head on her hand, her elbow perched on the passenger side door, wincing at the thought of how pitiful she must have sounded. Did something dart across Madeleine's face at her words? She couldn't be sure. Doing her best to hide the embarrassment at letting her thoughts slip out, she swallowed and tried to focus on dinner.

"I'm sorry. Asking what you would like to eat was pretty unfair of me, wasn't it?" Madeleine's tone was gentle but also teasing. Clearly she was enjoying Chloe's slightly altered state. Chloe couldn't even pretend to be embarrassed anymore, not when this teasing version of Madeleine was so much better than the guilt-stricken one she had seen for much of their urgent care visit.

"I know I should eat, but all I can think about is cuddling on my couch." Chloe slammed on the verbal brakes, swallowing the words "with you" that had almost leapt to her mouth. Christ, she was acting like a drunken fool.

"Fair enough. There's a sub shop here in Newcastle right on Main Street. I'll run in and grab some subs. You can eat yours cuddled on your couch." Pausing for a second to check traffic before she merged onto the road, Madeleine added in an afterthought, "You're lucky I took pity and made the decision for you. Try not to get used to it."

All Chloe could muster in response was a feeble "Mhmm." She barely registered the stop at the sub shop and must have dozed much of the trip home. She must have given Madeleine the address, but she had no recollection of that. She was surprised when the engine cut and she saw her own apartment. "I can't believe I fell asleep. You were right. I am pathetic."

Madeleine shook her head, hopping out of the car and coming over to Chloe's door. "Stop it. If taking Vicodin on an empty stomach didn't slow you down a little bit, I'd be concerned about where your tolerance came from. Now I know for sure you aren't Walter White."

Laughing, Chloe took Madeleine's outstretched hand and together they made their way into the house and down the hall to her apartment. Thankful that she had cleaned up the living room a bit this weekend, Chloe flipped on the lights, wincing a little as the brightness tugged at the remnants of the headache she had been fighting. Madeleine noticed, despite Chloe's best efforts to hide it.

"Easy, killer. Why don't you sit down on that couch that's been waiting for you." Madeleine placed a comforting hand on Chloe's back, melting away any resistance she might have mustered. Once she had her nestled into the crook of the couch, she switched off the overhead lights and turned on the lamp on the end table.

Grateful, Chloe leaned her head back and rested again. She heard Madeleine moving around her kitchen and tried to remember whether she had done her dishes yesterday. Madeleine's laughter made Chloe nervous, until she emerged from the kitchen with two plates of subs on one arm and two velociraptor mugs in the other hand.

"I see you found my fine china."

"I did. It was difficult, though, choosing between these and the other mugs in your cupboard. Are you a collector?"

Chloe laughed despite herself. The collection of mugs shaped like dinosaurs and storm troopers, Free Willy mugs and all the other wonderful and ridiculous things Hannah had bought her for every holiday certainly would be a surprise to any sane adult rifling through her cupboards.

Madeleine set their dinner on the coffee table and pulled it closer to the couch for easy access, minimizing the amount of moving Chloe would have to do. Chloe had grumbled about Madeleine insisting on making sure she ate, but it was actually really nice to have someone around tonight. Apparently reading her mind, Madeleine handed Chloe her sub just as it registered that she was indeed starving.

"Thanks." Chloe paused, slightly embarrassed for how much she was relying on Madeleine tonight. "I didn't mean to hijack your night. I really appreciate you driving me and feeding me and basically saving me." Taking a bite of the sub she had been holding, she couldn't quite contain the little moan that escaped as her mouth wrapped around the most perfectly toasted BLT she had ever tasted. Chewing quickly, she swallowed and continued, "This is absolutely delicious. I didn't realize how hungry I was. I love BLTs. You're wonderful." Feeling fireflies flitting about in her stomach, she took another bite, deciding that focusing on her sandwich was the safest course of action.

"You're welcome. But honestly, despite the fact that I feel absolutely awful for doing this to you, I had a lot of fun today. Thank you for being such a good sport with me and letting me assuage my guilt by taking care of you a little."

"Promise me you'll stop feeling guilty. I had a lot of fun too. I loved hanging out with you and now I'll add some mystique to my reputation with the kids. They're all going to be wondering what happened."

Chloe hoped some levity would put Madeleine at ease about everything that had happened. She couldn't really convey how nice it had been having her around for the urgent care visit. And now, relaxing and eating subs with her, it almost felt like a normal night of hanging out with a good friend. A friend, yes. One that was incredibly caring, smart, and attractive and *just a friend*, she reminded herself.

As they ate, conversation lulled into a comfortable silence. Chloe inhaled half of the giant hoagie, then reached for the mug of water, her hunger completely sated. She was feeling more like herself already; the food was taking a bit of the edge off the Vicodin-induced loopiness. Madeleine set her sub down, wiping her hands on a napkin and turning to face Chloe from the other end of the couch.

"These really are great mugs. Did you pick out all of the eclectic stuff in your cupboard?" The smile she wore told Chloe she wasn't weirded out by the incredibly nerdy selection of mugs and glasses she had accumulated.

"Not quite. It's become a kind of tradition now. I can't even remember how it started. I think I had found a mug with a baby beluga on it. Do you remember that song, 'Baby beluga in the deep blue sea'?" Chloe hummed a little bit of the song, hoping Madeleine might recognize it.

"He swims so wild and he swims so free!" Excited recognition showed on Madeleine's face.

"Yeah, that one! I don't even remember what show or movie it's from, but Hannah, my best friend from undergrad, and I cried until we laughed one night after trying to remember all the words to the whole song. I was shopping for her birthday the next year and found this mug with a baby beluga on it. I couldn't pass it up. Now I don't want to shatter any illusions, but I'm slightly nerdy, and Hannah, she's a lawyer, rivals me in my love for sci-fi, hilarious pop culture, and great books. So anyway, once I gave her that gateway mug it kind of turned into a tradition of getting each other amazing and weird mugs for holidays. Eventually anytime we traveled somewhere new we brought back the craziest and best mug or cup we could find."

"That's so great. It sounds like Hannah's pretty fantastic." Madeleine extended her legs and leaned back on the couch, her posture relaxed and happy. She acted genuinely interested in Chloe's life. Chloe marveled at how the day had turned out.

"She really is. She drives me crazy sometimes, but in the best way. I can't imagine not having her in my life. She's been with me through pretty much every shitty thing since I was first homesick at school."

"She seems fun, judging from the mugs. Do you get to see her much?"

"We make a point to get out to see each other as often as we can, but she recently started at a small law firm so her schedule is insane. We spent last weekend trying to plan her next visit. It was a nice distraction from waiting to interview for the long-term sub position for Marlene."

"I was meaning to ask you if you were going to apply! That's great news that you got an interview. How did it go?" Genuine excitement for Chloe was evident in Madeleine's enthusiastic tone.

Chloe hesitated slightly, gathering her thoughts. "It went really well as far as I could tell, Mark and the panel were very receptive throughout. Honestly it didn't feel much like an interview. It was more like a professional conversation." Chloe shrugged.

Madeleine nodded, momentarily pensive. "From the way Molly and Leah talk about you, I'd say the job's yours."

Chloe's face colored; she was helpless to stop it at Madeleine's compliment.

"Thank you. I hope you're right. I was pretty nervous about coming back to high school after so long away from it. College lectures are so much different." Chloe surprised herself, opening a door to a conversation she didn't think she was ready to have with anyone, much less Madeleine.

"What brought you here? I have this image of you as a college professor, mentoring little physics nerds. Why leave?"

Madeleine stopped abruptly, as if she hadn't meant to pose the question out loud.

Chloe worked to keep swirling emotions in check. How could she possibly explain everything without Madeleine losing any respect she might have for her? What could excuse her running away like a coward from a mess that was entirely her own making?

Madeleine seemed to sense her hesitation. How much more she could see Chloe wasn't sure. "You don't have to tell me if it's too painful. I know all about things that are too fresh to discuss."

Chloe was tempted to take the easy way out. It had been a long day, she was injured, Madeleine was offering her an out. She decided she should tell her something. Maybe it would help to put some useful distance between them.

"It's pretty fresh and I'm still not sure if I handled it the right way, so yeah it's tough to talk about." She cleared her throat. "There was a lot of tension within the department that I was oblivious to when I started out. For me it was all about the physics. I ended up in the middle of a departmental..." Chloe stumbled for a moment, unsure how to explain the mess that she became entangled in. "Well, an issue, I guess you could call it. My advisor hung me out to dry and I took a leave of absence. I guess I'm hoping to take this year to get a little perspective on the whole thing."

Throughout her explanation, Madeleine's eyes never left hers. It was comforting. Maybe it was the shared understanding of pain? Chloe didn't see any judgment in her gaze, which was nice, but Madeleine didn't know the whole story. Chloe was terrified what she might see reflected back at her if she ever learned it.

"I'm sorry you had to deal with that, but I'm glad you ended up here. Even if it's temporary." A sadness entered her eyes. Chloe instantly wanted to take it away. "I know a little about loss, so if you do want to wade through it, I'm here to listen anytime."

Chloe was touched by the offer. She could tell Madeleine was sincere, but she wasn't sure she could handle opening up to her about the situation. She hadn't even told Hannah the full story yet. Reaching for her mug, she took a drink, gathering her thoughts.

Madeleine had retreated into herself after putting up a good front while they ate. Chloe wasn't sure if she should interrupt, but she recognized the grimace on Madeleine's features. She was all too familiar with getting lost in the pain of her own thoughts.

"Do *you* want to talk about it?"

Madeleine jumped at the sound of Chloe's voice. Her fingers toyed with the frayed corner of a couch cushion. The surprise seemed to shake some of the clouds from of her features. "What do you mean?"

Chloe hesitated, unsure if this was something Madeleine wanted to talk about or something she wanted to talk about with her.

"Stop me if I'm crossing a line, but all this today took you to a pretty bad place." Pausing, Chloe was hesitant to voice her hunch for fear of severing the bond growing between them. Following her gut, she forged ahead. "I'm guessing it has to do with you or someone you care about and a big injury. I'm here to listen too if you want to share."

Madeleine's face closed and Chloe thought she was about to shut down completely. Nervous that she had presumed too much, she frantically backpedaled. "Don't feel any pressure to answer. I didn't mean to make it worse. I want to be here for you too. Not that you necessarily need it…" Chloe trailed off.

Madeleine's face was inscrutable. "It's fine. I don't handle concussions very well. Like I said they scare me. A concussion ended my career, and for some reason today put me right back there." Chloe had had a feeling that might have been the case, but she wasn't sure if Madeleine wanted to tell her any more about it. The silence stretched out between them, causing Chloe to second-guess herself with each moment. Finally, Madeleine went on.

"I haven't really talked about it much since it happened. Something about seeing you go down tonight…" She stopped, focusing her gaze on the hands folded in her lap.

Chloe considered her options, understanding the pain she saw in Madeleine's face. Could she offer her any comfort, considering the recent loss of her own career? Something that she considered to be her own fault? Madeleine's soccer career might have been taken away from her by something else entirely. She could at least listen. "What happened?"

Locking eyes with Chloe, Madeleine began. "I had always wanted to play for the national team. From the first time I ever saw them play. But I never told anyone that. It was too precious a dream to share. By my sophomore year, though, the national team coaches had reached out to me and wanted me to train with them. I couldn't believe it. It was more incredible than I had ever dared to imagine."

Chloe nodded, understanding that type of passion.

"I played with them for two years. After my senior season ended, I was invited to train with the Olympic team."

Unable to contain her enthusiasm, Chloe said, "That's amazing, Madeleine."

"It was literally living a dream. I got drafted into the NWSL in the first round. I couldn't keep up with the reality of it all. I made the official Olympic roster." She paused again, enjoyment lighting her face at this particular memory.

"Our first qualifying match was against Colombia. I was in the starting rotation. Things went really well. Syd scored in the twentieth minute off my assist. Then Carli put one in in the thirtieth minute. The Colombians were getting dirtier as the half went on. The left back was particularly nasty. She got a yellow somewhere around the fortieth minute, I think." Madeleine stopped, remembering the woman, no doubt.

"We went on one last breakaway as the two minutes of extra time were ending. My teammate sent a cross flying into the box as I made my break. I laid out, trying to get my head on the ball, and everything went black."

Madeleine teared up. Chloe wanted to reach out to her, but she decided she needed to maintain her distance—for Madeleine's sake and for her own sanity.

"I have no memory of a lot of this part. It's mainly from what people have told me. The back that had already been carded came flying across the box and kicked my head directly into the post. Apparently it was pretty clear she wasn't going for the ball. She was ejected immediately. I was lucky, apparently, to escape with only a little bit of memory loss. She fractured my orbital and I had a Grade Three concussion. I woke up in the hospital and my soccer career was over. It was too dangerous for me to play competitively again."

The tears Madeleine began to shed were too much for Chloe. She leaned forward and hugged her. She stiffened, but she eventually returned the hug. It was brief, but intense nonetheless. Chloe released Madeleine before she could enjoy the closeness too much and saw Madeleine's face lighten.

"I used to be pretty bitter about it, but I've come to terms with it, I think. I love teaching and coaching, and I'm still close with the team. I get gear and I talk to the girls on the road sometimes, but it's a little easier to retain my sanity if I maintain some distance."

"I can't imagine how hard it is to balance humoring people who want to know about your experience while trying to accept it yourself." Chloe couldn't help but reflect on her own current predicament.

"It's been hard. I didn't do myself any favors by trying to keep it to myself. Thanks for letting me unload some of it."

Madeleine clearly was ready to change the direction of the conversation.

"You didn't really unload all that much, but I'm really glad you shared it with me. It makes sense how my bloody face brought back a lot of memories," Chloe added gently, trying to apologize without saying as much.

"Don't even blame yourself," Madeleine chuckled, shaking her head. "I broke your nose and you're trying to comfort me. Always the brave one, huh?" Chloe grinned, glad to see Madeleine getting back to herself. A yawn surprised her. It was followed almost instantly by another wince at the shot of pain from the break that she had forgotten about.

"And that is my cue. You're exhausted and fragile, so I'll let you sleep." Madeleine stood, touching two fingers to her forehead in a casual salute.

"Exhausted and fragile—I'm glad I've made such a great impression." Chloe stood to let the laughing Madeleine out. Buttoning her coat, Madeleine shook her head.

"The jury's still out. And not to split hairs, but I did also say you were cute and pathetic." With that, she walked out the door to her car, leaving Chloe trying not to enjoy the way the offhand remark made her feel.

* * *

Climbing into bed, Chloe willed herself to relax after the eventful evening with Madeleine. It was difficult to process, though. Chloe could never be sure how to read Madeleine. The pain medicine tonight probably wasn't helping, but she wasn't wasting time feeling conflicted. What a pleasant side effect. Madeleine was always so composed, which in contrast made Chloe feel like a bumbling teenager. It was a nice change to be kept on her toes. The problem was she had absolutely no clue what, if anything, was happening between her and Madeleine.

Then there was the whole Landon question. He obviously was interested in Madeleine and they kept interacting with each other. That didn't quite fit with the fact that Madeleine pinged Chloe's gaydar. Though that was probably wishful thinking on her part.

The sound of guitar chords emanating from the top of her nightstand roused her from her musings. Seeing that it was Hannah, Chloe answered it. "You are so lucky you didn't call me three minutes earlier."

"Why's that, studly? Were you sweeping your straight teacher friend off her feet?"

"Why do you assume everything is about her?" Chloe countered.

"It's the way you try to avoid her in conversation and refuse to admit she's straight. Even if she isn't, you should convince yourself she is." Hannah went on, dampening Chloe's excitement. "Girls who are confused are trouble."

Chloe couldn't keep from interrupting. "It's only trouble when someone like you manages to flirt with seventeen different women at the same time. Someone realizing they are attracted to women is great. The more the merrier. Also, get over your biphobia. You're better than that."

"You raise a good point. But you can't blame me for not wanting something stupid to happen after everything you went through last year." The worry in Hannah's voice came through loud and clear.

If she knew the whole story she'd be even more concerned, Chloe thought. She had never found the strength to tell her everything about the reason she had left UMass. That would require allowing her to see how weak and dim-witted she had been.

Chloe resolved to dismiss whatever delusions she had been entertaining regarding Madeleine. She shook her head. It would be a struggle to quash the little crush she had been fostering, but she couldn't afford anything like that now anyway, not with all the baggage she was already carrying.

"You're right. So how was work?" she asked, redirecting the conversation toward Hannah's day at the office. Refocusing her thoughts, she listened intently as Hannah recounted a tale about a "pompous douche-man" that had come in demanding to speak with the owner of the firm, in the process rifling off some creative insults about the guy that she clearly had held back earlier in the day.

"Shit, Hannah. Tell me how you really feel about him."

"There's not enough time…" Her voice trailed off wistfully. "I do have some actual bad news. I was assigned to a new client because one of our associates went into labor weeks early. I'm swamped now and there's no way I'll be able to make it out this weekend. Can you ever forgive me?"

Chloe, though disappointed, totally understood. She knew Hannah was as disappointed as she was, but that she was also under immense pressure at work until she could make partner.

"Hannah, it's totally fine. I'll miss seeing you, but I'll have school breaks coming up, I'll plan on coming to you." Chloe paused, then decided it was time for another change of topic, and hopefully one that might lighten Hannah's spirits.

"Oh, by the way, something significant did happen here today. You have to swear you won't laugh," she said, knowing full well that Hannah wouldn't be able to resist when she heard about her newly broken nose.

"Spill!"

Chloe related the story of the shootout, filtering out any instances that Hannah might consider flirtatious. When she told Hannah about the backfire that caused the broken nose, Hannah struggled mightily to compose herself before she finally lost it.

"I'm sorry for laughing, but you know that's something that would only happen to you, right?"

"Yeah, I know. Madeleine took me to urgent care to get it set. I still can't believe it happened."

"Well, now we have to come up with some great stories for you to tell the kiddos tomorrow at school. I think one option should be that you stopped to get gas and saved an elderly lady from a falling piece of the overhang, only to get your nose smashed in the process."

The phone call quickly devolved into increasingly detailed, unlikely, and laughable accounts of heroism until, after twenty minutes or so, Hannah became distracted.

"Han, what's up?"

"It's nothing really. I need to find this paperwork for tomorrow, I know I had it earlier…" Her voice trailed off.

"Hannah, go find what you need. You should probably check the black hole you call your 'bag' again." Hannah had been one giant unorganized mess since freshman year. Though her workloads had increased with each semester, her organizational skills never did.

"Good night you. I'm going to go shower." Chloe was more than ready to relax and climb into bed.

"Take care of your nose and try not to beat yourself up for letting a lawn mower get the best of you."

"Funny. Good night, Hannah," Chloe said, cutting her off before she got any more insults in.

"Night," Hannah replied, still laughing at her own joke. "I'll talk to you later."

And with that, Chloe hung up and called it a night.

CHAPTER EIGHT

Thursday

"How's the schnoz?"

Chloe smiled at Taylor as she crossed the threshold of the classroom.

"Well, it definitely feels broken today."

Nodding empathetically, Taylor hopped onto the sturdy black countertop of the island at the front of the classroom.

"You're pretty badass with your double black eye combination. I overheard two students discussing the likelihood that you stole someone's girlfriend."

"Oh great. That's totally what I want floating around the school. Don't I come off more like someone who would save an old lady from a mugging?"

"These are high school kids, Chloe. Get real."

Acknowledging the truth in Taylor's assertion did not help her situation. She hadn't been exactly thrilled at the prospect of telling her students that she'd taken a soccer ball to the face so during first period she told them she would award extra credit to students who presented plausible accounts of what might have caused her new look, incorporating any of the principles they had covered so far in class. That had generated some seriously entertaining guesses.

Unfortunately they hadn't been eager to go back to work when Chloe wanted them to. In order to get them focused again she told them they had until the closing bell today to see if they could piece together the mystery, but if they kept talking about it in class she would add an extra, more difficult problem to the test scheduled for Friday. In theory it was a decent idea to leave them wondering, but in reality she was a little nervous about the outcome.

"In hindsight the extra credit scheme might not have been my best idea, but the kids were funny about it. I didn't get any 'soccer balls to the face' as guesses, but more than a handful of students speculated about my LARPing tendencies."

"Yeah, inviting high schoolers to speculate about your life isn't exactly encouraged in the teacher handbook. But neither is telling them you took a ball to the face." Taylor laughed heartily, then changed tacks. "So I have some good news to distract you. Landon wants to interview you."

"Sweet!" Chloe had no reservations about this particular interview. Coaching with Taylor was going to be amazing no matter what else happened, of that she was sure. Something was off in Taylor's face, though. "Is there a catch or something? You're nervous. Did you change your mind?"

"No, definitely not. There's no time to stew anyway. Your interview is in twenty minutes. He came to the gym and told me his schedule opened up and he wanted to move quickly on this. In Landon-speak that means he wants to surprise you with it and catch you off guard." Taylor frowned. "I don't really understand why he's being so ornery, maybe he…" She stopped herself, leaving Chloe curious about what she had been about to say.

With a shake of her head, she went on. "It doesn't really matter. You're going to nail this. I figured advising against taking his bait if he comes off as a chauvinist would be helpful though. I mean, he is one, but I need you to get this job. So be prepared for anything."

Chloe should have realized this was too good an opportunity for it to be straightforward. "I've dealt with plenty of that in the sciences. I want this job so I can put up with anything. Why don't we head over now?"

Taylor nodded, excitement lighting up her features. As they closed in on the gym, she nudged Chloe's arm. "Are you sure you're ready for this?"

Chloe knew Taylor wasn't questioning if she was prepared for the interview itself. She wanted to know if she was ready for Landon and all the weirdness she had tried to warn Chloe about.

"I'm as ready as I can be. I'm going to interview like I normally would, but I'm prepared for anything and everything inappropriate to come my way. I'll count to three before I speak if anything gets hinky. Sound like a decent plan?"

Nodding, Taylor responded, "Yes, it does. I really don't think he'll do anything stupid. He knows I want you for the job and he wants us to win. I also don't think he wants to have to deal with the union if he violates the discrimination policy, but he might not be that smart. Let's get this thing over with so we can officially start."

Turning the corner, Chloe ran into an unanticipated visual trigger. Landon was standing in the entrance to the office talking to Madeleine as she stood in the hallway. She had thought she was prepared for anything, but she hadn't expected to be pissed at the man before the interview even started.

Nothing about that scene should have bothered her, she admitted to herself. She had no claim on how Madeleine spent her time. But the thing was, she wanted to spend more time with her, more than she should. Seeing Landon eying her possessively made Chloe's blood boil.

As Taylor and Chloe approached, Chloe saw some barely disguised frustration on Madeleine's face. She got the distinct impression from her rigid posture and tightly controlled facial expressions that she would rather be anywhere else than standing there talking with Landon.

"Landon, how are you? Chloe, I'd like to formally introduce you to Landon Markfield, our athletic director." The warmth Taylor was injecting into her voice wasn't enough to overcome the serious amount of shade Chloe was catching from Landon.

"So nice to meet you. Taylor told me she is excited to interview you for the JV coaching position." While his words were supposed to be inviting, his tone was anything but. Chloe was picking up high levels of alpha male aggression.

Chloe had seen him on multiple occasions around the school. She had gathered that he had been one of the other English teachers before he accepted the position of athletic director. She extended her hand. Landon took it and applied a little too much pressure for the shake to be friendly.

Determined to get the job, Chloe ignored her gut and greeted him. "I've heard nothing but great things about you. I'm glad we're finally meeting. I'm very excited to talk with you and Taylor about the basketball program you have here. You all have done an amazing job with the it."

"Well, thank you." He inclined his head in what she assumed was supposed to be a humble acknowledgment of the compliment, though it came off as a bit pretentious. "If you two want to head into my office, I'll join you in a minute."

While his attention was still on Taylor and Chloe, Madeleine flashed a quick smile in Chloe's direction, mouthing "Good luck" with a thumbs-up. Feeling slightly cheered, Chloe turned to head into the office.

Landon turned his attention back to Madeleine, resuming their slightly strained conversation. Chloe tuned it out as she and Taylor walked into the office. She wasn't certain what the nature of his relationship with Madeleine was, but she was positive of two things: first, she wanted nothing to do with the whole affair, and secondly, Landon's feelings for Madeleine were very strong. Nearly all of the times she had seen him at school he was either with Madeleine or trying to find her.

Chloe couldn't find it in herself to believe that the Madeleine she had come to know actually enjoyed this creep's company. Still, much as she wanted to believe it wasn't a big deal, his presence provided another very good reason for her to keep things platonic with Madeleine. As long as she could maintain her composure, things would work out. A season of coaching with a great new friend, a fantastic work experience, and a direction in life—those were great reasons to keep herself out of trouble. Could she remember that during the interview and later when she was around Madeleine? That was the real question.

* * *

Chloe left the interview alone, leaving Taylor and Landon to discuss the plan moving forward. Despite Taylor's warning, the interview had been pretty uneventful, though he did manage to wonder out loud how she'd managed to embarrass herself by acquiring such "unsightly bruising." Chloe told herself she'd only imagined his happiness when he mentioned how much pain she must be in. That bit had been incredibly uncomfortable.

Landon was pretentious and condescending, but he did light up when discussing the sports teams at the school. It was evident that he wanted the program to be successful, and when Chloe and Taylor were discussing coaching philosophies he was pleased. The interview ended with a handshake and a promise from him to have a final offer for her by the end of the day. Chloe had been confident she would get the job, but the reality of securing it was even more exciting than she had imagined.

Heading back to her classroom with a noticeable increase in swag as she walked, Chloe couldn't keep the smile off her face. She didn't want to. Practice plans already forming in her head, she was mentally sifting through her favorite workouts, the best sprinting drills, types of offenses to try out. She could hardly wait to start writing everything out. She would also have to go out and get some sneakers to complement the red, black, and white gear she was going to load up on.

By the time she reached her classroom, she had a solid list of drills to diagram so that she could show them to Taylor. She had twenty minutes before she had to teach, so she sat down and hammered them out. When the bell signaling the end of the period roused her from her sketching, she'd made decent progress. The rest would come after she went home. Now she had to focus long enough to get through the rest of the day.

* * *

"All we need is your signature here on the contract." Chloe bent to sign the paper on Landon's desk. "And here too, this is the coaching policy. It outlines the school's standards and expectations. I'll email you a copy to keep. The rest of the employment paperwork we already have on file from your substituting. So, that's everything I need from you. Welcome aboard, Coach."

Landon's secretary was handling the tedious paperwork aspects necessary to finalize Chloe's acceptance of the position. He had congratulated her and formally offered her the position, explained the finer details, and then rushed off to show some support at the boys' soccer game. Chloe was glad it was only her and Michelle left in the office. She was a sweet woman in her late forties with two kids in the middle school. She had a caring demeanor and Chloe knew she was responsible for handling the real inner workings of the department, transportation, officials, scheduling.

"Michelle, I have it on good authority that this department wouldn't run without you, so I want to thank you in advance for making the season possible."

"Thanks, Chloe. I can't wait to see you and Taylor out there this season. I have a feeling the girls are going to have a lot of fun."

"Probably not as much fun as Taylor and I will have."

"You might be right about that," Michelle answered, nodding her head. "Well, you get out of here and enjoy your night! Congratulations again!"

"Thank you so much! I'm going to go celebrate by diagramming a few more drills!"

With that Chloe left the office. It was time to find Taylor and start making plans for the rapidly approaching season.

* * *

"Have I mentioned how much I love Manchetti's pizza?" Chloe called out to Taylor from her kitchen.

"You're welcome."

Taylor had found Chloe after school and asked if she wanted to grab some dinner and start the planning tonight. Chloe was more than happy to do that—she even offered to cook—but Taylor insisted on bringing the food. They had decided to meet at Chloe's apartment since it was on Taylor's way home anyway.

Bringing their drinks into the living room, Chloe settled in the armchair.

"So how're you holding up, champ?" Taylor asked nonchalantly as she reclined further into the couch with her slices.

"I'm jazzed about this season, but I'm not gonna lie. I'm a little nervous too."

"That's normal. If you don't feel a little bit of nerves, you're not really invested and shouldn't be coaching." Chloe nodded, and Taylor went on. "But you're going to do great. I can't wait. You respect the kids and the game and that's all you need to start with. I'll teach you the rest. I've seriously got zero concerns about your coaching. What I want to know is how you're holding up. Your life's been a bit of a whirlwind lately."

"I think I'm operating outside the conventional space-time continuum. My brain hasn't fully acknowledged the reality that I am living, that I could be a long-term sub for the rest of the year."

"But you're excited about that possibility?"

"Yes, excited and scared. It's a lot different from where I was this time last year."

Taylor spoke gently. "You know, some pretty wise people in my life finally got through to me that I don't always have to handle everything on my own, and I've been better off for that. We haven't been friends long, but I care about you, sunshine. You know I'm here for you, right?"

"I do, and I appreciate it more than you know. You know the same goes for you from me?"

"I do know that, but I think it's my turn to be the listening one. Anne's taught me well. You should have seen me before she came around. Subtlety of a moose."

Chloe couldn't help imagining a much younger Taylor dumbfounded by nuanced emotional responses. This Taylor was her sounding board, her straight-shooting, supportive sounding board. It was time to share a little with her, she decided.

"When I was at UMass the physics department was a good old boys club. Well, except for my advisor. I respected her so much. She was incredible. Or so I thought." Taylor listened but gave no indication that she might press Chloe for details. For that Chloe would be forever grateful.

"She really screwed me over. She totally violated my trust, pressured me for a relationship despite being in the closet and married. Then when I couldn't take it anymore, she recommended to my thesis committee that I take a leave of absence to 'sort everything out,' despite the fact that she was the one that needed sorting out. The worst part is, it's my fault it happened and I can't change a fucking thing."

Taylor sat, thoughtful for a moment.

"Chloe, you weren't living it alone. She was your advisor and if she was an active participant, it can't possibly all be your fault." Chloe nodded but remained silent. The fact was Elaine had done her fair share of contributing, but ultimately it was Chloe who hadn't stepped up, and that was the truth she would always live with.

Taylor went on. "Remember, when you want to get it all out there, I'll listen." Taylor's eyes took on a devilish gleam. "And until then I'll be coming up with the best insults you've ever heard to toss her way. Now, what do you want to do about tryouts?"

And with that, Taylor lifted a weight off Chloe she hadn't even known she'd been lugging around. She told her things were all right, and somehow she believed it. Maybe things would be okay after all.

Taylor went home around eight thirty, though they could have easily stayed up all night talking and laughing. They had hammered out a rough practice schedule, a timeline for when tryouts should be, and how long they should last and had reviewed and revamped the core principles the program was built on. They would spend the first three days practicing together, sharing a gym, going over fundamentals, and doing plenty of conditioning. They would have lunch every Saturday after practice to regroup and plan until games started; then they would spend even more time in the office preparing.

Fitting in her work at the Boatery had become a source of worry for her once the reality of her new responsibilities had set in, but Jacob had been so excited about her progress he suggested she switch to a seasonal position. She'd been so relieved. She didn't want to leave Jacob hanging, but the prospect of giving up every weekend did not seem sustainable. It turned out Andrew had requested more hours and summers were always the busiest months, so things were working out more smoothly than Chloe had imagined they would.

Coaching was going to be a big time commitment, Chloe knew, but she was excited by the challenge and by the assignment, especially the amount of freedom she was being given to develop an offense that worked for the girls on the team.

After saying goodbye to Taylor, she took the pizza box to the kitchen to place it with her other recyclables, wondering as she did so where her phone was. She hadn't even thought of it since Taylor had arrived. Her pockets were empty, so it had to be in the living room somewhere or in her coat.

Grabbing her jacket, she felt an extra weight in the pocket. When she fished the phone out, the blinking green light told her she had a text. Unlocking the screen, she saw a number she didn't know.

I got your number from Taylor, I hope you don't mind. How did the interview go?

Briefly confused, Chloe stared at the number until it hit her. *Madeleine.*

I don't mind at all. And I'd say it went pretty well. I'm the new JV coach.

CONGRATULATIONS! I knew you'd nail it. You're fantastic.

Chloe tried to tell herself her heart was racing because of how exciting it was to say that she was the new JV coach. As she was typing a response, another text came in.

If you want me to teach them how to take a charge, let me know ;)

Without hesitation, Chloe ripped off a response.

I think you misspoke. Your specialty is the actual charging part.

Chloe laughed out loud as she read Madeleine's response.

Now you're confused. Have you hit your head recently?

Chloe responded without hesitation.

You've got jokes. That's nice.

Pleasantly surprised by the speed with which Madeleine replied, Chloe felt her own silly grin widening.

I do and I'll be here all year.

Chloe wasn't quite sure how to keep the conversation going or if she should. Mercifully her phone went off again, pulling her from that train of thought.

Do you have plans after school tomorrow?

A totally innocent question should not incite such a visceral reaction. Regardless, a warm glow steadily spread outward from her center. Her nerves perked up, sensing the possibility of time with Madeleine.

Honest answer? I've got a hot date with a pile of papers. All my classes have a test tomorrow.

That is poetic serendipity. Would you care to double date in my classroom? Misery loves company.

Friends grade together. That had to be a thing, Chloe reasoned. Completely harmless, plus Madeleine was straight. Probably. Well, in any case, she wasn't out.

It's a date.

Chloe reread her text and stopped before sending it. No way could she let herself fall into this habit again. Pseudo flirting via text was a dangerous game and with Nora she had perfected it. It was easy to ignore the lines that were straddled when you sent a text. Flirting was ambiguous enough without the additional complication of texting. Erasing the text, she tried again.

I'm in.

Two words were all she could manage. Anything else that sprang to mind did not reside firmly in the friend zone.

Fabulous. I will see you tomorrow, and congratulations again!

Exactly what she was getting herself into was as yet undetermined, but Chloe knew her excitement at the prospect should worry her. The problem was, she couldn't muster nearly enough concern to do anything about it.

CHAPTER NINE

Friday

"What's up, sugar?"

Chloe's attention left the manila folder she held in her hands. The folder certainly felt real. This Taylor walking in to her classroom, complete with a never-ending supply of pet names, was too vivid to be imagined. All that still wasn't enough to speed up her acceptance of the reality of the last fifteen minutes.

"Uh, Chloe, don't take this the wrong way, but is there a reason you're looking like a drugged-out space cadet right now?"

"Yup. Right here." Chloe held up the folder. Taylor nodded immediately, her face suddenly serious.

"Ah, you're in deep with the Mafia and someone wants hush money. Got it."

"I got the job." Though she was still in disbelief, part of her was beginning to get excited about the possibilities this opportunity presented.

"Holy shit! It's official! You're on your way to becoming the real deal!" Taylor laughed and reached over, squeezing Chloe's arm affectionately.

"It is, isn't it. I'm signing the paperwork Monday, so I need to figure things out pretty quick."

"C'mon. Think about it. You've basically been doing the job for going on three weeks now. Nothing much is going to change other than knowing you're here for the duration. So you get to keep on keepin' on."

Chloe laughed at Taylor's ability to take everything in stride. It wasn't part of her makeup to let something rattle her for very long. "I seriously never imagined myself here, but right now I can't see myself doing anything else either." She shook her head. "Apparently this is what normal feels like. I forgot."

Taylor let out a laugh. "Yes, ma'am. Soak it up. It's a good damn thing you got the job too. I didn't want to have to adjust practice schedules for you to drive in from God knows where."

Chloe was already beginning to consider the small changes and additions she wanted to make to the semester plans Mrs. Flore had outlined.

A question from Taylor brought her back to the present. "So what were you doing before Dorman rocked your nerdy little world?"

"Nothing much. Organizing my life a little bit," Chloe said, gesturing toward the five stacks of papers and multiple notebooks spread on the bench in front of her.

"That's a thrilling Friday night plan. Could I convince you to ditch that right now and help me order some practice gear? I hear monotony can be a helpful coping mechanism."

Chloe laughed at Taylor. She was incorrigible. "Thank you so much for that generous offer. But is there any chance it could wait until tomorrow during lunch? I promised Madeleine I'd stay with her this afternoon so that we can both get some grading done. Otherwise we won't do it at all."

Letting out an exaggerated sigh, Taylor nodded her head in defeat. "Okay, get it done now so we can put together more practice plans tomorrow."

"Will do." What a way to spend the rest of the year, surrounded by friends *and* teaching physics. Granted, it wasn't the way she had originally pictured her academic pursuits panning out, but it was pretty fantastic nonetheless.

Chloe was laden down with tests from the three general physics classes as well as her messenger bag, workout bag, and water bottle when she finally made her way to Madeleine's room. Though she had walked by the room multiple times, she had never been inside it. The inside of a classroom could tell you a lot about a teacher. It was their domain and how it was organized and decorated spoke volumes about their personality and teaching style.

Madeleine wasn't in the room when Chloe arrived, but the lights were on and the door was open. Taking in the room, Chloe was not disappointed. What she guessed was a refurbished farm table served as Madeleine's desk. It held an assortment of books piled on it, her laptop, a sand Zen garden, and three potted plants. It was easy to imagine writing conferences taking place in the two comfortable chairs that sat beside it.

In the back corner was a reading den with three beanbag chairs and what had to have been a personal bookshelf. It was loaded with a library that Chloe wanted desperately to check out. The titles she saw ranged from *A Brave New World* by Aldous Huxley to the entire Harry Potter series. Chloe was excited to begin borrowing from the extensive collection. She loved the idea of students reading books from the vast assortment and she imagined Madeleine encouraging them to read whatever tickled their fancy.

The back of the room had an interesting array of student projects and a collection of signs. Walking to the whiteboard where the signs were posted, she read the first.

I like cooking my family and my pets.
Don't be a psycho, use commas.

Each sign she read grew more ridiculous. The next had two quotes with a cartoon of a scared grandmother. The text read "Let's eat Grandma!" and "Let's eat, Grandma!"

She lost it. *Punctuation saves lives.*

There was a Liam Neeson picture threatening students who didn't staple their papers when they handed them in. There were at least fifty cartoons and punny signs in all, some of them even handwritten.

As she was perusing them, she heard Madeleine enter the room. She turned. "I've got the perfect meme for your wall."

"Oh yeah? Care to share? Just so you know, I exercise supreme authority over what makes the cut."

"There's a prerequisite. You've seen *Star Wars*, right?" Chloe checked with Madeleine expectantly, eager to pull the meme up on her phone. When she didn't answer immediately, she was shocked.

"You've never seen *Star Wars*?" She was aghast. "How is that even possible? What kind of monster are you?"

"I know. It's a travesty. If you want to cut me out of your life, I understand."

"Seriously, how is that possible? I mean they're everywhere. It would be impressive if it wasn't so tragic."

"I never saw the appeal, and the whole Jedi business always felt a little culty to me. No one ever convinced me they were worth watching."

"I'll grant you there is a tiny cult feel to it, but they're so good. I'll convince you." She grinned, walking over to where her things were piled on the student desk. Glancing back at Madeleine, she smiled as she saw her shake her head at Chloe's conviction that watching the movie was now an inevitability for her. "How was your day?"

"Typical. Some dramatic readings, the seniors' papers were due, and then I was bullied over my taste in movies."

"Bullied is too strong a word. I would go with 'interrogated.' No maliciousness was involved."

"My apologies, I was *interrogated*. How about you? Did anyone accost you?"

At the sight of Madeleine's slightly crooked half smile, Chloe lost the thought she'd been forming. How could anyone think around this woman? What had she asked? Something about her day? "Not really, but I did get a pretty intriguing offer."

Madeleine gestured toward her table and the padded chairs.

"Here, sit down. Though they appear ancient, they're incredibly comfortable." As Chloe lowered herself into the chair, her knee brushed against Madeleine's thigh. Sliding her chair back to manufacture some distance, Chloe watched Madeleine's hand go to the hairband at her wrist. Today the accessory was bright yellow.

"So, what was this big offer?" Before Chloe could respond, things clicked into place for Madeleine. "You got the long-term position!" She grabbed Chloe's arm, squeezing it and beaming at her. Chloe's skin tingled at the contact.

"I did. It's official. I'm here all year!"

"Well, then, we need to celebrate. It's a shame we're at school and can't have a couple of celebratory margaritas." Madeleine frowned, appearing appropriately disappointed. "Why don't we finish some grading and then celebrate?"

Chloe agreed. Grading was about to become a central aspect of her time; she might as well dive in. Madeleine's half smile was back, and Chloe's ability to speak had vanished with its reappearance.

"Since coaching with a tequila hangover doesn't sound appealing for practice tomorrow morning, does a movie and popcorn in my in-room theater appeal to your sensibilities?" Madeleine gestured toward the beanbag chairs at the back of the room.

"Sounds perfect."

"Considering we're celebrating your new job, I'll let you pick out the movie." Madeleine paused, and Chloe jumped at her chance.

"I can't wait for you to see *Star Wars*. Then the 'Teacher took your phone, mine took my legs' meme would make so much more sense."

"Pump the brakes. I'm happy for you, but I'm not that easy. You've got to work for it. Make another selection."

Sighing, Chloe had to trust in her ability to wear Madeleine down eventually.

"I'm sensing some conditions here."

Madeleine shook her head. "Only that one. I reserve the right to veto any terrible choices."

"Well, congratulations to me! Are you sure you don't want to cut out the middleman and pick?"

"No, no, I wouldn't do that to you. Tonight's all about you." Electricity sparked to life in the air surrounding them. "After grading, of course."

Chloe stood, hoping that filling her hands with tests to grade would give her time to recover. She had never experienced such acute attraction in the simplest gestures. Madeleine, on the other hand, sat completely at ease. How in the hell was she going to be able to focus on her grading? She had to try.

Chloe brought the tests and her purple grading pen to the table after her heartbeat quieted to its normal cadence. Opening her own folder of essays, Madeleine began reading, her brows creased slightly in concentration.

Indulging herself, Chloe let her eyes follow slanting cheekbones down to the curve of impossibly soft lips. Madeleine caught the corner of her bottom lip with her teeth, stirring images in Chloe's mind of what she would do with those lips. Watching a slender hand bring a pen to her mouth, she could nearly feel those fingers on her own skin.

Knowing that she was playing with fire, she averted her eyes, put her head down, and began reading through the physics tests, grateful for something to occupy her mind. Ever since things had spiraled out of control with Elaine, she had been emotionally drained, incapable of connecting or even wanting to connect with someone again. Madeleine was drawing her in. That was dangerous. She had to shore up her resolve. Everything else was falling into place so nicely. She could not afford to have an epic relationship meltdown derail the progress she was making. Not again.

The calculations she was assessing helped steady and comfort her. That was the thing about Newtonian physics.

Everything was clear-cut. No matter who or what else was plaguing her, the formulas reminded her that order existed in the universe.

The students were doing surprisingly well, all things considered. Chloe hadn't been sure what to expect with this first test. She thought they were grasping the material, but that didn't necessarily translate into testing well.

It's odd, she thought. As a TA at UMass she had graded exams that other professors had written. This was different: it was the first test she herself had written, and it was for high schoolers as opposed to college students. She had never pictured herself in a high school classroom, but there was something about guiding students during their first exposure to physics that excited her in a way she had not experienced with undergraduates.

Lost in thought, she hadn't realized how long they had both been grading until her body reminded her. Madeleine was still leaning over her desk, the picture of concentration, two pens stuck through her messy bun and a third one being twirled between her fingers as she read. Chloe leaned back, stretching her legs. It was time for a mini break.

"Excuse me, but did every joint in your body just crack?" Madeleine wondered aloud.

"Pretty close to it. Getting old sucks."

"Right. Talk to me in a couple of years when you begin to know what it's really like."

"Does your body feel as old as mine does? I imagine after all of the national team work you did, you must be worse off than I am."

Chloe froze. Madeleine had told her how difficult dealing with her past had been and now here she was, referring to it as if it was no big deal. She peered over at her, afraid that she would see darkness clouding her face. Mercifully, there was none.

"They actually did a fantastic job managing our bodies. We had top-notch training and recovery. So it's not as bad as you might imagine." Madeleine's voice was clear, but she seemed to have noted Chloe's hesitancy. "I went back through the things that I had stored from my career after we talked. I realized I'd spent too much time being angry, sad at what I had lost. I forgot to think about all of the amazing experiences I had."

Chloe nodded, glad to see Madeleine moving toward making peace with her past. Someone should have closure—even if she couldn't.

"I suppose I should thank you for letting me break your nose to get me to talk about it. It was masterfully done." Madeleine's eyes had lit up, the hazel in them almost shimmering.

"I'm glad you're in a good place now or at least getting there. I'd let you break it again if it meant you could let go of that pain I saw you carrying around."

"Thank you." Madeleine faltered briefly. "It really did help, talking. I think I let a lot of it go the other night. You got me there, broken nose and all." She paused. "Not to mention that I have all sorts of material to work with when I trash talk at pickup now that I know of your soccer crushes."

"You can try, but they're old news. I've moved on," Chloe replied, carefully leaving out the bit about having found a different national team member to crush on. "Good news, though. I've decided on the movie I want to watch." Madeleine raised her eyebrows, interested yet suspicious about what Chloe had chosen.

"We're going to watch *Jurassic Park*. It's a timeless classic and one of my all-time favorites."

"I actually support that decision. I've been meaning to watch the original and I've heard good things."

Chloe sighed, exasperated but also excited that Madeleine was acquiescing. Madeleine let out a small chuckle. "I didn't get to ask, but do you have any dead-weight issues that you'd like to get off your chest? Any recent traumas, crazy exes?"

Despite the lightness of her tone, Chloe knew that Madeleine was making a genuine offer to listen and that she should level the playing field a little by sharing something. Anything she had to offer, though, was much too personal. It would be much better to talk about raptors and T-rexes.

It was as if the universe was listening, and it disagreed. A text came in on her phone.

Chloe, I could really use a friend. Please talk to me.

The universe has one sick sense of humor, Chloe thought, running her hand through her hair. Anything she did would leave her feeling guilty. Nora needed someone, but if Chloe tried to be her support, it would confuse her more. If Chloe left it alone, she would be hanging Nora out to dry. Running her hand through her hair again, this time more slowly, Chloe tried to relax. Madeleine was patiently waiting, clearly tuned in to the sudden uptick in Chloe's stress level.

"Seriously, is it anything you want to get off your chest?" she asked softly.

"No, it's just someone I knew from UMass. It's awkward. Totally my fault too."

"As difficult as it is to imagine, I'm not perfect, Chloe. Try me. I won't judge." Madeleine shot her a gentle smile, giving her an opportunity to keep the conversation surface level.

Could she really talk about this with Madeleine? Maybe this would be the perfect thing to create a little distance between them. Today had been amazing, too amazing to sustain. If Chloe couldn't do the right thing with Nora, at least she could steer Madeleine away from her own trolley of baggage.

The silence deepened as did the shadows filling the room now that the sun had sunk behind the trees. Madeleine, perhaps sensing Chloe's internal struggle, stood and walked to the door, closing it. Turning, she returned to her file cabinet and rummaged around in the bottom drawer for a moment. She emerged with two jar candles and a sheepish grin.

"You have to take a vow of secrecy. I know these are *technically* illegal, but I'm addicted. Burning them takes me to a happy place. I thought you could use a little happy."

"I love it. Two candles and we're living a Pinterest dream."

"I knew it!" Madeleine burst out. "You're a closet Pinner! You've got this swag about you that says you're too cool for crafting, but deep down, you're a total sap."

"You'll never know. Maybe that was just a clever cultural reference."

"Now that the mood is set," Madeleine replied softly, "do you want to talk about your UMass acquaintance?"

Chloe froze, still unsure if she was ready or if she even wanted to try to own this yet. What she found in Madeleine was welcoming. Too welcoming. Too safe. She had to make Madeleine see how damaged she really was.

"Well, it all comes down to the fact that I let an undergraduate that I was tutoring develop a pretty serious crush on me. I knew in the back of my mind all along that our tutor-pupil relationship was too friendly, but she was fun and I was an idiot."

Chloe stopped. Madeleine remained where she was, leaning back in her chair.

"Were you her professor or a school-appointed tutor?" she asked.

"Neither. My advisor referred her to me, but her parents paid me under the table."

"Was she an adult?"

"She was a junior at the time, twenty-one I think. But still, she was a kid."

Madeleine shrugged. "I'll grant you that, but she's an adult in the eyes of every institution, including the university. What do you mean when you say you were an idiot?"

Madeleine's face was unchanged, but she had begun playing with the green hair tie on her left wrist. Chloe was beginning to see a pattern there.

"I let things get too casual, too comfortable. We talked as friends, and I let my guard down. I told myself those same things. 'She's an intelligent twenty-one-year-old.' 'We can be friends.' I didn't want anything from her, not in that way. I wanted her to succeed and I genuinely liked her. But I could tell she was feeling more than that. I should have talked to her. But I was too caught up in my own nonsense. So I avoided confronting the issue."

Chloe paused, wondering how much damage she was doing to her own reputation with this story. Forging ahead, she added, "When she finally got blatantly flirtatious, to the point I couldn't ignore it, I panicked. She was doing fine in her classes and she didn't really need my help anymore. So I abandoned her without talking about it. And now she keeps trying to figure out what happened. I still haven't worked out how to handle it."

"I will admit that the tutor aspect complicates things a little, but it's not exactly something that hasn't happened before, and it's not scandalous. The best thing you can do now is try to clarify things with her. It won't be easy. Those types of conversations are never enjoyable, but I think you owe it to yourself and to her to be frank with her. If she's as intelligent as you say she is, she has to have an idea of what's going on. She doesn't want to, but she does. She's not going to be shocked."

"I know you're right. Now I have to force myself to face up to it. I hate confrontation, but to be a functioning adult I have to get over that."

"It would be advantageous." Madeleine's voice softened. "But hating yourself for making mistakes never helps. Believe me, I've tried that."

Chloe connected to what Madeleine offered so deeply that it frightened her. Why did she feel as if she understood her better than even Hannah did? She tried to conceal her intake of breath at the surprising intimacy of the moment. Time to change the subject. "You're not that much older than I am. How did you become so wise?"

"Oh, you know, a lot can happen in three years. Don't forget. I'll always have the age advantage on you," Madeleine responded wryly, following Chloe's bid to relieve the building tension. "May we both find emotional maturity by the time we're eighty. And now that we've both bared our souls, cue the popcorn and the movie and let's celebrate your new job."

CHAPTER TEN

October

Any worries Chloe had harbored about adjusting to teaching full-time at the high school had vanished in the flurry of activity. Despite having to stop working at the Boatery, she'd been able to spend a few lunches on her weekends with Jacob. He had been as thrilled for her about the permanent position as her own parents. He had certainly taken more credit for her appointment than they had. Their collective confidence in her was invaluable to her. She was looking forward to spending time with her family over Thanksgiving.

September finished in a whirlwind, and October began in much the same fashion. Thankfully Mrs. Flore was an incredibly organized woman. That fact made Chloe's life slightly less stressful in terms of planning and piecing together activities. Her years of experience meant Chloe could focus on changing things to fit her style rather than starting from scratch. That gave her time to unwind with occasional workouts and open gym sessions. She even caught a few of the girls' home soccer games. They were undefeated, and it was all but certain that they were heading for the championship. Chloe loved hearing all of the game recaps and projections for the next game from Molly and Leah.

Given all her other commitments, she had hesitated when she was asked to volunteer to help with the Science Olympiad team, which met once every two weeks after school to prepare for the competition that would be held at the end of March. She had never participated in the event herself, but the students talked about it with an enthusiasm that was contagious.

Despite her nervousness, the biweekly meetings had become something she genuinely looked forward to. Chloe was working with four different groups of students who had signed up for events that she felt confident coaching, Thermodynamic Detectives, Hovercrafts, Towers, and Write It Do It. Each event had a coach's manual and came with resources for students to prepare for the day of the competition, in which they would compete with other area students in activities which would be scored (like solving thermodynamics problem sets) or to which they would bring creations that they had designed and built in compliance with the regulations (such as the Tower Building event which required they "build the lightest tower, with the highest structural efficiency, capable of supporting a load of up to 15 kg"). The fact that so many students were participating in the science-based event was exciting on its own, but that six of her eight students were females thrilled Chloe.

On the days when she wasn't staying after with students who needed additional help, Chloe had fallen into a rhythm of grading and planning for an hour at the end of the school day. This was perfect on the days they were to have open gym in the evening. Often she would be joined by Madeleine, who, she discovered, was not only engaging, but wickedly funny. Occasionally Taylor would stick around too, though on those days they did more talking than working. The routine was nice.

Today, however, she was heading home as soon as possible. It had been a long day and she wanted nothing more than to be in sweatpants and veg out. Being busy had helped Chloe with the adjustment to her new routine, but that didn't mean she wasn't exhausted. It was hard to believe it was already October 20, but that at the same time it was *only* October 20. The thought of tackling an entire year at this pace was daunting. The basketball season started in November, and if planning for it took up this much of her time, actually being in season would require her to operate on an even higher level to get things done.

How Madeleine managed her commitments was a mystery. She was in the heart of her own season, teaching a full load, and outwardly unfazed. She always looked so fresh and confident. Chloe, on the other hand, felt as though she always looked as tired as she felt. Maybe by the end of the year she would figure out how to make everything appear effortless. Today was not that day.

By the time she was settled in on her couch, the evening was beginning to reflect her mood. Wave after wave of gray storm clouds moved in, threatening a cold rain. Chloe shivered, realizing the temperature had dropped and was likely to continue plummeting.

When she had gotten home, she'd managed to muster the strength to finalize her plans for tomorrow, clearing the rest of her evening of any responsibilities. While it hadn't been the highlight of her day, she was glad she'd taken the time to do so. The most difficult decision facing her now was which movie she wanted to watch.

Did she want something on Netflix or perhaps a classic from her collection? As she perused the movies on her shelf, she heard the rain begin to fall. By the time she had narrowed her choices down to *The Day After Tomorrow* or *Imagine Me and You*, the storm had kicked into high gear. The branches of the trees on her lawn were being whipped around mercilessly in the gusting wind while sheets of rain pounded the windows. She pitied anyone trying to drive through the torrent.

Returning her focus to the DVDs in her hand, Chloe decided on *The Day After Tomorrow*, inspired by the raging monster outside. She laughed to herself as she imagined her own fate if a climate-cleansing storm struck. She'd be in big trouble since her father did not have a high-level position with the government. She popped the DVD in and settled on the couch. As she was about to push the Play button she was jarred by a frantic knock on her door.

Who the hell is out in this? Opening the door, Chloe found Madeleine, soaked and shivering, arms wrapped tightly around herself. She hesitated for a split second, her mind adjusting to the unexpected visitor standing before her, then the howling wind moved her to action.

"Christ, Madeleine, you're drenched. Come inside!"

Stepping aside, she ushered her in and closed the door, cutting the volume of the storm's din in half. Which made it possible to hear Madeleine shivering. She wrapped her arms even tighter around herself.

"Today clearly was not the ideal evening for a long run."

"Yeah, not exactly the best conditions out there. Do you usually run out this way? I didn't think we lived that close to each other."

Madeleine checked her running watch. "Apparently it's about nine miles." Shaking her head, she went on, "I don't usually take such long runs. Every once in a while, though, I get lost in thought and keep running. Unfortunately today my stress landed me in the middle of the storm of the century."

Chloe watched, mesmerized, as droplets of water trickled down Madeleine's neck, traveling along an expanse of exposed skin before sneaking along the ridge of her collarbone and disappearing under the collar of her shirt. She blushed, realizing she was staring. *What the hell, stupid. Get a hold of yourself.*

"I'm sorry. You've got to be freezing, I've got plenty of clothes you can borrow. You're welcome to shower too if you want to actually thaw out."

"Oh, I don't need a shower. I'm really happy to be inside and out of that." Madeleine nodded toward the window, smiling. When a second, more ferocious shiver ripped through her, Chloe couldn't contain her sarcasm.

"That makes sense. Because I don't really have enough sweatpants or T-shirts that I could possibly spare any for you. You should be comfortable in what you've got on." Chloe rolled her eyes at Madeleine, prompting her little half smile to cross her dripping wet face. Chloe's jaw muscles tightened, her traitorous mind refusing to ignore the image of what it would be like to kiss along the path those raindrops were taking. Her mouth suddenly dry, she was relieved when Madeleine decided to speak.

"Okay, you're right. I'm freezing and a shower sounds amazing. You're a lifesaver."

After reining in her very active imagination, Chloe felt capable of speech.

"Perfect. The bathroom is down the hall. Help yourself to anything. Towels are in the closet." She gestured toward the bathroom. "I'll leave some clothes on my bed. You can see what fits. Most of it will probably be big, but it'll be warm."

"If I wasn't sopping wet, I would hug you. Thank you so much!" And with that, Madeleine headed to the bathroom.

As she attempted to find clothes for Madeleine, Chloe realized that picking them out invited wondering about the athletic body they would cover. It wasn't the first time she'd done so, which was atypical. Usually she was drawn to someone as a friend before she considered whether they were attractive. She had to admit that she had come to appreciate Madeleine's body more than that of any other "friend" she'd ever had. Never in her life had she been attracted to someone so powerfully. With her, the physical attraction was as strong as the emotional one.

She could picture even now the way her strong jawline would set stubbornly when she made up her mind to do something. The way her full, expressive eyebrows would raise slightly, to subtly question any fool who didn't believe in her. Then there was the way her entire face would animate, every feature expressing her enjoyment of a moment, and the way she moved on the basketball court, effortlessly, with her loose shorts sitting low on her hips and the definition in her arms visible, strong and yet distinctly feminine.

If she was honest, she hadn't even thought about anyone else since everything happened with Elaine. Now here she was considering kissing up the raindrops on Madeleine's neck. She shook her head. She could not, would not, jeopardize this opportunity for normalcy. Not after everything she had lost. Not even for someone as tempting as Madeleine. How she was going to curb the attraction, however, she had no idea.

She looked at the sweatpants, sweatshirts, T-shirts, and sports bra piled on the bed. They were all decent options. As for underwear… She added a pair of compression shorts. Thinking about Madeleine wearing her underwear or, worse yet, going commando was definitely not prudent if she wanted to keep things platonic.

Chloe purposefully sat with her back to the hallway, avoiding the potential for seeing Madeleine in a towel and reminding herself that, aside from occasional infuriatingly ambiguous comments, Madeleine had never explicitly expressed any feelings beyond friendship toward her.

Then again, there had been those comments, which could imply that potential existed for something more between them. Which dropped her again—bam!—into the murky depths of "gay or straight," "friend or more" confusion. Clearly something must be wrong with her. Hannah never had this much trouble navigating the lesbian gray area.

Shaking her head again, she turned her attention to the TV. Would it be rude to begin a movie while Madeleine was still here? She should wait and invite her to watch it with her. It was not likely that she had seen it before, given her less than impressive breadth of movie knowledge.

She decided to wait. Despite the emotional vertigo she was experiencing, she had to admit that it was nice to have some company in the evening. She wouldn't have called herself lonely, but the simple presence of someone else was comforting tonight.

Hoping Madeleine's music tastes were slightly more advanced than her taste in movies, she turned her Google music on shuffle and grabbed her book from the end table.

"There are no words to describe how much better I feel right now."

Madeleine walked toward the couch. The black St. Mike's hoodie she had chosen hung loosely on her lean frame. Chloe's gray sweats sat low on her hips with her feet barely poking out from the legs. Chloe smiled. Madeleine had picked her favorites.

"And you tried to tell me you didn't need to change."

"Keep it up and you'll never see this outfit again." Madeleine's eyes sparkled mischievously. Chloe did not doubt that she would try, and possibly succeed, to keep at least one of the pieces of clothing though she wouldn't let Madeleine win that easily.

"You aren't the first person to scope those out. Notice they are still in my possession."

"I don't know. These are amazing. It's like you broke them in just for me. I don't normally believe in fate, but this feels like it." Madeleine settled on the couch, curling her legs up beneath her. Lounging comfortably now, she changed the subject. "What exciting activity did I interrupt when I rudely washed up on your doorstep?"

"I had finally decided which movie to watch, one that I'm sure you've never seen."

"Go on and judge me. I'm not ashamed!"

Chloe shook her head, though she couldn't contain her smile. Madeleine interrupted the retort she was forming.

"I will confess, though. *Jurassic Park* was fantastic." Madeleine's admission hinted at her weakening resistance to the sci-fi/action/anything-most-people-would-watch genres.

"I'm as appreciative of your willingness to watch my movies as I am shocked by your pitiful breadth of experience."

"Thank you for that backhanded compliment. Really warms my heart."

"It slipped out." Chloe chuckled. "For what it's worth, it was genuine. I'm mainly bitter that you wear my favorite sweatpants better than I do. It's not right."

"Give it time. You'll get used to the sight of me in my new gear."

Chloe was grateful that Hozier was playing in the background. It covered her inability to formulate a sentence.

The easy friendship growing between them was becoming more comfortable every day. Chloe never felt pressed to come up with topics to talk about. They came naturally, from arguing over whether "moist" was a disgusting word to whether Emily Dickinson was worth anyone's time reading. Tonight was no different as Madeleine caught her up on where the soccer team stood and she commented on how planning with Taylor was going.

When another Hozier song played, Madeleine abandoned the sports talk altogether.

"This music is phenomenal. So far I've heard Adele, James Bay, Betty Who, and Hozier. Is this a playlist or is your library that impressive?"

"I wasn't really sure what you'd like to listen to, so I decided to see what my shuffle came up with."

"I love it."

Madeleine's smile buoyed Chloe's spirit. "Thanks." When she was around Madeleine she felt lighter, freer than she could remember being recently. She was overcome with a surge of gratitude at finding herself here. In an attempt to conceal the raw emotion, she stood and went to the window.

"This storm is incredible." Outside the wind had grown even wilder. Thick, gray clouds roiled in the sky. The rain, battering against the windows, was streaming down the driveway toward the nearest creek bed.

Chloe chanced a look back in Madeleine's direction. Pensive hazel eyes were taking her in, contemplative and unashamedly observing her at the window. Surprised by her own reaction to being watched, she again felt the need to do something.

"Are you hungry? I made way too much pad thai last night. You would be doing me a favor if you helped me eat some of it." Chloe tried to fight off the nervousness she was feeling.

"I love pad thai! I feel bad for crashing your night, though." Madeleine's voice trailed off, her face a mask. Chloe wasn't sure what she was trying to hide.

"Seriously, don't feel bad. You're interrupting a whole lot of nothing. It's nice having you over. I was actually going to see if you wanted to grab dinner sometime this week so we could avoid grading." The corner of Madeleine's mouth curved up slightly. They both enjoyed much of the work that they pretended to complain about together.

"It's settled. I'll warm some pad thai up for us. It's not fancy, but I thought it was pretty good." Chloe headed into the kitchen. She was glad she'd been ambitious the night before and tried a new version of the dish. It had been better than she'd expected. While the noodles were reheating in the microwave, she grabbed two giant mugs from the cupboard and filled them with ice water. Hannah made fun of her insistence on drinking everything out of mugs, but she stood by her love of the convenience of handles. Madeleine's voice from the doorway brought Chloe to the present.

"That smells delicious. Can I help with anything?" Wandering into the kitchen, she casually threw her hair into a messy bun, making use of the ever-present hairband that adorned her wrist. The simplest action and Chloe was putty. She had to stop staring, but Madeleine was so attractive in the most natural, effortless way.

You could help by letting me breathe when I'm around you. That might be nice, Chloe thought to herself, realizing she should answer out loud.

"There's not much to do, but if you want to grab some plates, they're in the cupboard to the right of the fridge." Saluting in confirmation of her duties, Madeleine slid past Chloe, lightly resting her hand on Chloe's back as she made her way to the cupboard. Suddenly the kitchen felt even smaller. Chloe felt every hair on her arms stand on end. Chancing a glance over her shoulder, Chloe saw Madeleine frozen in front of the cupboard, leaning forward on the counter on both hands.

The microwave chimed, announcing that the noodles had been reheated and offering something to distract them. She held out a hand to Madeleine, who gave a slight start, opened the cupboard, and pulled out two plates. Taking care not to touch her, she slid by Chloe again and headed back to the couch.

Regaining her equilibrium as she dished up their meals, Chloe followed Madeleine to the living room. It was nice, she thought. Being around Madeleine made her feel off balance, but she could talk with her for hours. Even though many of their conversations hadn't gone deeper than their current lives of school and sports, Madeleine always seemed to understand her and how she was feeling.

Looking up from her plate, Chloe found Madeleine considering her. She raised her eyebrows in question.

"You know, it doesn't feel like you've only been here since September. It's like you walked into exactly where you belong." There it was, Madeleine's ability to strike right at the heart of how Chloe felt but wasn't sure how to express herself.

"It does feel that way. I won't lie. It's a little disconcerting sometimes. Ninety-nine percent of the time I'm walking around dumbfounded that I landed here."

Madeleine was thoughtful again and Chloe could almost see the words she was going to say forming. Everything she said carried such intent, such purpose, as if she was always compelled to sift through until she found the exact way to give life to what she was thinking.

"I see that occasionally," she said, nodding. "It's as if you're struck with a reminder that this is nothing you had imagined for yourself, but you can't imagine anything else right now."

Chloe nodded slowly. Madeleine had seen exactly what she had been feeling lately. How much else had she seen?

"That's exactly how it feels. It's like I'm functioning and experiencing, but I'm processing everything on a delay—if that makes any sense."

"Absolutely. That's how I felt my first summer with the national team. You'll get used to it. And until then you can keep me company and lose to me at open gym."

"Keep talking shit and you lose the sweatpants and the company."

"Well, damn, that escalated quickly!" Madeleine threw her hands up in surrender.

Pleased with their exchange, both of them returned to their dinners, contentment stretching between them. After finishing hers, Chloe set her plate aside, her thoughts returning to when she interviewed with Landon for the JV job. She hadn't been able to shake the weird vibe she'd gotten from him. She wasn't sure where it was coming from, if he was a total homophobe or a misogynist or both. Since she was now working for him, she needed to get some insight. She decided to ask Madeleine about it.

"This is incredibly random, but I was wondering what your take is on Landon. I know he taught English before taking the athletic director job, so I assume you know him pretty well."

A shadow passed across Madeleine's face. Chloe knew there was something between them and that confirmed it. *Fuck. Time to take a step back.*

She tried to explain. "I can't get a great read on him, and since I'm working for him I want to understand why I feel like he hates me and thinks I'm a complete waste of his time. It doesn't feel like he's your run-of-the-mill chauvinist. Maybe those are my insecurities talking. I've seen him talking with you a lot, so I hoped you had some insight."

Something in Madeleine's face closed, a latch sliding into place, and Chloe realized she wasn't going to get any greater understanding about whatever was between them.

"He's all about power and control. It's his thing and until he asserts his authority he treats people like shit. He really has no power over Taylor. She's been at the school longer than he has, and everyone knew that the administration was planning on offering the athletic director position to her. She told them she didn't want the job, which would take time from being with Anne. I don't know if he's ever accepted the fact that a woman was preferred for the job. Let alone a gay woman. That's pure conjecture on my part, but still…"

Madeleine stopped briefly. Lost in thought, she bit her lower lip. "I think he's also pretty close-minded. As for him and me, he's not very good at taking no for an answer, but that's old history. I'm sorry. I don't think that was anything you didn't work out for yourself."

Chloe saw a glimmer of something Madeleine wouldn't say, but she decided to leave that alone for now.

"No, that was helpful. I needed some reassurance that I'm not crazy and he really is playing some power games here. I know he's an alpha male, but sometimes I've seen him in the hallway and the looks I caught from him..."

"That's pretty typical behavior for him. Don't let it get to you. Stick with Taylor and you'll be fine." Madeleine smiled, though Chloe noticed it had lost some wattage. The clock over the TV showed it was already almost nine. How had it gotten so late?

"Wow, it's late. I didn't mean to keep you here trapped without a ride."

"No, tonight was really nice! Thank you. For rescuing me and warming me up. I had fun."

Chloe was more than slightly proud that she had something to do with that. "Good, I had fun too. You're welcome to come over anytime."

The flutter of anticipation at spending more time like this with Madeleine settled directly in Chloe's core. She was getting dangerously used to that feeling. Pushing that thought aside, she stood and offered her hand to Madeleine.

"Let me drive you home. I'll even let you pick out the music, something which, I'll have you know, I don't offer lightly. Ask Hannah. It took her almost two years to earn that privilege. Then again she listened almost exclusively to electronica when I first met her."

Laughing, they gathered Madeleine's wet things and headed out into rain, which was much lighter now. Chloe's inner turmoil would still be there, waiting for her when she returned home.

CHAPTER ELEVEN

Friday

Autumn had officially claimed the region. Foliage on every road was changing hue, decorating streets with brilliant oranges, yellows, and reds. Championships were quickly approaching for fall sports, too, which also meant that Chloe's new, hectic basketball schedule was about to begin. An F. Scott Fitzgerald quote stuck with her, "Life starts all over again when it gets crisp in the fall." That was certainly how she was feeling. With her routine at school falling into place, she was excited to figure out how to incorporate coaching into the equation.

Taylor, on the other hand, was excitedly reminding everyone about the return of her and Anne's annual Halloween blowout. Apparently, the party had been postponed last year due to renovation conflicts and this year was going to be even bigger and better to compensate for that.

Chloe doubted that any gathering organized by Taylor would be boring, basing that purely on her magnetic personality and the dynamic group of people she surrounded herself with.

Her primary worry now was acquiring a costume. Taylor had been reminding everyone since early October to find one, but Chloe had procrastinated. It was now crunch time.

Chloe dialed Hannah, not even letting her answer before bursting out, "I need your help."

"Shocking. What is it this time?" Hannah replied. Chloe expected to catch some grief from her; it was her way of keeping Chloe on her toes. It was also her way of conveying that she would do anything for Chloe, given some leeway to gripe about it.

"Taylor and Anne are having a Halloween party tomorrow and I have no clue what to be. Everyone from pickup and all the cool kids are going to be there."

"All the cool kids, huh? Well then, you need to be someone hot. Who are the hottest homos these days?"

"Whatever you're imagining I'm not wearing it." Chloe knew she needed to slow Hannah's roll before she got a full head of steam.

"Fine, so you're going to the party as something lame. Maybe the incredibly witty junior-year basketball stud costume?"

"Come off it. I was broke and you know I didn't want to go out. That was like the day after I'd broken up with Abbey."

"That was a dark time for all of us…" Hannah said somberly, just barely maintaining a serious tone.

"Move on. I did." Hannah's laughter filled the phone until Chloe continued, "Now what could I pull off?" She was desperate for ideas and Hannah was not helping in the slightest.

"Well, you could do a Kill Bill. Uma Thurman is tall. But a wig on you would definitely be scary. And you probs don't have one."

"Now you're getting it. Keep going. Who else could be convincing?"

"Well, if you want to play it safe, you could pull off a convincing surfer. You could always be Jake from State Farm. The sheer number of khakis in your closet would make that easy to pull off." Chloe could hear the evil grin through the phone. "Hold the phone, I've got it. Lance Bass! No, wait. Miley

Cyrus! You could be every member of One Direction! Don't stop me. This is gold!" Hannah was cracking herself up now.

"Someone should stop you before you hurt yourself." Chloe couldn't help but laugh. Hannah's unabashed enthusiasm could lighten any mood. "How about a costume I might actually have?" she offered, trying to nudge this brainstorming session in the direction of something feasible.

"We could go down the pop culture spoof road, but that takes creativity and you're not giving me much to work with. How about some athletes?" Hannah offered thoughtfully. "What about cyclists? You can rock a pair of those spandex things they wear, and if it's yellow you could pull off a convincing Lance Arms…"

Chloe cut Hannah off, inspired by her mention of popular athletes.

"That's it! I have to have it somewhere. Hang on!" And with that Chloe was sorting through her trunk full of shorts and jerseys, praying she still had the jersey she needed.

"What, pray tell, is this masterful plan you've hatched?"

"Perfect!" Chloe shouted as she located the garment that was key to putting together her Halloween costume. "Remember when I went a little crazy over the U.S. women's soccer team? When all the gays were so hot and so fun to watch? I still have my Abby Wambach jersey, so I'm going to be her. I've got soccer socks somewhere." Chloe laughed at the memory that sprang to mind. "I could even use electrical tape like that one girl did in undergrad. Remember how she used to wrap it around her sock just below her knee and then fold them over so the socks would stay up? Shoot, what was her name, the beautiful one that you prayed was gay every night?"

"Ohhhhh, the love of my life. Lomax, Jessie Lomax. God, she was beautiful."

"Do you need a minute?" Chloe asked, still amused by Hannah's fascination with the old soccer star from college.

"I can't believe I never hit on her," Hannah mused, regretfully.

"There's no time to wallow. I've got a costume to put together and you're still beating the women off of you out there. I'd say that's more pressing than your old obsession," Chloe countered.

Wistfully, Hannah replied, "True. Ah well, maybe she'll find me when she works up the courage." She sighed dramatically. "Oh and you'll make a perfect Abby. Just don't try to actually play soccer. You could end up hospitalized this time."

"Don't cry too long over Lomax," Chloe said sardonically. "Gotta go now. I'm going to play dress up. I'll send you a picture of the final product. Bye!"

Hanging up, Chloe set about getting ready for the party, finding and trying on the full costume, jersey, socks, and matching blue shorts. She sent a picture to Hannah for her approval, then changed back into her sweatpants. She loved her apartment, but it was an old house and tended to be drafty, so she might as well be cozy. She would change into her shorts and a giant T-shirt for bed later.

While waiting for a response from Hannah, she grabbed a glass and some ice cubes and added a splash of the Blue Label Johnnie Walker that had been sitting untouched in the kitchen.

She studied the sleek glass bottle and gave a wry smile. It was the one thing from the entire Elaine ordeal she still could appreciate. As terrible as Elaine had been, she had been generous with her favored whiskey. She'd thrown away the other gifts Elaine had given her, but kept this, using the falling level of the bottle's contents as a gauge of what kind of progress she was making in putting that nightmare behind her. She rarely drank whiskey, though, let alone whiskey that carried so many memories along with it. She had a lot of whiskey left to drink, unfortunately. With luck, she'd find her way of coping long before the Johnnie Walker ran out.

The vibration from Hannah's incoming text distracted her before her thoughts could turn darker. Hannah was thrilled with the outfit and held out hope for Chloe yet. Relieved to have received her seal of approval, Chloe turned down the sheets on her bed, changed into her pajamas, and grabbed her latest read from the nightstand. Madeleine had recommended *A Brave New World*, shocked to hear Chloe hadn't read it before. It was hard to put down. So was the feeling that she was part of a community again. She could certainly get used to being understood and accepted.

The next morning the weather was clear and crisp, the perfect autumn day for Taylor's party. Taylor had said they'd have a bonfire, depending on the weather, but at the very least they would make use of the front and back porch for festivities as well. This was to be the first real party since a major remodel. She and Anne were thrilled to finally share their new digs with company.

The party was set to start at four, but as Taylor had said it was a "soft opening" people would be coming over any time after that. The food would be ready at six. Chloe was excited. Taylor had said most of the group from pickup would be there, some bringing dates, as well as a smattering of her and Anne's other friends. Taylor had also reminded her that nearly everyone would be crashing there. Chloe hadn't made up her mind whether she would stay over or not. Either way it would be fun to unwind with everyone.

The afternoon flew by. Chloe spent time talking with her parents. They had been excited to hear about her teaching gig and her appointment as the JV coach. They wanted her to be happy, and they were also glad to hear she would be staying closer to home. Nate, her brother, had moved to California last year after completing his master's in engineering. He'd done an internship on the West Coast in undergrad and they all knew he wouldn't be coming back east for a while. Her parents were holding out hope that Chloe wouldn't go so far away. As it was they hadn't been able to make the trip to Maine from upstate New York since she had moved. They were hoping to take a weekend off, but her dad's company was buying out a competitor and time off was hard to come by.

After ending their video call, Chloe went for a quick run and then got ready for the party. Sporting soccer warm-up pants that had been stolen from a basketball teammate and pulling a nondescript black zip-up over her jersey, she locked up her apartment and headed to Taylor's.

Taylor had given her directions on Thursday, but Chloe had never been on the water's edge near Newcastle before. The drive over was beyond picturesque. The forests hadn't lost their leaves yet, and brilliant shocks of orange and red and yellow danced in the light breeze. Sunlight was pouring in over the treetops, shimmering along the road in pockets of brightness, breaking up the shadows cast by the trees.

The house was tucked away on Brick Hill Road, right next to Dodge Point Preserve. It was secluded—they had only one neighbor. But it was all off River Road, a main road—if you used the term "main" loosely—which ran south out of Newcastle. She opened the car windows a touch to let in the fresh air. Once through the preserve, she spotted the nondescript dirt road Taylor had described and headed slowly down its slope. Though her Jeep was a four-wheel drive, she knew better than to trust any Maine road that she hadn't yet driven on.

The hill sloped sharply, and Chloe saw a modest colonial set back from the road in a large clearing. The crumbling stone wall on the front lawn betrayed the age of the house; the stonework had to be over a hundred years old. Taylor had said they were the last house on the road, though, so Chloe continued on. Adding a little speed as the road leveled out slightly, she rounded another bend and the cabin came into view.

The two-story cabin had been masterfully restored, the attached garage and addition to the back melding seamlessly with the original portions of the house. The cedar was a warm amber color, and the house was immediately welcoming. The cabin conveyed Taylor and Anne's warmth and charisma. The front porch was sturdy, with medium-sized logs woven together to make the posts and the railings. As per Taylor's fun-loving style the yard had been taken over by pumpkins and spider webs, while Anne's stylistic mark was evident in the luminaria outlining the driveway and porch.

Four cars already lined the driveway. As Chloe pulled in, Taylor strolled out the front door with two hard ciders in hand, prepared to welcome her next guest. Never one to disappoint, she was decked out in an Indiana Jones costume, complete with leather jacket, bullwhip, satchel, and authentic hat. Chloe grabbed the craft beer she had purchased and headed toward her on the front porch, praying her costume would hold up to Taylor's scrutiny.

"Welcome to my humble home!" Taylor exclaimed with a grand bow, offering Chloe a cider. "Did you find it easy enough?"

"Yeah, no problems. Taylor, this is incredible!" Chloe offered, gesturing with her hand to the house and the magnificent landscape.

"Thanks," Taylor replied, beaming. "I started thinking we might never see the end of the renovations, but they were worth it. You didn't have to bring the beer, but if it's good, thank you," she said wryly, leading her inside to give her the tour.

"This porch is amazing. I would never leave it," Chloe said in awe.

"Then you aren't allowed on the back porch. I never want to leave that one and I live here." Taylor was radiant, clearly in her element hosting such a warm gathering with her friends and sharing what she and Anne had built together.

As they crossed the threshold, Taylor began the tour properly, pointing out the original structures and the updates they had made. The open floor plan and comfortable furniture were inviting. The entire design seemed tailored to welcome anyone who walked in. The roughhewn walls added rustic character, while plush floor rugs and overstuffed couches were inviting. The back portion of the house opened to an enormous kitchen.

"Anne was completely in charge of the kitchen and it only cost me my life savings," Taylor began, only to be cut off when Anne entered from the back deck. She was dressed in baggy painter's pants with a fully stocked tool belt, flannel button-up, and work boots. She looked as if she just finished doing the renovations herself.

She slid her arm around Taylor's waist. "And it was worth every penny, right, sweetheart?"

Taylor feigned panic, then turned and kissed Anne's cheek.

"Maybe not every penny, but most of them."

Anne pushed Taylor away, laughing and pulled Chloe into a warm hug.

"I'm so glad you could make it. I wanted to tell you again that you are welcome here any time, with or without this one over here." Another quick peck on Taylor's cheek punctuated her statement. "I'll make you dinner and we can sit and commiserate on how Taylor torments us."

Returning the hug, Chloe replied, "That sounds perfect. I'll bring dessert and alcohol to drown our sorrows." Taylor interrupted, anxious to return to the Halloween festivities.

"You would both be lost without me. Let me continue my tour now so that we can get the costume charades started while it's still warm. We're only waiting on Madeleine, Jess, and Janae." Taylor leaned over to kiss Anne again, then led Chloe to the basement.

"We only finished this a month and a half ago. The stupid sump pump needed to be replaced and I nearly had a coronary on the spot. Anne calmed me down and now we have another usable room."

"This is fantastic!" Chloe said, genuinely admiring the finished product. There was yet another plush couch, a futon in the corner, another TV, and a spare room in the back.

"This will do the trick whenever we have drunks that need to stay over," Taylor noted, nudging Chloe. Taking one last swig of her cider, she took Chloe's empty from her hand. "Speaking of drunks, let's head out to the party. I'm pretty sure I heard a couple more cars pull up while Anne was accosting me."

"If that's what it's like to be accosted, your life is charmed," Chloe joked, pushing Taylor in the back.

Taylor nodded toward the back door. Sliding the glass door to the side, she waved to the guests milling about a fire pit located about twenty feet back from the deck. People were also grouped around the patio furniture on the enormous deck attached to the back of the house. The entire setup, house, deck, and both porches, was straight out of an HGTV makeover. Chloe loved every bit of it.

By the time Stacey, Anna, and a group of women she didn't recognize waved excitedly at her and Taylor, the dwindling rays of light were cresting the horizon, casting golden fall lighting on the partygoers. The candles added to the overall ambience. Everyone had lived up to Taylor's expectations, coming in full costume. Chloe counted thirteen women as she and Taylor approached the group drinking on the deck. It was surreal, as if she had stepped into a magical land of gayness populated by jovial women. Taylor, their effervescent leader, had guided her home from the tumultuous past year and a half. *Thank God for Taylor.*

They made their way to the fire pit. Stacey gave Chloe a huge hug. Beaming, she introduced her to her girlfriend, Molly, a much shorter, black-haired woman with friendly chocolate-brown eyes. Stacey was clad in a Steve Irwin costume, while Molly was a Jedi. Stacey informed her they had been introduced last year at Wiscasset's sectional soccer game against Newcastle, where Molly was the head coach. She'd never looked back.

Robin joined them, hugging each of them in turn. She was rocking a Rick costume from *The Walking Dead*, complete with sheriff pants and hat from Season One. After her arrival, they began talking about Taylor and Anne's house and the incredible renovations they had been doing. Chloe easily bantered with her basketball cohorts, the camaraderie extending naturally to new acquaintances. The discussion turned to the dreams they all entertained in regard to their own home building. Anne appeared at the sliding glass door. Taylor joined her, calling out to the women on the back lawn and gathering the group of fifteen or so together for formal introductions.

Chloe was thoroughly enjoying herself. She opened one of the beers she'd brought and took a swig, but not because she needed the alcohol to ease any first party awkwardness, she realized with a smile; there simply wasn't any of that. She was friends with nearly half of the attendees, and the rest were friendly and approachable. It was exactly the group of friends she had pictured Taylor and Anne would surround themselves with. It felt odd, but at the same time natural to be there, mingling with these women, being welcomed into their ranks.

The laughter and warmth was catching. Chloe felt at ease, at least until Taylor made the great pronouncement that each person was responsible for performing a charade for the group so they could guess their costume. Only after they were correctly identified could they introduce themselves to the group at large.

After planning their own skits, Stacey, Anna, Robin, and Molly offered to help with Chloe's charade. It was difficult to mime by oneself scoring a winning header.

Two of Anne's coworkers began the night. Both sporting orange jumpsuits, one with the trademark thick black plastic glasses, they were easily identified as Piper and Alex from *Orange Is The New Black*. Next came two ninja turtles, Meredith and Becca, college friends of Taylor and Anne's. One by one women were guessed and introduced. Chloe was surprised at how easily she was remembering names by associating them with their costumes.

Chloe gave a start. It was almost her turn. Stacey had suggested that Chloe score a header while Stacey mimed being the goalie. If no one guessed it, she would spin Chloe around and point at the name splayed across her back.

Once Andrea, the *Twilight* vampire with copious amounts of glitter all over her exposed skin, finished introducing herself as a physical therapist from Bar Harbor, Chloe and Stacey headed to the front of the group. A cursory glance on the walk up told Chloe that Madeleine was not here yet. Doing her best to quash the tiny knot of disappointment she had no right to be feeling, she carried on with Stacey. She had been excited about spending at least some of the evening with Madeleine. Then again, it was probably for the best that they didn't mix the carefree atmosphere of the party with alcohol and her growing attraction for the beautiful English teacher.

After ambling to the front, removing her soccer warm-up pants and unzipping her black Windbreaker, she mimed juggling a soccer ball and then, in her opinion, mimicked gracefully heading the imaginary ball past a fumbling Stacey. Before anyone else could guess, she heard a voice shout from the deck.

"Abby Wambach!"

Chloe's head snapped up as she recognized the voice. Her breath caught. Madeleine was standing on the deck wearing the most attractive Katniss Everdeen costume she had ever seen. Her hair, styled in a simple braid, framed her face, which was illuminated by the flickering light of the tiki torches along the railings.

The striking simplicity of the costume emphasized Madeleine's natural athleticism; the plain black ensemble hinted at the lean legs and sculpted physique it covered. It would have felt as if it were the most natural thing in the world if she grabbed the bow strung across her back and took down a deer. Chloe had never been a fan of hunting, but Madeleine made it look attractive. Very attractive.

Realizing she had been staring, Chloe scrambled to find words. When that failed, she decided on a grandiose bow, held for emphasis. Mercifully, the group laughed at her attempt. She regained her voice, then introduced herself.

"I'm Chloe Amden. I teach physics at Wiscasset, where about twice a week a bunch of us have the pleasure of beating up on Taylor on the basketball court." More laughter erupted around her. Most, if not all, of these women had at some point played with or against Taylor. They could certainly appreciate it when she was on the receiving end of some ribbing.

Trying to suppress the glowing excitement that had suddenly sprung to being below her navel, she returned to her spot near the back of the group. Stacey began to mime her own introduction. Chloe's attention, however, was immediately diverted when Madeleine arrived at her side. With one eyebrow cocked, Madeleine asked knowingly, "I clearly didn't get around to teaching you how to juggle the ball, did I?"

"Well, I would have asked you to, but my face got smashed in. There wasn't enough time."

"You tried, that's what counts. And now I know what to focus on if you ever let me near you with a soccer ball again." Chloe laughed and Madeleine continued, her voice lower. "Not to crush your dreams or anything, but Abby preferred brunettes. Luckily I happen to know a few players that are into the dirty blonde, tapered fade vibe." Madeleine reached out to tousle Chloe's hair. Instantly Chloe's pulse spiked and blood rushed to her cheeks.

Madeleine's voice trailed off and they laughed quietly together. Taylor finished off the introductions with a flourish, cracking her bullwhip and running away from boulders. She made a very enthusiastic Indiana Jones.

Ending with a sweeping bow, Taylor held the spotlight. "Now that everybody knows everybody else, it's about time we eat. Anne put together some killer food in the kitchen. It's all laid out, so go ahead and dig in. The booze is in the coolers out here on the deck. There's even a bar if you're feeling like making a mix drink. Now eat, drink, and laugh at all my jokes!"

At their dismissal from the group, everyone fell back into easy conversations, drinking and wandering in to get plates full of deliciousness. The five of them, Stacey, Molly, Anna, Madeleine, and Chloe, meandered inside to join the short food line. Out of the corner of her eye, Chloe watched Taylor take Anne's hand in hers and lead her toward the back edge of the property away from the rest of the party. It was clear how much Taylor loved Anne. It was in her eyes every single time she looked at her. Chloe wondered if either of them had felt truly whole before they had met.

Scooping a steaming portion of pulled pork onto her plate, Chloe let her mind wander. Surrounded by happy couples, she found herself considering Madeleine yet again, wondering what *her* relationship status was. No one ever talked about it at pickup or anywhere else for that matter. Chloe had a gut feeling she was gay, and she could count on one hand the number of times she had been wrong about that before. Was she just hopeful this time?

Making their way to a group of chairs around the only table on the back deck, they settled in. Chloe wedged herself in the corner next to Madeleine to make room for the others. Stacey and her girlfriend were adorable together, talking about something private. Robin was talking to Andrea, the *Twilight* vampire, about the city of Syracuse. Apparently Andrea was not a fan, and Robin was defending her old stomping grounds. As Chloe wondered if she would ever find out Madeleine's relationship status, a loud shout tore her attention away.

"She said yes! Hot damn! Everyone get a drink and raise it up! We're getting hitched!"

The entire party shouted in unison, and a boisterous toast went up, with everyone adding their congratulations to the couple. Hands entwined, the couple walked back to the party. Anne was the picture of happiness and contentment. Taylor was like a kid at Christmas.

The announcement infused the party with even more life and drinks began to flow in earnest. Chloe lost track of time. By her fourth beer she was happily buzzed, sitting around the fire between Madeleine and Robin, content. The talk at the fire turned to tales about Taylor and Anne's relationship history, everyone wanting to know about their first date, who asked whom, etc. It was essentially a drunk version of the Newlywed Game.

Chloe had wondered if the pair had had a reason for putting off getting married. If anyone should be married, it was these two. Anne was a balancing force for Taylor's vivacious personality, though she was equally intense in her own right. Listening to them tell stories, finishing each other's thoughts, was priceless.

Slowly the tide of conversation shifted toward horror stories from everyone's dating history. Stacey had met a girl once who on their second date insisted they name their future children. She had been completely serious about it. Taylor dated a girl on her team in high school who had broken up with her for scoring on her in practice.

It was a little bit frightening to hear about the prevalence of deranged ladies out there, though Chloe was thoroughly entertained by Robin's story about a teammate who took a girl out on a date only to wake up the next morning to thirty-eight texts from her. Somewhere around the fifteenth text she had lost all interest.

As the women shared more anecdotes, Chloe was hoping to hear something from Madeleine's past. Before that could happen, though, Taylor announced that she needed to go find her fiancée, who had gone inside much too long ago for her liking. She emphasized the word fiancée with gusto and with her departure effectively broke up the larger group into smaller factions that moved away from the fire, taking advantage of the fact that it was a warm autumn evening that was perfect for being outside.

It was easy to lose track of time out here, tucked away in Taylor's little corner of the world, surrounded by interesting women, women who were happy with who they were and what they were doing with their lives. When was the last time that had been true for her? Before she had ever met Elaine. When her studies were fulfilling and anything was possible. She had messed that up royally. But here, things felt different. Nothing was completely sorted out, but if Chloe didn't know any better she might think she was recovering a little bit of her own happiness.

Struck by a desire for some quiet time on her own, Chloe grabbed her beer and left the group. As she entered the door to the porch, she met Anne, who was walking back outside. This was the first time since the proposal that Chloe had caught her alone.

"Anne, I am so happy for you two. I've never seen Taylor happier than she was tonight."

"Thank you so much, Chloe. I still can't really believe it. I had no idea she was even thinking about proposing tonight."

"Leave it to Taylor to find a way to surprise you. Did you guys get a chance to talk about plans or did she go to shouting from the mountaintops right away?"

The pride shining from Anne's face at the mention of Taylor's excitement at their engagement, even after being together with her going on six years, was a beautiful thing to see.

"Well, I've always said I would love a winter wedding, but that's the most we had ever discussed. So maybe this winter we will have another excuse to come out here and drink!"

"I don't need an excuse, but that sounds amazing to me!" Chloe paused, wondering if she should ask Anne what was on her mind. "Anne, earlier at the fire when we were all talking about dating, Madeleine was silent. Is there something I shouldn't ask about with her? I don't want to put my foot in my mouth." She finished the thought sheepishly, realizing that this attempt was likely completely transparent to Anne.

"She's always been very tight-lipped about her dating history. We've just accepted it and don't press her about it. It's almost an unwritten rule. I'm not really sure who she confides in, to be honest, but I never wanted to push, so I'm pretty much useless."

"You're not useless. I was just wondering. I've never met anyone that didn't at least let some detail slip. It's impressive, honestly." Chloe paused. "Where has your fiancée run off to? Last time I saw her she was headed inside to look for you."

At the mere mention of the word "fiancée," Anne's face radiated joy. "She's just behind me. We were on our way back to sit at the fire." Chloe smiled at the slight blush she saw cross Anne's face. Apparently they had taken a few minutes to celebrate together.

"You should probably go check. You know, make sure she isn't lonely."

Anne laughed, shaking her head as she turned back to the house.

Chloe, still smiling, turned and walked through the screen door to the porch. Spotting a guitar leaning against the small sofa there, she scooped it up, sat on the couch, and contemplated the gorgeous expanse of countryside sprawling out before her. The moon was shrouded by wisps of cloud cover now, though its light was still illuminating the landscape.

It was difficult not to be calm here. Unable to resist, she started quietly picking out the chorus for "Give Me Love," playing it from memory. She wasn't sure how long she had been sitting there strumming when the sound of someone else entering the porch interrupted her solitude.

"Do you usually sit alone in the dark?"

Chloe turned at the sound of Madeleine's voice and felt her face break into an unabashed grin. "Only when the dark is too beautiful to turn on the lights," she replied, surprising herself. Usually she would have come back with some smart-aleck remark. Apparently, she was feeling romantic. She wasn't used to witnessing marriage proposals, she guessed. Alcohol might be playing a part too.

"Good point. God, it is so gorgeous out here." Madeleine walked to the screen and stared out, her silhouette draped in soft yellow moonlight. "This view is breathtaking."

"I could definitely get used to this." Chloe wasn't sure whether she was talking about the porch or Madeleine's company. She decided to not try to figure that out. It was better that way.

Then Madeleine turned around and the connection between them became almost palpable. Chloe was utterly captivated. It felt as though Madeleine saw every single piece of her. It felt like... She bit her lip and tried to recall one of her favorite songs. Focusing on the guitar in her hand was much safer.

After a pregnant pause, Madeleine continued, "These two deserve the world. I'm so thrilled for them. And for us. The wedding should be an even better party than this one."

"Anne told me she has always wanted a winter wedding. Can you imagine this view covered in snow?"

Madeleine sat down lightly in the seat next to Chloe, bringing with her a sweet mix of smells, including the faintest hint of cider and a citrus shampoo.

"There's something so romantic about a winter wedding. Beach weddings have nothing over a white wedding."

"I went to a destination beach wedding once. It was terrible. I mean the ceremony was beautiful, but I didn't think I was going to make it through the vows without an IV drip and a box fan." Chloe shuddered as she remembered sitting in the sweltering heat at Hannah's mother's second wedding. The sound of the ocean in the background had not been worth the discomfort in her opinion. "I'm with you. There's nothing prettier than a fresh snowfall as the backdrop for some vows."

"Maybe there is hope for you yet. I was worried; scientists are a weird bunch." Even in the moonlight Chloe could clearly see her playful grin.

"I know we have our quirks, but can we please talk about the crazy that runs wide and deep through most writers? Poe, nuts.

Tolstoy spiraled off into depression. Vonnegut was a complete weirdo. Don't even get me started on Emily Dickinson."

Her rant pulled a short burst of laughter from Madeleine. God, even her laugh was appealing, full of life and energy.

"True. I suppose we're all just weirdos trying to find other compatible weirdos. Though it seems from that guitar you're holding that you've got a lot of musician in you as well as scientist, and I don't think I need to list off the vein of instability that runs through there."

"It's okay. I embrace it. It adds to the mystique."

"Intrigue and madness. There's an interesting combination." Madeleine's voice had dropped slightly lower. The banter was decidedly light, but Chloe couldn't help but wonder if they were dancing around another topic here.

Maybe it was the fact that Madeleine had left the group to join her or maybe she had just lost her mind. Either way, Chloe felt emboldened. Madeleine was the most relaxed Chloe had seen her and her openness exerted too strong a pull for her to resist.

"I was surprised you didn't have any stories to share at the fire."

"Oh, Mademoiselle, weren't you the one talking about mystique just now?"

Chloe nearly melted when the unexpected silkiness of Madeleine's French accent reached her ear.

"Touché. But you clearly have achieved that. Wouldn't the natural progression involve you sharing a story with the intrigued party?"

Chloe hadn't dared to test the limits of their friendship this way before, but after months of radio silence regarding Madeleine's dating history or preferences, she was too curious to resist. All she needed was a pronoun, one casual word, and she would let it rest.

A heartbeat of silence passed and Chloe felt panic threaten.

"Well, in the interest of fairness, you shared nothing at the fire either."

So, this was going to be a verbal chess match. Who could maneuver the conversation best? Chloe wasn't certain, but she wanted to find out.

Her tone certainly suggested she was enjoying herself, but something about the way Madeleine was sitting, relaxed and yet poised, reminded Chloe of her potential to change direction without warning on the court. Chloe wished she could see her face more clearly, maybe catch a glimpse of what was going on behind her eyes.

Madeleine brought her drink to her lips, temporarily derailing Chloe's thoughts. When she finished it, she placed the bottle on the floor and Chloe remembered what she intended to say. She set the guitar aside. "I think we should do something to break this stalemate."

Madeleine's eyebrow shot up, signaling her interest, and her hand went to her wrist. Chloe couldn't see the hair band, but she knew Madeleine was probably fiddling with it as she did when she was nervous or flustered. A small part of Chloe hoped that she was the reason Madeleine was playing with the band tonight. The thought was exciting.

"One of my friends in undergrad created this game of sorts, 'Interview with Fran.' We would have these girls' nights dedicated to staying in and drinking wine together. Francis was an RA with a wicked sense of humor and a nonexistent filter." Chloe stopped to shake her head. She had yet to meet anyone like Fran and she was confident she never would. "Anyway, it's basically a quid-pro-quo question-and-answer session. You come up with a question, it can be anything, but whatever it is the other person has to answer. The catch is you also have to answer the question."

Madeleine sat forward, looking interested.

As an afterthought Chloe added, "Any evasiveness can be matched with an equally evasive answer, and there's no repeating questions. Are you up for it?"

"I think I'm going to like this game." Madeleine spoke clearly, the timbre of her voice making Chloe question if she had just bitten off more than she could chew.

"Since it's your first time, you can have the first question."

As Madeleine considered her options, nibbling the corner of her bottom lip gently, Chloe's heartbeat reverberated in her own ears. Madeleine hadn't asked her anything yet and she already was worked up.

"What quality do you find the most attractive in someone?"

Chloe swallowed, relieved that the first question wasn't asking for deep dark secrets.

"One quality? I don't know if there is any single one."

Madeleine interrupted, gesturing with her hand. "There has to be something."

"I mean…well, humor is obviously attractive. And intelligence. Both are must-haves." She considered when she had been most attracted to people in the past. Images of Kendall working out, Nora lost in thought with a tough physics problem, Madeleine coaching and teaching. Suddenly, it clicked. "It's got to be passion. Passion for what you do, fully committing to what you believe in? Yeah, that's it."

Madeleine nodded, looking as if she had just learned something important. Chloe wondered if Madeleine's answers would be as enlightening for her.

"And you? What's yours?"

"Since you named three, I'll follow suit. I'll give humility third place, humor and intelligence are tied for second place. I would have to say authenticity takes first. When someone knows who they are, and they live in that without reserve, that's incredibly attractive to me. And yes, I realize I cheated."

They laughed. Chloe wasn't disappointed that she got more information than had been asked for and, clearly, Madeleine wasn't dissatisfied with Chloe's response either.

"My turn." Chloe grinned. "I'll flip it now. What's your biggest turnoff, that one thing that shuts it all down?" She was eager to hear the answer; it would tell her a lot about Madeleine.

Madeleine answered swiftly, no hesitation in her voice. "This is easy. Lying. Someone lies—nope, it's over." The edge in her voice gave Chloe the distinct impression there was a lot of pain and experience fueling that answer.

"I agree with that," she said, realizing it was her turn, "but I'm going with condescension. Thinking you're better than someone, hell no, I'm out. Uh-uh, no thank you."

Chloe shook her head vehemently, reaching for her drink, hoping to slow things down a bit, but Madeleine already had her next question ready.

"This is ridiculous, but I want to know. Where was the best kiss you've ever had, and why was it the best?"

Faint color painted Madeleine's cheekbones as she asked the question and Chloe couldn't speak. All she could imagine at the moment was what it would be like to be kissing the woman across from her. That would definitely be the best kiss she could ever have.

"Technically, that's two questions," she said, buying some time to come up with a response that was more circumspect. "But I'll give you a pass this time." She was being ridiculous. She needed to come up with an answer and now. Sorting through her memories, she found it.

"I don't think it gets more stereotypical than this. It was in our locker room in college. My teammate and I were there. She offered to massage a knot in my neck. I was a puddle. I remember thinking I might want to kiss her, and she whispered in my ear that she'd like to kiss me. It was perfect."

"That's really cute. Did you guys date?"

"Yup, but for less than a year. She ended up transferring, but it ended well. I got lucky. Your turn." Chloe was incredibly interested in this answer too, more than the first two if that was possible. What would Madeleine share?

"You're not going to like my answer." That was not what Chloe had been expecting.

"How could I not like it? It's your kiss. Which one was the best?" Chloe didn't understand the problem.

"I haven't had a best kiss. Honestly, none of them were all that special. I can't even think of one to tell you right now."

"Come on. You've got to had at least one that was better than the rest. You're incredible. You've probably got people waiting in line for a chance to kiss you."

The words tumbled out of her mouth before she could even contemplate shutting up. Flushing in embarrassment, Chloe reached again for her drink, disappointed to find it empty. As she began to regroup, she was relieved to see that Madeleine had not realized she was one of the people standing in that line. Instead, Madeleine seemed to be sincerely struggling to come up with something she was willing to share.

Chloe had an idea. It would be safer to let Madeleine make do with a tame, uninspired kiss, if that was the truth. It would be more interesting, though, to hear the answer to a related question.

"Okay, fine. What's the best kiss you can imagine?" Chloe heard the eagerness in her voice. She hoped Madeleine didn't as well. This was personal, but it was also playful. It was only fair that Madeleine answer something.

"That's technically a second question," Madeleine countered. "But I'll give *you* a pass." There was a teasing tone to her voice as she repeated Chloe's earlier words. Then the tone turned serious. "Give me a minute."

"You think. I'll get us more drinks." Chloe walked out to the cooler, wondering whether she was setting herself up for a torturous night. When she returned, a cold beer in each hand, Madeleine looked ready. She handed her a bottle and sat down again on the couch.

"I've got it, but I don't quite know how to describe it. I've never been asked this before."

"You're an English teacher. I think you can manage," Chloe bantered, hoping to lighten the moment, if only slightly.

Madeleine faltered, then began to dish. "I want to be consumed by desire that explodes out of nowhere, to be astonished and drawn in completely, unexpectedly." Madeleine was far away for a moment. She went on. "For some reason, I imagine it happening at work. They throw open my door and back me up to the wall, pinning me without even touching me. I want to be kissed breathless."

Chloe was inundated with thoughts she tried desperately to ignore. She had been having enough difficulty with the way her body reacted to Madeleine under normal circumstances. Being able to picture a scene like this only exacerbated the problem.

Madeleine groaned, reminding Chloe she was not alone in her daydream. "You do realize now you've got me wanting that type of kiss. My students are going to start asking why I'm zoning out in class and it's all your fault." Her chuckle cut through the thickness that had blossomed in the air.

Chloe coughed. "Oops? Okay, moving on. My question again. Have you ever been in love? Not infatuation. Genuine, meaningful love."

Madeleine's jaw clenched quickly along with what looked like every muscle in her body. There was a story here. Chloe wasn't sure if she wanted to hear it.

"I thought so. I was wrong." The way she said it closed the door to further discussion. "How about you?" The ball was back in Chloe's court.

"I loved Kendall, in that I cared about her. But I don't know that I've really been in love, the deep, lasting kind. I want what Taylor and Anne have." Glancing at Madeleine, who was looking like she could bolt at any minute, she added, "And I really want it with Sara Bareilles."

The amusement that melted the iciness in Madeleine's expression was priceless.

"So she's your celebrity crush, huh?"

"I mean, there's a short list, but I think I would have to say she's it. Emma Watson *is* making a play for the top spot, though." Madeleine's laughter warmed something in Chloe she hadn't thought about in a long time. "Your turn, sunshine. Who's your crush. Let me hear it."

"Well, I could spend every waking moment with Adele."

Chloe swore Madeleine knew she was toying with Chloe. She had to. Adele was a safe answer. She was clearly straight, beautiful, and her voice could seduce anyone. If Madeleine had picked anyone else, Chloe might have been able to confirm or deny her potential for gayness, so this reply still did not offer any substantiation. "You're up."

"Aside from not proposing to Sara yet," Madeleine said, "what's your biggest regret?"

Even the buzz Chloe had been enjoying wasn't enough to prevent the surge of guilt that engulfed her. Judging from the way Madeleine stiffened, her face must have reflected the uncomfortable memory. How could she explain this? She had to try.

"I let myself get drawn into…" What could she call it? A relationship? That word insinuated it was mutual. Then again, she had been a participant, at least initially. "Well, a relationship of sorts, one that I knew wasn't healthy. I mishandled the entire thing, and I'm still living with that."

That answer would have to suffice, as vague as it was. Apparently realizing that Chloe had things she didn't want to discuss either, Madeleine offered her own answer.

"I would say mine was being overly trusting. It won't happen again, though. Live and learn and whatnot."

Chloe raised her beer, offering a toast. "Hakuna matata!"

The ridiculousness of the toast was just enough to lighten the mood again. Chloe was relieved. Riding the emotional roller coaster this had turned into was exhausting. She designed her next question to be much less intense. While Madeleine took a swig of beer, Chloe forged on.

"So, what feature do you notice first when you're attracted to someone?"

"Oh, you mean, am I a sucker for nice smile or a sculpted physique?"

Chloe flushed, knowing that she thoroughly enjoyed Madeleine's aforementioned assets. "Yes. It can be anything." She took a swig of beer. "Fran apparently had a thing for nice teeth."

Madeleine nodded her acknowledgment. "In that case, it's definitely the walk."

"The walk?" Chloe could not remember being attracted to someone's walk.

"Don't start judging now. When someone walks up to you, you know that slight swag, not too much. A confident, athletic, whole body appeal. Gets me every time."

Chloe raised her eyebrows, considering if she had ever noticed anyone's gait before. Thinking of it in terms of "swag," an athletic body in motion—that made some sense. To be fair, Madeleine herself had a pretty sexy walk.

Madeleine interrupted her musing. "So what's yours?"

"This is tough. If I had to pick one thing, first thing I'm attracted to? It's got to be the smile. A good smile and some pretty eyes, I'm in."

"I know what you mean. If you pass the walk test and you've got nice eyes, I'm in trouble."

Chloe tried hard not to wonder if Madeleine had ever assessed her walk and eyes and if they had made the grade.

"Okay. Now, stick with me for this next one," Madeleine said. "What's your physical weakness? The kryptonite that turns you to jelly every time. For me, it's definitely having my hair played with. Throw in a hand tangling in my hair to pull me into a kiss…" Madeleine blew out her breath, shaking her head.

Chloe reached for her beer again, desperate again to hide the desire that she feared was apparent on her face. Draining the bottle to buy time and a little cover, she sat up, a pleasant wobbliness accompanying the motion. That was her last beer, she promised herself, but in the meantime it would help her answer.

"Mine is definitely my neck."

"Explain, please."

"Have you ever had someone run their fingers along your neck?" Chloe trailed off while gesturing toward her own neck. In the scant light from the moon it was hard to tell, but Chloe swore Madeleine's eyes darkened.

Her voice lowered. "I'm not sure I know what you mean."

"A light touch on my neck, maybe drawing designs. I just, well, I get chills…"

When Madeleine responded, Chloe had to lean in to hear her. "No one has ever given me those."

Chloe acted. There was no thinking involved, though a vague awareness that she was doing something she shouldn't hovered in the background. She quelled the feeling. This was just a silly exchange between friends, nothing more.

"Turn so you're facing the deck," she said quietly. Madeleine did.

Chloe reached up to her neck, brushing the braid and loose tendrils of hair to one side and exposing the skin on the back of her neck. She breathed in deeply, savoring the smell of Madeleine's shampoo. She leaned forward, her lips a breath away from Madeleine's ear, and heard a subtle change in her breathing. Concentrating on maintaining the tantalizing distance between her lips and Madeleine's inviting skin, she whispered, "It can be the feel of breath on my skin." She stopped, breathing deeply to keep her focus. "There's a sweet anticipation." She paused, noticing the fine hairs standing up on Madeleine's neck.

She moved her mouth closer, breathing gently on the soft skin there. Bringing her hand up, she carefully traced a path along Madeleine's neck, starting at her jawline and slowly winding her way down. The contact was electric, sending chills rippling down her arm and causing Madeleine to shudder almost imperceptibly and lean back into her touch. She sketched patterns across the base of her neck, then shifted forward in her seat. Her heart was racing. She was moving her hand slowly upward, toward Madeleine's hairline, when she realized that if she continued, if she tangled her fingers in her hair, made use of what Madeleine had just told her, she'd be crossing the hazy boundary she'd set in her mind about their relationship. She stilled her hand.

"Something about my neck," she said in a hoarse whisper. "I just melt."

Neither of them moved, the attraction between them charging the air around them. Chloe took a shallow breath and slowly removed her hand, her fingertips tingling where they had touched Madeleine's skin. Fear gripped her. She wasn't ready for this. She eased herself back on the couch, struggling to find the words that might remind them both that this was just frivolous banter.

When Madeleine turned around, those thoughts scattered to the wind. Madeleine's eyes were smoldering, at once inviting and terrifying. She couldn't pull her gaze away. The moment stretched out further and further—and then something shifted in Madeleine's face. She leaned back casually, breaking their connection.

"I can see how someone might enjoy that." She grinned and made a so-so gesture with one hand. "Maybe."

Chloe shook her head, welcoming the return to more casual conversation. "Don't come to me asking for a massage," she said with a smile. "Since it's clear now that your neck is completely devoid of feeling."

"I will admit it was enjoyable—if you promise not to write off any future massages."

With one sentence sparks began flying between them once more. Chloe couldn't imagine giving Madeleine a platonic massage and keeping her sanity. Then again, if this exchange was any indication, having an excuse to touch her might just be worth losing her mind. She struggled to get the conversation back on safer ground.

"Okay, but you might have to watch *Star Wars* to get any future massages."

"Still holding onto that I see. You're fighting an uphill battle, but a massage might be a good enough reason to watch." Madeleine stopped, her face pensive. "You know, I'm curious. I've never actually asked you. What's your favorite movie? Is it *Star Wars*?"

"There are so many good movies out there, I can't pick one. It usually depends on my mood." Chloe continued after a moment's thought. "You can't go wrong with sci-fi thrillers. I'm not much of a scary movie fan, but I will watch any science fiction flick at least once." She paused, trying to decide if she had a clear favorite. None came to mind. "*Star Wars* is up there with *Jurassic Park*."

"I never watch those—well, aside from the time you broadened my dinosaur horizons."

Chloe stared over at her, astounded. "Give me a minute." She shook her head. "I thought the *Star Wars* miss was a fluke. Now I think I'm in shock. There's really no science fiction in your life?"

"Those movies never really interested me. They're so long and…"

Chloe could not let her finish. She brought her hand to her face, covering it. "Movies are long to you, but you will willingly sit down and power through something like *War and Peace* for days on end. That makes complete sense…"

Shaking her head again, Chloe made up her mind. "I can't let you keep hating on these movies without at least trying to watch them. It will happen. I will make it so. If I have to unleash the hounds of hell, I'll do it."

"Whatever you say," Madeleine responded. She furrowed her brow. "So if you can't pick a favorite movie, then what's your favorite song?"

Chloe shot her a bemused look. "There is no way I can possibly answer that. There are too many. I can list off dozens for you, but I could never pick just one."

"Well, then, play one on the guitar and I'll be satisfied."

"Wow, easy to please. I'll have to remember that." Chloe cringed, knowing that no one on earth could have heard that response and not immediately recognized it as flirting. Maybe Madeleine was buzzed enough to let it slide. There was nothing for it but to forge ahead. She picked up the guitar beside the couch and paused. "Any requests?" she asked as casually as she could muster.

"How about Ed Sheeran? You listen to him, right?" The teasing tone of Madeleine's voice didn't suggest that she had been put off by Chloe's slipup.

Firmly reminding herself to be good, Chloe warned Madeleine, "Good choice. Though once I start I'm likely to butcher his whole album."

"Fantastic. I'm all ears."

Madeleine pulled her legs up onto the couch, curling them underneath her. She turned her body toward Chloe and leaned back, ready to listen. They were on opposite ends of the sofa, but Chloe felt Madeleine's presence as if it were a tangible thing, from the weight of her stare to the faint smell of citrus that clung to her.

She couldn't remember the last time she'd been so nervous. She summoned all of her concentration, focusing on remembering the opening to "Photograph." After the first bar chord, she slipped into a comfortable rhythm, gradually adjusting to being the sole object of Madeleine's attention though the energy in the air was difficult to ignore.

After her fourth or fifth song, Chloe heard a shuffling sound next to her. Madeleine was repositioning herself, draping her legs over Chloe's. Fighting the urge to rest her hand on the knee that was now resting on her thigh, Chloe channeled her energy into the last song.

While her powerful response to being around Madeleine was terrifying, wondering how Madeleine felt about her was infinitely more frightening. Setting down the guitar, she chanced a glimpse at Madeleine's reclining form and gulped. She was even more beautiful in sleep. Strands of hair had slipped from her braid and were lying softly on her cheekbones. She looked so peaceful. Chloe brushed the few stray hairs from her face, then slowly slid out from underneath her legs. Completely intrigued by the puzzle that was Madeleine Levit, she moved to grab the blanket off the back of the couch, partly to cover her up, partly to manufacture some distance between them.

Once she was sure that Madeleine was comfortably settled on the sofa, Chloe seated herself in the rocking chair across from the couch, wrapping herself in the extra blanket she'd found. As sleep claimed her too, she wondered how on earth she was going to maintain the emotional distance she so desperately needed in order to keep from messing up again.

* * *

Chloe opened her eyes slowly. The sun was up, but barely, and Madeleine was still sleeping soundly on the couch directly across from her. Her pulse picked up as memories from the party resurfaced. Why in God's name had she brought up Interview with Fran? More importantly, how was she supposed to interact with Madeleine now? It felt last night as though something had changed, that Madeleine had given as good as she got during their time together. Rather than risk an awkward encounter, though, she decided to slip away without saying any farewells. Perhaps she could pretend on Monday that she hadn't blatantly been flirting with her.

As she entered the kitchen, she was roused from her musings by the sight of Anne washing dishes.

"Good morning! You're up early."

"I can never sleep in late after parties," Chloe replied. "I was always the kid bored in the morning while my friends snored in their sleeping bags. Can I help clean up a bit?"

"Honestly, there isn't too much left to do. Stacey had to leave last night so she helped me box up the leftovers and throw out the plates and whatnot."

"Good, so you and Taylor can relax and celebrate today!"

Anne set the pan she'd rinsed in the dish drain and wiped her hands dry.

"If by celebrate you mean lounge on the couch while Taylor prepares for basketball practice Monday, then yes, we're going to get crazy here."

A shiver of excitement went up Chloe's spine at the thought of their first practice. She couldn't wait to meet her players and get to know them. Playing sports had brought her so much joy throughout her life, she could only hope to share that with the girls on the team this season.

The shuffling of feet on the stairs surprised Chloe. She assumed Taylor would sleep in this morning. Chloe hadn't pegged her as an early morning riser.

"Did I hear you say practice?" Taylor rounded the corner in the kitchen.

"I did, sweetheart. Chloe was wondering how we would celebrate. My money is on you putting together a practice plan with your JV coach."

Taylor went to Anne, wrapping her arms around her fiancée and placing a kiss on her cheek. "Actually, we've already talked about tryouts, so you're in luck, lady." Turning to Chloe, Taylor switched gears. "Are you heading out?"

"Yeah, I want to get a run in and go over some of the drills we talked about."

"Let me walk you out." Taylor kissed Anne gently, tenderly touching her cheek, before stepping away.

"Thanks for having us all over, you two. Last night was incredible."

"I'm so glad you could make it. It was a pretty special night," Anne said. "Now drive safe and I'm sure I'll see you here this week after practice!"

Chloe headed outside with Taylor.

"So how are you really feeling about tomorrow?"

"Honestly, I'm so excited I forget to be nervous. Most of the time anyway. I just want to make sure these girls have a good experience. I want them to take something away from the season besides better shooting form, you know?"

Taylor nodded. Chloe unlocked her Jeep, and opening the door, leaned on it.

"So, I don't know everything about coaching," Taylor said, "but I can tell you what I know for sure. The most important part of being a high school coach is teaching kids how to be good people. That's also the most rewarding part. It's all about fostering respect and commitment. If you can show them you care, about them and about doing things the right way, then you're doing it right."

Chloe nodded and Taylor went on. "I know you know basketball, but more importantly I know you're good people. If you respect every single player, they're going to respect you. Then you can teach them about basketball and have some fun in the process. Just be yourself and follow my lead. This is going to be fun, don't you worry."

Chloe took a deep breath, grateful for Taylor yet again.

"You're right. This is going to be fun, isn't it?"

"You bet. Now get out of here before I start asking what happened between you and Madeleine last night."

Chloe jumped into her Jeep before Taylor could ask her anything she didn't have an answer to. Pulling out of the driveway, she couldn't suppress the seed of optimism taking root within her. She might not have any answers about where she stood with Madeleine right now, but she was beginning to enjoy the ride.

CHAPTER TWELVE

November

Chloe stood at half-court, waiting for everyone to finish their free throws. Since the first practice they had ended with each player shooting ten. Every time they had to shoot with a different partner than the one from the previous practice. The girls would report to Chloe if they made fewer than seven shots. Each one under seven was a sprint. Chloe told them if the team shot a combined seventy percent, *she* would run a "forty-eight." None of her players had ever heard of the sprint, but after running eight court lengths in under forty-eight seconds the first time, they were not eager to do it again. The possibility of watching their coach run one definitely helped to motivate them. This drill was difficult, but it was a good lesson on the importance of both foul shooting and supporting your teammates. The conditioning element was an added bonus.

While the pairs of girls milled around mid-court as they finished, it made Chloe proud to hear them cheering on the last pair of shooters, Amanda and Claire. Neither of the two had played much basketball before this, but they were eager to learn. Today, Amanda had finally hit the sixty percent mark, cheering like crazy when her last shot went in. While her form was not pretty, she had come a long way in two short weeks.

"So what's the final number ladies?" Chloe called to the pair.

"Coach, I went six for ten!" Amanda's excitement eclipsed the fact that there were still a good number of sprints to run.

"Great work!" Chloe shouted, holding up a hand and waiting for a high five from her. "Stick with me and you'll be shooting ninety percent in no time!"

Amanda beamed and the rest of the girls high-fived her.

"All right, balls in, and get to the line, ladies. You've got five full-court sprints or one suicide. Your choice."

Collective whining ensued. The girls mumbled good naturedly, talking amongst themselves to discern the lesser of two evils. Macy, one of Chloe's most animated sophomores, convinced the girls the five sprints were better, primarily because running suicides went on forever.

With the group on the line, Chloe gave them their instructions. "Forty-five seconds. Anyone in after that shoots a free throw. A miss means another sprint for everybody so pick your teammates up. Ready…"

She blew the whistle and the girls were off. She was already so proud of the group. There was a lot of work to be done, but they had all embraced her coaching style as well as each other. She had high standards and expected one hundred percent effort at all times, but they knew she was invested in each one of them and gave them her respect. Chloe celebrated the victories of each of her players with enthusiasm, jumping up and down and emphatically pumping her fists. Nothing compared to seeing their excitement when they succeeded. Watching them hustle, drill after drill, she saw that they were starting to believe in themselves now too.

The girls had ten seconds left and Emily was just reaching the far end of the court.

"Ten seconds, ladies!"

Suddenly cheers burst out. Despite their own fatigue, they yelled words of encouragement to Emily to finish strong.

Grimacing, Emily ground out the final sprint. She squeaked in at forty-four seconds, flopping her body against the wall to catch her breath.

"Bring it in, everybody," Chloe called, and the girls jogged in to center court. "Great practice today! If you guys keep this up we're going to have a lot of fun this season!" She paused. The girls were exhausted but excited. *Perfect.*

"Tomorrow Coach Rafferty is going to be bringing us the pinnies and we're going to start to put in some of the offense, if you can all stay focused!" The girls nudged each other excitedly, ready to start seeing the practices become less like summer camp and more like a real team practice. "And don't forget, we're at six tomorrow. Hands in, Emily. Count us off."

Emily leaned in, putting her hand on top of everyone else's. "'Together' on three. One, two, three…"

"Together!!"

With that, the girls headed to the sidelines to get their bags, chatting amongst themselves before heading off to ride home with their parents.

Walking over to her bag on the bleachers, Chloe searched for her phone. She needed to check to see if Hannah had texted her. They were going to Skype tonight to catch up and Chloe expected to be asked to describe her team in detail, along with the offense she was planning on installing. Sure enough, she had a text from Hannah asking if eleven was too late. Chloe told her she should be free. If she fell asleep Hannah should just call her until she woke up. Tossing her phone back in her bag, she went to lock up the cage of balls. Macy was still on the court shooting, though, so Chloe stopped. The rest of the girls had left, so she decided to head over and talk to her.

"If you're still up for shooting, practice wasn't hard enough," Chloe called to Macy as she made her way across the court.

"No, we definitely ran enough. I didn't realize I was joining the track team."

"Hey, if you made more foul shots you wouldn't have to run as much. Maybe you should be shooting those instead of threes?"

Chloe teased, only partially kidding. Macy laughed, defiantly taking another shot from behind the arc. Her personality was coming to life more and more at these practices.

"Why aren't you sprinting out of here to go eat like everyone else?"

"I don't think my mom's here yet. Plus, I kinda wanted to ask you a question."

"Shoot," Chloe offered, watching as Macy took a jumper from the elbow. Her rebound bounced toward the opposite wall, and she took her time walking after it. Chloe was curious what had the sophomore so pensive.

Walking back, Macy lobbed a pass to her coach. Chloe took the shot from where she had been standing, four feet behind the arc. When the shot went in, hitting nothing but the net, Macy groaned and Chloe knew she would feel the need to hit a three of her own. Hoping that her competitive spirit would lessen her anxiety about sharing whatever was bothering her, she let her take her time formulating her question.

"This is random, but I think I might like someone. It's sort of complicated. How do you know if a crush is the real thing?" Macy spit out hurriedly.

"Well, I guess that depends on what you're feeling," Chloe said tentatively, unsure where this was leading. Macy had pinged her gaydar from the first practice.

Chloe knew she had to tread lightly. She wasn't sure yet what subjects were okay to discuss with a high school student. She had been accustomed to speaking with college students with a greater degree of freedom. What were acceptable high school student conversations? She caught a glimpse of Macy's furrowed brow as she dribbled around the paint and her concern peaked. She vividly remembered what it felt like in high school to be crushing hard on a close friend, unsure if it was possible for those feelings to be reciprocated. Not to mention the fear of disclosing to someone else something that was so confusing.

For Chloe, saying it out loud, verbalizing that she was gay, had made it more real. It had forced her to deal with her "otherness." Or at least what had felt like otherness back then.

She didn't know exactly what she could or should say, but she wanted to provide Macy someone to talk with at least.

"I don't know, Coach. Never mind, it isn't important," Macy mumbled, dribbling toward the baseline.

"Macy, I'm really glad you said something to me. You probably want to get out of here, huh? Because talking about what's going on in your head makes it more real and that can be scary. But it can help to talk it out, and whatever you say here stays right here between you and me." She paused. "I have a feeling you haven't said anything to anyone about this even though you've wanted to." Chloe raised her eyebrows at Macy questioningly.

"How did you know?" Macy asked, her hands gripping the ball so tightly her knuckles were turning white.

"Give me a little credit. I survived high school once," Chloe said gently. Macy's death grip relaxed slightly. "So, why is this crush throwing you for a loop?"

"Well, because I don't know if it's a crush. I haven't felt this before. And never with, well, with someone like this." Macy shot a three and missed badly. She chased down the rebound.

"Okay." Putting her hands up, waiting for the pass, Chloe contemplated how she might steer the conversation. "Can you try and give me some more hints about why this is a problem?" Chloe caught Macy's pass and dribbled to the right wing.

"I don't know, Coach. I don't know if it is a problem. I don't know how my friends will react or if I even want to tell them."

"Well, the first thing you have to figure out is how you're feeling, don't you think?" Chloe asked, turning away from Macy to shoot the jump shot. She recognized the cautiousness, the way Macy danced around the main issue. The painstaking way she avoided using pronouns and chose phrases that were purposefully vague. She had talked to her own friends in high school like this when she was chewing on the idea that she might be gay. Even when she had come out to her brother she had talked in hypotheticals at first, building up the courage to spit it out.

"Yeah, I guess so." Macy caught the ball as it came through the net and began dribbling around the perimeter to choose a spot to shoot from. "It's scary because I can't tell if it's just friend zone or if sh…" Macy froze, with her back to Chloe. She left the thought hanging in midair, instead taking another shot which hit the back rim. She bounded cross court after the rebound.

"Deciding if someone else feels the same way you do can be terrifying. But you've got to remember, no matter what, it's okay to feel for someone. No matter who they are or who you are."

Chloe hoped she was getting her message across without outing Macy. She didn't want to scare her away by calling her gay before Macy had a chance to accept it herself.

"A lot of people don't think so," Macy mumbled, clenching her jaw and averting her eyes.

"Well, a lot of people can be wrong. Back in the nineteen fifties people were still protesting and rioting over interracial couples and marriages. How foolish do they look now?"

Macy took her time to digest that tidbit, shooting a free throw, which just rimmed out.

"I'm nervous people are going to start talking about me."

"Why would they talk about you?" Chloe nudged her closer to the issue.

"Because they're assholes."

"Hey, watch your language. You can't call someone that in front of a teacher."

"Unless they really deserve it."

"I guess I can let that slide this time since right now I'm the coach and I make the rules in the gym. And you're right."

"Sorry, Coach, it just makes me mad that I have to worry about everybody else when I don't even know anything…" Macy trailed off.

"Macy, the first thing you have to do is be happy with yourself, with who you are. Which, by the way, is not defined by who you have a crush on. You're a smart kid, although with a sailor's mouth, and you could be a great basketball player if you would listen to me and jump stop once in your life."

"God, enough with the jump stopping!" Macy barked, exasperated, but finally smiling.

"And," Chloe went on, "you are many other things. Try to focus on who you are, and you'll realize who you click with doesn't define you. Once that sinks in, everything else will be a little bit easier. Don't get me wrong, that might be the toughest part, but that's why you have the best coach in the universe here to talk to."

Chloe spun to her left and drained a deep three, nearly from the coach's box. Out of the corner of her eye she watched Macy process what she had said. Was Chloe imagining it, or was she standing a little bit straighter?

"Thanks, Coach. I'm still not going to jump stop, though," Macy said, laughing.

"Well then, get comfortable on the bench, kid!" Chloe yelled as she walked to fetch her rebound.

"Yeah, yeah, yeah. I've got to go. I think my mom's here! I'll see you tomorrow!"

And with that, Macy ran over to the sideline, grabbed her bag, and jogged out the door toward her ride home. Chloe shook her head, hoping she could be a support to Macy as she figured out who she was.

* * *

Awareness gradually seeped into Chloe's consciousness. Cloaked in sheets, she stretched, various parts of her body clicking and popping. A yawn escaped her before she could even open her eyes. Somewhere around two her restless mind had conceded defeat to her exhausted body, but just for five hours. Only now, slightly more rested, did she even realize how poorly she had been sleeping lately. For the past week she had been thrashing about in her sleep, her restless body keeping pace with her mind.

Hannah would tell her she needed to talk it out. She always advocated talking. Chloe didn't know how to talk about this, though. The high school was becoming a home for her. But beneath the stability and pleasure it gave her an undercurrent of unease was gaining ground. Wiscasset was a haven, a port in the storm that her life had become, but none of the things that had brought her here had been resolved. In fact, everything was becoming more complicated.

Thinking of things that were complicated conjured up thoughts of Nora. *There* was something she could fix. Well, if not actually fix, at least address. Doing so might resolve some of the guilt and, who knows, it might even help Nora.

Sliding into a sitting position, Chloe tried to decide if changing out of her boxers and sleep T-shirt would be a form of procrastination or the reinforcement she needed in order to own up to Nora. The conversation she was about to have did not need to be any more intimate than it already was going to be, she decided. She made herself move, showered, and put on jeans and a fresh T-shirt. She made the bed, sat atop the covers, and checked the time. It was a little early, but Nora was an early riser. It was now or never.

"Hello?" The voice on her phone was tentative but recognizable, though it was also clear that something had changed. In truth, everything had changed.

"Hi, Nora. It's Chloe. How are you?" She wondered if the question sounded as inane to Nora as it did to her.

"I'm all right."

Chloe paused, unsure how to proceed. "Have you started your comprehensive yet?" She tried for neutral ground, hoping something might click into place.

"Yeah, I'm working on the literature review right now. It should be pretty interesting." Nora's voice was steady, if not totally even. She was either masking any hurt she felt or she had done better than Chloe at moving on.

"Nora, I know this is probably the last thing you care about hearing right now, or maybe ever, but I wanted to call and apologize to you. I am genuinely sorry for hurting you. I, well, I'm ashamed of how I fucked everything up and hung you out to dry in the process."

Silence followed, and Chloe could feel the enormity of the chasm between them. Painfully aware of the void now existing where easy friendship had once bubbled over, she continued. "I'm sure you don't care to hear my explanations, but I hope you can believe me when I say I care about you. I always have. I shouldn't have shut down on you without any explanation."

"Why are you telling me anything right now? I got your message loud and clear when you didn't respond to any of my texts."

"That's the thing. I think you got the wrong message, and that's entirely my fault."

"How gallant of you, taking responsibility for everything."

"I deserve that. And more. I'm sorry. I really do care about you, but I can't be with you. I think you know that now and you knew it then. I should have talked to you as soon as I thought you felt something more, but I was selfish. I loved being around you, and then all of the sudden I couldn't focus on anything outside myself."

Chloe heard the silence again, but this time the distance between them felt smaller somehow.

"What happened with Elaine, Chloe?"

Chloe froze, unsure how to answer or if she even could.

"Listen, Chloe, I've spent way longer than I like to admit being mad at you. I realized that you didn't want me. And you were always very careful to keep things friendly. But things changed so fast and you shut down. That's what hurt the most. You just cut me out. I thought I was at least your friend. I had chalked everything up to you being a complete ass, but then some rumors started spreading. I think I have an idea now about what really happened."

Chloe's breath caught. "What rumors?"

"Apparently an undergrad is bringing charges against Elaine, and word is that a PhD from Berkeley is on the lawsuit as well. She got her master's here the year before you got here."

This time it was Chloe who was silent. Could she finally own up to everything to Nora? Only one way to find out. "What are you doing today?"

"I don't have anything planned."

It was now or never. She needed to know what was happening for her own sake, and she owed as much to Nora. They both deserved closure.

"Let's get lunch, and if you want to hear it, I'll explain everything." Nora's breathing was the only sound from the other end of the line. Chloe wondered if she had pushed too fast.

"Sure, that sounds good. Why don't I meet you at Charro's? Around one?"

"All right. See you soon."

"Chloe?"

"Yes?"

"Thanks for calling."

Chloe smiled. "Thanks for answering."

* * *

It didn't take Chloe long to dress and get on the road for the four-hour drive to Amherst. Making up her mind to face Nora had forced her to accept the reality of what had happened rather than run from it. That didn't mean she was excited about owning up to her mistakes, but a peacefulness had settled upon her after making the decision to talk to her, and truthfully she didn't hate it.

What she hadn't quite been able to wrap her head around was the fact that there was a lawsuit pending against Elaine. Her manipulation sure as hell hadn't been professional. It had certainly hurt her and been damaging, but she hadn't ever stopped to consider if it was actually criminal. None of that had factored in her decision-making when everything had spiraled out of control less than a year ago.

It was difficult to sulk on such a gorgeous day. She was on the road by nine fifteen, I-95 was completely clear, and with any luck she would be pulling into Charro's around one. Her phone call with Hannah about halfway into the trip had buoyed her spirits as well. Hannah's elation at finding Chloe actually facing some of her demons had given her the boost of confidence and reassurance she needed to commit herself to clearing the air completely with Nora. She'd caught Jacob in a free moment too. They'd chatted about her students and her season starting.

The pride in his voice at her transition to Wiscasset was even more pronounced than Hannah's reaction had been. They hung up after agreeing to find a time to get lunch in the near future.

As she navigated her way through Amherst, Chloe felt as though she was experiencing everything for the first time. The streets of the city were the same, but they felt different. She felt different. Charro's, the best burrito place in the city, hadn't changed at all, though. The small black and red sign still hung over the door of the nondescript building at East and Finley. She hadn't eaten a burrito since leaving Amherst. Smelling the fresh tortillas and spices now, she was reminded of what she had been missing.

Pulling the door open, she was hit with a wave of nostalgia. She had stopped at this place more times than she could count on evenings when she didn't feel like cooking. Scanning the room, she spied Nora sitting at a corner booth, blond hair casually thrown into a bun. Her bright blue eyes were clearer than Chloe remembered them being. When she looked up and saw Chloe, the cautious smile that spread on her face was so endearing that Chloe finally allowed herself to admit that she had genuinely missed her.

"I had almost convinced myself you weren't coming." Nora stood at Chloe's approach, a glint of disbelief evident in her eyes.

"Hey, stranger."

Nora shook her head gently. "Why don't you go order? It'll give me time to accept that this isn't some strange alternate reality."

"That I can definitely do."

Chloe reacquainted herself with the menu and returned to the table with a giant burrito a short while later. The size of the thing was intimidating, but also awe-inspiring. She hadn't finished an entire burrito in one sitting during her time in Amherst.

"I forgot how enormous these were."

"You probably blocked it out, trying to cope with not having any out in the middle of nowhere." Nora was as naturally enthusiastic as Chloe remembered.

"I think you're right." She nodded, unsure how exactly to proceed.

"I honestly didn't think I would see you here again, and if by some miracle I did, I definitely imagined feeling some type of way about you being back. But truthfully, it's good to see you."

The nerves that had been causing Chloe's chest to get tighter and tighter relaxed a little, loosening their hold. It was really good to see Nora, though the prospect of sharing with her what had remained unspoken thus far didn't appeal quite so much.

"I have to agree. I've been pretty anxious about this, but it's nice being here again." Chloe was encouraged by the way Nora was leaning back, taking everything in. She exuded a confidence Chloe hadn't seen before.

"So, how are you? How are things going? You look really good, happy."

"Thanks. I *am* happy. It's strange, your timing."

"Why is it strange?"

"Well, I was pretty pissed at you for a while, but then I started spending more time with Jenna. She's a biochem major. I finally got up the nerve to ask her out and it's going… Well, it's going fantastic, to be honest." Her happiness was infectious; Chloe couldn't help but be impacted by it. She was grateful to hear that Nora had been able to move on, to find someone who was right for her without Chloe blocking her view.

"She must be special. You're cheesing so hard. I love it. That's awesome."

"Yeah, I'm not gonna lie. It's pretty fantastic." Nora sat quietly while Chloe made some headway with her burrito. "I can tell you all about her later if you want."

"Definitely. I want to hear all about this lady who makes you so happy."

Nora took a few bites of her own burrito, apparently content to let them sit together in companionable silence for a moment or two longer, then spoke again.

"I really need to know what happened, Chloe. I'm not stupid and you know it. You didn't really lead me on, but you made me think you were my friend and then you kind of shit all over that. Tell me why." Nora hesitated, a flash of anger surfacing. "Please."

"I know you didn't think that back then, and you probably don't believe it now, but it wasn't about our friendship. I wish I could go back, but I just…" Chloe ran a hand through her hair, gathering her thoughts. "I didn't want you getting dragged into it. So I shut you out." She stopped, so many thoughts and emotions coursing through her. "I'm sorry for hurting you. I know I did, but I think you're better for not being involved at all."

"That's bullshit. Yes, I'm younger than you are, and no, we weren't dating. But you can't argue that we didn't have a solid friendship. I actually believed you when you said that you wanted to stay close no matter where I went after UMass."

"That's still true."

"Then talk to me. If I know you, and I think I do, you've been all stoic and you haven't really talked to anyone. I'm here to listen. I want to understand. You forget—I saw what this did to you. I also know more than you do now about what she's done to other people."

Struggling to keep her emotions in check, Chloe took a deep, steadying breath. It had been almost a year since everything started, and for that entire time, she had not divulged the whole story to anyone, not even Hannah. "I don't know if I can."

"I do. I think you want to. You wouldn't have driven here if you didn't. I'm not going to judge you. If I wanted to, I could have done that already. I didn't. I tried to understand why you did what you did. Help me know what you went through. You can lean on me here."

"Jesus, Nora. I'm supposed to be your mentor, not the other way around."

Nora's laugh was refreshing. "Dude, you were my mentor and then my crush, then my friend. I'm an old soul."

Chloe returned Nora's smile, though she wasn't yet able to speak.

Nora didn't let the silence grow for long. "I guess my biggest question is how did everything start? How did she put herself in a position to be so close to you? She was your advisor, not your classmate."

Nora's sincere desire to understand finally pulled the words from Chloe, words that had been straining to get out for far too long.

"Well, for starters, once I was in her lab, we were working together every day. Her lab was so different from Gossler's or Jenk's. Maybe because she was the only woman, I don't know. But we were working together all the time. She was the most casual and informal advisor I had ever seen and I liked that. She treated us like peers and she was—well, she still is—a phenomenal physicist."

"I know what you mean. I was in her class last semester. She's charismatic and wicked smart. I can see how you would respect her and trust her."

Chloe nodded. Nora had seen the side of Elaine that she put on for everyone, the side that made her the "cool" professor and the sought-after advisor.

"She would host dinners and barbecues for the entire lab at her house. She would stay in the lab all hours while we were stuck on something, and it wasn't strange for any one of us to be there with her and order takeout when we got hungry." Chloe had thought she would hate sharing this, but finding understanding in Nora's eyes rather than pity was reassuring.

"She was so funny and we could talk about things like the existence of God or sexism in science. I felt like she respected me for my ideas the same way I did her." Chloe paused to gather her thoughts. "I started to feel something different, though. I don't know really what specifically it was, but I knew we weren't just colleagues anymore. Things were more personal. I was stupid."

"Well, that's where you're dead wrong. You trusted your advisor. That's what's supposed to happen. She was the one who needed to maintain *some* level of professionalism."

"Have you been talking to my friend Hannah?" Nora smiled, confident in her assessment. She was right, Chloe knew, but only to a point. She didn't know everything.

"We started getting into more personal territory over lunches and dinners. More and more it was only me and her. She asked me about old girlfriends. I told her all of it. By that time, she had told me she believed in connections between people that ran deeper than romance or marriage, that were in celebration of the universe itself. Christ, what bullshit." Chloe shook her head, castigating herself again. She let the momentum that had built lead her forward. The story was flooding out of her now.

"She effectively told me she had had multiple affairs with women and that John, her husband, was clueless. When I didn't flinch at that, things got intense." Chloe hoped Nora knew this was a plea for understanding. "I needed her. Without her I had no mentor, no lab, and no future in academia. I had crossed into a weird personal place with her, and I wasn't sure I could find any way to go back to a professional relationship. So I listened to her. I tried to dodge the flirty comments and ignore the fact that she was constantly finding reasons to touch me. Every time she did that, though, she followed up with a compliment on my research. I felt the unspoken threat."

"Chloe, you aren't the only person she's done this to. You have to stop blaming yourself." Nora had grown so much, Chloe thought, but she was still so naïve.

"You don't understand. She might have preyed on other people, but I let this happen. I tried to convince myself things were fine, but I let her kiss me. I kissed her back. I used excuses to keep things from going anywhere, but I let it drag on. She moved in slowly but surely, and I let her. I even convinced myself she was a catch."

Chloe dropped her head into her hands, hiding the emotion pouring out of her. She had said it, had admitted to reciprocating with Elaine. She had consented in her own way, putting herself at Elaine's mercy. "I crossed the professional line too. I made a choice that put me in an untenable position. She had me and she knew it."

Two strong hands were on hers, their softness surprising her. Ice-blue eyes pierced hers.

"Chloe, your advisor manipulated you. She made sure to remind you that she had all of the power and you didn't. Did you actively seek out or initiate an intimate relationship with her?"

"No, but…"

Nora cut her off. "No, and you didn't want one. But she maneuvered you into a position where you felt like the best plan was to go along. That's not consent. It's *sexual assault*. It's not your fault that you liked her and trusted her. She had the power and she used it to her advantage. End of story."

Chloe pulled up short, the validity of what Nora had said finally hitting her. This *was* the end of the story or could be. She had the power to end it. It wouldn't be easy, but she had to work through it and let it go.

"You were a victim, Chloe. I know you don't want to admit it, but you were abused by someone in power. It was emotional and probably more physical than you want to admit. But every time you tell the story, you reclaim some of the power she tried to steal from you."

"I'm an idiot." Chloe shook her head again, though for a much different reason this time.

"Seriously, were you listening?"

"I was. I'm an idiot for not talking to you sooner."

Nora shrugged. It was incredible the difference a couple of months had made in her.

"I hope you can understand why I did what I did. I wanted to protect you, but I couldn't face my truth. I hope you can forgive me. You've already worked to understand what I went through, but I was too caught up in myself. I was so intent on trying to keep you out of the mess that I didn't own up to the fact that I was hurting you until it was already done. I'm so sorry."

"Chloe, thank you. But that's the last apology, okay? I'm sorry you've been going through this alone. And I'm really glad you are talking to me again."

At Nora's offer to move past the old hurt, Chloe felt something start to heal inside her. It was only the beginning, but it was a beginning she hadn't anticipated this morning.

"I am too. You're too perceptive and level-headed for a senior in college." The eye-roll that comment elicited solidified their return to friendship status. "Now can you please tell me about Jenna and then all about the lawsuit, in that order?"

CHAPTER THIRTEEN

December

Chloe jogged to her apartment after the game, exhausted but too wired for sleep. Stepping through the front door, she brushed the snow off her coat, then shook out her hat; it was really coming down outside. Waves of white blanketed everything; over six inches of snowfall was predicted.

Welcome home, winter. Might as well make yourself comfortable, Chloe thought.

She reflected on her day. Four games completed already. How had that happened? The JV team had just won its second game—when no one predicted they would get their first win until over halfway through the season.

Macy had come into her own. She was a force on the perimeter, leading the team in points per game and, more importantly, assists per game. Her spunk and confidence provided the spark that got the rest of the girls going. Since her talk with Chloe, she had come out to her family and then to the team. Chloe had nearly cried at the unwavering support the girls had given her. They hadn't batted an eye, normalizing the whole thing.

Amanda had far and away been the surprise of the season. She was dominating the post. Her finesse was a work in progress, but she was a competitor down there, pouring in six points a game. Better yet, she was averaging eight rebounds a game!

Chloe couldn't decide what she was the proudest of. The girls were really learning how to be teammates now. They'd developed a collective toughness that she hadn't seen in many of the groups she'd played with; they never gave up on her. She would never give up on them either.

They had played so well tonight. They had absolutely deserved their victory. The other team had size on them, but they had executed the zone as planned and pulled out the win. Chloe had been thrilled that she'd been able to get every one of them some minutes. Even Claire had played for nearly five minutes, her tenacity on defense earning her time on the floor.

It felt as if it was only last week that she had been interviewing for the long-term sub position. She shook her head, so grateful. Her life was surreal. Even her Thanksgiving had felt like one that had been pulled from a Lifetime movie.

When her mother had called to tell her they were going to visit with Nate in California, Chloe had had to tell them dejectedly that due to the academic and athletic schedules there was no way that she could go with them. She had resigned herself to a quiet holiday consisting of watching football and cooking for one until Taylor had invited her to spend the day with her and the gang at their house.

Taylor and Anne had been itching to have people over for their first Thanksgiving in the finished house. The camaraderie they had all shared—laughing themselves to tears, relaxing, and even getting Madeleine to watch football—that was their own brand of family.

Madeleine. Chloe's thoughts drifted to her now as they so often did of late. She couldn't spend enough time with her. No matter how often the little voice in her head warned her, she kept returning for more, even though she couldn't decipher what everything between them was.

Giant white puffs of snow were swirling in the wind. It was time to break out the snowboard again. Unsure if any of the gang was big into skiing or snowboarding, she had asked at Thanksgiving, and Anne had informed her that they all tried to go together at least twice a month. If their schedules allowed, they would get out every weekend. They were scheduled to go on the first trip of the season this weekend if the snow held.

Chloe had been more than a little disappointed to find out that while Madeleine was going along, she wouldn't actually join the group on the slopes. She typically spent her time at the resort reading and would join them for dinner after their day on the mountain.

Chloe had been shocked and said so. "I cannot believe you never learned to snowboard or ski. How did you make it this far in your life, born and bred in the Northeast, without learning to?"

Being on a snowboard was one of the most prominent memories of Chloe's childhood. Nate complained to her all the time about how much he missed being able to get up and go to the mountain whenever he wanted. She didn't feel too bad for him, though. Now he was catching waves instead. Thinking on it, she didn't know anyone in the area that had not at one point been skiing, snowboarding, or both.

"My parents were transplants. They never had an affinity for it, so neither did I. My friends went, but I was more than happy to spend my time on the trails with my Yamaha."

"Well, that helps your cred slightly, but still..."

Taylor nudged Chloe, interrupting her. "Keep it up, JV. She hasn't tried to learn any other time I've offered. With encouragement like yours, maybe now she *never* will."

Chloe scrambled to rectify her approach and regain any chance of spending a day on the slopes with Madeleine.

"I'm sorry! Come on. You've got to try it. I know you'll enjoy yourself." Chloe pressed on. "If you hate it, you can break my nose again."

Madeleine seemed conflicted. Finally, though, she must have come to terms with the internal issue, whatever it was.

"Okay. But only because you were a good sport when I needed you to play goalie."

Chloe cut in before she could continue. "Great. You'll come with us, no one will laugh at you, and I promise I won't break any of *your* bones!" She watched Madeleine try and fail not to crack a smile.

"No more broken bones jokes," she warned. "Or I might be liable to inflict other bodily harm."

Chloe had the feeling Madeleine was seeing right through her, reading emotions she herself didn't even understand. She *should* keep her distance, but the animation in Madeleine's eyes was impossible to tear herself away from.

* * *

Having offered to provide everything Madeleine would need for the weekend, Chloe was glad once again that she had insisted on purchasing a Jeep despite her mother pulling hard for a sedan. With the seats flipped down there was plenty of room for two boards, helmets, boots, and the bag filled with pants, gloves, and wrist guards. Now there was nothing but a two-hour drive between her and Black Mountain Ski Resort. Snow accumulations there were just shy of a foot and the weather promised a great day of snowboarding. Taylor and Anne had reserved a suite of adjoining rooms, offering to share with anyone who wanted to stay to maximize their time. Chloe had eagerly accepted, offering money which Taylor immediately refused. Stacey had already booked a room; Molly was getting in Saturday night and would join the group on the slopes Sunday. Jaysa was planning on skiing both days, but since her partner Ben was away this weekend, she'd be commuting to take care of Major, her completely spoiled Australian shepherd.

Before long, the sign for the resort was popping up on the horizon. As she pulled into the parking lot, she was reminded of the mountain where she learned to snowboard. Her family had spent countless weekends there. A central part of her childhood, it had had a tiny lodge and lone chair lift. Black Mountain was bigger, but it had the same sort of community vibe. The gravel parking lot was surrounded by a simple wooden log fence. The welcoming lodge, located at the base of the slope, had a cool blue exterior that was set off by exposed beams and roughhewn logs.

Families milled about in the parking lot, with young skiers eager to learn and older siblings just as eager to head off on their own. Chloe spotted Taylor in the far corner leaning casually against her Rav4. She perked up when she recognized Chloe's car, waving her over. She jumped her before she'd even gotten out of the Jeep.

"Hurry, let's go buy our passes and make Anne wait for the other hoodlums."

"That's perfect. Is Madeleine here yet? I want to buy her pass for this weekend."

Taylor didn't press, though her knowing glance let Chloe know she was intrigued.

"You're the first one here, which—I'm not going to lie—shocked me. You're never this early." Taylor playfully elbowed Chloe as they walked toward the lodge.

"I love this place, reminds me of home."

"It's one of our best kept secrets so we get the trails to ourselves. Plus, the kids learning are fun to watch. A little dangerous, though. Sort of like drunken pinballs flying around the mountain, but you get used to that," Taylor finished with a shrug. Chloe smiled. She had been one of those drunken pinballs once upon a time. She'd been lucky to survive her adolescence.

"It's a great place. We considered having the wedding here as a matter of fact. They renovated parts of the lodge over the summer and put in a gorgeous restaurant downstairs. You'll see it tonight. That's where we're eating."

"God, Taylor, that would be beautiful! Do you guys have a date or a place yet?"

Taylor's face lit up brightly.

"Well, it's not official, but we heard back from the venue we finally picked. It's fucking perfect. Marianmade Farm. It's a small operational lavender farm right on the water in Wiscasset. Amazing views, gorgeous barn, finished inside with exposed beams and the perfect rustic feel to it. The barn holds like one hundred and forty. We want to keep it under one hundred. You're lucky you're on the list."

"That sounds amazing. You'll be in khakis, right?" She could picture Taylor clearly, standing in her khakis and T-shirt waiting for Anne in her gorgeous dress. Taylor could too, judging from her laughter. "Seriously, though, you have to let me know if you guys need anything, I'm happy to help."

"Thanks. I know you are. But honestly, with it being so low-key, it's basically a dinner with some friends and nice flowers. We're locked in for the first weekend in January, so clear your schedule."

"Got it. But let's be honest. All I do is coach my kids, grade papers, and spend time with our fellow basketball players and skiers. I'll make it work." Their laughter followed them to the window where they purchased their lift tickets. On the walk back, Taylor briefed Chloe on which were the most challenging runs and the best for learning and what time to be back at the lodge for dinner.

As they approached the car, they found Stacey and Jaysa chatting with Anne.

"Any sign of Madeleine yet?" Taylor asked.

"Nope, she probably got scared off again," Jaysa called back. Apparently, no one had seen or talked to her this morning.

"Why don't you guys go find the rooms, change, and get your tickets?" Taylor suggested. "Chloe and I can be Madeleine's welcoming committee. I'll give her a call and make sure she didn't back out."

Laughter followed as the three women headed to the lodge to suit up for the day. Taylor turned to face Chloe with a more serious expression.

"So…what's going on with you and Madeleine?" Apparently, Taylor's patience had finally been maxed out. Chloe had wondered if, and when, this conversation might happen. What was there to say?

"I don't know. I mean I love being around her, and if I'm honest, there's been some harmless flirting. But it's nothing."

"From that vague response, I think there's more going on than you want to admit. I guess I just want to know what *you* want. Do you know?" Concern emanated from Taylor.

"That's the thing. I finally feel ready to move forward, really let go of the past and be happy. I want the works, a solid relationship and someone who's ready to do that with me. But that doesn't mean I want that from Madeleine right now, you know? I just feel good when I'm around her."

Taylor's smile held a glimmer of sadness. Chloe could practically see the cautionary words that were coming before she gave voice to them.

"You seem really good, more like a whole person than when I first met you. And yes, I'm perceptive enough to recognize that. Anne may have hinted at a few things, but that's beside the point."

Chloe chuckled, imagining Anne offering insights to Taylor out on their porch.

"I guess I just want to make sure you've got both eyes open here. I don't think Madeleine has made the same peace with her past that you have." Taylor was thoughtful for a moment, then added, "And I'm obligated to tell you that, hard as you're trying, you're totally transparent. I see how you swoon every time you see her."

"Oh wow, thanks, Taylor. That settles my nerves right down. You're so helpful."

Chloe was spared a retort from Taylor by Madeleine's impeccable timing. Jostled by the less than smooth parking lot, her little hatchback was bouncing its way over to them.

"Welcome! Glad to see you're on time as always." Taylor laughed, pushing her way past Chloe to open Madeleine's door.

"Being sarcastic now isn't the best way to keep me here, darling." The two laughed and Madeleine turned her attention to Chloe.

"If I survive today, can we call it even on the broken nose front?" She tilted her head, one brow arched, and leaned into Chloe's orbit, causing quite a ruckus in her abdomen. Temporarily lost for words, Chloe nodded and tried to ignore Taylor. Madeleine took in her surroundings.

"So—I'm new to this, but I believe I have to purchase a lift ticket. Where would one find such a thing?"

Smiling sheepishly, Chloe pulled the ticket out of her jacket pocket. "Right here. I've got you covered. Welcome to your all-expenses-paid lesson of a lifetime." Chloe bowed, assuming her most regal and gracious demeanor. Madeleine's and Taylor's laughter told her today might just turn out to be fine.

"You two get your gear together. I'm going to the lodge and find the other three. I've got to tell them you showed up. I think they were placing bets earlier." Taylor turned and walked away, leaving Madeleine alone with Chloe. Moving to the back of her Jeep, Chloe began gathering the necessary gear.

"You didn't need to do this," Madeleine said softly as she attached the lift ticket to her jacket and joined Chloe at the back of the Jeep.

"I know, but I wanted to. I remember how panicky I was at the thought of playing soccer in front of you. I can't imagine having to pay to be that nervous."

"I wouldn't say I'm nervous. I've resigned myself to the reality of experiencing prolonged and repeated embarrassment."

"Madeleine, I promise you, this isn't going to be as bad as you're imagining. I guarantee you're going to have fun, and as a bonus I won't force you to admit it when you do."

Returning her attention to the gear in the back, Chloe grabbed the small duffel and checked to make sure everything Madeleine would need was inside. She felt Madeleine's eyes on her and a corresponding tug near her navel jumped to life. There was a softness in Madeleine that she hadn't seen before, an openness that drew her in. She felt her knees weaken. Shakily, she extended the bag of clothing to Madeleine.

"These are for you. There's a base layer and some leggings, a pair of my favorite socks, and snow pants. The wrist guards and helmet are in there too, but don't worry about those until we get on the slope." The words fell from her mouth in nervous clusters, Madeleine's nearness nearly eclipsing her ability to speak.

As Madeleine reached for the bag, their fingers brushed. Heat rushed to Chloe's face, and her skin tingled from the contact. She saw Madeleine's eyes dart down to their hands. The electricity of their interactions was creating a magnetic field stronger than any electromagnet Chloe had ever studied. It kept pulling them closer. Chloe felt herself leaning forward, then, realizing that the electricity was swelling beyond their ability to control it, she pulled back. She needed to figure this out before they both had regrets.

"Why don't we head over? They're probably waiting for us. You can change and I can get you set up with a locker." Madeleine nodded, and they began walking toward the others.

* * *

Sitting on a wooden bench between the back deck of the lodge and the path to the lift, Chloe took several deep and calming breaths. She began stretching her legs, trying to loosen her knee, aware of just how tight she was, already loaded with nervous energy. Stacey sat down next to her. Leaning in to Chloe so that no one around them could hear her, she whispered, "It doesn't matter if she doesn't make it down once today. We both know you're the reason she's out here instead of inside reading."

Casually, she straightened up, and it registered with Chloe that everyone in the group suspected that things were happening between them. *Great. Just great.*

"Stacey, I love you to death, but I don't think that's true. Plus, even if it is, is that supposed to make me less nervous?" Chloe's exasperation only caused Stacey to laugh loudly, drawing the attention of a group of tiny little ski girls walking by.

"Just have fun today. And no, the group hasn't talked about anything that might or might not be happening. But speaking for myself, I like seeing you guys together. You're both happier. That's all I'm saying." Stacey threw her hands up in a gesture of surrender.

"We only gravitate toward each other because we're the single losers," Chloe muttered halfheartedly.

Another full laugh was the only response she received. Stacey stood, patting Chloe's shoulder comfortingly, and beckoned her forward to join the group, which was walking toward them. Chloe's fears were confirmed when she saw Madeleine. Even in snowboarding gear, she was a knockout. Her hair, braided again, lay over the collar of her ski jacket. Her form, despite layers of padding, still pulled Chloe in. Chloe's mouth went dry. She had been pointedly trying to focus on anything other than her desire to be around her. The attraction was so powerful and so distracting that she wasn't sure it would allow her to convey even the basics of snowboarding.

"Madeleine, I'm telling you right now, if Chloe isn't cutting it, find me and I'll take over. You'll be making full runs in no time." Jaysa's bouncy energy was contagious.

"I'm holding you to that." Madeleine nodded in J's direction.

"And I'm telling you, when and if you would like a break from the experts, I'll join you in the lodge for a nice snack." Anne's disarming quip was perfectly timed, as usual.

"Thanks, everyone, for the votes of confidence. But right now there are a few too many cooks in the kitchen. You guys head up, enjoy, and we will see you around." Chloe shooed the group away, which allowed Madeleine to relax marginally.

"Now that they're gone, come sit with me for a second."

Madeleine's face relaxed almost completely at the prospect of gathering her thoughts.

"We can take this at whatever pace you feel comfortable with. I honestly just want you to give it a shot because I think you're going to really enjoy it."

Madeleine nodded, encouraging Chloe to go on.

"So, here's my thought process. The best way to learn this is to just do it. I'll be with you every step of the way, but first we should cover some basics. The best spot for that is flat ground." Chloe stood, offering a hand to Madeleine and shivering a little when its addictive warmth hit her system. Today was going to be sweet, sweet torture.

Walking to a flat patch twenty yards off, Chloe began explaining the mechanics of the boards and the boots. Madeleine picked that up instantly, easily clipping in and out.

She then moved to having them practice getting up on the board from a sitting position. Madeleine stood staring questioningly as Chloe sat on the ground, both boots in her snowboard.

"I'm not doing this to be cool here, as hard as that is to believe," Chloe teased. Madeleine cracked a half smile, though she still didn't join Chloe.

"The reality is you're going to fall today. And there is nothing worse than feeling like a beached whale up there, not able to stand back up or flailing around and falling back and forth every time you try it." When Madeleine didn't respond, Chloe pulled out her last bit of persuasion.

"It's either try it a couple of times down here until you're comfortable or try it halfway down the slope with gravity pulling you forward and experts zooming past you." The idea of avoiding potential embarrassment was enough to convince Madeleine. She clicked in and joined Chloe on the ground.

After Madeleine spent about ten minutes practicing hopping up, walking with the board on one foot, and mastering the awkward stopping motion, Chloe decided she was adequately briefed to make her first foray on the mountain.

"I know it's intuitive, but this is all about balance, using your core and muscle memory." She paused. "If you can force yourself to take it slow in the beginning, it'll be worth it in the end. I promise I'll get you to enjoy it." Chloe saw a question in Madeleine's eyes and amusement at how those words might be taken in a different context. *Shit.* Well, that hadn't been what she meant, but it was pretty solid advice. They headed for the lift.

The sky was bright, though not blindingly so, and she could see rolling hills and lush Maine countryside for what felt like miles in either direction. A faint breeze rustled the treetops.

"This view might just be worth it. If I hate this, can I ride the chair lift all day?"

Chloe saw through Madeleine's joke, glimpsing an open vulnerability, and felt her resolve to remain distant begin to waver. Each new view of Madeleine was more intriguing than the last.

"You could try, but I don't think the staff would approve."

Shaking her head, Madeleine resumed her appreciation of the view as they bounced along up the mountain. Desperate for a distraction from the warmth Madeleine had stirred within her, Chloe steered the conversation back to snowboarding.

"Do you have other questions? We went through it a little fast, but you're picking everything up really quickly."

"I don't have specific questions necessarily. I'm probably the least confident about getting off this stupid lift and the whole process of turning and stopping. You know, nonessentials."

Chloe giggled in spite of herself, then added, "I know it doesn't feel like it, but you know enough to start. The best way for me to explain it is to have you doing what I'm saying as I'm saying it. I'll be with you the whole time, I promise."

Madeleine shook her head and turned away with a sigh.

"What?"

"I don't know how you do that."

"Do what?"

"Make me think I should trust you."

Chloe's breath caught. She didn't know why Madeleine was so leery about trusting others, but those fears must be deep-seated, and that scared her. What had happened to make her so wary? She wanted her to trust her, more than she could ever say. When she was with her it was as if they had been together for ages. And her laughter…

Chloe was well on her way to losing herself in their connection when the clanking of the chair lift reminded her that they needed to get off and soon. She got herself ready and then turned to Madeleine.

"Okay, are you ready for this?"

"No."

"Yes, you are. Remember, stand when I say to and keep pushing with your other foot. Ready? And…stand!" Together they leapt off the lift, though toward what exactly Chloe was not certain.

* * *

By the time Madeleine showed she was comfortable on the board, long shadows were stretching across the mountain. She had picked it all up so easily. She had spent the morning familiarizing herself with the feel of the board, the basics of getting back up, catching a few tough edges, and finding her balance. After lunch, though, something had clicked, and she was making it down the bunny hill every time without falling.

As they moved up in difficulty on the various trails, Madeleine grew more and more confident, her enjoyment of the challenge evident in her movements. It felt as though they had laughed their way through the day, periodically joining with Stacey or Taylor to show off her new skills. Madeleine had taken that break Anne had promised, too, sitting with her while Chloe, Taylor and J took two runs down Digger's Peak.

Now that the lights were coming on, the pair decided to attempt one of the steeper trails that swung around the outer edge of the mountain. From the mouth of the trail, a wide clearing gave them an unobstructed view of the sky, which was growing progressively darker. Madeleine slowed to a stop at the precipice, her breath blooming in clouds of moisture in the cold night air.

She turned to Chloe, her face completely open, without a trace of hesitation, conflict, or fear. Chloe knew now what utter contentment felt like. Sometimes things were unequivocally good.

"Are you up for this?"

"Absolutely."

"I'm thinking you should start as fast you want. That way you can watch me finish." Realizing the words again could be taken in a different context, Chloe grinned. Madeleine's corresponding blush told her that apparently her mind had gone to a similar place. Though tempted, she decided it was best to leave well enough alone. "I'll be waiting with open arms." She made her escape without watching Madeleine's reaction.

The freedom she experienced on each run was intoxicating. She always felt so powerful as she sliced her way down a slope, the whole mountain sprawled before her and snow beckoning her forward, a feeling amplified tonight by Madeleine's presence.

All too soon she found herself at the base of the trail. She turned to watch Madeleine's final descent. She was maneuvering with apparent ease, nearly halfway down the run. Fluid in her turns, she was graceful and confident, nothing like the tense bundle of nerves that had walked out of the locker room in the morning.

The mountain was getting busy, Chloe noted. It had been lively but not crowded during the day, but traffic had picked up when the lights had switched on. A group of kids was about fifty yards behind Madeleine, trying out tricks on their skis.

Madeleine was on the final stretch now, joyful exuberance on her face. Even as she delighted in this utterly relaxed version of Madeleine, though, Chloe found her attention being pulled to the teens behind her, who were gaining on her with reckless speed. Their vector pointed directly through Madeleine's path. The force with which they were hurtling down the hill was alarming and increasing with their acceleration. Judging from how much smaller they were, two of them had to be in middle school. They were less than fifteen yards behind Madeleine now. Her eyes darting between the young skiers and Madeleine, Chloe mentally calculated their trajectory and prayed Madeleine would speed through the last stretch; she was in a race without knowing it.

Ending her run, Madeleine threw on the brakes three yards from Chloe and stopped, her back to the trail. Relieved, Chloe slid over and was getting ready to congratulate her when a flash of movement on the hill caught her attention. On instinct she dove behind Madeleine, intercepting a rogue skier as he sped toward Madeleine's exposed back. She wrapped her arms around the boy, her body twisting at the impact. Turning her body in midair to keep from landing on him, she slammed into the ground, her shoulder taking the full weight and force of the collision. They slid past Madeleine and on for another couple of yards. When finally they came to a stop, heat and pain converged on her collarbone.

Shit. Please don't let it be broken. I can't deal with another surgery.

She sat up slowly, relieved when she was able to do so without debilitating pain, and focused on the skier lying on his side next to her. He didn't seem hurt physically and had been wearing a protective helmet, but he wasn't more than ten years old, and his round face was blank with the shock he was feeling at his wipeout.

Chloe caught Madeleine's attention as she started to rush over to them, waving her off with a shake of her head. Madeleine stopped, nodding as she realized what Chloe was trying to tell her. Returning her focus to the boy next to her, Chloe addressed him quietly.

"You know that was way too fast with so many people out here, right? And that you might have hurt yourself or someone else very, very badly?"

He nodded his head. Glistening tears pooled beneath his eyes and Chloe's heart melted. Her voice softened. She stood up and reached out to help him up, ignoring the throbbing pain near her shoulder.

"Now that that's out of the way, are you okay?" A quick nod was all she got as he accepted her right hand and sat up.

Hoping to calm him down before his friends got there, Chloe leaned forward, whispering so that only he could hear her. "Your friends might pick on you, but that's only because they're jealous you crushed them." She leaned back and was finally rewarded with a giggle. He would be fine. She hoped he had learned a little something from his wipeout too.

"I think you should probably apologize to my friend here and we can call it even."

"Okay. Thanks for breaking my fall. Sorry I smashed you."

Chloe nodded and he stood, righting himself in order to ski over and apologize to Madeleine, who was talking to the group of older boys at the spot where she and Chloe had been standing moments earlier. Chloe knew it would take a lot of courage for the little guy to apologize in front of his friends, but it needed to happen.

Interested in how the apology would play out, Chloe stretched her left arm forward to push off the ground and stand up. An explosion of pain in her collarbone took her breath away. Instantly retracting her arm, she carefully redistributed her weight so she could stand without using her left side, then slowly stood and went to gather up her board, cursing her luck. For all the injuries that had plagued her in the past, she just wanted to be a *normal person* for once and stop finding creative ways to break things. Chloe wiggled her fingers, then bent her elbow. She didn't have any numbness or tingling, all of which she had learned meant there was a problem.

"Well, that certainly wasn't the ending I had planned. Are you okay? Did you hit your head?"

As Madeleine silently appraised her for signs of injury, Chloe eased her hand into her jacket pocket, hoping she wouldn't wince. She refused to have to acknowledge another injury in front of her. This was getting ridiculous. Not to mention the fact that she couldn't even contemplate what a trip to the ER would cost her. She was still paying off her last visit to urgent care.

"I'm fine. I just landed hard on my shoulder. It'll be sore I'm sure, but that's all that hit. How was the apology?"

Madeleine quieted, temporarily mollified and distracted by the memory of the boy.

"It was cute. He was nervous and embarrassed, but he powered through it. His brother and cousins, that was the group he was with, apologized to me before he even got over to us. They had been teasing each other and said they would race, but Clark there apparently didn't realize they hadn't meant a race to the death."

"Kids are dumb. I know, I was the dumbest."

"I can only imagine. How did you ever make it out of adolescence with all of your limbs? You're perpetually getting slammed into or broken."

Chloe laughed, Madeleine's consternation reminded her of her mom's habitual worrying throughout her childhood and then her college basketball career.

"I mean, I always thought I had things under control, but you know the saying, I break even. Eventually. I think it's a positive outlook. Mom on the other hand likes to point out that regardless of the outcome I always manage to break something. It's a bit of a mantra for Dad, something he reminds me of every time things don't go as planned."

"Well, I'm just glad I've only seen one of the aforementioned breaks. Your nose was traumatic enough." Madeleine shook her head, though she didn't shake the smile from her lips. "How did you even get there in time? He must have been flying. You guys went about eight feet, if not more."

"They had been gaining on you for most of the trail so I knew they had to be moving. There's a little mini ramp up the hill from here. I saw him mishit it. It was a blur, but I reacted just in case. Better safe than sorry."

"I'm sorry you took a hit, but I appreciate it. I don't think I would've bounced back so quickly after getting blindsided by a human cannonball. Plus, my parents are still getting over my last injury. They would have shown up here tomorrow if I'd been leveled. They've always supported me and my dreams, but they both consider worrying a competitive sport. It's how they show love. Suffocating at times, but genuine all the same." She paused, again studying Chloe, clearly attempting to discern the level of truth to her claims at being uninjured. "You're sure you're all right?" She eyed Chloe suspiciously, apparently not convinced that there wasn't some damage. She moved to close some of the distance between them. Chloe's ability to breathe declined rapidly, and her heart rate skyrocketed. She swallowed twice, hoping to find words that made sense.

"Honestly, I'll be sore tomorrow, but I'm fine for now."

It wasn't the whole truth, but it was partly true, she rationalized. She was fine in that she would survive. But she was also in considerable pain. Maybe she was convincing herself she didn't need to be looked at, but she simply wanted to be okay for once. Madeleine didn't need to know the details.

She needed to withdraw from the world for a moment, find a place to think and to wince without witnesses. Chloe turned. "Let's go find the others inside. I'm sure they're waiting for us."

With the majority of the crowd dispersed to their rooms or the restaurant, the lodge was relatively quiet. Walking toward the locker rooms, they spotted Taylor and Anne sitting and talking in two overstuffed chairs next to the fireplace in the grand foyer. They were already changed. Anne waved them over.

"Are you two ready for dinner? You're the last ones in."

"Which is code for 'hurry the hell up and change so we can eat.'" Taylor waved both hands, gesturing toward the locker rooms impatiently. Madeleine laughed and walked in, but Chloe lagged behind.

"Anne, do you have any pain meds? I landed pretty hard out there and I know I'm going to need to take some of the soreness out ASAP."

"Absolutely, it's up in the room. I can go get it."

"Babe, she's going up there to change. She can grab it." Turning her attention to Chloe, Taylor went on, "It's in the brown leather case on the bathroom counter. Just dig around, it's my bag so don't be shy. But hurry, I'm wasting away here."

"I'll be back in no time. Don't wait for me. I'll find you in the restaurant."

As Taylor and Anne nodded in agreement with the plan, Chloe turned and began the trek to the room. The second floor suddenly felt very far away. She was grateful she'd bought herself some extra time. She was going to need it.

The restaurant downstairs was magnificent, though Chloe was sure she was missing many of the finer details due to the persistent ache plaguing her. She prayed the ibuprofen would kick in soon, but she had brought two Tylenol with her to take if it didn't abate shortly. Bouncing back and forth between pain and pleasure, her thoughts were doing little to encourage her appreciation of her surroundings.

After a hot shower, she had felt limber enough to carefully maneuver into a black sweater and soft white T-shirt, forgoing a bra that might put pressure on her collarbone. She'd paired them with black skinny jeans.

By the time she made it to the group, everyone had ordered drinks and an appetizer sampler was on the table. Molly had joined them. Stacey was completely enamored with her, that was apparent. Thankfully Jaysa had agreed to stay and eat before heading home to Major, otherwise the couple aura would have driven Chloe past her breaking point.

"The hero returns!" Jaysa called out as she greeted Chloe. Laughter met her. Taylor spoke up.

"Drinks are on me. Not only did you manage to make sure Madeleine had fun and was returned uninjured, she just agreed to come back next time!"

"I'll drink to that!" Stacey raised her glass in salute, and Chloe blushed. She took the final seat in the wraparound booth, sliding in to the left of Madeleine and reaching for the drink Taylor had mentioned. Maybe alcohol would calm the waves of attraction and nervousness she was feeling. It wouldn't hurt to try. She took a sip of the amber liquid. The distinctive taste of a whiskey sour was a welcome surprise.

"So, Molly, how was your family?" Anne's question brought conversation back to life around the table, giving Chloe a chance to settle in. She was taking a second sip of her drink when Madeleine leaned in. Keeping her voice quiet, presumably to keep the conversation between them, she whispered.

"I thought the sweatshirt I stole from you was my favorite piece of your clothing, but that outfit is definitely my new favorite."

The compliment sent a flood of sensation throughout Chloe's body.

"You can borrow it if you'd like. Just promise I'll get these back." Chloe pointed to the jeans she was wearing. "They're my favorite jeans and you've already stolen my favorite sweats."

Madeleine inched forward, her voice dropping even lower to deliver her reply.

"No, you should keep them. I definitely prefer them on you."

Chloe knew she should say something. But the top two buttons of the loose-fitting white oxford Madeleine was wearing were open, revealing an expanse of skin that begged to be explored. She took another fortifying sip of her drink to avoid getting caught staring even longer.

The alcohol didn't dissipate the connection sizzling between them. Chloe wished they were back outside, where physical contact had been a given. She had had innumerable reasons there to be close to Madeleine when she was helping her up, steadying her. Here there was no excuse for doing that, and Chloe was sure she would explode.

"What are you drinking?"

"It's nothing fancy, dark rum and ginger beer served over ice and garnished with a slice of lime. Called a Dark n' Stormy?" By name alone the drink was appropriate for Madeleine. "Ever had one?"

"I haven't. Maybe I'll order one later. This whiskey sour is delicious, though."

Over the course of their conversation, Madeleine had inched closer to Chloe, leaning in and narrowing the gap between them. The subtle scent she was wearing was fresh and light, intoxicating like Madeleine.

"Taylor wanted to order you a gin and tonic. I had to step in. I was pretty sure I know your taste better than Taylor does."

Chloe's gaze fell to Madeleine's mouth and the seductive smile spreading there. Bringing her focus back to her eyes, she found an intensity within them that simultaneously shocked and thrilled her.

"I think you're right."

Madeleine's hands encircled her glass, gentle fingers drawing patterns in the condensation, and she leaned dangerously close to Chloe. Chloe took a deep breath. Being around Madeleine felt like standing on a cliff. Easing away from the edge, she leaned back, weakening their connection, though not severing it. Their exchange had lasted only a few minutes, but it felt much longer.

Returning her attention with effort to the table talk, Chloe caught the end of Molly's story about her nephew's birthday party. Apparently, it had gone well until Banjo, the family dog, had demolished the cake her brother, Devin, had left on the counter.

Their meals arrived and everyone dug in, hungry from a fun but tiring day. The salmon Chloe had ordered was delicious, but cutting it with one hand was proving to be a formidable task. Thankfully nearly everyone else was happily buzzed and deep into their second or third, drink and didn't notice her trials.

Conversation continued between savory bites. Molly hadn't been to any of the gang dinners in a while, so they were taking turns filling her in on the various sports seasons, life at school, the usual. Midway through Taylor's recap of the progress of the basketball team, Jaysa interrupted.

"Hey, did any of you see that dope Landon out there today? He's your athletic director, right, Taylor?" Taylor, intrigued, nodded her head at Jaysa.

"He almost plowed me over just before I came inside. Dude's a tool bag if I ever saw one." Jaysa shook her head. A chorus of "No's," uttered in faux surprise, and general agreement about his temperament rang around the table.

Though it was fleeting, Chloe had felt Madeleine's body tense. The subject of discussion shifted yet again, but Chloe's focus remained on Madeleine's obvious discomfort. Her entire demeanor had shifted. No one else seemed to have noticed.

Concerned, Chloe tried to gauge how Madeleine was doing. She didn't appear to be in great distress. But there was a new set to her jaw and the slight crease between her brows. Working awfully hard to appear casual, she had begun to cut up her vegetables with forceful strokes, her gaze fixed with laser focus on her plate.

Chloe leaned into Madeleine casually and remained there. Speaking only loud enough for Madeleine to hear, she asked, "Did broccoli wrong you as a child?" Madeleine's knife stopped in midair. "I don't mean to interrupt, but that floret is taking a real beating."

Madeleine let out a short-lived chuckle. Lowering her silverware, she dropped her hands to her knees and took a deep breath. Chloe felt it was safe to push on.

"Seriously, I'm here if you want to vent."

Chloe wasn't sure what made her do it. Maybe it was the conflict so evident in Madeleine. Or her mounting suspicion about Landon's constant presence in the periphery, which strongly reminded Chloe of her own experience with Elaine. Something made her reach out. Finding Madeleine's left hand, Chloe set her right hand on top of it and gave it a gentle squeeze, hoping she would not pull away. She didn't. The rush that accompanied that realization nearly took Chloe's breath away.

"Don't hold it against me, but I've got a particularly shady past with cauliflower myself."

Their joint laughter drew the attention of some of the others, primarily Taylor. Chloe knew she should remove her hand before her lapse in judgment became more noticeable. She lifted it, experiencing palpable loss as the contact between them was severed, and gave a dismissive wave.

"Nothing to see here, folks. Just some vegetable humor."

"Oh, God help us all. Madeleine's met her match."

A chorus of light-hearted agreement circled the table, and Chloe felt heat rush to her face. Not only had she grabbed Madeleine's hand, but Taylor had called her out on it in her own charming way. So much for keeping her distance. Apparently she had used up all of her willpower in deciding to leave UMass.

By the time the waitress brought them their checks, Chloe's pain had been reduced to a level that no longer impacted her breathing or overall functioning. She was confident that all she would have to show for it in the morning was a nasty bruise.

In the meantime, she had pain of a different kind to deal with. Something had changed in Madeleine. She was withdrawing, carefully avoiding any physical interaction with her. Chloe couldn't understand what was driving this strange yo-yoing, but as a result she was barely hanging on.

As they all stood, extricating themselves from their places at the table, Taylor gathered the group. "Who's up for another drink with me at the bar before we call it a night?"

Stacey chimed in first, beaming at Molly. "We're in, right, babe?"

Chloe wanted to stay and try to figure out what was happening between her and Madeleine. Since that was out of the question, she decided to settle for a quick walk and a comfortable bed.

"I'm getting a bit sore. I'm going to get a little fresh air and then hit the sack. Thanks for a great day, everyone." Hoping for a final connection, Chloe casually reached out and slid her hand onto Madeleine's toned shoulder. Her pulse quickened as she felt the taut muscles there bunch beneath the soft fabric of her oxford.

"Have one for me. I've got to go nurse my aging body back to health."

Madeleine bit the corner of her lower lip, looking as if she had wanted to respond, but she caught herself at the last moment. Chills raced up and down Chloe's spine. If Madeleine had asked her to jump off a cliff in that moment, she wouldn't have hesitated. God, this woman was dangerous.

Turning away slowly and with purpose, Chloe made her way to the sanctity of the deck that looked out onto the mountain. The lights on the trails had been turned off, leaving the flickering lights from inside the lodge and the fireplace as the only sources of illumination. Spotting a nearby wooden bench, she seated herself gingerly on the back of it, planting both feet firmly on the sturdy seat. Taking deep breaths, filling her chest with crisp air, she felt some of her worry fade.

Today had certainly been an adventure. Madeleine had been her typical enticing and perplexing self. Despite her initial wariness, she had accepted the challenge of mastering her snowboarding skills eagerly. The first time she had fallen hard, she popped back up and continued down the hill without hesitation.

And on the ski lift, she'd asked Chloe how she felt her work with Science Olympiad was going. She had listened intently, asking specific questions about each different event despite not sharing Chloe's passion for the laws of thermodynamics. Chloe was being steadily drawn into deeper waters, pulled out to sea as if by a rip tide. She was fully aware of the danger she was in. Captivating though she might be, Madeleine also was constantly wavering, open one moment and closed off the next. Chloe didn't know what was worse—being held at arm's length or the risk that Madeleine would let her in.

She sighed. Everything had been so simple not so long ago. Find a job and maybe figure out where to go next. But now? She had a job, yes. As for the question of where to go next, she was nowhere nearer to answering it than she had been four months ago. The pain she felt at the thought of losing the connections she had made with her students and her team made her realize she had a pretty good idea of what she wanted. Would she be able to pursue it, though? Would teaching and coaching allow her to pay back her student loans?

"Young Clark may not have broken any of your bones when you stopped him from plowing into me, but hypothermia is a thing, you know."

Madeleine's voice from out of the darkness was as smooth as the velvety blackness in the sky. Chloe patted the empty stretch of bench next to her.

"I'm wearing a sweater, you're the one in a button-up. I can't imagine it's very warm."

"Don't you know alcohol is the best sweater? I'll be fine."

Chloe heard the playfulness in her voice, but she was wary. With the unpredictable push-and-pull routine Madeleine had been giving her lately she couldn't know when the playful Madeleine would disappear and closed-off Madeleine would make her appearance again.

As Madeleine perched deftly next to her on the back of the bench, Chloe found herself reflecting on how easily and openly she'd interacted with the kids on the slope. She had an amazing capacity for connection with kids. She treated her students and her players with respect and in return they respected and adored her.

Chloe couldn't help but wonder what kept her from that level of connection in adult relationships. Whatever it was, she doubted she would find out tonight.

"I'm really glad you came today." *Good, keep it simple. Simple is good.*

"I am too. Today was fantastic, and I know it was all because of you. So truly, thank you, Chloe."

A shiver made its way down Chloe's spine, a visceral reaction to hearing Madeleine say her name so sincerely.

"You're welcome. I had so much fun. I'm yours anytime."

Chloe cringed. Had she seriously just said that? She stood and stepped down off the bench. Her only hope was to move. Madeleine followed suit, a few steps behind. Halting at the railing, Chloe centered herself again, focusing on her breathing. She discovered that measured breaths were all she could manage; anything more resulted in waves of pain radiating from the vicinity of her collarbone.

She glanced at Madeleine, registering smooth, calm features illuminated by the soft light emanating from the windows of the lodge. The firelight was dancing on her skin. She looked back toward the darkened slopes. She needed separation, something to break the spell she was falling under once again.

"Did you have any idea Landon was coming today? It was weird I never even saw him out there."

Icy tension rippled out of Madeleine. *Mission accomplished. Spell broken.* Not to mention the wonderful rapport they'd enjoyed on the slopes. A dozen words or so and she'd again managed to piss Madeleine off completely. *Great.*

"I had no idea." Her clipped tones invited no response. Not that Chloe felt like giving one. If Madeleine was going to be so evasive, she refused to feel bad about referring to aspects of their shared reality. She let the silence sit, wondering if this was always going to be the way Madeleine reacted to mentions of Landon. Then, remembering her own irrational and self-destructive behavior of late, she softened. She hated to think this was how Hannah had felt when dealing with her last year.

"Madeleine, is everything all right? Something is going on and I wish you would talk to me."

"Everything's fine."

"Okay, I just feel like…" Chloe wasn't able to finish that thought.

Madeleine's voice canceled out her own as she spun into Chloe's personal space. "Just leave it alone. Jesus."

Taking a breath, Chloe eased back. "I don't believe you don't want to talk about it. Just know I'm here when you do, okay?"

The sag in Madeleine's shoulders broke Chloe's heart. Though she had absolutely no idea what was happening between her and Landon, it was as if she witnessed the weight of the world draping itself on her. Without thinking, she reached out, needing to lend Madeleine a physical show of support. She brought her hand to Madeleine's shoulder and gently squeezed, feeling cords of muscle taut with emotion.

As it had the first time they were close to each other, the air shifted and Chloe felt her heartbeat throughout her body. She struggled to focus.

Madeleine turned into Chloe's touch. She closed the distance between them, her eyes molten. Chloe's breathing hitched as Madeleine's face came closer, tantalizing lips parted and expectant.

When the contact came, Chloe was stunned. As soft, sweet lips danced with her own, Madeleine pulled her closer, a hand in the middle of her lower back bringing their bodies into contact and loosing a cascade of pleasure. Her hips pinned Chloe to the railing. She gasped, pain mingling with exquisite pleasure.

Chloe cupped Madeleine's jaw, holding her face tight against hers as Madeleine explored her lips hungrily. A low moan escaped between them. Had it been hers? Madeleine's? Chloe didn't know and she didn't care. She wasn't sure where one of them ended and the other began. It didn't matter. She never wanted the feeling to end.

Catching Chloe's bottom lip with her teeth, Madeleine tugged gently, sending shockwaves through her system, and placed burning kisses along her jawline. She traced a path to Chloe's earlobe, which she gave another gentle tug to before shifting her focus to Chloe's exposed neck. She heard herself grind out a low moan. Madeleine's hands found their way to her waist, slid under her shirt and beneath the waistband of her jeans, seeking her hipbones. A tug of pressure on her neck from Madeleine's teeth ripped another moan from her throat. Madeleine's answering whimper shattered her control. She reached out, finding the front of Madeleine's shirt, and tugged her face back toward her own, and resumed their scorching kiss. Madeleine slid her thigh between Chloe's legs, and she gasped, the pressure nearly undoing her. Her head reeled, her back arched. Madeleine pressed herself more firmly into her, moving her hands to Chloe's sides and sliding them upward along Chloe's ribs, exposing bare flesh. She rocked her hips slightly and whimpered again, this time more urgently.

A door slammed in the distance, ripping Madeleine's attention away from Chloe and bringing everything to a halt. Chloe couldn't have moved if she wanted to, trapped by the ecstasy she felt from being pinned by Madeleine. Madeleine, on the other hand… She quickly removed her leg from between Chloe's, the color draining from her face. Feeling exposed and rejected, Chloe swallowed painfully.

"Fuck." The whispered curse escaped Madeleine's lips. She stepped back abruptly, the passion that had been smoldering in her eyes now tinged with fear and worry.

At a loss for what to say, Chloe pushed off from the railing, but pulled up short as pain sliced through her upper torso with a vengeance. Madeleine took another step backward. Bringing her fingers to her mouth, she traced her lips with them as if reliving what they had just shared. Shaking her head, she lingered for another instant. Then she was gone.

Chloe swallowed again, aching at the loss of her touch, a single word bouncing around her head. *Fuck.*

* * *

The digital clock in her adjoining room in the suite showed 4:13 a.m. Taylor and Anne were surely sound asleep at this point, but Chloe was giving up the fight. She had slept for a grand total of forty-five minutes by her reckoning. The pain in her collarbone had kept her from getting comfortable, but it hadn't kept her from wondering about what the hell happened between her and Madeleine. Despite having initially planned to stay over, Madeleine had left without even bothering to give Anne or Taylor an excuse. That didn't fill Chloe with confidence.

To top things off, every time she moved now pain jolted her, bringing with it new questions and worries. She was glad she had thrown a book in her duffel. Now was the perfect time to crack it open. She sat up gingerly. She would spend the next few hours trying to read, since sleep was not an option. Leaving the bed, she opened the curtains, revealing an unobstructed expanse of star-filled sky. At least the view was magnificent. She stood there, silently taking it all in. She lost track of time, transfixed by the mountain in darkness.

Moving away from the window, she contemplated her clothing options. She hadn't had the energy to change out of her white T-shirt before collapsing in bed. It would have to do. She dragged herself to her open bag and managed to put on clean sweatpants and socks. Tossing the comforter back on the bed, she piled some pillows against the headboard and began to read.

The light knock on the adjoining door a few hours later got her attention. Mercifully, the reading had distracted her enough to feel almost comfortable.

"Come on in."

Anne appeared in the doorway, carrying matching cups of coffee from the little café in the lodge. The smell wafted to Chloe. She let out an audible sigh. Anne's eyebrow lifted. As she came close enough to take in Chloe's appearance, concern appeared on her face.

"Rough night?"

"I guess. I didn't sleep well. That smells divine and, incidentally, reinforces my belief that you *are* an angel." Anne's chuckle quieted as she watched the cautious way Chloe readjusted herself on the pillows in order to take the coffee from her outstretched hand.

"You're moving pretty carefully. Are you sure you're all right after your spill?" Anne's features revealed all too clearly that she hadn't believed Chloe's insistence that she was fine last night. Chloe knew Anne would see through her bluff; that was literally part of her job.

"I don't think it's anything to worry about." Chloe shrugged but immediately regretted it. Anne stood next to the bed, sizing Chloe up.

"Let me see it."

Anne being forceful was an entirely new experience. Chloe instantly understood how this mellow woman kept pace with Taylor. Conceding defeat, she contemplated how best to allow Anne access to her collarbone. With Anne's help, she managed to slip her T-shirt over her head. It revealed a pretty nasty sight. Chloe hadn't looked closely at her body in a mirror since the collision, so she hadn't anticipated seeing a protruding bump where her collarbone normally lay flat.

"Well, I stand corrected." Anne sat down next to her on the edge of the bed. "I told Taylor you had a good head on your shoulders. Clearly I was wrong. You didn't think this needed a doctor?" Anne's disbelief was almost laughable. The genuine concern in her voice convinced Chloe that laughing was a bad idea, for a variety of reasons.

"Anne, I swear to you, I didn't realize it was this bad. I mean, I didn't really examine it closely last night. Yeah, it hurt like hell, but I figured I was going to be sore." She decided to leave out the part about how being near Madeleine had singlehandedly short-circuited all other brain function and she hadn't been thinking clearly since then. Anne was already questioning her sanity as it was.

Chloe was met with temporary silence as Anne contemplated her response.

"It's just… I have been to so many doctors and had so many surgeries I honestly thought I would be okay. I didn't lose feeling or have any tingling. I wanted to have a normal weekend without being fucking hospitalized."

Though apparently accepting Chloe's rationale, Anne set her face again with that formidable determination. "We are going to see a doctor. There's a very good chance you've fractured your clavicle and it's displaced. If you're lucky you'll get away with just a sling, but I want an ortho's opinion. Depending on the X-ray, you might need surgery."

Resigned to her fate, though secretly relieved at the prospect of getting something to ease the pain, Chloe allowed Anne to help her get ready and take her for another visit to another urgent care.

CHAPTER FOURTEEN

As her fourth-block students made their way out the door heading for their lockers, Chloe began cleaning off the whiteboard. Each swipe jostled her sling, though the pain was fading. She had left the urgent care with some decent pain medicine, managing to avoid surgery entirely. It had been almost a week, though, and she was ready to rip the sling off. She was also considering locking Madeleine in her classroom to get her to talk to her, but she had so far resisted both temptations.

Returning her attention to the board, she considered today's class session. She reserved the last half hour of one block a week for groups to work on homework problems together with little or no input from her. It gave them practice at sorting things out with others, and listening to their discussions helped her gauge what she needed to spend more time on with them. Her own group review sessions in college had been where she had really solidified her knowledge.

She had been pleased with how today went but was also frustrated that at the very end Kirk kept insisting they do the problem his way—a method that Chloe had explicitly described as incorrect earlier in the block. She kept quiet, though. She would find a way to bring it up with him next week. She considered how best to approach him. He was smart, but incredibly stubborn and at times insufferable. Not wanting to write off a student that way, she decided to give him the benefit of the doubt. Again. Maybe this time she'd get through to him.

As she continued erasing the board, her thoughts turned to Madeleine—as they had been doing consistently since the skiing trip. She'd been fighting her attraction to her since they met, attributing her foot-dragging to the turbulent state of her professional and personal life. Now, however, there was nothing to hide behind anymore. Employed full-time and moving past Elaine with unexpected help from Nora, she finally felt clarity in what she wanted personally.

Madeleine obviously didn't have that. Running away from a kiss like that without a word didn't exactly scream "emotionally available." She hadn't imagined the signals Madeleine had been giving off; the attraction was mutual. But the way Madeleine had run from her, from their kiss, had hurt. She couldn't help but wonder how to proceed.

"I never asked you if things worked out with your UMass tutee."

Madeleine's voice made Chloe jump. She hadn't seen her at all on Monday. They'd crossed paths at lunch on Tuesday, when Madeleine had been surprised to see her in a sling and wished her a speedy recovery. Her solicitation was comforting, but after she'd made sure Chloe was all right physically, she left lunch early, citing some papers that needed grading. Chloe hadn't seen her since; she got the distinct impression she was being avoided.

"I'm surprised you remembered. It feels like forever ago that I told you about that."

"It does, doesn't it? I still wanted to check in, make sure you're either happily single with no guilty conscience or newly coupled up."

"So, it was a morbid curiosity that brought you. I get it."

"No, it's definitely concern that's motivating me to ask, but curiosity may have been a small factor." She held up her thumb and forefinger, separated by a millimeter. "Seriously though, how have things been in that department?"

Biting the bullet, Chloe decided to jump right in.

"Well, I went to visit her a couple of weeks ago, after the Halloween party."

Something flashed across Madeleine's features too quickly for Chloe to be sure what it was she saw. Immediately it was replaced with a calm expression. Chloe swallowed her annoyance. Madeleine had no right to feel jealous, and she definitely shouldn't be getting a thrill from the possibility that she might be.

"How did that go? I didn't realize you wanted to make the trip."

"I hadn't planned on ever making it again, honestly. But that felt like the one thing I still had some control over. Something I could still do something about. You were right, by the way, I owed it to Nora. So I met her for lunch. And I'm so glad I did."

Madeleine remained quiet, taking in what Chloe was saying.

"She has moved past the crush, I'm happy to say. She took time to focus on herself, and she's got a new girlfriend who sounds pretty incredible. She doesn't resent me for shutting down on her without explaining anything, which in itself is a miracle."

Madeleine's features lightened again as she dealt with the information Chloe was providing, filling in gaps and making connections. Soon words began forming on her lips. Chloe was amused watching the process unfold.

"What's your question?"

"I'm trying to understand. What drove the final wedge between you? What made you run away? I know you said you abandoned her, but was there something else?"

Almost a week without talking, no mention of their kiss, and Madeleine unknowingly opens the subject of Elaine? How could Madeleine be so skilled at delving into the most nuanced, complicated elements of Chloe's past, but unable to even touch the topic of their shared kiss?

Chloe was having trouble keeping up. Making the task infinitely more difficult was the fact that Madeleine consistently impressed Chloe with her perceptiveness and her empathy. She had a grace about her. She worked to untangle and understand other people's truths, making everyone around her feel truly known.

Take now, for instance. Chloe hadn't talked with her about Elaine; she'd simply mentioned during their exchange on Halloween that in the past she'd been drawn into an unhealthy relationship. It was one of her least favorite subjects, but something had compelled her to talk about it with her.

Chloe considered her options: ignore the truth of the thing or make the story her own, claim it like Nora said. She took a deep breath. "My old advisor, she crossed a lot of personal boundaries, and I didn't want Nora involved."

"'Personal boundaries'?" Madeleine asked cautiously.

"She wanted a relationship and she wasn't above using her power to make it happen. So it did. When I finally said no, well, she didn't take it well. I wasn't the first, unfortunately. Nora told me there's a lawsuit being filed against her now."

"I'm so sorry."

"Don't be. It was over a year ago and it wasn't your fault."

A tear sprang forth, unbidden. *Damn!* She had managed to talk about Elaine with Nora without crying, and here she was falling to pieces around Madeleine. Chloe turned, battling for composure. A hand on her arm pulled her back around and into a chair. Madeleine sat down beside her.

"Hey, Chloe, it's all right."

Five simple words. The tenderness in her voice as she offered her company and support was Chloe's undoing.

Madeleine moved to pull her into a hug, and Chloe felt herself stiffen. When Madeleine didn't relent, though, her resolve weakened. Madeleine's chest rose and fell in sync with her own. There was strength in the arms that cradled her, solace in the rhythmic patterns that her hands were drawing on her back.

As Chloe sank deeper into the embrace, Madeleine's hands took more sweeping strokes up and down her back, trailing her hands along the curve of her spine and the expanse of her neck, then slowly brushing the hair out of her eyes. Her touches left chills in their wake, but the contact was as soothing as it was stimulating.

Gradually Chloe let go of the anger she'd been clinging to, allowing it to empty out of her. Now there was only Madeleine, tracing the path of the single tear that had fallen down Chloe's cheek before returning her hand to her back.

She cherished the lingering contact. She wasn't alone. She allowed that fact to wash over her, focusing on her breathing, maintaining a slow and steady rhythm. Resting her head on Madeleine's chest, she heard Madeleine's breathing catch and become choppier and uneven.

Chloe's body was humming. Reveling in the sensations Madeleine's hands were rousing, she remained as she was, not wanting to break the moment. Madeleine continued to explore new paths, tracing more boldly along her neck, the line of her jaw, upward into her hair. Chloe closed her eyes and lifted her chin, inching closer, picturing Madeleine's face, a breath away from her own, the tanned skin, her gently sloping cheekbones golden in the late afternoon light.

She looked up, her green eyes meeting Madeleine's hazel ones. She dangled helplessly on the edge of indecision, terror preventing her from what she wanted to do, temptation urging her onward.

A cough in the hallway ripped both of them from the moment and into the next. Landon stood in the doorway, seething with rage. Chloe nearly leapt out of her chair in her haste to make the embrace end. Madeleine, however, simply straightened up, stood, and addressed him.

"Can I help you with something, Landon?" she asked seriously in a tone that did not encourage small talk.

"I was coming to check in on the progress of Chloe's season, offer some advice or help if she wanted it. Make sure she hadn't broken any more bones. Apparently you are helping her enough, Madeleine," Landon spat out, his condescension magnified by his anger. Chloe saw through his lame excuses. He hadn't been dropping by to chat. He'd been stalking Madeleine.

"I'm all set. Thanks, though," Chloe replied, recovering from the interruption. He remained standing in the doorway, glowering. The muscles in his jaw were working nearly as hard as the vein pulsing in his neck.

"Anything else?" Madeleine asked, her desire for him to leave evident.

"No, that's all. Don't let me interrupt," he taunted, lingering for a moment as if contemplating throwing a few more accusatory looks their way. Apparently satisfied that he had conveyed his disgust, he turned slowly and walked away.

Chloe was reeling. Madeleine was back in her room for ten minutes and they had picked up right where they had left off on the mountain. But now she was sitting on the counter near the window. Silent. Shutting her out again. Chloe's disquiet twisted into knots with every passing moment. Was there any way to salvage what was happening between the two of them, whatever that was? She had to know. Weighing her need for answers against her fear, she broke the silence.

"Madeleine, what's going on?"

Madeleine responded with more silence, though she did turn to face her. After waiting an eternity, she spoke. "What do you mean?"

Gathering her thoughts, Chloe narrowed her questions from a thousand down to the most pressing.

"Well, what's in your head? Or what's going on between you and Landon? I mean is he following you? What's going on?"

Madeleine's eyes were stormy, pain and want gathering there. Chloe wanted so badly to reach out to her, but the pain she felt at being repeatedly abandoned kept her rooted to the spot. Perspiration gathered at her temples.

"Nothing's going on with Landon." Chloe couldn't help but notice Madeleine refused to look directly at her when she told the lie. At least she knew it was a lie too.

"I don't believe that. And neither do you."

Madeleine's jaw clenched. She'd finally pushed too far.

"There's nothing. Let it go."

It took every ounce of strength she possessed to swallow the things she wanted to say. They would fall on deaf ears and pushing harder would only guarantee more of this icy silence. Corralling the thoughts galloping around in her head, she focused on slowing her heart rate. By the time she was able to breathe deeply enough to settle into herself, enough of the icy distance separating them had thawed for her to ask a different question.

"Okay, what are you thinking about?"

The pregnant pause that followed made Chloe wonder if she should even follow this through. Did it matter what Madeleine was thinking if she wasn't going to share it or do anything about it? Something was on her mind: her hand was at her wrist again, playing with the navy hair tie there.

"You."

Chloe stumbled. That was the last response she expected. Her pulse, unpredictable whenever she was near Madeleine, was off to the races again.

"What do you want from me here, Madeleine? I want to be here for you, but you keep shutting me out."

Madeleine's angst was etched on her features for a moment, and then it was as if a switch had been flipped. Her features were set and all evidence of the attraction to her that Chloe had glimpsed was gone. Only anger and resignation remained.

"I don't want anything from you. I can't. I'm sorry. I have to go."

And with that, Madeleine walked out, leaving Chloe floundering in her wake.

* * *

Chloe had never in her life been more thankful for basketball. The focus and energy it took to manage her team as well as help Taylor with the varsity was propelling her through the days remaining until winter break. If she could make it through this week, she would have a full week to see her parents, relax, and sulk before she had to face Taylor and Anne's wedding. While she was looking forward to celebrating their marriage, the prospect of doing so with Madeleine also in attendance was agonizing.

They had pushed their highly charged interactions to the periphery of their consciousnesses during the school day. When occasionally they showed up for lunch with Taylor on the same day, they were both pleasant, but there had been a fundamental shift between them, and it was becoming impossible for Chloe to ignore. Knowing what it felt like to kiss Madeleine reignited tortured memories every time she saw her. Knowing how much Madeleine was hurting tormented her when she went home. She got some sleep each night, but it was barely enough to keep her going.

She hoped that retreating from Madeleine would help her move on, that maybe it would dampen the attraction, emotional and physical, that she had been harboring for her. What else could she do? Madeleine was able to laugh and joke with her comfortably. Chloe had to do the same. They could be friends again—if she could just pull it together.

She was happy to say that teaching was going better than her relationship with Madeleine. Today had been a really good day, in fact, even though the students had been buzzing about the holidays ahead. There was only so much she could do to make curvilinear motion and centripetal force more exciting than the impending break. By the time she'd made it to her last class, however, she'd decided their youthful enthusiasm was warranted. She didn't have the strength to rein them in anyway. She had caved and let them start on their homework fifteen minutes early. There was a lot more talk at the tables about gifts and family festivities than there was about the problem set, but, truthfully it was kind of cute to see them so jazzed about break. They needed it nearly as much as Chloe did.

Grabbing her bag now and shutting off the lights, she headed toward the gym, grateful that there was a thirty-minute after-school window before team practice started. Now that she didn't have to wear the sling, she was more than ready to get her full range of motion back. She wanted to shoot for a bit before the girls got there. She decided to go there by way of the English hall. Stupid, but Madeleine hadn't been at lunch today and at this point she'd settle for a glimpse of her, just to make sure she was doing okay. Instead of Madeleine, though, she ran into Taylor.

"Taylor?" Chloe couldn't remember ever seeing her in this hall.

"Perfect. Now I can give them to both of you. Come in here. I told Anne I was hand delivering these. I'm not paying postage when I see you both every day." Taylor beckoned Chloe into Madeleine's room. Pushing down a tiny thrill of excitement, Chloe tried to set her face in a relaxed expression.

Madeleine greeted them from her desk as they walked in. Chloe couldn't help but smile at the sight. Seeing Madeleine in her element would always make her happy.

"Hey, guys. How's it going?"

"Oh fantastic, I've got you both here. Anne will be happy to learn that I did not, contrary to prediction, lose the invitations before I had the chance to deliver them. I would like to cordially invite you to our wedding. Sorry they aren't mailed, but I think it's stupid, considering."

As they all laughed together, Chloe felt genuinely comfortable in Madeleine's presence for the first time since she had run out of her classroom the previous week.

"Thank you kindly, Taylor. I'm honored." Madeleine's delight didn't make it all the way to her eyes. Was she imagining things?

"You're welcome. Chloe, I have to go get some stuff from my car, the new pump and needles. The gym's full of Kurtz's kids. They needed the gym to film some class project so you'll have to wait until they're done to get in there. I'll meet you in the locker room." With that, she left.

Chloe took a breath and tried to relax. Madeleine had started out as her friend; they could get back there eventually. They had to.

"How was your day?" That was innocuous enough to start out with.

"Have a seat. I feel like I've seen you only once or twice lately. It's been weird."

Chloe kept her thoughts about that to herself, waiting for Madeleine's answer about her day.

"Today was one of those days that I wanted to be over before it really got started. Right now I want a bottle of wine to myself."

Chloe laughed, knowing exactly what she meant. She relaxed a little. After some initial awkwardness, things were settling into a relatively comfortable normal.

"I know that feeling. My day wasn't that annoying, but the kids were practically vibrating in their seats all day long. I'm ready to get home and veg out."

"That sounds fantastic. But first I want a hot shower."

"Preach. Why was your day so terrible?"

Madeleine's face clouded, and Chloe sensed that something was on her mind. Not wanting to press the issue, she waited for her to divulge what had happened.

"Nothing earth-shattering. Landon came in the weight room this morning when I was working out. Not the ideal start to my morning."

"What did he do?" Chloe felt a knot of worry forming. Whatever was coming was not going to be good.

"Nothing serious. He's just being an immature pig." Madeleine tried to dismiss Chloe's concerns. Chloe knew if she was willing to bring this up, however, that something had happened, something she needed to get out. She wanted to believe that Madeleine was turning to her because their connection was deep enough that she knew she could confide in her. The other possibility was that whatever happened was bad enough that she couldn't keep it to herself. That worried her immensely.

Several moments of silence passed before, finally, Madeleine gave in to the urge to spill.

"I had finished running on the treadmill and was stretching for a cool down when he came in. He just stared at me. Gawked, actually. It made me nauseous, but I ignored him, refusing to acknowledge it."

Chloe felt her anger stirring. Landon believed he could do whatever he wanted without reproach for two reasons. First he was a man. Second he was close with the district administration, his uncle being the superintendent of schools and all. Something he mentioned with some frequency.

Madeleine continued, her account only adding to Chloe's unrest and mounting fury. "He came over to me when I started lifting, trying to start up conversation, all while taking his shirt off. I barely got out one-word responses and told him I needed to focus."

"You need to tell him he makes you uncomfortable!" Chloe interjected, feeling helpless to prevent Madeleine from experiencing what she had with Elaine.

"I know," Madeleine stated flatly. "I didn't think it was necessary, until he started trying to help me with my form. He came up behind me and started trying to do adjustments. I just walked away from that lift and told him I was fine. He came over one last time while I was doing curls, ran his hand from my thigh up to my ribcage, and said my form was flawless on this one, but he was available at all hours to help me perfect it. I told him thanks for the offer and kept lifting."

Madeleine's dismissal of the blatant sexual harassment tore Chloe up. Ignoring it would only lead to bigger problems later on; Chloe's flight from UMass was a testament to that fact.

"Madeleine, I'm so sorry. I really think you should talk to someone about it. He's not going to stop if you don't." Chloe knew she risked pushing her away again, but she had to take the chance.

"Right, thanks. I've got that," Madeleine snapped.

"I can't watch this happen, not to you," Chloe burst out with a ferocity so intense Madeleine could not hold her gaze. Before long, Chloe's temper won out. Being patient was probably the way to go, but her concern for Madeleine eclipsed her rationality. She walked out. It was all she could to do keep from sprinting down the hallway.

Madeleine was caring, empathetic, sweet, and smart. She was independent and strong. Chloe respected her so much. Despite all of that, or maybe because of it, her situation brought rushing back to Chloe the sense of complete helplessness she had felt when she was unable to stop what was happening with Elaine. This time it was magnified by the fact that this was hurting Madeleine and once again she could do nothing to fix it.

Looking around, Chloe found herself near the gym. She headed for the nearest exit in the side hallway near the entrance to the locker rooms. She needed to get outside and calm the inferno inside her. As she reached for the handle, Madeleine's voice stopped her.

"Where are you going?" she demanded.

Frozen, Chloe didn't answer. She didn't turn around; she couldn't. She heard Madeleine take a few steps toward her, but still refused to turn around.

"Why are you so upset by this? It's not your problem!" she demanded again, beginning to lash out.

"Because I care about you." Chloe paused, searching for the words, "I can't make you, but I want you to handle this so you don't…"

The rest of her sentence was swallowed up by Madeleine's outburst as she closed the gap between them. "How would you like me to do that? Handle it the same way you did with your advisor? I can't run away!" Her voice was filled with anger and fear; she was nearly shouting.

Though Chloe knew she had thrown the barb because she was hurting, she couldn't keep herself from responding. She spun herself around with such force that she knocked them both sideways, pinning Madeleine against the wall. Though they remained separated by a few inches, it was not enough room to allow what she had intended to say to fall from her lips.

Chloe slammed her right hand onto the wall to Madeleine's left, steadying herself. Her skin tingled from the adrenaline coursing through her and the hairs on her neck stood on end. Held in place by her own confusion, she felt her anger barely receding—and the fire in her veins growing.

A yell from within the locker room shattered the moment and shocked them into action. "Chloe, where in God's name did you put the scorebook?" Taylor's voice echoed off the tiled floors.

Chloe immediately stepped back, searching for something to say to ease the ball of awkwardness insinuating itself between her and Madeleine. Nothing came to her. She wouldn't apologize for wanting her to take this seriously. She decided she could allow herself to apologize for losing her temper instead, then changed her mind.

"I've got to go help Taylor. Drive safe in the snow and have a great holiday."

With that, she stepped sideways and walked into the locker room, reminding herself as she did that she didn't need or want these kinds of complications in her life. Before either of them could damage the other more than had already been done, she needed to pull herself out of Madeleine's orbit. Her only option for doing that was to change her own trajectory. She hoped she had enough strength to do it. She'd made a career out of studying the laws of the physical universe, but she couldn't explain the power with which Madeleine drew her in, physically and emotionally.

CHAPTER FIFTEEN

January

Saturday

"Chloe, I love you. And I'm glad I know I can outsource my work to you. But it's literally been two weeks, and you've avoided talking to me about that giant elephant over there. I'm taking a stand here."

Chloe set down the mason jar she had been working on, knowing what was coming next. Taylor had been patient, as had Hannah. She, on the other hand, had been brooding and moody—basically impossible—since she'd left Madeleine's classroom two weeks ago. It wasn't that they hadn't talked; they had interacted. The problem was the impenetrable wall Madeleine had thrown up with regard to anything that wasn't work-related. Chloe hadn't reached out to her and she wasn't planning on doing so, having decided that it was best if she simply accepted that Madeleine wanted to forget, to put what they'd had out of reach. She needed that. That put Chloe in such a miserable place, though.

"Put the centerpiece down and no one gets hurt." Startled from her thoughts, Chloe realized she had spaced out yet again. She pushed the glass jar away and raised both hands in surrender. Taylor appeared satisfied.

"Now that I have your attention, I'm going to drop some truth bombs."

"Taylor, I…"

Taylor cut Chloe off, raising her hand and turning her head away, not willing to listen to any more of her lame excuses.

"You and Madeleine connected. She's been pretty shut off to anything personal like *that* since she got here. I think someone hurt her pretty badly before and I hope you've realized the same thing."

Chloe nodded, unsure if she was allowed to speak yet.

Taylor continued. "So, just so you know, I know there was something happening between you. I mean, I called you out on it before we skied and since I have fucking eyes I saw you two at dinner during your 'vegetable moment.'" Chloe chuckled. Taylor's version of things was so matter-of-fact.

"What I need to hear from you is what the hell happened to drive the wedge between you and what you're going to do about it." Chloe opened her mouth to speak, but Taylor silenced her again. "Because I love the piss out of you and Madeleine, and you know I want to help you figure it out. That being said, I'm marrying the most incredible woman on the planet and I want—no, I need—you guys to figure out how to coexist in T-minus four days."

The guilt that hit Chloe was so powerful she lost the train of thought she'd been on. Even though she had spent nearly every night after practice for the past week or so trying to help Taylor and Anne in whatever ways she could, she'd blocked out the fact that the distance between her and Madeleine could impact others at the wedding. *Shit!*

"Taylor, I'm a terrible friend. I'm sorry."

"Oh, shut up. You're not a bad friend. But I thought it was high time for a little perspective and now you need to tell me what the fuck happened so I can talk to Anne and then come back to you with some good advice."

"Great. I'll even pretend the advice came right from you."

"Perfect. Now what happened? Things were all cozy at Black Mountain."

"Well, the day was really good. We both had a lot of fun."

Taylor raised her eyebrows, clearly impatient to get into the meat of the issue.

"I don't know how to describe it, Taylor. It was like things were moving in a good direction. We laughed and talked. She told me about the national team, I talked to her about some of my baggage. There was some flirting going on, but she would pull back periodically. I felt like I was on a fucking roller coaster."

Taylor nodded, her expression interested, as if she was piecing together some sort of puzzle.

"That night in the restaurant she got visibly upset over Landon being at the resort. Which makes sense, considering he continues to pursue her despite her rebuffing him. It's sexual harassment at the very least, although to me it seems like it has escalated to stalking, but I don't know all of the details. So that's happening."

Chloe stopped short, frustrated with the situation, but also with herself for telling Taylor without Madeleine's permission. She couldn't take it back now. She would have to trust Taylor to keep her confidence. She charged forward.

"When you guys went to the bar, I went outside and she joined me a bit later on the deck. I pushed her a little about what was happening and then out of nowhere she kissed me."

Chloe stopped, unable to say any more. It almost didn't feel real to her that the kiss had happened. She wanted to keep it safe.

"I'm gonna need a little context here. What happened? A first kiss doesn't usually shut everything down when you're two consenting adults."

"Well, it wasn't your average kiss. Jesus, Taylor, it was so intense. I've never been kissed like that before. And she was the one in charge. But when things got going, she backed off, terrified. She basically ran away and didn't talk to me for a week."

"Okay, this is making a bit more sense to me now." Taylor nodded, understanding clicking into place for her. Chloe was irritated. Taylor was trying to help, but it felt like she was leaving her in the dark.

"Well, I'm glad it makes sense to you, because last week she came into my room asking me about UMass. I told her even more about last year and basically broke down in front of her. She almost kissed me again, Landon interrupted us, and then she ran again. I'm getting pretty sick of feeling like I'm on some jacked-up soap opera."

Chloe was almost yelling by the end of her tirade. She hadn't meant to take it out on Taylor, but reality was catching up to her. This wasn't going away, and she didn't have any hope that it would get better. A noise in the hallway drew her attention. Anne walked through the doorway with three beers in her hand. Casually setting them on three coasters amidst the wedding explosion that was the coffee table, she chose the armchair to settle in, grabbed some supplies, and started crafting quietly. Chloe shook her head. She couldn't be too embarrassed here. Anne was the most perceptive person she knew, and it was highly likely she was already twelve steps ahead of her and Taylor, waiting for them to catch up.

"Thanks, babe. You're the bees' knees, you know that?" Taylor inclined her beer at Anne, blew her a kiss, and took a long swig from the bottle. Returning her focus to Chloe, she motioned toward Chloe's beer.

"Take a drink. I don't want you to lose your voice for the game." Chloe tried to hide her amusement. God, Taylor was ridiculous. She was also a unicorn sent from above to keep her sane, as was Anne.

"So basically, she's falling for you, but she's scared shitless. Things are good, my friend. You're going to go to the wedding, be yourself, dance with the girls, and let her come to you. If she doesn't, I'm saving the heavy artillery for after the honeymoon. When we get back, I'll sic my bride on her."

"I love you, but please don't refer to me like some sort of rabid attack animal," Anne said quietly. Taylor smiled sheepishly. Anne went on. "I have to agree with Taylor. I know it doesn't sound easy, but I think if you focus on enjoying the wedding things will settle down a bit. Then you two can find time to talk when she's ready."

"I don't know if I can wait until she's ready." Voicing her fear out loud shook Chloe to the core. Here she was thinking she had done so well putting the past in the past, and now she was in that same pathetic, vulnerable place all over again.

"If you don't want to wait, you've got the best wingman on earth to help you move on."

Anne chimed in, "Yeah, basketball. And when that doesn't take your mind off things, you can come over here and entertain Taylor."

The laughter surrounding her was a soothing balm. Chloe only wondered if she could really pull herself together in time for the wedding.

* * *

It had been nice spending Christmas with her family. Chloe had hoped they would be enough to keep her mind occupied, but even a warm house filled with cousins, aunts, uncles, and both sets of grandparents hadn't been able to clear her head completely. Letting her concerns slip to Taylor had been a relief in the moment, but now she was worried about having violated Madeleine's trust. She wanted to help, but Madeleine needed to handle things her own way. That didn't make it easier to stop thinking about Landon's abusive behavior. Complicating things further, thoughts of how rapidly things had deteriorated with Madeleine kept sneaking in all break. When things were right, they should come naturally, simply. The frenetic volleying back and forth with Madeleine certainly didn't seem simple.

While their situation had left Chloe distracted for most of the break, she did have the upcoming wedding to look forward to—sans the part where she and Madeleine might have to interact. She was overjoyed to be involved in helping Taylor and Anne cement their union and optimistic enough to hold out the hope that she might be able to reestablish her friendship with Madeleine after she gave them both a reprieve from their highly charged interactions. Oddly enough, that thought was always much more convincing when she was miles away from Madeleine.

Going to the wedding had meant figuring out what to wear to it, another useful, though challenging distraction. She had decided the week before to wear a pair of light gray dress pants, slim fit and closely cropped at the ankles. She had purchased them over the summer when she realized she had no properly fitting dress clothes. Going for broke, she had had them tailored; she could never find anything off the rack that fit her for length as well as in the waist. She was planning on pairing them with a matching vest and a chambray blue button-up.

Unsure what shoes she was going to wear, she had gone shopping during the break to find the perfect pair and had fallen head over heels for a pair of vintage light brown leather oxfords with a brogue design. They were one of the best pair of shoes she had ever owned, she had to admit, but they had made her wallet cry. Casting fiscal caution to the winds, she went for broke and got a dark blue pocket square as well. For Anne and Taylor's wedding she had to step it up.

When Saturday afternoon arrived, Chloe was all sorts of jittery. Hoping to burn off a little of her anxiousness, she went for a run on the old treadmill that her landlady had set up across from the washer and dryer in the unfinished basement. She had told her she was welcome to use it any time. It wasn't exactly state-of the-art, probably never had been, but the even footing it provided was better than trying to navigate the town's icy streets. With her luck, she would slip, fall, and end up in urgent care again, this time with a broken leg instead of a broken nose or collarbone.

She stretched out, set the speed to four miles per hour, and began to run, reflecting as she usually did on her relationship with Madeleine. If she was honest with herself she had known early on that the friendship that was forming was never going to be purely platonic. She had wanted it to be, sincerely she had. Well, maybe she had wanted it to be platonic after the shitstorm Elaine had caused.

She did not enjoy having her emotions tossed about like a cat's plaything each time she encountered Madeleine, for better or worse. It made the work she had put into dealing with that grad school mess, focusing on herself and what she wanted, feel almost wasted. Her life was becoming another lesbian stereotype: wounded gay girl falls for unavailable, closeted coworker.

Grabbing her towel, she dragged it over her face as she continued to run, imagining she was clearing her thoughts along with her sweat.

Tonight I am going to celebrate for Taylor and Anne. I am going to enjoy the great company, and I am going to feel great in my outfit. I will laugh and I will see Madeleine, but I will make it clear that I only want to be friends.

How many times had she said this very thing to herself? And yet she kept letting her emotions take the reins every time she saw her. Punching the button to increase the speed of the treadmill, she pounded even harder on the machine, hoping it would last a couple more minutes. Jacob's voice drifted into her consciousness as she sped up, "Que sera, sera." *Preach, Jacob,* she thought and, finally feeling a sense of reluctant peace, she finished her run.

Walking up the stairs later, she was glad that she made the time to exercise. The hour-long workout had taken some of the edge off the anticipation that was mounting within her. A quick shower would nudge her closer to the serenity she was chasing, she hoped. She immersed herself in water and music, taking full advantage of the speakers Hannah had bought her for one of her last birthdays.

Chloe studied her reflection in the mirror as she toweled her hair dry, glad she had found World Hair on a spur of the moment trip to Brunswick. Drawn to the eclectic salon by the sight of stylists with plenty of tattoos and piercings, she had decided to give it a shot. Sam, a friendly young woman with a bright blue bob, had given her a fantastic fade, texturizing the top so that she could style it easily. She would definitely be scheduling more appointments with her. Would Madeleine notice her haircut?

Chloe laughed. *Ah well, even if everything falls apart, at least there's an open bar. Jack can help me through the night. It'll have to do.*

The invitation had offered a plus one, but she would be going stag. She would give anything to have Hannah here for the night, but she hadn't been able to come due to work. Out of desperation she'd asked Jacob to come. He was out of town with his new girlfriend. Which meant Chloe couldn't even be mad at him for not joining her.

How am I going to be in the same room with her? Playing with her hair, attempting to get the blond strands to submit, Chloe reminded herself that she and Madeleine had barely talked since before break. No sparks would be flying tonight.

She took a fortifying breath. Time to make this all about Taylor and Anne. It was the least she could do. They deserved all the happiness in the world.

This is really happening.

Thankful for the warmth of her coat, Chloe hustled to her Jeep. Puffy white flakes swirled in the wind, accumulating quickly on the ground. Local forecasters were predicting an overnight snowfall of about a foot, but it was early afternoon. The plows had plenty of time to get ahead of the storm.

Approaching Marianmade, she turned down a driveway lined with mason jars filled with white lights dangling on miniature shepherds' hooks that offered soft guidance up the long drive. The beams supporting the covered entryway were wrapped in similar white lights, she saw, with the tops of the windows draped in more of the same the length of the building. Simple, beautiful, and welcoming, the wedding venue embodied the love Taylor and Anne already shared with the world.

Chloe's nerves were eclipsed by her eagerness to celebrate that love. *Tonight needn't be complicated*, she reminded herself. She parked, hopped out of her Jeep, and made her way through the falling snow to the building. The view was incredible, the dark gray building illuminated and shining in front of Casco Bay.

She was completely swept away when she walked inside. The barn doors opened directly into a small entryway, where a second set of sliding barn doors gave way to the main barn. Hanging her coat on one of the wrought-iron coatracks, she slid open the second door and stood in awe.

Cream-colored walls were accentuated by natural wooden beams, exposed and crisscrossing their way across the ceiling. A walkway that ran about twenty feet opened to the opposite end of the barn where the ceremony would take place. The barn felt intimate, with fifty simple wooden chairs arranged on both sides of the aisle. Small bouquets hung at the end of each row. A table with candles and more flowers was placed at the front where Taylor and Anne would exchange vows. Every detail felt right. Chloe hadn't realized it, but this was exactly what she had expected.

There were only a few guests present so far. Knowing it would be more than forty minutes until the ceremony began, she moved to check out the views further; they did not disappoint. Though it was freezing, she stood just outside the door to take in the landscape, watching as the snow fell and darkness crept closer. It was so peaceful. When her fingers began to tingle from the cold, she turned to find her seat.

"Chloe?"

Chloe's mind went blank as she recognized the voice. Madeleine stood mere feet away, her face a study in vulnerability. Fear, nervousness, and worry were swirling across her features.

Chloe's heart leapt into her throat at the sight of Madeleine, her long, lean legs disappearing under the hem of a short black dress that peeked out from underneath a gray wool coat. Madeleine brushed a stray hair back into place, and Chloe's fingers twitched, wishing they could take the place of hers.

"Hi, Chloe." Madeleine took two steps forward, extending her hand nervously. Chloe looked at it, confused, then reached out and took it, warmth flooding her fingers at the touch. Her brow wrinkled in confusion. A handshake?

"I wanted to reintroduce myself. I'm Madeleine Levit. I was hoping you might want to become reacquainted with the real me, not the self-absorbed ass you dealt with recently who was so ruthlessly efficient at lashing out at people who simply want the best for her."

"I thought you looked familiar." Chloe allowed her impassive façade to break into a grin and watched in delight as Madeleine's fears melted away.

"It's good to see you again. It's been a while, but I think we were getting pretty close. You know, what with me breaking two of your bones and all." Madeleine took another step forward, bringing with her the sweet smell of her perfume. She slid her arm around Chloe and pulled her into a quick hug. Holding her for a long moment, she whispered quietly, "Thank you for caring, friend."

* * *

Chloe leaned back in her chair and sighed contentedly, watching as Anne and Taylor slow-danced together joined by several dozen other couples. The ceremony had been short and powerful. Anne wore an ivory dress with an empire waist and minimal lace detailing. The gown was fitted, with a slim silhouette and highlighted Anne's classic beauty. Taylor, in her burgundy herringbone trousers and cream button-up, complemented Anne perfectly. The two had elected to write their own vows and Chloe was willing to bet that every guest had teared up at least once during the exchange. Dinner had been delicious and the celebration that followed felt more relaxed and comfortable than any other wedding Chloe had ever been to. All of the guests either knew one another or were connected somehow, which gave the event the feeling of a gathering of old friends here to celebrate together.

Stacey and Molly had joined Chloe, Madeleine, Jaysa, and her boyfriend Ben at a table. Stacey and Molly were serious enough as a couple to be able to talk of a wedding in the future without suggesting that that day would come anytime soon. Ben and Jaysa had been together long enough that he knew all the dreams—and specific requirements—she had for that special day. It had been hilarious to listen to them talk about the mishaps and misunderstandings they had weathered as they hammered out potential wedding plans.

They had all danced too, Chloe considerably more than usual. It was easy to dance without a care when surrounded by people who were doing the same. She stifled a yawn. It was about time to head home so that Taylor and Anne could head off for their mini-honeymoon. She saw that a few other guests had had the same idea and were heading to their cars. She was going to follow suit, but a new song started playing and she decided to hold off. She couldn't leave during a Sara song. No way.

As she tried to decide whether to listen or join the group on the dance floor, Chloe spotted Madeleine walking back to the table from the restrooms. They had had a wonderful time together, one rooted firmly and reassuringly in the friend zone, but this, she realized, was her first unobstructed view of her. What she saw made her heart pound. The short, simple black dress was stunning on her, and the two- to three-inch black heels she was wearing were incredibly sexy. She looked around, surprised not to see fireworks popping off somewhere. She could have sworn she heard some.

As Madeleine approached, that delicious half smile of hers made another appearance on her face. Chloe knew she had been caught staring, but it didn't appear that she was in trouble for it. In fact, Madeleine appeared to be enjoying the interest she was showing.

"I was wondering if you wanted to dance. You have to dance to at least one Sara song, don't you, given your history with her?" Madeleine said, giving her a wink.

Chloe uncrossed her legs, attempting to alleviate the pressure that was building between them. Dancing with Madeleine might prove to be her undoing, but she didn't have the willpower to say no. "I think you're right."

She followed Madeleine to the floor, stopping short of where she stopped in order to allow her to set the tone of the dance. Madeleine stepped closer, wrapping her arms casually around Chloe's neck, leaving six inches between them. Careful

not to infringe on the gap between them, Chloe slid her hands
into position on Madeleine's lower back. Instantly, as if no time
had passed, the connection between them reignited and Chloe
was remembering the feel and taste of the kiss they had shared
at the resort.

Slowly they began to dance, swaying to "Send Me the Moon"
by Sara. Chloe guided them around the floor, heat creeping up
her neck and onto her cheeks. Sure that Madeleine could hear
her heart thundering out of her chest, she tried to come up with
something to say to distract her. Before she could say a word,
Madeleine closed the distance between them, resting her head
carefully on Chloe's shoulder. Quietly, she whispered, "Don't be
nervous, Chloe. Just be here with me."

Chloe breathed deeply, taking everything in: her scent, the
grace with which she moved, the feeling of her body in her
arms. All the other emotions, all her worries, melted away. She
was with Madeleine, if only for one song. That was enough. It
would have to be.

All too soon, another song began and reality reasserted itself.
Thankful that there was no awkwardness, Chloe led Madeleine
back to the table. She was about to ask when they planned to
head out when the music faded and Taylor stood to make an
announcement.

"I don't want to have to do this, but we just got an update
from the weather service and we've got to call it a night. There's
a ton of snow coming and a weather advisory for no unnecessary
travel. We can't stay here, obviously, but if you've been drinking
you can leave your car here. We've cleared it with the owners. If
you're driving and have a reliable ride, consider putting together
a car pool with someone who lives near you. Let's everybody
form a plan. Come find me when you know who you're driving
or riding with!"

"I had no idea it was that bad out there," Stacey said. "I
thought they weren't calling for the storm to pick up until the
early hours of the morning!"

"Where are you two headed tonight?" Chloe asked.

"We took my Subaru, so we're going back to my place. Do
you two want to ride with us?" Molly was sweet to offer, but to

drop her and Madeleine off they would need to go the opposite direction of Stacey's place in Newcastle.

"Thanks for the offer, but I don't want you guys to have to double back to take me home. You should just get yourselves home as soon as you can." Directing her next remark to Madeleine, she continued, "My Jeep has four-wheel drive and new snow tires. I can take you home and we can get your car sometime tomorrow if you want."

Madeleine nodded. "That makes sense, Chloe. Thanks. Taylor will feel better knowing there are fewer people on the road. I'll tell her we're all set."

Gathering their things quickly, they told Taylor of their plans and said goodbye. The storm was definitely no joke Chloe saw when she waded out to her Jeep. Well over a foot of snow had fallen in the four hours they had been there. Thankfully the owners of the farm had been plowing the driveway during the reception, so cars could at least get out. The roads, she predicted, would be another story entirely.

Chloe drove up to the entryway where Madeleine was waiting to be picked up. No sense having both of them hike through the snowdrifts, especially with Madeleine in heels. She grabbed the spare blanket from the back seat and, allowing herself a quick, tantalizing glimpse of Madeleine's legs, draped it over her once she was situated in the passenger seat. "My heater is slow and this might take a while. You should at least be warm and comfortable."

With the snow still falling steadily, driving took up nearly all of Chloe's concentration, though not enough to prevent her subconscious from bombarding her with visions of the two of them getting snowed in together. Those thoughts would have to wait while she tried to figure out where the curbs were, though, and whether the snow-encrusted stoplights were signaling red or green. Luckily most of the area inhabitants had had the good sense to stay home, so traffic was close to nonexistent.

Chloe was relieved to see that Madeleine's driveway had been plowed within the past few hours. There were only a few inches lining it. The walkway to her front door was a different story. Chloe saw her shovel parked safely on the porch, out of reach, and laughed.

"Wait here for a minute. I'll clear a quick path so you can get to your door without snowshoes."

She quickly changed from her oxfords to the Keen snow boots she always kept in the back seat, then, closing the door on any objections, quickly grabbed her own shovel from the back of the Jeep. Making light work of the short path, Chloe returned to the car, offered Madeleine her hand, and helped her step out. As they walked to the front door, snow swirled around them, giant flakes steadily falling, and the thick blanket of white covering the neighborhood shone brightly, reflecting the moonlight that had broken through the clouds. Chloe stood on the porch, enjoying the view as Madeleine fished her keys out of her purse.

"Chloe, thank you for everything. Seriously, you've been amazing."

Unlocking and unlatching the door, Madeleine let it swing open. The snowflakes on her coat, in her hair, began to melt, leaving droplets glistening on the ridge of her sloping cheekbone. Chloe reached out, mesmerized and, softly, with the pad of her thumb, brushed them away. She stopped, anxious not to overstep again, but when she looked at Madeleine she saw her own desire reflecting back at her. She took a step closer.

"I'm not asking you for anything more tonight, but your eyes are telling me to kiss you. And I'm going to listen to them."

Gently, seeking permission, Chloe barely brushed Madeleine's lips with her own. She pulled back slightly, but unable to resist, returned, meeting Madeleine's soft lips again. Tenderly they kissed, drinking each other in, trading sweet kisses until, feeling her desire threatening to bubble over, Chloe slowed herself and pulled back. After tracing Madeleine's jawline with her thumb, she took another step back, then another.

"Good night, Madeleine."

As she made her way through the thick snowfall back to the car, she couldn't tell if Madeleine was still waiting on her porch and watching. It didn't matter. Chloe had finally had the guts to put herself out there, to go out on a limb with no guarantee that it wouldn't be sawn off, and it felt incredible. Normally she would have been petrified. Tonight, she felt…liberated. She was able to almost completely disregard the tiny bit of fear still churning around in her belly.

She slapped the steering wheel and grinned at herself in the rearview mirror. *Way to go, Chloe!* Too many times she had been content to let things happen only when she was comfortable, letting them come to her, or to ignore things, hoping they'd just go away. What was happening here, though, was too important to leave to chance. Chloe waited as a dark pickup drove down the street, then pulled out of the driveway and began the trek home, making a mental note to call Madeleine tomorrow to arrange to take her back to fetch her car.

CHAPTER SIXTEEN

Monday

"You did what?" Hannah's voice was incredulous and rightly so, Chloe had to admit. She'd rationalized not calling her earlier because she knew Hannah had been busy over the weekend. It wouldn't have interfered all that much to steal her best friend away from her work for a little while and update her, but something had held her back. She had wanted to savor the moment a little longer, keep it private so no one else could judge it.

So she'd waited until Monday evening to break the news. She might have put it off even longer if Madeleine had been around to distract her. But she wasn't. She had texted Chloe on Sunday to let her know that after having lunch with Jaysa, they had picked up her car from the farm. That was the last she had heard from her. She was absent from school Monday, and that was conspicuous. Apparently she had not taken a sick day in the three years she had been employed at Wiscasset. Afraid it had more to do with her than with some germ, Chloe had needed to talk to Hannah.

"You heard me," she said, a little defensively. "I thought you would be a little bit more proud of me, considering I was channeling some of your confidence and all."

Hannah's audible intake of breath was not a good sign of what was to come.

"So after everything that's happened, you decided the best plan was to kiss her one more time, just to make *sure* she's going to fuck you over?"

Ouch. Chloe hadn't really considered it from this perspective, but in light of the fact that Madeleine hadn't come to school today, Hannah's point of view had some legitimacy.

"Come on, Hannah. You said it before. 'Why not try something different for once?' I've never done anything like this."

"Finding the most emotionally unavailable woman in a fifty-mile radius and trying to seduce her is not the 'something different' I was referring to."

"Fine, I'll give you that. But it doesn't have to mean anything. I kissed her and now I can move on. You're ruining my buzz here."

"Right, she's out of your system just like that. Did you see her today?"

"Well, that's the other thing." Chloe braced herself for Hannah's reaction. "She called in sick."

The line got quiet. Chloe waited for the surge of censure she was sure would follow. Madeleine's absence today had eroded all of her confidence. Though she didn't know if she wanted to tell Hannah that bit.

"How are you feeling?" Hannah said quietly, her concern for her friend eclipsing her earlier consternation. She was completely keyed into Chloe's feelings. Not surprising since they'd been friends for so long, but Chloe couldn't help feel grateful for her understanding and support.

"I'll survive. It just sucks."

"The waiting bullshit is the worst. I wish I could tell you to let it go, but I know that's not where your head is."

"Exactly. I felt great all weekend, but now I'm going back over everything, second guessing."

"Chloe, I love you, so I'm going to tell you how it is. You made your move—which, by the way, was pretty damn smooth. I'm impressed, I won't lie." Hannah's laugh broke up the seriousness of their conversation. "That being said, you're objectively smart and funny, not to mention attractive as hell. If she doesn't know enough to at least talk to you, then you need to move on. And I will help you do that. I am your wingman after all."

"I know you're right. If she can't talk to me, then I have to accept that. But right now I want you to distract me, okay?"

Sensing that her message had been received, Hannah obliged, relaying the details of her weekend, including the spontaneous date she had gone on with the doctor she had introduced herself to at their shared coffee shop last month. Chloe relaxed into her couch. Some things would always remain the same.

* * *

When Madeleine was nowhere to be found again on Tuesday, Chloe's fears crystallized and her concentration evaporated. She realized she was in for a long day when she found her usually enjoyable juniors nearly intolerable. Clenching and unclenching her jaw repeatedly to prevent herself from snapping at benign questions from them, she had prayed she could make it to five o'clock. All the running she would do during practice would help de-stress her.

By the time she blew the whistle to signal the end of practice, she was ready to crawl into bed for the night. Disappointed didn't touch on how frustrated she was with herself. Coming unglued over a woman was a rookie mistake, one that she had no intention of allowing to continue. Madeleine eventually would come back to the school, and when she did she would face her head on.

Wednesday

Chloe wiped down the whiteboard as her fourth-block students filed out. She was proud of herself. Today had been closer to normal. Though she hadn't seen Madeleine, the fact that she hadn't tried to seek her out either had reassured Chloe about her willpower, which had been on a hiatus as of late.

And now for something completely different, she thought. She switched her focus to her practice plan. The season was almost over and she wanted to end on a win. If they were going to do that, they had to take better care of the ball. As she contemplated how to prepare the team to do that, Chloe barely heard the knock on her door.

"Are you terribly busy?"

Chloe froze for a second, then turned, drinking Madeleine in. Her face was still except for a slight smile. Chloe loved that smile.

"Not terribly, no."

Nodding slightly, Madeleine walked over, hopping up on the table on the other side of the teaching bench from Chloe. Her hands were folded and her head bowed in an uncharacteristic show of nervousness.

"Are you feeling better?"

Madeleine hopped back off the bench and crossed the classroom, closing the door. When she returned, she stopped at the window. She remained silent.

Chloe had no idea how to proceed. She joined her at the window, hoping that might help Madeleine share what was on her mind.

Madeleine sighed. "I want to tell you something, but I need to know it will stay here between us. At least for now."

"Whatever it is won't leave this room," Chloe said, even as her mind began to buzz with possible topics. Could this be a wholesale rejection? Coming clean about her past? Fear warred with a glimmer of hope and worry about Madeleine. Her sigh had physically pained Chloe, revealing the depth of exhaustion she was experiencing.

"I wasn't sick these past two days. I came in to speak with Mark and then had to meet with my lawyer."

Chloe's stomach bottomed out. *One kiss—okay, a few—and she's filing a complaint?* Realizing that Madeleine would hardly be talking to her if that were the case, she started to assess other possibilities. *Or...is she resigning?* She was opening her mouth to object when Madeleine turned to face her, instantly quieting the retort.

"I have filed a sexual harassment complaint about Landon with Mark, who urged me to secure an order of protection against him as well. The school is opening their own internal investigation."

"Madeleine, that's..." Chloe stopped short. Having the courage and conviction to face this, to reclaim the power... Telling Madeleine how she felt about her doing that was beyond the scope of her expression. She struggled to find words.

"You are absolutely incredible, Madeleine."

Silence. Madeleine responded to Chloe's encouragement with a shake of her head. She understood. Nothing she could say would erase the turmoil Madeleine was facing, but that didn't mean she couldn't try.

"What you're doing, it's so important. For you and for all of our girls. I hope you realize how much you're doing for them, for the community, beyond how much you're doing to take care of yourself."

"It's not an answer. It's only the beginning, but I had to do this. For me."

Chloe faltered, imagining Madeleine agonizing over this decision for so long. Alone. She had no right to be hurt that she hadn't confided in her. Why then did she feel offense creeping in?

"I hope you don't feel like you have to go this alone." She made her quiet comment before she could consider whether it was wise or not.

"I'm not alone. I have my parents and Nate. They've all been great sounding boards this weekend. Mom and Dad offered to come out this week. Plus Mark is being so supportive."

That stung. Chloe stamped the feeling down, trying hard not to make this about her.

"As long as you know you have people here who care about you."

Madeleine nodded, her mouth set in a line. Chloe would have thought taking this action would have lightened Madeleine's worries, but the crease in her brow showed anything but relief. She shifted gears.

"If you don't want to talk about it with me, that's fine. I know everything is just starting right now. But I have to ask. Did you get an order of protection?" She pulled herself away from the window, moving toward her chair at the front bench.

"Chloe…" Madeleine took two steps after her, then stopped. She flicked her eyes toward the door.

Chloe kicked herself for being so stupid. Of course Madeleine would be worried about where Landon was now that she had gotten the authorities involved. She moved toward her office. "Let's talk in here."

Nodding, Madeleine followed her into the small office. Chloe sat in her own chair and offered Madeleine the one next to her desk, the one used if a student ever came in to talk. Madeleine sat lightly, leaning back, setting her left arm on the edge of Chloe's desk. Her posture was more relaxed, but Chloe still sensed some nervousness. The office suddenly felt incredibly intimate.

"I'm sorry I didn't talk to you about this, but I had to do it on my own. You pushed me before I was ready. But you were the one person who helped me get to this point. I kept thinking about how you said this wasn't going to stop if I didn't talk to someone. And I knew you weren't just saying it, you've been here. I'm so grateful for you, I want you to know that."

"Madeleine, I didn't…"

She raised her hand, cutting Chloe off. "You did. You were here for me. You gave me the room I thought I needed, but you challenged me to be stronger, to learn from you. And I'm trying."

Chloe would never cease to be impressed by this woman. She sat in the silence, relieved, but still concerned about how tense Madeleine was. Reaching out, she gently took her hand in her own.

"It's going to be okay, you know."

"How do you always make it feel so easy?"

The words were barely a whisper. Chloe tilted her head in confusion. Always?

"Madeleine?"

Silence. Chloe felt like she was ten steps behind in this conversation. Madeleine closed her eyes, leaning her head back against the wall behind her.

"I was engaged before."

Unsure what to make of this new information, Chloe waited.

"Her name was Emma. We hadn't been together long, just over a year and a half. She was vibrant, always moving or laughing. She surrounded herself with people and energy all the time. It was infectious. We met junior year, started dating over the summer. I was captivated."

Madeleine sat forward, opening her eyes, though still avoiding eye contact. Chloe watched the rise and fall of Madeleine's chest, willing her own muscles to relax as she waited. A war was raging inside Chloe, the urge to comfort vying with the need to understand.

"We were moving so fast. It was a whirlwind, and I was happy to be consumed. With training kicking into high gear for the national team, I was spending all my time with the girls on the road. Emma wasn't the axis for my orbit anymore, like she had been after the season senior year. When she proposed, I was shocked, but thrilled. Everything was going so well." The dark laugh that followed sounded so hollow.

"She moved into my apartment. It made sense. She would live in it while I traveled. I would come home to her. I was so consumed by soccer, I never realized..." Madeleine left the thought hanging, unfinished.

"When I woke up in the hospital and realized I was never going to play competitive soccer again, the only thing I could think was that I was lucky to have a fiancée who could help me through. That was until I was released from the hospital a day early and walked in on her with her ex."

"Oh my god, Madeleine." Her burgeoning feelings for Madeleine slammed into Chloe with physical force.

Madeleine turned her shoulders, finally facing Chloe again. Her face was filled with fear—and a longing Chloe hadn't ever seen before. Standing, she pulled Madeleine into her arms. She held her tightly to her, her heart racing as she felt Madeleine's cheek pressed to her chest. Chloe was sure Madeleine could hear the blood pumping in her veins, the drumbeat that was her heart.

Slowly Madeleine pulled back, then released herself from the hug.

"I don't know if I can do this, Chloe, but you make me want to. You make it feel so easy but…"

Chloe's heart lurched in her chest. The roller-coaster ride clearly was not over yet.

"But I lost everything all at once before and now it feels like it's happening again."

Chloe was opening her mouth to speak when Madeleine shook her head, resignation replacing the confusion from before.

"You aren't even mine to lose." She walked out of the office. "I've got to go."

Chloe stood there, reeling. Was it possible to hate a woman she didn't know? Nausea bubbled up in her stomach. Emma was a fool. A selfish, heartless fool. But Madeleine was better off now, and that was the important thing. Chloe wanted to be with Madeleine, but above all else she wanted to see her happy. But what could she do to help her find that happiness? What did she truly want?

Madeleine was a virtuoso at sending mixed messages, but hadn't she consistently come back, invited Chloe in emotionally? Their ski trip, then the wedding, reintroducing herself, even now opening up about Landon and her past. The words she'd said as she left haunted Chloe. "You aren't even mine to lose." Wasn't it obvious that she cared about Madeleine? She had made it clear, or so she thought, when she had kissed her after the wedding. But a kiss could mean a lot of different things. She hadn't *told* her what she was feeling. She had been afraid to admit it even to herself. How could Madeleine know with any certainty where she stood? It was now or never.

She took out her phone, typed a message, hit send, then threw the phone on the desk. The only thing left to do was go back to getting ready for practice. And wait. She was never very good at waiting. But there was nothing else for her now. She had played her cards, had finally taken the step that was necessary to make it clear to Madeleine she wanted to be with her. It was up to her to decide if she was ready.

Relationship troubles also would not get her a pass from her players, who expected her to help them win their final game. Checking her watch, Chloe saw she had an hour and a half before the boys' practice ended. Returning to her office, she pulled her duffel bag from beneath the desk. Placing her practice pad on the front lab bench, she looked over the rough outline she had made of drills they could work on. They needed to be ready for the half-court trap that Bar Harbor was known for. Tonight she would concentrate on passing-skill work drills under pressure and live action. To the extent she could concentrate, that is, and not obsess about how Madeleine was reacting to her message. She gave herself a mental kick in the pants and tried to block out all thoughts that were not related to basketball.

She picked up a pen and started writing out potential drills to incorporate for specific objectives. That always helped her get a feel for where she wanted a practice to go. Inevitably she would end up cutting drills on the fly based on what she was seeing and how the girls were doing, but having a solid plan made things run smoothly. Conference championships were right around the corner, which meant she only had the girls for another week. Once JV practices were over, Chloe would be serving as Taylor's assistant.

As she tucked her notes into the bag holding her practice gear, Chloe realized her sneakers were missing. She distinctly remembered putting them in her duffel. They must have fallen out of the bag on the drive in this morning. She decided she might as well go get them now.

She was turning for the door when it burst open and Madeleine strode powerfully over the threshold, closing the door firmly behind her. Her expression was hungry as she walked confidently across the room. She did not slow down as she reached Chloe, instead maneuvering them both backward, pinning Chloe to the wall and claiming her with a ferocity unlike any Chloe had ever known. Sensations erupted, her skin drinking in every inch of contact.

Chloe began kissing back, exploring every inch Madeleine offered. Madeleine's lithe body moved in waves, lean muscle pressing her harder against the wall. Madeleine's hand snuck under Chloe's shirt, blazing a path to her ribcage, setting Chloe on fire.

Pushing off from the wall, locked in an embrace, Chloe steered them into her office. Madeleine bumped into the desk, and Chloe lifted her onto it, inserting herself between Madeleine's legs. Gradually, remembering where they were, Chloe slowed the pace. Their urgency turned to languid exploration. Chloe tangled her hand in Madeleine's hair as she kissed her deeply. Madeleine's hips pressed forward in response. Her chest was soft beneath Chloe's, her breathing labored as Chloe purposefully gripped her hair, determined to make *this* the kiss Madeleine had always wanted.

Madeleine's mouth shifted to Chloe's neck, and Chloe's mind emptied of everything but the feeling of Madeleine on her skin. She was everywhere and it was still not enough.

Returning to Chloe's mouth, Madeleine brought both hands to Chloe's face, resting them there. Chloe finally ended the kiss, resting her forehead on Madeleine's, her eyes still closed.

"You make me want to trust you." Madeleine's voice was husky, sending a chill down Chloe's spine. "But I'm not sure I remember how to."

Chloe swallowed, regaining her voice. "I know how hard it was for you to open up to me, Madeleine. I'm going to make it worth the risk you took. I promise."

Madeleine's face was open with want and something more. She was scared, Chloe could see, but ready at last to move forward.

"Do you think you could start by doing dinner tonight?" Madeleine asked.

Chloe nodded. Wrapping her arms around her, she silently thanked the universe for this moment. Unending moments of pleasure later, Chloe remembered that she had a practice to run and grudgingly broke their kiss.

"I would love to make you dinner, and I would love to cancel practice to do it. But I have to walk outside and get my shoes right now or I won't ever leave for practice."

Groaning, Madeleine squeezed Chloe quickly, running her hands up her back, then down the sides of her ribcage. Chloe moaned and pulled away, bumping into the back wall of the office. Madeleine crushed what little willpower she still had.

"You are not helping my resolve."

"Neither are you, standing there like that." Chloe's pulse skyrocketed at Madeleine's words. They had opened Pandora's Box. She never wanted to shut it.

"Okay. We are going to make a plan so that I can keep my job and also feed you. Practice is in twenty minutes. I'm going to get my shoes and try to coach. Try and fail, because I'll be focused on you."

Chloe snaked her hand out and pulled Madeleine flush to her again, torturing herself as much as Madeleine. She placed a searing kiss in the soft hollow between her jaw and ear. She whispered, "As soon as I'm done with my kids, I'm going to meet you at my place. We can do dinner, talk, and do whatever else comes to mind."

The chills that she saw rippling across Madeleine's skin gave Chloe a heady rush of pleasure. God damn, she didn't want to go to practice. Taking a deep, steadying breath, she straightened and released Madeleine.

"Seriously, we have to walk out now, because I'm thirty seconds from canceling the rest of the season."

Madeleine's blush was as unexpected as it was adorable.

"What time should I meet you?"

Without hesitation, Chloe responded, "Seven twenty-four. Not a minute later." She squeezed Madeleine's hand, then let go and watched her walk out of the classroom. Elated, she returned to her office to gather her things. Now ready to head to practice, she scooped up her phone from the table at the front of the room. Glancing at the screen, she smiled again, rereading her last text.

I am yours, if you want me.

Chloe hadn't realized how much emotional energy she had been expending every day on the yo-yoing between her and Madeleine. As she walked through the school to her car, the memory of Madeleine's lips on hers, enfolding her body in her arms, played over and over in her mind. Her heart swelled when she thought of Madeleine coming back to her, of them taking a real step toward something, together.

First, though, she had to get through this practice and that meant running to her Jeep in the biting wind to get her shoes. What a cruel world this was. Chloe laughed as she swung open the door to the outside. There were still a surprising number of cars in the lot.

"I don't understand how you think what you're doing is acceptable."

The deep voice came from behind her. Chloe turned to see a visibly agitated Landon closing the distance between them. This was definitely not an encounter she wanted to have, not after the way he had treated Madeleine.

"What am I doing?" Chloe asked. "I don't know what you mean by that, Landon," she responded coolly, seeking to defuse the situation. She kept walking.

"Listen, your act isn't going to fly here." His brow was furrowed, and his face teemed with a dark cloud of emotions. Something had set him off. A flicker of panic crossed her mind. Had he seen them in the classroom just now? She hadn't exactly been paying attention to anything except Madeleine. But no, the door had been shut. Regardless of the trigger, it was obvious that right now he was dangerous. She answered as calmly as she could.

"Landon, I really have no idea what act you're talking about." The indignant laugh he let out was tinged with determination and anger. She was becoming frightened. With him following her to the cars, she was running out of space to get away should things escalate. His voice was raised and she hadn't the faintest clue how to calm him down.

"I saw you and Madeleine snowboarding, then near the gym. I know you took her home after that gay ass wedding. You just can't keep it in your fucking pants. Just because you're a dyke bitch doesn't mean any girl you want is."

"Landon, I don't want to fight with you. There isn't anything going on." She hated having to deny her relationship with Madeleine, but this wasn't the time or place. He was ready to snap. If he hadn't done so already.

"Don't fucking patronize me, you whore!" Landon gritted out, his voice raspy and dangerous. In one breath he closed the gap between them and pinned Chloe to her Jeep. They were confined now to the space between it and someone else's SUV. Landon was livid, the vein in his forehead pounding, his face flushing. The hatred in his eyes made Chloe shudder.

"I tried to tell you I wouldn't put up with you. I knew you would pull this. I just didn't think you would be stupid enough to try it at school. I saw what you did to her in there, you freak." He spit the words out.

"Landon, I don't know what's going on. I certainly didn't mean to upset you. I'm sure we can work this out. Obviously there has been a misunderstanding." Her voice never wavered, though it took all of her composure not to let her temper or her fear show.

"No, now you misunderstand me. What I'm going to do now is teach you something about men. Maybe give you a real reason to hate us before you go back to screwing girls."

The words crackled in the air, his spite a venom directed at her. The harsh whisper took forever to register in Chloe's mind. She realized his intent a second too late.

He brought his hands roughly up to Chloe's chest, squeezing her with all of his strength, leaning into her with the length of his body. Shocked, she reacted on instinct, bringing her knee up directly into his crotch. She connected full force, knocking the wind out of him as he stumbled backward. She barely had time to move, though, before he recovered enough to slam a giant fist into her face, connecting with a nasty crunching sound.

The force of the punch jarred her senses, shooting blinding pain through her nose and cheekbone. She was blinking furiously, trying to regain her bearings, when another fist sent a blow to her ribcage. The momentum of the swing sent her crashing back into her car.

Thankful for something to keep her upright, Chloe struggled to stop the onslaught. Everything was a blur, though the pain coursing through her was undeniable. As she turned to face him again, he landed another punch, his knuckles cracking against her skull. She staggered back into the side of the Jeep once more, reeling and desperately trying to bring three blurry Landons into focus.

Knowing she would not be able to stop him with a punch, Chloe desperately kicked out with all of her strength, aiming for the leg all of his weight was planted on. Mercifully her foot connected with her target. At the contact his knee buckled, hyperextending completely. A sickening popping noise coupled with his scream let her know she'd momentarily stopped him. She had to act fast. As he fell to his knees, she seized the opportunity to strike. She stepped into her next swing, crashing her fist into his throat and feeling him choke. His hands immediately went to his windpipe, the rage on his face mixing with panic as he struggled to pull in his next breath. Unwilling to take the chance that he'd recover, she grabbed the back of his head and slammed it with all her might face first into the side door of the Jeep.

Letting go of him, she stumbled backward into the car, pausing only long enough to study Landon's limp form and make sure he was unconscious. Moving to distance herself from him, she took three slow steps backward and took several deep breaths.

Reality came in fragmented sensations. The wind was bitterly cold. That thought was the one that registered first. As the seconds dragged out into minutes, she began to feel the pain. Her face was on fire. Throbbing, stinging, aching, and pains she had never felt before were barraging her senses. And when she took a deeper breath to gather some semblance of control, a stabbing pain from her ribs sent her reeling for support.

She leaned against the Jeep, adrenaline coursing through her. Most likely it was the only thing keeping her standing. Finally, the haze in her brain lifted, she remembered her cell phone, and everything lurched into hyperspeed. With shaking hands she fished the phone out of her pocket, noticing in the process that her right knuckles were beginning to swell.

Her hand should be hurting, but she felt disconnected from her body. She didn't want to see her face or her ribs, which were continuing to smart noticeably with each breath.

Slowly she unlocked the phone screen and dialed 911. Her body was still operating on high alert when she spoke with the dispatcher. They responded immediately to the dazed sound of her voice, dispatching a car to the school even before they heard her whole story.

Chloe waited, somehow remaining standing, until a uniformed officer arrived. That was the exact moment when she lost consciousness.

* * *

Chloe drew a breath, confused about why the air in her nose felt so cold and also so clean. Taking another slow breath, she realized that there was a two-pronged intrusion in her nostrils. The kind of thing they gave to people in the hospital to help them breathe. Fighting off her fear and her confusion, she opened her eyes to take stock of her surroundings.

The room was dark, but three people were talking quietly in the chairs to her left, lit by light from the hallway. She blinked two times in rapid succession, assessing the level of damage to her face, which felt six sizes too big for her skin. There wasn't a lot of pain. No doubt she'd been given some medicine, which had taken the edge off.

She wiggled her fingers and toes, determining that her extremities were fine. Breathing deeply, however, was limited by the searing pain in her ribs. It was time to find out what happened.

"How long was I out?" she croaked.

Madeleine reacted the most visibly, nearly jumping out of her chair, covering the two feet to her bedside in what had to be record time. Chloe's heart broke. Madeleine's features were drawn, and she had prominent dark splotches under her eyes. She hated to see her so upset.

Madeleine brought her hands toward Chloe's face but hesitated, apparently unsure of where to touch. Chloe flipped her left hand, palm up, and waited expectantly for her to take it. Thankfully, she didn't have to wait long to feel the warmth of her hand in hers. Grounded by the contact, she relaxed more deeply.

Anne's voice broke into Chloe's awareness.

"You were out for about four hours. You have a fractured orbital, seriously bruised ribs, and some pretty nasty bruising on your face. You have a Grade Three concussion, but your intracranial pressure has stabilized so you're going to be okay."

Chloe nodded, thankful for the candid report from Anne.

"You had us pretty worried. We got a hold of your mom and dad. They're on their way now. Taylor stepped out to call and let them know you're awake." Anne's tone softened even more, allowing her emotions to seep into her professional demeanor. "How are you feeling?"

"I'm assuming they gave me some meds, because I can kind of feel the things you talked about, but it's not terrible. My head hurts now that you mention it, but the worst is my face. It feels enormous."

"I'm sure it does. I'm so glad you're awake, Chloe." Anne shakily released her breath. Chloe felt surging guilt at scaring everyone. "Don't worry, the doctors don't think you'll have any permanent damage to your face. Once the swelling comes down you'll be looking more like your usual self."

Taylor's laughter broke into the worried tension that had been crackling in the air.

"I've always told you you've got a big head, champ, so nothing new there. But I'm getting pretty sick of seeing your face black and blue, you know. Stop trying to be Jason Bourne already. Makes me feel a little less than. I don't like it."

Their shared laughter felt normal. Chloe smiled or tried to at least.

"Thanks for being here, guys. I didn't mean to scare you all."

"It's okay. Just don't let it happen again." Taylor arched her eyebrow, her smile warm but muted.

"Deal." Wondering what she was worried about, Chloe looked around. *Ah.* There were police officers waiting in the wings. Anne took the lead yet again.

"So we forced our way into the room and got to be your welcoming committee, but now they need to get your statement. Are you okay to give it to them now?"

Chloe felt Madeleine's grip on her hand tighten, and her heart fluttered in response. Now that she finally had Madeleine by her side, she didn't want her moving anywhere. Her anxiety must have shown.

"Would you like me to stay in here with you?" Madeleine's question was tentative, but the need in her voice told Chloe all she needed to know. Squeezing her hand tightly, Chloe made up her mind. She might want her here, but Madeleine didn't need to hear everything she would have to report, not right now.

"Thank you for the offer, but I don't want to traumatize you with the details. Seeing my mug like this has to be hard enough."

Sitting down, Madeleine pulled her chair closer to Chloe. "Chloe, he almost killed you. Don't ask me to walk away after that, not right now. Please."

She realized there was nothing to protect Madeleine from. She was as invested in this as Chloe, more so because of her charges against Landon. She would end up talking to her about it eventually. Well, that is if she still… *No.* Chloe shut down those thoughts. There was all the time in the world for them now. First, though, the police. Nodding, she gripped Madeleine's hand tightly with one hand and gestured the officers inside her room with the other.

* * *

When the officers left, Chloe felt herself relax. Madeleine hadn't wavered, sitting silently by Chloe's side, holding her hand as she related the events to the police. The worst part of it all, actually, had been when they had taken pictures of her injuries, documenting every bruise, holding up their little ruler with every click of the camera. The authorities knew what had happened now, and the Landon saga was truly over.

Madeleine returned to the chair once the officers walked out, and Taylor and Anne popped back in the doorway. "Tell me you're as hungry as we are," Taylor called out, clearly hoping to identify something productive to do. Thank god, she and Anne were so perceptive. *Well, mainly Anne.*

"You know, I didn't realize how hungry I was until you mentioned it. I'll eat anything right now."

"We're on it. Madeleine, keep her dumb ass in that bed at all costs. We'll be back with a delicious dinner. It'll have to be something compatible with your meds, I suppose, but we'll be looking for something greasy probably and definitely unhealthy. You broke your face, your arteries are fine. I'm sure Anne will agree just this once."

Chloe laughed despite the pain, knowing that they all needed some laughs to break through the fear they had all been through in the past four hours.

"Taylor, your humor needs work, but at least you're useful. Anne, I stand by the assertion that you are an angel. Thank you so much, I'm starving. I'm sure you all are."

They waved and walked out of the room in search of dinner, enabling Chloe to turn her full attention to Madeleine. Nervous that she might pull away again out of some misguided sense of guilt, Chloe decided that it was now or never. She had done enough waiting and wondering. She was done with that. Madeleine was here, and Chloe needed her to understand.

"Madeleine?" No response. "So…I realize that this is probably giving you all sorts of fits in there." Chloe reached up and tapped Madeleine's forehead, wincing slightly as she extended the bruised ribs. Despite Madeleine's concern, she went on. "But I'm going to try to clear some of that up for you. I want us to be a couple. I hadn't said it before, but I'm saying it now. I want to be the one you can trust, the one who earns that right and who proves to you every day that that trust isn't misplaced. I'm not going to rush you, which I think shows some impressive restraint on my part. But I also know that I don't want to wander around lost anymore and that you're the one person on earth who helps me feel like I'm going somewhere."

Pausing, Chloe swallowed and pushed on, "Call me greedy, but I want the chance to get lost in you."

Well, that was that. She had no more falling left to do. The realization would have terrified her if she didn't see the same truth looking back at her.

Madeleine's brilliant smile outshone everything else. Closing her eyes, Chloe pulled Madeleine to her. Their kiss was emotional, hungry and yet patient. Reaching up, Chloe wove her hand into Madeleine's hair, pulling her closer. The tiny moan Chloe heard sent her heart racing, sending jolts of energy through her body. She could spend forever trying to make Madeleine feel loved.

Sensing perhaps that this was heading somewhere that Chloe's bruised and battered body was not prepared for, Madeleine slowed the pace, placing some final, sweet kisses on Chloe's lips before pulling back completely. Unwilling to sever all physical contact, she traced her fingertips along Chloe's jawline, avoiding the bruising, and danced her way down Chloe's neck, leaving searing pleasure in her wake. Chloe knew her smile was ridiculous, but she no longer cared. She wanted Madeleine to see exactly how happy she made her.

"So, not to belabor the point, but can I really call you my girlfriend?"

Madeleine slipped her hand back into Chloe's and leaned forward. Chills rippled through Chloe's body as she spoke.

"I'm sure you're going to call me many things, and I can't wait to hear them all." Catching Chloe's earlobe in her teeth, she gave it a slight tug. Chloe felt her body respond instantly, the surge of arousal immediate and powerful. What torture had she signed up for? As Madeleine leaned back, that smile dancing on her mouth, her eyes a heady mix of enjoyment and attraction, Chloe knew she was toast. But god, how amazing was it going to be keeping up with this woman?

"Not only can you *call* me your girlfriend, I'll even *be* your girlfriend." Madeleine's teasing lit up her face. "I'd love nothing more than to be with you, Chloe Amden. And that includes meeting your parents for the first time in this damn hospital. Not to mention figuring out a way to explain to them that I seem to push your luck when it comes to breaking even."

Chloe laughed, aware of Madeleine's nervousness and still completely certain that there was nowhere else in the world she would rather be. She'd done better than break even this time, she had to say. In fact, anyway you looked at it, she was miles ahead.

EPILOGUE

"I cannot believe that you've known me for, what, three years now? And you still think you're allowed to change the channel during a Harry Potter marathon?"

"Chloe, sweetheart, it's Taylor's house. You can't always be in charge of the remote you know." Madeleine leaned over and kissed Chloe's cheek as she groused at Taylor.

Taylor's maniacal laughter drew Anne in from the kitchen. Walking over to her wife, she placed her hands on Taylor's shoulders. "Honey, do you know that every time I hear that specific laugh, I know you've been off work for too long and I begin to make lists of summer projects for you?"

"Guys, I've been made." Taylor dropped her head forward in defeat, earning her a shove from Anne before she joined her on the love seat.

Chloe found Madeleine's hand to hold. Three years ago she had moved to Boothbay to escape. Now she was teaching here and living the life she never realized she wanted.

"Chloe, I know you're probably still upset about Harry Potter, but remember how you've been whining about catching fireflies for past two weeks? It's finally dark enough you can see them all out there." Taylor winked at Chloe as she watched Madeleine's focus swing to the window. Chloe nodded in response and stood.

"I guess you made up for your mistake. Just try not to make it again."

Offering her hand to Madeleine, Chloe helped her off the couch and over to the back porch where mason jars sat waiting on the table. As they stepped off the deck with jars in hand, the field opening up before them, Chloe slipped her hand back into Madeleine's, as caught up in the beauty of the moment as she was.

"Nothing could be more perfect," Madeleine whispered.

Lingering at the mouth of the path, the two remained still, hands linked, enjoying the company and the incredible view. Thousands of fireflies lit up the meadow, twinkling brightly. The moon was a sliver in the night sky, providing enough darkness to showcase the fireflies and starlight, the breeze was light, dancing on the tops of the grass along with the twinkling insects, and stars dotted the entire sky. Together they made their way through the grass, laughing and filling their jars with as many blinking bugs as they each could manage. Chloe, finished with her jar, walked back over to Madeleine.

"Hey, I love you more than all these lights and all those stars, you know that?" She leaned in for a soft kiss, drinking in the sweetness of Madeleine's mouth. She could feel the happiness, the contentment there in that kiss. Now was the time. "I think I caught more than you did," she said to Madeleine, offering her jar up for inspection.

Madeleine brought the jar close in order to get a better look, her eyes widening as she spotted something glistening at the bottom. It most definitely wasn't a firefly. She cocked her head, thoroughly intrigued by the round, silvery object inside the jar. Chloe continued, somehow getting the words out past her tightening throat.